SEDONA CONSPIRACY

Borgo Press Books by JAMES C. GLASS

Imaginings of a Dark Mind: Science Fiction Stories
Sedona Conspiracy: A Science Fiction Novel
Toth: A Science Fiction Novel
Touches of Wonder and Terror: Tales of Dark Fantasy and Science Fiction
Visions: A Science Fiction Western
Voyages in Mind and Space: Stories of Mystery and Fantasy

SEDONA CONSPIRACY

A SCIENCE FICTION NOVEL

JAMES C. GLASS

For Glenda, best wishes,
James C. Glass

THE BORGO PRESS

MMXII

SEDONA CONSPIRACY

DEDICATION

This one is for the good people of Sedona, Arizona, and the beautiful place where they live.

CONTENTS

CHAPTER ONE
LIGHTS IN THE CANYON

The rain started at midnight, and by eight in the morning was still coming down in sheets. It was one thunderstorm after another as a line of cells moved through the Sedona area. A thousand waterfalls cascaded down red rock buttes surrounding town, and thick mist shrouded the canyons.

Martin looked out his motel room window towards the southwest. "Might be brightening up out there. Let's get going."

Doug was lying on his bed, watching CNN. "I'd rather go to town. Red dirt can suck your boots off after a rain."

"Don't you back out on me," warned Martin. "The permit's for one night, and I didn't drive a hundred miles to shop for new-age junk. Up-and-on, before trailhead parking fills up."

Breakfast was two power bars; they picked up coffee at The Planet, and then made the short drive west into the butte country. Boynton Canyon was the most popular trail, but as they'd hoped the trailhead parking area was empty, people scared off by the rain. Even in their four-by-four the red hardpan in the lot had turned to mud slippery as ice.

Rain lessened to mist by the time their packs were on and the car locked. The sky was definitely lightening up in the southwest, but only a hundred yards along the trail red muck was already reaching their bootlaces. They slogged to Katchina Woman, a spire sacred to the Apache. A gnarled tree there was said to be a vortex site that concentrated local magnetic energies. New age folk came there to meditate. Doug was into the local culture, and wanted to pause for a quiet moment, but Martin insisted they press on and he promised they'd stop on the way back in the morning.

The first mile was a boring slog, squishing through muck on the flats, then up steep rock pouring water on their boots as they skirted the edge of a resort with lawns and expensive condos right up to the wilderness boundary. A faint side trail leading up to nicely preserved cliff dwellings was now a waterfall, and so they headed straight into the canyon and the quiet serenity two miles beyond the wilderness boundary sign. Canyon walls were first distant, then close, towering masses of red rock turning pink and orange in the diffused light, colors that artists often struggled to duplicate.

The sky brightened above them, and the summits to their right glowed orange. A soft breeze chilled their faces and filled them with the scents of pine and mesquite. Ahead, through a tangle of trees, they could see rough cliffs and jumbled spires at the canyon's end. They came to the clearing where they would camp for the night. Logs had been placed in a large square there, a pile of stones making an energy pyramid at its center.

The tent was up in minutes, gear stowed and stove gassed. With the day brightening, Martin and Doug slung daypacks and headed to trail's end up a steep, scree slope at the headwall half a mile from their camp. On a shelf high above the canyon floor they munched trail mix and watched the colors change with progression of the day. A dozen red-rock cairns graced the shelf around them, all placed during someone's spiritual moment. The two men sat silently; in this magical place, there seemed no need to talk.

So it was that when the sound came, the shock of it made their hearts hammer hard.

It filled their ears, and the rock slab beneath them vibrated noticeably. It was as if a commercial jet was taking off just behind them, but there were only towers of rock there, and beyond those a wilderness of buttes and mesquite-covered flats.

"Jesus!" shouted Doug, and clapped hands over his ears.

The sound went on for several seconds, and cut off as sharply as it had begun.

"Airport's the other direction," said Martin, and pointed east towards Sedona, "and they don't let anything that big come in anyway."

"I still hear something," said Doug.

There was a faint whine, lowering in pitch, then a rattling sound, but in a few seconds the complete silence of the canyon had returned.

"I want to take a look," said Martin, and stood up to hoist his daypack.

"Climb to the top?" Doug shook his head. "It's off trail, and straight up."

"Maybe. We have the time."

"Four miles to the car is a long crawl with a broken leg."

"Well, I'm not going to be stupid about it. Come on." Martin started across a faint game trail on a shelf inclined upwards along the sheer wall above them. "We'll follow the animals."

Doug followed reluctantly. All he'd come for was quiet contemplation in a sacred place, not a rock climb. But the sound intrigued him, excited him, for there were many stories about strange happenings in the canyons and on certain buttes. New age poppycock, many said, but what he'd heard was the sound of a jet or even a rocket engine in the middle of a wilderness, and it had been real enough.

They only climbed for half an hour before giving up. The game trail faded to nothing at a foot-wide ledge, crossed a sheer wall with a fifty-foot drop to a boulder field, and they didn't even have a rope. They bouldered up a hanging canyon next to the wall, but were stopped in the end by smooth towers rising another hundred feet. No hand or foot holds, no cracks, straight up. They stood there in frustration, for beyond the tops of the towers there were faint sounds again: a steady, muffled beat of some kind of engine, and a hammering sound like someone cracking concrete.

"Must be a ranch out there," said Martin. "Maybe someone's

digging a well."

"With a jet engine?" said Doug.

"No, but this is a waste of time; we can't get any higher, and I want to look for ruins on the other side of the canyon this afternoon. Let's go down."

"Fine with me. I'm gonna tell Bob Terrell about this when we get back to town."

"The UFO guy? Don't even tell him I was with you."

"Not just UFO sightings. Military base stories, too, maybe fifty years back."

"He makes a good living writing books about it. That's your thing, Doug, not mine. I wasn't with you. Got it?"

"Sure," said Doug, and smiled. "I can't help it if you don't have any imagination."

They picked their way down over boulders and scree, and spent the afternoon brush busting the other side of the canyon to find one old Yavapai site on a ledge forty feet above the floor, but finding it made Martin's day complete.

Dusk was early in the canyon, and they'd seen no other hikers during the day. Sprinkles continued off and on until dark. They ate a freeze-dried stew dinner at five, read paperbacks by flashlight, and turned in at nine. Sleep came quickly in a place without even birdsong at night, but it seemed only minutes later they were startled awake by a sound immediately familiar to them, and a bright flash of light washed over their tent.

"Helicopter?" said Doug in the darkness. "Sounds close."

Martin was already out of his bag and crawling outside. "Lights up above the headwall. Hovering right now. Sure sounds like a helicopter."

Doug crawled out of the tent behind Martin, and looked up. The canyon headwall loomed above them, a black silhouette seen through the bare branches of deciduous trees. Bright lights flickered in and out there, one very bright, a V-shaped pattern of six red, fainter lights below it. The pattern seemed to rotate while the two men watched, and once again the bright light flashed over their tent.

Doug blinked, eyes adjusting quickly to darkness again. He pointed. "There, above that center peak. See the dark shape?"

"I see it. Helicopter, all right. A big one, and something is hanging beneath it."

Whatever it was headed west at that instant and was lost from view, the flup-flup engine sound fading, then gone.

"Oh, boy," said Doug.

Martin sighed. "Don't even get started. Some kind of construction going on over there. No little green men, just a helicopter carrying a prefab wall, or something."

"In the middle of the night?"

"Why not?"

They crawled back into their sacks. Doug was bursting to talk about what they'd seen, but Martin was snoring the instant his head hit the pillow. Doug didn't drift off for nearly an hour, his senses on high alert, but eventually he succumbed to a light sleep, once or twice barely awakening to what he thought might be helicopter sounds again, and the second time it was already starting to get light.

They slept in longer than they'd planned to, and hurriedly broke camp around nine. The tent was folded, ready to be rolled up, and they were stuffing their packs when Martin heard a crunch and looked up to see two men descending the trail from the headwall. They moved lightly and balanced, a mark of experienced mountaineers, hair long and tied in ponytails. They saw Martin and smiled, stopped on the trail a few yards from the campsite and exchanged sips on a single water bottle between them. The taller of the two spoke, the other just listened. Both men gave Martin a steady gaze with startlingly blue eyes.

"You camp here last night?"

"Yep. Came up yesterday morning. You must have come in before dawn."

"Pretty close to it. Nice hike. I didn't know camping was allowed in here. Beautiful place for it."

"Pretty limited, but you can get a permit at the Ranger's station."

"Nice looking rock here," said the taller man, and his partner nodded in agreement. "We'll have to bring our gear next time. Bet it's real quiet here at night."

"It was last night. Slept like a baby," said Martin, and cast a sidelong glance at Doug, who was staring at him.

The taller man capped his water bottle and stuffed it into his partner's rucksack. "Well, you have a nice walk out, now. Couple more canyons we want to see today."

A friendly wave, and the two men turned back to the trail, walking with a brisk pace until they were out of sight in the trees.

"Slept like a baby, huh," said Doug.

"After a while," said Martin, and smiled.

Martin was strangely silent on the way back, and seemed to be studying the trail all the way. Walking was easier than it had been the day before, but the trail was still spongy from all the rain. They stopped at Katchina Woman, and Doug spent half an hour meditating by the gnarled tree said to be a focus of magnetic energies in the region.

By the time they got back to the car, people were already coming in on the trail and the parking lot was full. The two hikers they'd seen at their campsite were not there. Martin dumped their packs into the four-by-four and offered Doug a drink of water.

Doug took a sip, then, "Okay, what's going on? You haven't said more than ten words on the trail today."

Martin frowned. "I was studying the trail. Noticed our tennis shoe tracks from yesterday, saw some fainter boot tracks going out. Our tracks were fainter, too. Ground's not so soft today."

"So?"

Martin paused, then looked at Doug darkly. "Those guys we met at camp this morning didn't come into the canyon this morning, at least not from this parking lot, and I'm not aware of any other trail in. They came in from somewhere up by the headwall. Now, I ask, how would they do that?"

"And why?" said Doug, and smiled. "I'm telling all of this to

Bob Terrell before we leave town, Martin, but I promise I won't mention your name."

"Okay," said Martin.

They got into the four-by-four and drove back to town to find Terrell.

CHAPTER TWO
REACTIONS

The helicopter came in at tree level and dropped towards a concrete pad surrounded by green lawn. Twin rotors synchronized and pitched for stealth, the black polymer fuselage landed gently without lights. Darkness came early in the Catalina Mountains of Arizona, and a single window was dimly illuminated in the sprawling silhouette of the ranch house. The figure of a man was standing there, looking outside.

Gilbert Norton came down three steps from the craft, briefcase in hand, and was met by two men who nodded a silent greeting and escorted him shoulder-to-shoulder to the front door of the main house. One of two guards there, dressed casually in jeans and woolen shirts, opened the door and Gilbert left his escorts behind. Inside, the foyer was in gloom; Gil passed four men who watched silently from chairs and a sofa, and walked directly to the line of small night-lights leading down a long hallway to a closed door. He knocked four times, paused briefly, and opened the door.

Log walls and a high, beamed ceiling glowed in the light from a hissing fire in the great stone fireplace. Two leather sofas, a chair and a massive oak desk were the furnishings, and two walls were lined with books from floor to ceiling. A man sat behind the desk. He smiled.

"Good to see you, Gil. Have a good trip?"

"I did, Mister President. Thank you. Because of your encouraging phone call the report arrived on time. I have it here." Gil patted his briefcase with one hand.

"Good. Well, do sit down, and take off that overcoat."

Gil took off his coat and draped it over a sofa before sitting down in a leather chair in front of the desk. The heat on the back of his neck felt like it was coming from a blast furnace. He was immediately thirsty, but said nothing. He took a thin folder from his briefcase and pushed it across the desk to his host.

The President of the United States opened the folder and began reading. Gil watched stoically, rigid in his chair. Sweat was running down the back of his neck, and his mouth was powder dry. Suddenly the President looked up at him.

"Sorry, Gil. Got the fire too hot tonight. There's a bar just right of the fireplace. Why don't you fix both of us a scotch with plenty of ice? We need to talk this thing through leisurely."

"Yes, Mister President."

"It's not a breach of protocol to call me Arthur in this room, Gil."

Gil smiled. "I realize that, Mister President. It's a matter of respect, sir."

Arthur Evans shook his head. "Just for that you can pour yourself a triple. Me too. One page into this, and I'm already irritated."

Gil went to the bar and made their drinks while his President read. When he returned with the drinks he found Evans frowning at the open file in front of him.

"It gets worse and worse. Now the Green Party is pissed at us. That makes it unanimous. The Reds and the Blues have opposed cooperation from the get-go. Nothing they do surprises me, but I've never heard such strong language from the Greens. We can't let their military be involved, Gil. It's an open invitation to anarchy."

"I realize that, sir. I see it as a security issue, and some sloppy leadership. There's pressure for quick results, and testing has not been either safe or secure. There was another civilian sighting last week. The fringe folks are on to it, and it'll be on the web any day. Security is a shambles, sir, and our colleagues are only pointing this out."

"But they're asking for a change of command, Gil, and I'm not going to authorize it. We have too many insiders as it is. NSA should be putting pressure on Davis to tighten security, not me. Officially I don't know anything about this operation, remember?"

"Yes, sir. We have a man in place, but Davis has the authority and is pushing hard. The Pentagon is pleased with that, and has not been sympathetic to my complaints."

"Bradley and his OSS mentality again," said the President. "I'll give him a personal call in the morning. This operation will be secure, or the leadership moves to Langley."

"I appreciate that, Mister President. I think we're better trained to run operations this deep, anyway, but we're always ready to give advice if the military is willing to listen to us. There's another concern, sir, if you'll read further."

Arthur Evans scowled at him, but read on rapidly, riffling pages. He raised an eyebrow, tapped the file with a finger. "So, when did these little 'accidents' begin?"

"Two months ago, maybe earlier. Little things at first: parts missing, inventory errors, some backup disks mysteriously erased. Lately it's more serious: mislabeled fuel lines, weld breaks in a sodium loop, and then a broken cable nearly lost a lift pod for us in the main bay. It's more than circumstance, sir. I think it's planned, and so do our allies. the Reds in particular have denied any efforts to block technology transfer, even though they've vocally opposed it. The Blues say they won't dignify such an insulting accusation with an answer."

"Personal opinion, Gil," said Evans.

"I think one or both groups are lying, sir, though I can't see them working together on something like this. It could also be a few people in their ranks. I think the incidents are planned, and project Shooting Star is in danger. We can't afford delays of any length, and if the Greens feel their interests are threatened our window of opportunity could be closed in an instant. Even your good will won't be able to prevent it, Mister President."

"There was a time when I could talk to them," said Evans.

"That was when you had my job, sir, before the senate years and the presidency. These aren't the same people you were dealing with then. You're a stranger to them."

"That's why I have people like you around me, Gil. I can squeeze the Pentagon to tighten base security, but these other things take a different kind of fix. I see a lot of finger pointing in this report. This has to stop. We need to restore the Greens' confidence and excise the bad guys if there's active sabotage going on. Give me some ideas on how to do it." Evans steepled his fingers in front of his face, awaiting an immediate answer from the man he had trained two decades before in a previous life.

"I want to send in a new field operative, sir. He's very deep in our structure, one of five men who've worked indirectly with the Greens in East Europe. Our people know him as an outstanding data analyst, but he's killed for us on two occasions. I want to send him into the base as a support analyst to speed up tech-transfer, but his parallel mission will be to find out who our enemies are in Shooting Star and to neutralize them."

"You think one man can do this?"

"It's pretty much a closed shop, sir. Any more than one new person could be suspicious. And the man I'm considering is a lone wolf at his best."

"You don't need my authorization, Gil. Do what you think is necessary, but get us that technology, the plane, the generator, the whole package intact. I don't have to tell you how much we need it."

"I understand, Mister President. My operative will be on his way by tomorrow evening. I'm seeing him in the morning."

Evans smiled, and downed the last half of his drink in a gulp. "Anything I can do, Gil. Keep me in the loop."

"I will, sir."

"I miss it, you know. The challenges, action, even the fear. But I was a lot younger, then."

"I know the feeling, sir. All I fly now is a desk, but I have good people to do the work and I try to stay out of their way. A good man once taught me that."

Evans smiled again. "Finnish that scotch, then, and join me for a sandwich and coffee before you have to leave. It's been a while, Gil. I want to hear all about those grandkids."

They retired to a dining room with a long oaken table lit by candles, and a military chef served them slices of rye bread and a plate heaped with pastrami. They talked until midnight, renewing a friendship going back three decades, a common heritage going back to childhood in the desert country of the southwest. And when the helicopter lifted off, Gil looked outside, saw the silhouette of his president and friend standing behind the dimly lit window, and he contemplated the loneliness of great power.

The helicopter sped him to the base where he would don pressure suit and helmet for the Mach 4 flight back to Langley. Gil only glanced at the bright stars in a clear Arizona sky, then took the file of Eric Price out of his briefcase and began to read. It was a thick file, full of a rich history of both brilliance and violence, the history of a complex man with multiple personalities living together under an uneasy truce.

Gil needed all of those personalities to work together this time. He searched for a way to encourage it. By the time he got back to Langley, he actually thought he'd found the answer.

* * * * * * *

The ceiling of the cavern was a hundred feet above the red-rock floor, and two cranes moved along hanging tracks there, preparing to move cargo. The port wall itself was now darkened and transparent, and the lights behind it flickered like distant stars. It was already cold, and the men waiting in front of the wall hugged thick parkas to stay warm.

The cranes were dropping their great hooks toward the floor when a baffled door screeched upwards in a far wall of the cavern, and an electric switch engine pushed two flat cars inside on another set of tracks to receive cargo. As they came to a stop, the port wall suddenly turned green, then blue with flashes of red, and rolled upwards like another great door. Behind it was pitch-blackness, then sudden movement. Packing crates eight feet wide and equally high came out of the darkness, each carried on a hydraulic lifter operated by a single man. The men awaiting their arrival rushed to attach webbing and lift-eyes to each crate, and the cranes dutifully moved each across the cavern to the receiving flatcars. There were ten crates, and in twenty minutes they were loaded and the switch engine backed slowly out of the cavern with its precious cargo, the door closing behind it. Ten men pushed the hydraulic lifters back into the darkness, the port wall shimmered green, and was transparent again.

Nobody noticed that eleven men had come in with the lifters.

The cranes moved back into their resting positions in the corners of the cavern, the operators descending in one-man elevators in clear plastic tubes and joining the rest of the receiving crew. A military flatbed truck came to get them and drove them out of the cavern along an open tunnel curving out of sight near the train tracks.

High above the floor, a long window looked out onto the port wall. Figures moved there. The lights in the cavern went out, leaving only the star-like flickers of blue behind the port. The light behind the window went out. Silence descended on the cavern, and remained there for several minutes.

Suddenly, a red light bloomed by the port wall. The light was carried by a man who went straight to one of the elevators, and lifted himself to the control cabin of a crane. An electric engine whirred, and the crane's great lifting hook was lowered to the floor. The man descended from the cab, went to the hook. A second light flared, this one white and hot, and the man played it over the crane's lifting cable at a single spot for only a few seconds. He ascended the elevator again, and the crane's hook was lifted back to its resting position. The electric engine ceased to whir. Again there was only the red light as the man came down the elevator and went back to stand at the port wall. The red light flicked out. Blackness and silence returned to the cavern, but not for long.

The port wall suddenly shimmered green, and then blue and red as it soundlessly rolled upwards. The silhouette of the man was briefly visible before the port closed again, and the man was gone.

The cavern was empty again.

CHAPTER THREE
ERIC PRICE

It wasn't as if he'd planned to come home early, a trick to catch Jenny doing what he knew she'd been doing for months. No, the assignment had come out of the blue, and he had a late afternoon plane, and some things to pack for cold weather where he was going, so he caught a cab home and there was the guy's Mercedes sitting right in front of the house. He let himself in with the stealth of his profession and went up the stairs without a sound, past Gia's bedroom, their little girl, their love-child, down the hall to the master-bedroom and half-opened door and sounds of rising pleasure, and there they were, tangled in the sheets, humping and grinding and moaning, and he slammed the door back on its hinges and they freaked.

Jenny screamed, and the guy came out of her, pop, like a cork out of a bottle, and his eyes were the size of poker chips. Eric smiled, pulled the Smith-forty-five from his shoulder holster and pointed it at the sweating couple. "Now," he said, "The only question is, which one of you do I kill first?"

Jenny burst into tears and was pleading with him to understand; the guy just babbled and frothed at the mouth. Eric went ahead and shot both of them, Jenny first, then the guy, right in the forehead, and their blood sprayed over the wall from floor to ceiling. But when he paused to admire his handiwork there was a shrill scream from behind him, and when he turned there was Gia in her teddy bear pajamas, Annie-doll clutched tightly, and she shouted, "You didn't have to kill mommy! You're a *bad* daddy! I'll never speak to you again. Never, never, never!" She ran back to her room and slammed the door behind her.

And Eric Price finally awoke.

He awoke sweating, and disgusted with himself. The bedcover was on the floor, and the sheets were a twisted mess around his legs. He untangled himself, got his feet on the floor, put his head in his hands and sat that way for a minute, coming back to reality. No, he hadn't killed Jenny, but a part of him still thought about doing it. There'd been no surprising a happy couple in bed. He'd simply come home from a three-month assignment in Bulgaria to find a house empty except for his clothes and a few personal things and a note lying on the floor by the front door.

You're never here, and you don't care about us. I've found someone who does. My lawyer will contact you. Jenny.

Seventeen years ago.

The dream disgusted him, the product of a brain-part he despised, the part that hated and plotted and killed. It was not Eric Price, not now, not at this moment. It was an evil, rancid thing, deep inside, but alert to anything that threatened or abused him.

He knew what had triggered the dream again. The day-old memory instantly brought an ache to his chest, a constriction in the throat, a burning in the eyes. A phone call while he was gone, the message left by a daughter who had refused contact with him for seventeen years.

Daddy, this is Gia. Mom will be furious if she finds out I called you, so please don't tell her. I'm getting married in two weeks. Michael is giving me away, of course. Mom insisted on that. You probably don't care, but I'm letting you know anyway. Maybe someday things can be different between us, but not now, so I'm not inviting you to the wedding. I don't feel good about that; I guess that's why I'm calling. But I missed you again. You're just never there, daddy. You never were. Bye.

Eric wiped his eyes dry, then showered and dressed for the day. Breakfast was toast with peanut butter, and coffee. The limousine arrived for him at nine. He got in, and never saw his driver. The windows were totally blackened, but his trained mind followed the turns and measured the distances by instinct as they drove out into the Virginia countryside. Later, if required to, he would be able to locate the meeting place within a mile or two, but it was unlikely that Gil would ever use the place again.

One hundred and thirty four minutes later the car slowed, then stopped. A man wearing a black suit with a power tie opened the door. The loosely fitting suit failed to hide the bulk of a shoulder holster from an experienced eye. "Follow me, please," said the man.

They were in a garage of concrete with a steel-baffle door already closed and a personnel door to one side. They went through it into what looked like a private residence with Georgian furnishings in dark woods and brass. The windows were covered with blinds, and lights were on. Gil sat on a couch in a lushly furnished front room, and several files lay open on a glass-topped coffee table. A silver tray was there with a press-down coffee server, and two glass mugs.

"Morning," said Gil, and patted the sofa where Eric should sit.

Eric sat. "Nice place."

"Borrowed from a friend," said Gil. "Pour yourself coffee if you want it. We'll be having lunch in an hour. This won't take long, and you can do most of your reading on the plane. There'll be a two week prep period in Phoenix before you go into the field."

"I thought this was for data analysis."

"It is, but it's also a cover for something deeper. You'll be living in town, so you need a cover, and that's what the prep is about. You're going to be an art dealer."

"What?"

"Sedona is an art center. You're getting a crash course in contemporary art represented there. You work out of your home, connected to galleries all over the country. You're going to have an active social life."

"Why can't I work at the base? This is a military problem, not civilian."

"The man we have there now thinks otherwise. He thinks there are commercial interests in the technology, interests that have compromised some of the leadership. There are several problems here, Eric, and they all affect base security. We want you in a position to see the overall picture, and that means playing two roles."

"You have a lot of people experienced in domestic operations. Why me?"

Gil smiled. "Your record in data analysis and tech evaluation is top-notch. We have to be sure we're being fed accurate information because we're dealing with three factions, and two of them are resistant to giving us anything. You've spent over a decade in Eastern Europe, and you know how they love anarchy in their private business dealings. The technology is important to us; you need to find out if it's real, accurate, and who the hell is trying to keep us from getting it. The bad guys might include American business interests who want it for their own. That's enough challenges, even for you. Security prevents us from giving you much help. We have one man inside, and that's all you'll get. You'll have to recruit your own allies without dropping your cover."

"What about command-chains?"

"Once you're settled, we'll contact you regularly, but you run your own day-to-day operation."

Eric's eyes narrowed. "And what if it becomes necessary to neutralize someone?"

"That we will have to talk about," said Gil firmly. He opened a lower-left drawer, withdrew a manila envelope stuffed tightly by its contents, and pushed it across the desk for Eric. "This is for starters: local cultural material, maps, and some bios of key people you'll be dealing with. The rest will be waiting for you in Phoenix. You're flying out this evening."

"I'd like to get a few things from home to take with me."

"Give me a list. You're staying here until the plane is ready. All that you need is packed and ready. Your apartment is being cleaned and secured. You could be gone for several months this time."

Eric thought of Gia's wedding, and frowned. Gil seemed to read his mind.

"Sorry about your daughter. I didn't see my kids much either while they were growing up, but I was lucky enough to have a wife who stuck with me."

"You heard the recording?"

"We heard it when it came in; you know that. Time heals a lot of things, so for now just let her be happy. Do your job; it's what you have. Okay?"

"Yeah, it's okay—for now." Eric took the envelope from the desk and looked at Gil darkly. "Not for much longer, I think."

Gil nodded. "We'll talk about that. It happens to all of us. It happened to me. Don't worry about it. Just do the job this time, and then we'll talk."

Eric nodded. "What now?"

"Coffee, lunch, and a quiet room where you can read. You leave in four hours. Good hunting."

They shook hands, and a security agent arrived to take Eric away again.

CHAPTER FOUR
WARNINGS

The office of World Arts was always closed and locked during business hours, its occupant coming and going at all times. Leon Newell was said to be computer-linked with business partners who did acquisitions and shipping in Phoenix, New York and San Francisco. His concern was setting up domestic and foreign markets for fine and cultural arts from the U.S., Europe, and Asia. Like many other entrepreneurs in Sedona, he preferred to live and work in a lovely small-town setting and commute one or two days a week to his regional office in Phoenix, doing much of his business by computer. At art openings he appeared in thousand-dollar, tailored suits, but otherwise was seen publicly in jeans, silk shirts and alligator-skin boots.

Leon was a small man, slim, a chiseled face with green, piercing eyes and carefully trimmed, red hair. He was meticulous about his appearance: clean-shaven face, nails cleaned and polished, and every hair in its place with fashion purpose. It was said his academic training was in art education, but he demonstrated a wide knowledge of history, anthropology and physical science, and had deep interests in all aspects of new-age culture. This made him a welcome guest among the socially elite in town and the target of more than one sophisticated and available woman there. Leon's somewhat affected speech and gestures only charmed them, and suspicions of the men about Leon's sexual preferences quickly evaporated as they got to know him better.

He lived in a two million dollar Santa Fe-style adobe on two acres west of town. The house was nearly invisible a hundred yards off Dry Creek Road, hidden by a forest of cactus, shrub mesquite and juniper. It was owned by World Arts Corporation, and paid for in cash, no specific names on the title. The property was surrounded by a rail fence in metal painted olive green, and was entered through an electronically controlled gate. A security system included floodlights activated by the motion of something as small as a mouse, it was said, but the neighbors were also wealthy, and understood the privacy of the rich. They did not complain. Leon came and went in his yellow Humvee, gave a few, lavish parties for the chosen among them, and otherwise lived an unobtrusive life.

He was regarded as an important member of the community, and so people were naturally excited when they learned that one of his business partners would soon join him in their little town.

Leon, on the other hand, had been given the news earlier at home, and was not so much excited as he was disturbed by it.

The news had come to his home via satellite in the regular morning's transmission from Washington. Eric Price was both a program and technology analyst with the highest credentials from operations in Europe and Asia. The man's extensive file was attached. All the man's work was with the military, and there was no mention of direct links to CIA or NSA. A Pentagon operative, perhaps, career military. Gil had simply counter-signed the order, and forwarded it without warning. Perhaps he hadn't had any. The Pentagon was reacting to the security problems, and slow progress at the base. They were taking steps to speed things up. Perhaps. Leon had received the notice indirectly, since he was not a link in the military chain of command.

There was a way to check the information flow. Leon picked up his cell phone and dialed the private number of Colonel Alexander Davis, linked to him by military satellite. The call was answered on the second ring.

"Davis." The voice was low, and soft.

"Leon. I just got word about the new analyst they're sending out for Shooting Star. I suppose you know about it."

"Yesterday morning. How did you find out about it?"

"NSA Phoenix sent me a copy of the Pentagon order. We're providing his cover in town."

"I saw that. I asked for this help months ago. I don't see why they can't house him at the base. Everything he needs is here."

"He's not just a tech analyst. Half his record is for restructuring programs and rebuilding security networks. Didn't you get his file?"

"I got it. He smells like a CIA operative to me. When I asked the Pentagon about it I was told the question was not relevant. Isn't he one of yours?"

"No. His record is military. I have nothing to do with his operation except to provide his civilian cover while he's here. I'll probably learn more when he arrives tomorrow. We're putting him up in a house close to mine, and he'll have a place in my office in town. I'll let you know anything new that comes up."

"I appreciate that, Leon," said Davis. "We've had a good working relationship up to now, and I wouldn't like to see someone come in and mess it up. We're getting close, you know, close enough that someone is trying to slow things down. I have my own people to dig them out; I don't need Washington sending in someone to do it for me. If this guy Price even smells like a field operative to you, I want to know about it. Accidents can happen, and there's too much at stake for both of us. You remember that."

"Oh, I remember. That's why I called you."

"Good man. I'll be able to get out of here Saturday. Let's have a drink on it. I'll call you early morning."

"It'll have to be late. I have an opening to attend at eight at Frago's. There's a bar just down the street from it. Working class, no art patrons."

"Sounds good. I'll call to verify. Gotta go, now. Keep your eyes open."

The line went dead.

Leon turned off his cell phone. There was a queasy feeling in his stomach. Accidents can happen. That was going too far, but worrying now was premature. Meet the man; find out who or what he is. Time for maneuvering later.

Leon went to the bathroom and spent over an hour preparing an appropriate fashion statement for a day including luncheon with proper, wealthy ladies of the local garden club.

* * * * * * *

Eric Price arrived at exactly seven in the evening, as prearranged by telephone. The entry-com beeped, and Leon jumped to answer it.

"Yes?"

"Eric Price to see Leon Newell. I'm expected."

"Park behind the Humvee. I'll meet you at the door." Leon pressed a button to open the heavy gate, went to the door and outside to stand on the porch. It was late dusk outside, and red rock bluffs stood in silhouette, but a few bright stars twinkled overhead. Light from inside the house spilled onto the porch, and a yard light mounted above the garage door illuminated the Humvee sitting there. A black BMW sedan came up to the garage, tires crunching rusty scree as it came to a stop behind Leon's vehicle. The man who got out of the car was tall, slender, wore a dark suit and carried a briefcase. When he came up on the porch he did not smile, but extended a hand.

"Eric Price. You must be Mister Newell."

Leon extended a limp hand. "Please, it's Leon." He suppressed a flinch when Price ground his fingers together in the handshake. "Welcome to the new-age capital of the world."

Price regarded him somberly with dark eyes. "Haven't seen any UFOs yet," he said.

Leon laughed. "Oh, you will. I'll teach you how to look for them. Come in, before you get cold out here. We're nearly a mile above sea level, you know."

Price followed him inside, looked at the beamed ceiling, the leather furniture, the paintings on the walls, the small assemblies of sculpture and glass arranged on tables and shelves. "Very nice," he said.

"The company has good taste. Something to drink?"

"Coffee is fine," said Price, and then gave Leon an appraising look. "You come out of Langley, or Washington?"

"Neither. Let's say I'm on loan to a needy agency. How about you?"

"Likewise. Let's leave it there. When do I go to the base? That wasn't in my package."

"Soon enough. Get settled, and I'll introduce you around. We can't just spy on people; we have a business to run."

"The company actually sells art to people?" A faint trace of a smile came to the hard face of the man. Nicely hewn features, but eyes so dark brown they seemed black. His speech was even and direct, and there were no nervous gestures..

"Of course. We do rather well, in fact. It's certainly more satisfying than fighting with political cretins for senate appropriations. This Sunday there will be a party in honor of your arrival. It will be your introduction to the opulence here, and the people who live with it."

"And what does that have to do with the problem I'm here to solve?"

"Nothing, or everything, I don't know. There might be outside influences involved, and it certainly can't hurt to befriend the shakers and movers in this town."

"I suppose," said Price, "if they understand I'm not a sociable person. It's not an ordinary part of my job. That's why I asked."

Leon poured steaming coffee into two mugs and offered one to Price. "A perfectly legitimate question. Rely on me, and I'll have you charming people in no time at all. They should include that training for all field agents, I think."

"I'm not a field agent; I'm an analyst," said Price, a bit quickly. "I don't even own a weapon. I climb logic trees and crunch numbers, and I'm supposed to evaluate a technology I haven't been told about yet. Who's going to do it? You?"

The man's look was so direct and focused that Leon felt the hairs move on the back of his neck. It was not the look of a data analyst, he thought.

"I can do it, but I'm surprised you weren't briefed beforehand. What *did* they tell you?"

Eric blinked once. "A project called Shooting Star is being run at a hidden base near here, another area fifty-one, and apparently it's so deep it's considered beyond black ops. They've obtained an advanced aircraft of some kind, and can't get it to fly for them like the Pentagon wants. I'm here to find out why that is. Is the technology Russian?"

"We don't know. The people who brought it out to us claim to be eastern European, but won't identify their country. Very slight accents. Could be Slav."

"You don't have any original documentation? No plans or manuals?"

"Nothing. It's all been done by word of mouth from a few people who arrived with the aircraft."

"Let me guess. They don't know how to fly it."

"Apparently not. Our guess is they stole it. We've spent a year probing around east Europe to see if anyone, particularly the Russians, is missing anything. The report I've seen says the entire craft arrived in one piece on a Swedish-registered ship, and was airlifted here. Look, these are questions you should ask at the base when we get you there. You just got in; relax a bit. At ease, soldier."

"I'm not a soldier," said Price, "and neither are you. It seems both of us are on loan to Gil's office, and he's the only boss we have in common. So quit fishing. I'm not happy about being here in such a stupid situation, and I like to be well briefed before I begin an assignment. That isn't happening."

Leon thought of the file he'd read on Price, and thought, *Ph.D. prima donnas can be such absolute pricks.* "Then I suggest you complain about it to Gil right away. He'll explain to you I'm only a liaison to the base, and what you want will come from Colonel Alexander Davis, who heads the project. My function is to integrate you with the civilian community, get you settled and up to speed on our communications with Langley and Washington. And I really do hope we're going to get along personally, If not, then you can drive back to Phoenix and fly away to wherever you came from. There will be no solo players in this operation. I won't stand for it, and neither will Gil, and I just realized I've told you I'm not some tiny cog in the wheel of this operation."

Price was smiling at him. "Honesty is best. Gil told me I'd be reporting to you, but you weren't telling me that."

"Well done, Mister Price. I'll remember it. Can we start over? Welcome to Sedona."

"Could be interesting. I *was* pulled from a nice assignment in Germany to come here. That aircraft must be important."

"It's more than an aircraft, Mister Price. It can fly in space at great speed if we can ever figure out what powers it out there. Colonel Davis will do the briefing. Have you been to your house yet?"

"No, I came straight here from town."

"You passed it, then, the next house down, about five hundred yards. We can walk there if you wish."

"It's getting dark out there," said Price.

Leon smiled. "I'll show you another way. Come with me, and leave your briefcase. We'll come back later for your car."

Price's eyebrow rose, but he said nothing and left his briefcase on a table. Leon led him through a kitchen with stainless steel appliances and blue slate counter tops to a door that led downstairs. There was a game room with a pool table, an alcove behind glass with two circular openings in the wall. Two cylindrical conduits ran twenty-five meters to bull's-eye targets on metal frames, well lit. Leon gestured casually at the conduits. "You're welcome to practice here anytime; I'd like the company. Just give me some warning."

"Like I said, I don't have a weapon," said Price.

Leon smiled. "No problem. I have plenty for both of us."

They went to another door, which Leon opened with dramatic flair. "Our own, private walkway, good in any weather."

A tunnel ran straight ahead a hundred meters before turning to the right and out of sight. Pipes ran along the ceiling, and there was an orange light every few meters, high on the wall. The floor was dirt-covered, with sections of metal grating that clanged hollowly as they walked.

"How far does this go?" asked Price.

"It only connects our houses. Quite a job putting it in."

The walls were solid red-rock, broken by ventilation grates every fifty meters. There was a faint humming sound coming from them.

"You'll have a key to the entrance at my house in case of emergencies."

"What emergencies?" asked Price.

"One never knows in our business. And it's convenient for contact without outside observation. I can never be sure the office in town is secure."

Price blinked slowly at him, and Leon knew the man thought he was being overly dramatic. "Nothing is done here without reason, Mister Price."

"That's Eric; we're supposed to be partners, at least in business."

Leon did not like the innuendo when he saw the twinkle in Price's eyes. "That's all it is, I assure you. And don't let my little affectations fool you; appearances can be very deceiving, even dangerous in the wrong situation."

"Just getting to know you, Leon. No offense intended."

"None taken," said Leon, and smiled sweetly while pinching the thumb pad of his left hand with a fingernail because he'd allowed the man to pull his chain again. Price was more than an analyst, that much was certain, and there was a cruel side to his psyche.

They came to the end of the tunnel. The steel door there was locked. Leon unlocked it, and handed Eric the key. "It fits both ends of the tunnel. Both doors are kept locked, and there's no other way out of the tunnel."

The basement was dark, and Leon switched on a light.

Empty shelves floor to ceiling, and an oil furnace. They went up wooden stairs to the main floor. Beamed ceilings, Santa Fe style, but smaller than Leon's house, two bedrooms, front and dining rooms, nicely but not richly furnished. A notebook computer sat on a bar counter in the kitchen. Fish swam lazily on the screen. Shelves were stocked with food, and the refrigerator was full. Two garage door openers were on the dining room table. One was for the gate. "Motion sensors all around the property," said Leon, "and any alarm will be relayed to me." He pulled open a drawer in the dining room hutch. A Beretta 92F automatic was there, loaded and locked, hammer forward, safety off. "Something familiar, right out of school. Just for emergencies, of course, but you might consider carrying it."

"Lots of precautions for a data analyst," said Eric. "I assume the reasons will be made known to me soon."

"Tomorrow, when you're settled. We start at eight, at the office. You know where it is?"

"I passed it on the way."

"I'll have the entire file there on what I know so far. Here are the house keys, front and back door, garage door to the house."

They went back to the basement, leaving the upstairs lights on. The walk back seemed shorter. Eric picked up his briefcase again and Leon led him to the front door, stopping there before opening it. He looked up at Eric, and was suddenly coldly serious.

"In the coming weeks or months, however long it takes, I will try to be as honest with you as I can, and I will expect the same from you. This is not to say we must share information about our individual backgrounds, training or agencies. We each have our own agendas, I'm sure, but we must share where they overlap or this operation can turn out badly and even have tragic consequences. You'll have to decide what you can tell me, and I will do likewise, but please believe me when I say we've been assigned to work together to save a project of high value to our country, and that's what we're going to do."

Leon smiled, and extended a hand. "Beginning tomorrow

morning."

Eric nodded, and shook his hand. "Fair enough. Your grip has improved in the past hour. See you at the office."

Leon let him out, and waited at the door until the big BMW had cleared the gate, and then he went inside the house and placed a phone call to Colonel Alexander Davis to tell him what he'd learned about the new man.

* * * * * * *

Eric made the short drive to his house, and put the car in the garage. It was near midnight when he finished unpacking. He left the Beretta in the hutch, but kept his own forty-five-Colt-Modified in its holster, and put it loaded and locked, hammer on half cock, in the nightstand by his bed. The Walther PPK went under his pillow. He sent an e-mail to a sister he didn't have, saying he'd arrived home safely and that Uncle Leo was doing fine, then fixed himself half a pastrami on rye from the refrigerator and washed it down with water. It took him over an hour to get to sleep, his senses alert to every sound, every creak and groan of an unfamiliar house settling in for the night. Twice he thought he heard footsteps in the dark hallway outside his closed bedroom door. The yard lights flashed on several times, alert to any motion: mouse, snake, perhaps a javelina on the prowl. Exhaustion overwhelmed all of it, and after an hour he slept without remembered dreams, awakening refreshed to begin his new assignments.

A few hundred yards up the road, Leon Newell's night passed as well, but not without disturbance.

* * * * * * *

Davis listened politely, but reserved judgment until he'd met with Price. He was inclined to agree with Leon that the man was a CIA field operative, and not just an analyst. They spoke for only a few minutes, since it was getting late.

Leon went through his nightly bathing and manicuring ritual and sipped a glass of warmed brandy before crawling into bed around two in the morning. He set the alarm for seven, and lay awake for several minutes thinking about Eric Price, his words, expressions, stillness of his posture, and the focus of his eyes. It was vaguely like being in the presence of a predatory cat, he thought, not a man of science and mathematics. The real man was not well hidden, not from the view of a professional, and Leon Newell was a professional. He could swish with the best salon dandies, offer the limp hand to ladies and talk to them like a sister, but he'd killed seven times in the service of his country and also to meet his own agendas. And in just an hour, Price had been able to get a glimpse of what lay beneath the surface of the man he was supposed to trust. That made him insightful, and potentially dangerous, a condition that could be tolerated only to a certain point before Leon might be called upon to neutralize him.

The warm brandy took effect, and Leon gradually drifted off into a light sleep, a quiet place between wakefulness and dreams. Leon rarely slept deeply. It was a result of his training, and years spent in situations where a moment of careless preoccupation could result in death. He rested quietly, was not oblivious to sounds inside and outside the house, or the beating of his own heart. He was not oblivious to the texture of his silken sheets, or the lingering scents of lavender and fried meat in the air.

Hovering above the abyss of dreams, Leon first noticed a sweet odor, something familiar, like myrrh. His head began to swirl gently, a peaceful descent to a place dark yet safe, the place where his true self, his higher self, dwelt in contemplative solitude. He met himself there, his naked body glistening gold, sitting in lotus position, hands out from his sides, palms upwards. He opened his eyes, and they were black, and he smiled to himself.

"Welcome," he said to himself. "I believe you have a truth to tell me. You may do it here safely, for only the one of us is here."

"And what is that truth?" asked Leon.

"There is a new person in your life, and you have deep reservations about your association with him. You must bring these feelings forward and look at them with a quiet mind. They may be real, or an illusion."

The black eyes blinked once. Leon felt peace.

"I have judged by instinct based on past experience. The man is more than what he says. He is a killer. He can be dangerous to the movement if he discovers what it really is."

"Then you must watch him closely, and share with us what you learn, and I will guide you along the proper course. I will speak to the angels, and they to me, and the higher self of the one whom you speak of will also be consulted. Together we will choose the correct path. Together, we are in harmony with The All."

Leon felt a kind of euphoria, an uplifting, and the golden man faded from view. The sweet scent returned, and he felt a cool breeze on his face, arms and chest that brought him near a waking state. He opened his eyes. The room was in deep gloom, but the silhouettes of tall figures surrounded his bed. One leaned over close enough for Leon to see a glow of reflected light in two large eyes, and the man's voice was barely a whisper.

"Sleep now, friend, and return to the golden one, for it's he who will guide you. We will be watching."

A faint hiss, a burst of sweet odor, and Leon drifted away, thinking, *these people are friends, and they have come to me before. They ask questions, and I must answer them, but always it's things I've talked about with Colonel Davis. Why don't they just ask him?*

He awoke refreshed in the morning, and remembered nothing that had happened after Eric Price had left him the previous night.

CHAPTER FIVE
AGENDAS

The meeting room was one level down from the surface, and had a high ceiling. Six men sat around a large oaken table in dim red light coming from panels above them. They were cloaked and hooded for anonymity and wore earphones connected to a translator module in the center of the table. Two others were not present, but participated via closed circuit television; a camera and video monitor were mounted at one end of the table where the others could see everyone. Heat flowed into the room from floor grates, and a humidifier sprayed a fine mist from one corner of the room. This was in answer to the requests of two of the council members who were suffering uncomfortable skin conditions aggravated by the Arizona heat.

"All are present, so let's begin," said Mister Brown, the chairman. "Mister White will read the minutes of the previous meeting."

The man called Mister White, also a Green, like his chairman, read the minutes, pausing occasionally for the translator to catch up in transmitting his words in four different languages for the council members."

"Are there any corrections or additions?"

There were none.

"Under new business, I have an announcement. A new analyst has arrived to participate in Shooting Star. There's some disagreement among our American colleagues as to what agency he works for and why he's here. If you check your files you'll see he's a top program and technology analyst, involved most recently with the Ju-67 lifter package, which surfaced in Sophia. Excellent credentials, and he's worked for several agencies, including the military, a situation I personally do not find unusual, but the Americans are suffering from their usual paranoia."

"Well, there *have* been problems here," said Mister White. "I don't think they're accidents, and neither do you. I can assure all of you the Green Party is not involved with the problem, but it *will* participate in the solution. I know we have differing views on how and when the drive technology should be revealed, but we all agreed it would eventually be done, and sabotage, either overt or covert, will not be tolerated."

"Are you pointing a finger at anyone in particular?" asked Mister Jones.

"Are you speaking for the Reds today?" asked Mister White.

"I am."

"The Americans have a saying that if the shoe fits you wear it, so I suppose—"

"Nobody is being accused, Mister Jones," said the chairman. "You must admit, however, that any saboteur involved can only be a member of the project and have access to internal correspondence."

"Witness the damage done to the field generator. Only this Council and Colonel Davis knew when that was coming in," said White.

"So maybe you should accuse Davis of something besides his usual corruption."

"It would hardly be in his best interests to damage the technology his corporate masters would like to get their hands on. Whatever Davis does, he can always be diverted by money. He's not the problem here. Someone wants the project slowed, or stopped. It's logical to suspect those who have vocally opposed those goals after agreeing to our initial plan."

"It was your plan," said Jones.

"But you agreed to it. You all did," said Mister Brown. "If

you've changed your minds, then you should disassociate your-selves from the project. We *can* proceed without you."

There was a pause, then, "I doubt you're prepared to pay the political price for that kind of arrogance," said Jones, and he looked down the table towards the television monitor. "I'd like to hear something from the Blues about now. Mister Smith?"

Again a long pause, and then a soft reply from one of the two-seated figures shown on the video screen, a kind of mumble quickly transformed into the metallic speech of the translator.

"We have nothing to gain personally by the success or failure of this project. Our objection from the beginning has been brought against giving any kind of technology to a political system we basically despise. In the end it will make fortunes for a few, and the common people will see little value from it. Our decision to participate was based on developing rela-tions between the governments represented on this council, to show that after a century of squabbling we could actually work together on something. We have done that until recently, and now we're squabbling again. Instead of pointing fingers regarding transfer of a technology that is already a generation old we should be asking who will benefit the most if we go our separate ways again."

"Are you prepared to suggest someone to us?" asked the chairman. "It seems to me we were only having a discussion, not divisive argumentation."

"But people who oppose the project for various reasons should not be equated with saboteurs who endanger or end lives. That was being inferred. I have no person or party in mind, but whoever it is has access to council discussions and physical access to the base. It could be one person, a group, or a govern-ment. It could be one or more of the Americans. This new man just arrived, this Eric Price, I think we all agree he's more than a scientist or mathematician. The need for better and faster data analysis has been around a long time. When the sabotage began, he is suddenly here. I think he's here to solve the problem for us, and we should not waste our time here with pointless accusations. We should be talking about getting a new airframe and converter in here to replace the one our American friends so stupidly damaged in the recent test. And we should at last give them the manual in simple English they can understand. That, at least, is in keeping with our agenda for this meeting."

Chairman Brown quietly bit his tongue to divert an emotional outburst. "Point noted, Mister Jones. You can be certain the sabotage issue will be on next meeting's agenda. And if there are any further unusual incidents, I'm sure this council can put together its own team of agents who won't bother to deal with the perpetrators or their supporters in a humane way."

"And we'll we willing to contribute to that effort," said Mister Jones.

"On to other business, then," said Brown, and they moved on to discuss the logistics of bringing in all the necessary parts to replace what had been damaged or destroyed in the Americans' hastily arranged and ill-fated test. Eric Price was added to the assignments of the watch team, and there was a report on the deuterium separation facility under construction two hundred miles east of Fiji.

The hour ended, and the meeting was adjourned. The video monitor was shut down, and everyone returned to their rooms before their American hosts had risen for a new day.

Mister Jones did not retire so soon. He went directly to his computer, selected one of four channels, addressed a short invitation for a private meeting, and sent it. A minute later the reply arrived on the open channel, voice mode, blank screen.

"Thank you for answering so quickly," said Jones. "You can imagine how irritating the meeting was for me. I tried hard to hold my temper."

"You did well, under the circumstances." The voice coming from the computer was gravelly, slow-paced, and required no translation. "I'm not displeased with you."

"I think the Greens are looking for an excuse to bring in their own military, sir. The man's arrogance has become provocative. He practically dictates policy to the council."

"In time it will trap him. The Blues are also displeased by his attitude. I've just heard from them. I think there might be an opportunity for an alliance."

"But what do we do about the sabotage?"

"The perpetrators must be found, of course. We should all clean our own houses, but the Americans must not be a part of it. We cannot allow our structure to be revealed. And if the new agent they've brought in gets too close to our identities, even at the council level, he'll have to be killed. It'll be easy enough to blame it on the Americans. They're already suspicious of him."

"Any specific orders for me, sir? I truly regret my outburst today."

"Do not be so critical of yourself, my friend. Be my eyes and ears, avoid provocation, but let the Greens know they are not going to define policy for the council. Tactfulness is desirable, but firmness is required."

"Yes, sir."

And the connection was broken.

Jones went right to bed, and was awake for only minutes. He was confident he was doing all that was required of him, and Control had even called him friend. That was a good sign.

* * * * * * *

Leon ordered lunch uptown at Burger Heaven at eleven, before the weekend mob of tourists got hungry enough to descend on the place. Quarter-pounder with curly fries and diet cola were ready in ten minutes, and he was the only person in line. He took his tray over to a rough-hewn table in the mall way between clothing and new age shops, and sat down facing the street. People crowded the walkway, and wandered in and out of the shops. Angelic music came from one doorway, along with the odor of aromatic oils and burning incense.

Leon ate slowly, starting with his fries. He was halfway through with his burger when a balding, heavyset man with a round face sat down opposite him. The man wore jeans, cowboy shirt and black Stetson. He placed a large cup of coffee on the table, took off his Stetson and put it on the bench beside him.

"Nothing to eat?" asked Leon.

Alexander Davis, Colonel, United States Army, scowled as Leon took a big bite out of his hamburger. "That thing you're eating would stay in my stomach for a week."

"Too much stress," said Leon coldly, but smiled to make it a joke.

Davis uncapped his coffee, and took a cautious sip. "Price acknowledged my message. Pickup is at oh-five-hundred Monday."

"Does it *have* to be so early? The party will run after midnight."

"I don't care about your party. I have a schedule to keep."

"If it'll make you happier, you could tell me who your corporate friends are, and I could send them an invitation. Nataly is the best hostess in town."

"They contact me; I don't contact them," said Davis, "and all you are is hired help. Remember that."

"As long as I'm well paid," said Leon. He chewed thoughtfully while Davis took another sip of coffee, then, "So, when are you going to have something else for me?"

"Probably late next week. Our guests are preparing an instruction manual that covers the entire system. After the last test I told them we wouldn't proceed without it."

"Ah, so they really do know how that thing flies."

"We'll see. It could all be lies, and we'll have to test everything, but a copy of the manual should be sent out right away. The usual way, from Phoenix, and if you send it to anyone except our clients I'll know about it."

"Of course," said Leon, but thought, *you just think you know things, asshole, but you don't know jack-shit about what's going on.*

"Just reminding you," said Davis, and then he softened, reached into his shirt pocket and took out a small envelope, folded in half. He handed it to Leon. The envelope felt soft, and bulky. "That'll make you feel better. You'll get the same in two weeks, and so on, as long as you do your job. Enjoy it. Buy a painting, or something."

Leon pocketed the offering. "Give me some warning about delivery of the package."

"Of course," said Davis. "Well, gotta go. It'll be a month before we can meet again like this. Check your P.O. box every day."

Leon nodded. Davis got up and walked away behind Leon's back.

Leon finished his cola leisurely, then went to his Humvee and drove directly to his bank to make a deposit.

CHAPTER SIX
SOCIAL GRACES

Leon picked up Eric at exactly seventeen hundred. Eric buzzed the Humvee through the gate, and was waiting at the garage when it pulled up. The mini-opener on his key ring let them out again. Leon turned right on Dry Creek Road and headed back to 89A, left to the Y, then right to the creek and out of town. Traffic was heavy, the weekend crowd from Phoenix just starting to head for home. All around them the spires and buttes were turning yellow-gold and red-oxide in the light of the setting sun. Hardened to travel all over the world, Eric nonetheless thought he'd never seen so much beautiful, surreal scenery in one place.

It was slightly spoiled by Leon being obnoxious again.

"I know it's not part of your nature, but tonight you're going to be absolutely charming to everyone and laugh at all their stories, no matter how boring or trivial they are."

"Can't I just listen politely?" asked Eric, with what he hoped was a sarcastic tone of voice.

"Not without positive affirmation or a clever response, especially when it comes to their artistic tastes. These are the people who keep our galleries open, dear boy, and they've come from as far away as New York just for this party. Nataly is simply fabulous, and just wait until you see the house."

The narrow road curved sharply several times, and came out onto a sloping plane. Ahead, the multi-spire complex of Cathedral Rocks was a black silhouette against a red and yellow-streaked sky. Leon turned right onto Back-o-Beyond Road, and followed the winding course up into a canyon guarded by red-rock massifs on both sides. Sprawling Santa Fe-style homes were perched grandly on ledges high above the road.

"Definitely the high-rent district," said Eric.

"Five to eight million, most of them. Nataly's is more." Leon turned onto a scree road that climbed steeply and went around four hairpin curves before coming to a closed gate flanked by two guards with holstered automatics. A third man watched from a little kiosk on the other side of the gate.

"Hi, Sam," said Leon to the guard who peered in at them. "Eric Price here is one of the honored guests tonight."

The guard checked their names off a list on his clipboard. "Have a nice evening, gentlemen," he said. A wave of his hand, and the gate opened. They drove through it, around another curve, and came out onto the terraced summit of a butte at eye level with the summits of Cathedral Rocks, a thousand yards distant.

The entire summit of the butte was a single estate built in several layers with a sprawling, single story dwelling at the top. A graveled area was nearly filled with cars. A sloping forest of prickly pear and other cactus led to the edge of an endless pool fed by waterfalls cascading down red rock, and up to a balcony the size of an ordinary house. Festive globe lights in several colors were suspended above the balcony, and a noisy crowd was talking, drinking and enjoying the spectacular views in all directions. Eric followed Leon up red-rock steps to the door of a Spanish-style mansion with red-tiled roof and stucco stained reddish brown. Eric was reminded of Celtic patterns by the ornate carvings on the door. The door was open; they walked right in, and were immediately assailed by those who'd heard about Leon's new partner and wanted to meet him. The women wore designer clothing from jeans to gowns, their men in casual wear to match, and nothing off the rack.

Eric met dozens of people in just half an hour. He shook their hands, listened politely to their small talk, verified over and over again that, yes, he was a single man with nobody special in his life. He smiled until his jaws ached. Leon watched closely and occasionally raised an eyebrow to show his approval. In just half an hour, four women came on to Eric, one whispering how nice it was to see that Leon's new partner was, as she put it, straight as an arrow. The noise level was deafening, and the strain of trying to hear an individual conversation was exhausting. Someone put a drink in his hand without asking. It was scotch, with too much water. He sipped it and smiled and raised his glass to toast things he couldn't hear in the din. His head began to ache. Leon had abandoned him by now, and was nowhere in sight. A woman around forty, tall and elegant, caught his eye from across the room and began edging through the crowd towards him.

Eric fled.

He pretended not to notice the woman coming at him, shouldered his way to the buffet table and filled his plate with prime rib, a roll with butter, and two knishes with some unidentified stuffing. The balcony was within reach, the woman gaining on him. He squeezed past the open, sliding door and fled down a winding staircase to a path descending past the waterfall towards the pool. In seconds he was out of sight of the balcony, hiding like a schoolboy and feeling stupid about it.

The pool was still and beckoning, reflecting the red and orange colors of a sky at dusk. He went to it, eating a few bites from his plate, and sat down in a lounge chair close to the waterfall. Mist cooled his face, his senses calmed by the white noise of splashing water.

He'd been sitting there for several minutes when there was movement in his peripheral vision. He looked right and saw a woman descending the stairs. She wore an orange, Asian-style, sleeveless dress with a slit up one thigh. Her long hair was coal black, draped over a shoulder, and her skin seemed to glow in the day's last light.

Eric stared without conscious thought, for she was the most beautiful woman he'd ever seen. She saw him, then, and smiled.

He averted his gaze, looked towards the pool, but she came close, and he smelled scented soap and lavender.

"Leon said I'd probably find you here. A person can't hear himself think upstairs, but everyone is having such a good time. Aren't you?"

Eric dared to look at her, and swallowed hard. Up close, her eyes were nearly as dark as her hair, her skin so white that fine, blue veins showed in her forearms. "I'm afraid I'm not very good in crowds," he managed to say, and was thankful when his voice didn't quaver. "Introvert, I guess."

"Me, too," she said. "I'm most comfortable one-on-one with people. And I think it's very peaceful down here."

Eric was trying to think of a profound reply when there was a shout from above him. He looked up; saw Leon hanging well out beyond the corner of the balcony to be able to see them past the waterfall. Leon waved merrily, hanging on tightly to the railing with one hand.

"Hi, Nataly. I see you found him. Do try to coax him back upstairs again."

Eric rolled his eyes, but Nataly just waved at Leon. "I promise," she called, and Leon disappeared from view.

"He thinks he's my mother," said Eric, trying to be clever.

Nataly sat down beside him, looked out at the pool. "He's a complex man, so flamboyant, but beneath the surface is something else, don't you think?"

"Something else?"

She turned to look at him, and he felt himself blush, hoped it was hidden in the rapidly dimming light.

"Yes. Something still, focused, even dark. It's in his eyes. I can see things in people's eyes."

Eric averted his gaze, gestured around him with one hand. "This is an incredible place you have here."

"It's comfortable, and I love the views. I can detach myself from the physical plane here, go where violence and tragedy don't exist, at least for a while." She stretched out a slender arm and pointed towards Cathedral Rocks. "You see the three spires to the left? Somewhere in there is a portal from another dimension. Beings come and go there, aliens or angels, depending on your beliefs."

"You actually believe that?" asked Eric.

She smiled with her eyes. "I think it's possible, and if other people believe I must respect that. I'm exposed to many strange beliefs by people who come into my shop."

"New Visions? I thought it was a gallery."

"It's going to be soon, but the front half is my store."

Eric's response was out before he could stop it. "Business must be good," he said, and hated himself.

"I do well," she said, after a pause of two heartbeats, "but it's a hobby for me, like the art. Creative, imaginative people intrigue me, and I cater to their wishes. Come in, sometime, and we'll find a crystal that resonates with you, or maybe a relaxing fragrance. I don't do it for money. My late father provided for all my physical comforts, including this estate, but like anyone else I try to provide for my own mental and emotional needs. I see people every day who haven't been able to do it. I see the pain in their eyes, and hear it in their words. They've lost touch with a higher part of themselves."

Eric tried hard to look her straight in the eye, and failed. "The new-age culture is totally new to me. The artists I've dealt with in the east are more pop than new age. I guess I'm really a left-brained accountant at heart, but I'm willing to learn."

Nataly's eyes widened beautifully. "Ah, well, that's a start." She stood up, extended a hand. "Now, before I throw you to the hordes again, let me take you on a tour of the house. Two of our local artists will join us, and they want to meet you. Leon has not given them the attention they deserve."

He escorted her up the stairs, her hand on his arm. People watched them, and Leon was grinning. Indeed, she took him on a house tour. Two artists, young, followed them. Wakefield and Enrow were both painters, early thirties, and both had agents. Eric gave each of them his card. The house was monstrous, each room huge, terra cotta stucco, brown beams at the ceilings, three fireplaces, furnished in dark leather and Santa Fe western. Wall niches held collections of pre-Colombian and contemporary Indian art, walls decorated with red-rock paintings in gilded frames, Navaho blankets and a few, small sand paintings. Each room had arrangements of quartz, calcite, halite and other crystals in intricate displays with the overall shape of a pyramid, and in the main bedroom a huge brass bed faced a painted, golden eye on the opposite wall. The aroma in each room was different, aromatic oil burners and sticks of incense spewing lavender, sandalwood, Egyptian musk and myrrh. And through all of it, Nataly's hand never left his arm.

As promised, she took him back to the crowd, and he endured more hours of inane conversation and prying questions with Leon right there to watch and coach him. He kept looking for Nataly, but she had disappeared as her guests consumed more alcohol and became even louder than earlier.

Finally, even Leon had had enough. It was nearing midnight, and Eric would have little time for sleep. Leon steered him straight towards the front door, and suddenly Nataly was there. She smiled, and stepped out onto the front porch with them. Leon kissed her hand, but she was already turning towards Eric; her eyes fixed on his, and wouldn't let go.

"Nice meeting you," said Eric, smiled, and held out his hand. She took it in both of hers, and stepped close. Up close her eyes were the deepest of brown. "Drop by the shop sometime, Mister Price. I hope you'll like our little town. And if you stay here long enough, I think you'll experience the healing you've been looking for."

She squeezed his hand, turned, and melded back into the crowd.

Eric stood there for a moment, feeling a variety of emotions. One of them was anger.

Leon sped him home in the Humvee and mercifully made few efforts at conversation, sensing Eric's mood. "Be ready at oh-five-hundred. A black SUV will come for you, and I won't be coming along. You'll be having an audience with Davis himself.

That's all I know. Brief me when you return."

They pulled up in front of the gate to Eric's house. Eric got out, clicked open the gate, then Leon said, "What'd you think of Nataly Hegel? Isn't she a beauty?"

"Maybe so, but I think she likes you, or at least finds you interesting."

"Yes, in a spooky sort of way."

"Like a lab rat. She tried to psychoanalyze me."

"Go for it," said Leon, jerked the steering wheel sharply, backed up in a spray of dirt and was laughing when he drove away.

Eric wasn't laughing. Another woman passing judgment on him, trying to change him, just like Jenny. How easily women bailed when they didn't get their way. Taking the children with them, turning them against their father. It seemed he'd had a lifetime of it. He didn't really like being alone; the feeling was stronger with each passing year, but for each woman he'd chanced a relationship with it was always the same. There was a shortcoming, some kind of defect in his character that had to be changed. And it was never the same thing twice.

The first sight of Nataly had taken his breath away; he'd barely missed being struck dumb by her presence, but in the end she was like all the others. She only wanted to change him. Did his bitterness really show that much?

I'm not looking for healing, lady. I'm here to do a job. To hell with you.

Eric unlocked the door, and entered his new house, and immediately knew that something wasn't right.

Nothing seemed disturbed, and he heard no strange sounds, but a scent in the air hadn't been there before. Something musky, like wet fur. It was strongest near the door, fading to nothing a few steps beyond, and replaced by something faint and sweet. Only a minute, and Eric didn't notice it anymore, but the musky odor remained by the door. He was not imagining that one, at least. He went to every room in the house, checked the windows, the back door. All locked tight. In the basement, the tunnel entrance was locked tight. Nothing seemed out of order. He unlocked the door and opened it, his heart jumping with a surge of adrenalin.

The tunnel was empty. He knew it was silly, but his reflexes were jumpy, the hair bristling on the back of his neck. Instincts. His instincts were trained by experts and honed by years of dangerous experience, and they were telling him something.

It was nearly midnight. He had to sleep. He closed and locked the tunnel door again and got ready for bed. He feared his heightened senses would keep him awake, but they didn't. He drifted off only minutes after the lights were out. He did not sense the sweet odor that gradually permeated his room, hear the creak of a board under footfall, or see the dark, moving shadows that came to stand by his bed for a moment before leaving without a sound.

He only slept four hours, but awoke in the morning quite alert, and amazingly refreshed.

CHAPTER SEVEN
UNDERGROUND

A black SUV with heavily tinted windows rolled up to his gate at exactly five in the morning, and Eric buzzed it in. The SUV pulled up to his garage and sat there, engine running, windows up. Eric tried the front passenger door, but it was locked. The rear door wasn't. He opened it, and got in.

"Good morning, sir." A driver in military fatigues looked at him in his rear view mirror as Eric closed the door. There was a thick, polymer barrier between them.

"A bit early for that," quipped Eric.

The driver smiled. "You're working with the military, sir. Up and on."

Eric thumbed the gate shut as they went through it. They turned left, and headed away from town, accelerating rapidly.

"Seat belts, sir. You have an oh-six-hundred with Colonel Davis, and I'll have to hammer it."

"That far?" asked Eric, and snapped in lap and chest belts.

"A ways, sir. There's a thermos of coffee on the seat left of you. Hope you drink it black."

Eric uncapped the thermos, poured, and sipped. The liquid burned a path down into his empty stomach, the caffeine giving him a welcome jolt. The sky was beginning to glow outside, but was dim through the tinted windows, and they were suddenly veering left, bouncing once as they hit a graded, red-rock road. A mile in they came to a ranch, went around the main house and accelerated again as the road reappeared past an empty cattle pen. Eric's mind was on autopilot, judging speeds and directions, calculating distances.

Four miles later they came to a water tank fenced in next to what looked like a garage. The fence gate and garage door were opening for them as they reached it, and closing as they entered the area. Lights came on as the garage door clanged shut. They stopped by a pedestal with what looked like a phone pad. The driver reached out and punched in some numbers, then closed his window again.

Two seconds, a loud thump, and the coffee in Eric's stomach seemed to float for an instant. The entire vehicle was descending, and for several moments the only light came from the dashboard panel.

They came to a stop facing a bright light floating somewhere above them. The car pulled forward as Eric calculated, estimating they were now around ninety feet beneath the surface of the ground. They came out into a tunnel, two lines of ceiling lights coming together in the far distance left and right, a two-lane road of steel grating on red dirt. A military jeep buzzed by them, heading right. They turned, and followed it. The car was traveling around forty, and they drove for fifteen minutes, the jeep remaining ahead in view. No traffic passed them going the other way.

They stopped at a cutout in the tunnel, a parking area large enough for twenty cars, quick count. The tunnel itself went on straight ahead, and out of view. The jeep had parked there, and two soldiers with military police armbands were waiting for them.

"These men will take you to Colonel Davis," said Eric's driver. "Have a good day."

One of the military policemen opened the door for Eric, and he got out. "Colonel Davis is expecting you, sir. Please come with us."

The men walked on either side of him. The air was dry, smelled of oil and salt, and fine, red dust particles floated in the air. Behind two large vents in the ceiling, something hummed loudly.

An elevator door opened for them. The interior was polished brass. They descended for only a few seconds, perhaps another sixty feet, and suddenly stopped. The door opened, and they could have been in any office building in a large city. There were rows of offices along a green-carpeted hallway, both men and women in military fatigues hurrying to assignments. They stopped at a door like any of the others, this one marked 'Commander'. Three knocks on the door brought an answer from inside.

"Come!"

"Mister Price is here, sir."

"Send him in!"

A policeman opened the door, and Eric stepped inside.

A heavyset man, balding, sat behind a polished, mahogany desk. He was in army fatigues, and his sausage-like fingers moved over a computer keyboard briefly before entering something with a single keystroke. He gestured at a chair in front of his desk, pulled a thick file out of a drawer and pushed it across the desk as Eric sat down.

There were no preliminaries. "I'm Alex Davis. That's Colonel Davis. You'll report to me directly. What we have so far is in the file. You should read it in order. You'll need historical perspective to see if the information we're getting is consistent. I hear you're very good at that."

"You think the data you're obtaining might be false, then? Is that why the delays have become long enough for the Pentagon to be concerned?" Eric opened the file, and riffled a few pages. The file was the thickness of a ream of paper. Graphs, equations, diagrams of a delta-shaped aircraft flashed past his eyes.

"Could be. We've had problems at every stage of testing, even in conventional flight."

"Conventional?"

"Sub-sonic. It's all summarized in the file. I couldn't brief you if I had the time for it. A list of people you're allowed to talk to is on page one. Don't deviate from that list without consulting me first."

"My clearance is orange card."

"I don't care about your color. Need to know, and I'll decide that. Everyone at this base has top clearance, but only a handful of us have an overview of the entire project. Everyone else works on a small part of it. They know it's an aircraft we're working with, but nothing beyond that."

"And how much will I be allowed to know?" Eric's eyes narrowed. "You have my file, and my orders. I consult with you. It's protocol, but the people I report to are at the top of the command chain. I do what they want done, and if I don't get what I need they'll ask why and I'll tell them why."

There was a faint smile from Davis. "You'll have what you need as long as you don't leak information to someone who shouldn't know it while you make inquiries. Consulting with me isn't advised, it's required."

"I understand that."

"Good, then here's the drill. You read that file and develop a plan for both technological and program analysis. You have four days, and then we talk again. Most of the tech staff lives in town; that's why you're based there. Communications will be primarily by closed cable to your home machine. You'll spend little time here, primarily for face-to-face briefings with me. And no staff member will be interviewed until I've approved it."

"My understanding was that I'd be spending a great deal of my time here, and have access to all parts of the base. I can't just look at sketches, I have to see hardware."

"Maybe later. You're aware I have some security problems here. I don't want anyone new sniffing around and alerting the person or persons we're trying to ferret out. My own security people are on it."

"I'm here to analyze data and evaluate foreign technology, Colonel. I can't do it without laying hands on that technology."

"Later, I said." Colonel Davis' face flushed red. "I'll decide when."

Eric snapped the folder shut in his lap. "My first report goes out tonight. I'll tell them what my situation is, and leave it to you to explain it to them. I'm sure they'll understand."

"I'll explain it after they tell me why you're really here. Our analysts are good enough, we don't need another one, and I didn't ask for new personnel. Impressive file, Mister Price, or should I call you doctor? Physics, computer science, all the right prep, and a long record as an analyst, if it's real. I've got twenty-four years in the military, and a lot of it in covert ops. I know a field spook when I see one, and until I'm told why you're really here you'll be working on that file in town."

Give it up for now. "Okay, I'll file my report, and the pentagon will decide what happens to both our careers. I'll work through the file tonight, but that's as far as I go until this situation is resolved. I can't develop any procedural plans without the access I want."

Davis smiled slightly. "Probably true, if you're what I think you are, so we're both taking a chance here. Nothing personal, Price."

Eric gave him the dark, predatory look of a young, hungry boxer. The look would have made a normal man shudder, but Colonel Davis didn't even flinch.

"If it turns out you're hiding something you shouldn't be hiding, Colonel, then it will be worse than personal, and it'll be a matter of national security."

Davis leaned over his desk and glared back at him. "And if you knew the situations I've been dealing with, you'd know why I'm not even afraid of that. File your report, Mister Price, and let's see what happens. For now, you'll report back to me four days from now about the contents of that file, Four days, at oh-five-hundred. Be ready."

Davis sat up straight. "Sergeant, Mister Price is ready to leave."

The door opened, and an MP stood there. "This way, sir," he said sharply.

Eric nodded, stood, and followed the guard out the door

without looking back, and another guard closed the door behind him.

They marched him straight to the elevator without a word, ascended with him to tunnel level, and the black SUV was waiting with the same driver who'd picked him up earlier. Half an hour later he was ascending again to the garage and the water tower and the high, chain link fence, then racing back to his house on red dirt and pavement, the driver totally silent and Eric making no effort at conversation. He was already writing his report in his mind, and had no time to waste in absorbing the file in his possession.

Eric went into his house and sniffed the air. Slips of paper he'd put near the base of front and back doors were undisturbed, and there were no unusual odors. He sat right down at the computer and wrote a terse report to Gil about the suspicious way he'd been received by Colonel Davis. The man was either uncertain or insecure about his position, or he was trying to hide something. Eric would have total access to the base, or request reassignment. The entire report, single spaced, was less than a page long, and Eric sent it on its way with a keystroke.

The telephone rang. Eric picked it up on the second ring.

"Oh, you're back already," said Leon.

"Surprised? You didn't tell me Colonel Davis is a complete asshole."

"Let's talk. Your place. I'll let myself in from the tunnel, so don't shoot me."

The phone went dead.

So, he can get in here from the basement. Yes, we need to talk.

Leon must have run the entire way, in minutes the tunnel door opened as Eric watched from the top of the stairs. Leon locked the door behind him. "I don't see a gun, so I guess I'm welcome."

"I don't have a gun," said Eric.

"That's right, Analysts have no use for them. So, what happened with you and Davis?"

Eric went down the stairs. He and Leon stood by the furnace in orange light to talk. Eric told him what had happened, in detail. Leon shook his head.

"He's never acted like that with me. We've even had some drinks together. You must have said something to spook him."

"I know I did. I want total access to the base, and he doesn't want me there."

"Do you need that for tech evaluation?"

"I have to see and handle the hardware, Leon. You sound like Davis."

"Didn't he brief you on 'Shooting Star'?"

"I have the file here."

"So study it. Maybe everything you need is in there. Slow down a bit; you just got here."

"Fine, but I can't speed up progress on the project if I can't get what I need. I have to see the aircraft, get my hands on the metal, and Davis knows it. What's he so suspicious about?"

"I don't know," said Leon.

"I just sent in my initial report, and it's not complimentary to Davis. Either I get what I want, or I'm out of here."

"I wish you'd talked to me first."

"I don't report to you, Leon. Christ, first Davis, now you. Everyone wants to be a boss. Well at least I have the file. Now why don't you get out of here so I can read it."

"Okay, but you don't have to play prima-donnas with me. Read the file. Maybe it'll show you how important this project really is. We can talk in the morning. I'll be in the office by ten."

"Goodbye," said Eric. He thought about stomping a foot for emphasis, but decided that would be pushing things too far.

Leon turned away, opened the door to the tunnel and closed it loudly behind him. Eric immediately locked it, making a show of temper. He went up the stairs, taking deep breaths, letting them out slowly.

Well, I think I've stirred up things enough for one day.

He made coffee in the kitchen, made a ham and cheese sandwich and took it all to his desk, where the file awaited him. For the rest of the morning, all afternoon and early that evening he read it, studied it, making notes, talking to himself on paper with each discovery he made.

It was not just an aircraft, but also something more. It was delta-shaped, flat like a lifting body and huge, with extreme dimensions of a seven-twenty-seven. A crew of five in a spacious controls area at the sharp nose of a smooth fuselage not designed for stealth. No missile pods to be seen, nor was there a bomb bay, yet the overall shape of the craft suggested military. The drawings showed four jet engines, but no specs or manufacturer were given. *Could be a lifting body for something smaller, he thought, then, no, the aft cross-section is much too thick, the taper forward too extreme for a lifting body. The whole thing looks aerodynamically unstable, must be fly-by-wire.*

There was nothing in the file to tell him where the thing had come from: no markings, no manuals in a foreign language, no history about how it had been obtained. There was not even a photograph of the aircraft, only drawings. One detail drawing showed a strange, internally cantilevered section to the rear of the craft that, when lowered, made it look even more unstable, and there was nothing to show what was in that section or what purpose it served.

The great bulk of the file was table after table of test data, all taken in a laboratory setting: wind tunnel data to Mach one, vibration and stress tables on wings and fuselage, thermal and electrical conductivity data over selected sections of the aircraft. There were no records of any performance testing, not even a record of a flight.

What am I supposed to do? Come up with a plan to put all this crap together so it says something? Why would anybody want to sabotage such a messed up project?

Eric closed the file in disgust, and took himself to town for dinner at The Planet. He had a Saturn burger with fries, and someone who had been at Nataly's party tried to interest him in buying a timeshare. When Eric politely declined, the man told him about a program at the Creative Life Center just outside of town. Some expert on UFOs was speaking there. It would be an opportunity to meet some of the new age crowd, many of whom were devoted patrons of the arts. Perhaps Eric could salvage a bad day by developing his cover as a man of art.

He drove to the center after dark. A sharp turn off Schnabley Hill Road took him to an interesting structure built in a sort of vertical helix with modern art appointments in bronze and glass. He walked up a spiral walkway from the parking lot, bought his twenty-dollar ticket at the door, and got one of the last seats in a large lecture hall filled with people talking loudly. A man was introduced, claiming to be a physicist. He talked for an hour about UFOs from other planets and other universes, the many groups of aliens now living among humans, their various agendas, some good, some bad. Eric fought to listen; it was all so absurd. The man showed UFO photographs, most of which could be staged with little imagination. When photos were shown of flying saucers sitting in the front yard of a man's house during a Swiss visitation, Eric had to bite his tongue to keep himself from laughing out loud.

Midway through the talk, he had a strange feeling he was being watched. Eric turned around to look over his shoulder and saw Nataly Hegel standing at the back of the room, arms folded. She'd been frowning, but when she saw him looking at her she smiled, and he quickly faced forward again. His heart thumped forcefully, and he heard little of the rest of the talk. After it ended, perhaps she'd have coffee with him.

When the talk ended he looked for Nataly, but she had left.

Eric went home that night feeling strangely depressed.

* * * * * * *

Leon fumed all the way back to his house. *If that was a phony snit, then he did a good job of it, but I'm not so easily fooled, Mister Price.*

He went straight to his desk, sat down at his computer and dialed in a series of numbers on his telephone. The machine buzzed three times, a pause, then three more times.

"Yes, what is it?"

"Leon. Can we talk?"

"Yes," said Colonel Alexander Davis.

"I just talked to Price. What in the hell do you think you're doing? Price just filed a complaint because you won't give him base access, and we could have a whole platoon of deep ops people here in a day. Are you crazy?"

"I'm trying to find a saboteur, Leon. I don't need a new face here to probe around and warn the bastard."

Leon's voice rose in pitch. "There could be a dozen new faces at your base in days because of your hair trigger ego. If you'd think for just one minute you'd see your suspicions are telling you that Price has been sent to do exactly what you want done. My bet is he's better at it than any ten men you can put together."

"I don't think—"

"That's right, you don't think! Shut up and listen for once! An NSA team will sniff out our arrangement in a week. With only one man we have some control. I'll call my boss; reinforce your claim that analysts don't need total base access, but that if Eric is also here for the security problem his orders need to be clarified so that access can be granted. If they deny he's here for that purpose, we're in trouble. We'll know quick, and I'll call you back."

"You spooks need to be educated about military protocol," said Davis. "That's what caused this problem."

"Fuck your military protocol. You caused this problem," said Leon, "and it had better not happen again. You like to talk about accidents. Be careful one doesn't happen to you."

Leon stabbed the keyboard and broke the connection before Davis could answer the threat with one of his own.

He sat there for half an hour, composing thoughts, rehearsing arguments, then dialed Gil on his cell phone. He was prepared for tough arguing, maybe even a chewing out for not properly preparing Davis.

What he got was a cheerful Gil who quickly agreed to clarify

Eric's orders and be totally open about the man's assignments. He even gave Leon a small pat on the back for moving so rapidly to remove a logjam in the operation.

Leon hung up, relieved but confused. There'd been no real discussion. It had all been too easy.

Thinking about it kept him awake that night.

* * * * * * *

"Our man is in, Mister President. There was a problem with the details of his orders, but it's all taken care of. I'll bring you summaries of his briefings as they come in."

"That's good news, Gil. Let's get this show on the road for sure. I want to see that plane flying by the end of the year."

"You'll have it, Mister President," said Gil.

CHAPTER EIGHT
REVELATIONS

There was little he could do in the way of a plan, but in two days he organized the existing laboratory data into a coherent state through graphical display in three dimensions. Stress tolerances and conductivities were shown as colored surfaces superimposed on an external drawing of the aircraft, and he added a red, variable surface showing applied stress from the wind tunnel work. There were no anomalies to be seen, the aircraft perfectly designed mechanically up to mach-one, but like a bumblebee it was totally unstable aerodynamically, another fly-by-wire design. The cantilevered section aft remained a total mystery to him, and was first on a list of questions included in his report for Davis if he was ever allowed on the base again.

He didn't have to worry about it for long. It was nine in the morning, his second day in the little office near the south edge of town. Once upon a time it had been a workingman's bar, and Leon swore that in the heat of summer the walls sweated beer, the odor impossible to get rid of.

Eric was proofing the final draft of his report when the telephone rang. Leon hadn't arrived yet, so Eric answered the call.

"World Arts, this is Eric Price, how may I help you?

"You can do what you were sent here to do. This is Colonel Davis. You've got what you want, but I'm still going to watch you like a hawk. Two days, oh-five-hundred. Be ready to impress me."

The line went dead before Eric could say a word.

How I love the sound of an arrogant man who has just been given a new asshole by a superior, he thought. *I just hope they didn't tell him everything about me. A person thinking they're dealing with a common field agent is the best protection I can have.*

For a moment, he enjoyed a kind of smugness over his victory. Gil had done it again.

Leon arrived at ten, and Eric told him what had happened.

"There you are, see? There was nothing at all to get upset about. Everything's going to be fine." He removed his jacket and hung it carefully over the back of his chair before sitting down at his computer. He pointed at Eric, and said, "Today, I will show you how to sell art, or to at least appear to be doing it. When you're done with your military thingy, I have a list of dummy galleries to go over with you."

Again the floppy wrist and affected speech, but Eric had already been with the man long enough to know it was all a lie.

The phone rang again a few minutes later, but this time Leon answered it. "Oh, hi," he said. "I bet you want to talk to Eric. He's right here. Hold on." He put a hand over the receiver, and whispered.

"John Coulter. Just play along, and meet him. I'll explain later."

Eric picked up the phone. Leon did not hang up, listened with his hand over the receiver.

"Eric Price. How may I help you?"

"John Coulter, Mister Price. We met at the Nataly Hegel party, and shared an appreciation for the cheese knishes at the buffet, remember?"

"Oh, yes. Leon introduced us."

"Leon and I go back a couple of years. We share an interest in pistols, and also in art."

"Are you a collector?"

"Not really. I'm in imports and exports, Mister Price, a wide range of products, including art, and even guns on occasion."

The hair bristled on the back of Eric's neck, and Leon raised an eyebrow at him.

"Guns?"

"Well, sporting weapons, really, but paramilitary favorites as well, all semi-automatic, of course. I'm interested in anything that can be sold abroad, Mister Price, and I'd like to acquaint you with my connections. I think I can provide some fine markets for you. Can we meet over coffee or lunch sometime and discuss it?"

Leon was nodding vigorously at him.

"Of course. Lunch would be best. How about the Coffee Pot?"

"This Wednesday—at noon?"

"Fine. I've put it down, Mister Coulter. See you then."

They hung up. Leon smiled. "Nicely done, short and sweet. Now, when you meet, be a good listener and you'll discover a new element in this mystery you're here to solve. It seems our dear Colonel Davis also has friends in the commercial sector who are most anxious to get their hands on the new technology we've acquired. They've made him a lucrative offer, and Davis has offered me in turn a generous stipend to aid him in his quest for wealth. Can you imagine the audacity of the man in bribing a federal employee and patriotic citizen such as me? I have accepted his offer, of course. John Coulter will eventually present to you a similar offer, if you seem willing, and you will be willing. If John is liaison to the commercial interests involved with Davis, we might learn the identity of the people or companies involved and turn the information over to Gil for whatever action he wants to take. And from the look in your eyes right now you might even want that assignment. Death to those who commit treason, and all that."

"Davis should have been turned in for court-martial as soon as you discovered this," said Eric.

"Ah, but we need him, at least for the moment. First things first, Eric; first the saboteurs, then the technology, then those who'd like to steal it. Interesting, don't you think? And you also get to go to nice parties and meet beautiful women."

"Stop it, Leon. I don't need the act."

Leon laughed, turned back to his desk, and they worked the rest of the morning in silence. When Eric finished proofing his report for Davis it was nearly noon. Leon had brought a sack lunch, and was deeply engrossed in his work. Eric was hungry. "Think I'll hit the deli at the grocery store," he said, and Leon didn't even look up.

Safeway was several blocks away, Nataly's shop three blocks closer, and the impulse, when it came, was overwhelming. Eric didn't fight it, pulled into the little parking lot in front of New Visions. A few cars were there, Arizona plates, Phoenix area. The front window display featured museum-quality crystal clusters, Tibetan singing bowls and dream catchers the size of dinner plates. When he opened the door a dozen exotic scents, sweet and musky, assailed him. A pretty, young girl in a sleeveless, silk blouse and peasant skirt smiled at him from behind the counter as she checked out another customer. Golden hoops dangled from her ears, stretching the lobes, and a small, white crystal glistened from the right side of her nose.

It seemed at first that Nataly wasn't there, and Eric didn't dare to ask for her. He wandered around the shop like any other customer. Glass shelves held little boxes with crystal and mineral specimens; he paused to examine several of them. Locked cabinets held larger, pricier pieces, many of them scepters of clear quartz and amethyst, and a red garnet the size of a baseball. Incense sticks hung in bags on a wall, near a display of burners, black sand, charcoal disks and little pouches filled with nuggets of frankincense, myrrh and Egyptian musk. Angelic choir music came softly from two speakers in the back corners of the shop where shelves were lined with books on alternative religions, mythology and UFOs. Several related to strange sightings in the Sedona area. Eric pulled one from the shelf and had begun leafing through it when a soft touch on his elbow made him jump.

Nataly was standing next to him, very close, looking up at him with fathomless eyes.

"That's a very interesting book," she said. "Bob Terrell has written a series of them. You might want to meet him sometime. He's local."

Eric pretended to study the book. "Oh, I don't think so. I've never seen a UFO and, quite frankly, I don't think they exist if we're talking about little green men. People do see strange things, I admit, but I think they're all natural phenomena if you take the time to figure them out.

"Ah, a skeptic," said Nataly. "That's good when you're seeking the truth, but even scientists are trained to keep an open mind about the possibilities. Terrell's like that; he reports what people have seen, and suggests possible explanations for each case. And it's not just UFOs that he talks about."

She reached across him and pulled another book from the shelf. "Here, this one is about the military base we think is still somewhere in the backcountry here. No little green men in this one." Her eyes twinkled, her smile playful as she handed the book to him.

Eric felt a shock, and hoped it didn't reach his eyes. He opened the book, leafed through it and saw no pictures.

"People have seen black Humvees, black helicopters that make no sound, even armed military people in the backcountry. Some of the encounters have been hostile, people turned back on hiking trails. Years ago there was a huge fire in the backcountry beyond Boynton Canyon. The Sedona fire department went out to fight it and were turned back by armed soldiers dressed in black, and the fire burned on for several days, maybe weeks."

"I'm not aware of any restricted air space around here," said Eric.

"It's not necessary if the base is underground."

Eric forced a chuckle. "I don't think so. I'm sorry; it doesn't make sense to me. A secret base so close to a major tourist center is even too stupid for the military."

Her dark eyes moved slightly, as if scanning his face, then made solid eye contact and held him there. A slight pause, then, "You don't really believe that, and you don't think our firemen lied about what they saw."

"No, they could have run into some right-wing paramilitary outfit playing commando in the desert, for all I know. It doesn't have to be a government conspiracy; that's all I'm trying to say."

Nataly cocked her head to one side, considering what he'd said. The look on her face was both focused and ethereal. Eric swallowed slowly, but hard. "Look, I actually came here to see if you'd like to take a break for coffee or lunch." He glanced at his watch. "I have to head back to the office in forty-five minutes."

"Oh, I can't leave the shop with Marie alone here," she said quickly. Eric's heart sank, and he looked away nervously.

"Why don't we eat right here?" Nataly added. "I have bread, meat and cheese in the back, and there's green tea."

Now his heart jumped. "Well, I suppose—"

"Good. Marie, I'll be in the back! Ring the bell if there are any problems."

"Yes, ma'am," said Marie.

Nataly pulled four paperback books off a shelf, and put them into his hands. "Consider this a loan, and promise me you'll read them. A lot of people here believe what's in those books, and you need to know what that is if you're going to be a resident in Sedona."

Her seriousness made him smile without conscious thought. "Okay, but I could be called back to Phoenix anytime."

"They'll just have to do without you," she said, then put a hand on his arm and guided him to the back of the shop where a curtain of glass and bamboo cylinders covered an open doorway. In the back were boxes floor to ceiling against two walls, a table with two chairs, a refrigerator next to a sink and counter. "No atmosphere, but quiet," said Nataly. She put a teapot on a hot plate, and made ham and cheese sandwiches while the water heated. They talked about little things: the traffic in town, the weather. For a moment Eric felt as if he'd drifted off for a while. He returned to consciousness and watched silently until she served him at the table.

"This is very nice of you," he said.

"It's nice to have adult company. Marie is sweet, but we have little in common outside of the shop. Different generations."

"She must be well into her twenties." *And you look thirty, tops,* he thought.

Nataly sat down opposite him and took a bite of her sandwich. For the first time Eric noticed how long and slender her fingers were. "I'm much older than Marie, Mister Price," she said.

"Eric," he said, and made eye contact.

"Eric. You have such interesting eyes. I'd like to read them sometime."

"Read them?"

"Iridology. Several of us are practitioners here."

Her gaze was direct and intense; she was studying him.

"You're a forceful person. I see a suggestion of danger, and there's a sense of sadness. I see so much of that, the things people do to hurt each other."

"That's life," he said, and heard the bitterness in his own voice.

"You're alone, or at least you think you are." Her voice was a near whisper.

Eric bit down hard on his sandwich. "I was married, but it ended in divorce. My only daughter will be married soon, and I'm not invited to the ceremony. I probably deserve it. Hurt goes both ways."

"I'm sorry," said Nataly. "But there's goodness in everyone."

"How about you? Anything personal isn't any of my business, of course, but you must have an active social life with your position in the community."

Nataly rolled her eyes. "Oh, yes, lots of parties, and flirting, and offers to satisfy my wildest desires. I've been tempted more than once. People like to say I'm too particular, that I'm going to grow old alone, but they're wrong. I'm just patient about finding the right man."

"Good advice for anyone. Divorce is nasty," he said.

"I can see that." She reached over and touched his arm. For a moment, her hand lingered there. "If you open your mind to them, many healing arts are available to you here. I can show you some of them, if you like."

Again, a slight smile came to his face without thought. He felt suddenly relaxed in the presence of this woman, without the sense of being judged or threatened. *God, she is lovely.* "If you want to take a chance with a pragmatist, sure. I'm told I'm a professional skeptic."

Nataly smiled then, and brushed back errant strands of black hair from the side of her face. "Any good student asks questions on the road to truth."

Eric shook his head slightly in wonderment.

"What?" she asked, and now she really smiled, and he felt a shortness of breath.

"I've never met anyone like you," he managed.

"Ah, then I'm an adventure. Tea?" She held up the ceramic pot where tea had been brewing, and arched an eyebrow at him.

"Sure, why not. I've become addicted to coffee."

Nataly poured. "Nice aroma, but too acidic. I love both the tastes and scents of tea. I think it's important to stimulate all the senses." As she said it she handed a cup of tea to him, one finger absently touching the back of his hand. "I believe in balance in everything. That's not easy for me to do in my position. People see me as a wealthy party giver and patron of the arts, and I'm more than that."

"Yes, you are." *My God, did I just say that?* The uncontrolled blush that came to his face instantly dismayed Eric.

Nataly's smile softened then. Her eyes widened, and fixed on his. "I like you, Eric. I don't really know why yet, but I'd like the opportunity to find out. I know you've been hurt in the past, and the hurt is still there, but you seem willing to take a risk in coming here. You've seen me in my castle, and now in my little shop. What do you think?"

"I think you're fascinating," he said, and felt good about saying it.

"And you intrigue me. We should meet again. Do you like exotic foods, or are you a meat 'n' potatoes man?"

"My tastes vary. I've been around the world some."

"I'll want to hear all about that. My chef is German, but he can do anything European. My house, say seven a week from this Friday? Casual dress, and just the two of us."

"Sounds nice. I'll call you here if some business thing comes up." Eric had no idea what hours he'd be spending at the base. Friday at seven he could be a hundred feet underground.

Nataly thrust out her lower lip in a pout. "Oh, that would be a shame if money matters interfered with our dinner. I'll leave that decision to you. For now, Marie must be getting hungry, and I have to take my turn at the counter, and you have to go." She pointed at her watch.

He'd been in her shop over an hour, yet it seemed they'd only talked for minutes. "You're right. I'm late."

"If Leon scolds you, tell him it was my fault. He plays the bon vivant, but I'm sure he can be very hard when he wants to be. Don't forget your books."

He'd nearly walked away from the books she'd loaned him. He retrieved them, said, "Thanks again." His mind went blank, his feet refusing to move until Nataly took his arm and escorted him to the door. She waved goodbye, and disappeared from view.

Eric drove back to his office, feeling the giddiness of a juvenile anticipating his first date, and seeing nothing strange about it at all. The euphoria lasted all day and through the evening. By bedtime he was feeling a bit silly about it, and managed to go over his report one final time.

It was likely a mistake to do that, because his sleep was restless all night. He had dreams of Leon shouting at him, and Davis pointing a pistol at him and accusing him of being a spy. Towards morning, Nataly appeared in a vivid dream that woke him up. He remembered sitting up in bed. The lights were low, and dark shadows were moving around the room, circling him, and then the door burst open and Nataly was standing there like an angry angel, shouting, "Get out! All of you get out of this room right now!" And the shadows fled.

When he was awake, sweating, he was certain he could smell her musky scent in the room.

CHAPTER NINE
THE PLANE

Davis seemed resigned to the Pentagon's decision, but was clearly disgusted by it. "This is what happens when desk jockeys micromanage field operations. Only good I can see is our saboteur might lie low for a while. I'll be keeping a record of every place you go, every person you talk to, and when. One slip of the tongue from you, anyone hears something they're not supposed to and you're out of here, I guarantee it."

"Understood," said Eric, and pushed a folder across Davis' desk. "There's my report, such as it is. Now I want to see the plane."

"Sergeant!" said Davis loudly. The door opened, and an MP was standing there in fatigues with beret and sidearm. Short, but solidly built, the man had strangely colored eyes, a kind of blue-green.

"Take Mister Price to Area Five. I'll call to have Johnson meet you there. Do not leave this man's side, and use the journal forms I gave you."

"Yes, sir. This way, Mister Price."

Davis was opening Eric's report file and said nothing as they left his office.

"Sergeant Nutt, sir. I'll accompany you wherever you go, and arrange your schedule here. Please don't ever go off on your own; I don't want to be a private again. It's for your own safety, sir."

"You have a first name, sergeant?"

"Alan, sir."

"I'm Eric. I forget the sergeant, and you forget the sir. I'm a civilian."

"Yes, sir."

Eric laughed, stuck out a hand, and Alan shook it. "The Man is a stickler for protocol, sir. Got to follow it. You ever in the military?"

"Rangers. That was a long time ago. I was younger than you."

"Get a chance to kill bad guys?"

"Yes, I did. That's all I can say about it, Alan."

"Understood, sir. A van has been assigned to us. Look for number three stenciled on the rear door. It's waiting."

They took the elevator down to the lot where Eric had first come in. The van was there, with a driver. Eric and Alan got in, sitting behind an MP with his M16 mounted vertically on the dashboard. As soon as the door closed, the van jerked ahead, moving deeper into the base than Eric had been before.

"It's just a few minutes," said Alan. Eric looked over the front seat, saw the speedometer hit forty and hold there. "How big is this base?" he asked.

"There are really eight bases in one, sir, all connected by tunnels like this one. The entire complex runs seven hundred miles north to south, spreads out as much as sixty east and west." Alan took out his clipboard, and wrote something down on it.

"Are you going to write down every question I ask? Use a tape recorder."

Alan grinned, took something the size of a cigarette lighter out of his pocket, and held it up for inspection. "Got it, sir."

Eric grinned back. "Are you going to tell me where your camera is?"

Alan pointed to a point at the center of his beret, above his forehead. "Video, Israeli-made. State-of-the-Art, sir."

"Good. I feel much safer, now."

The trip took exactly four minutes. Another parking area in a broad recess carved out of solid red rock, and a floor of black, metal gratings. Light panels in a high ceiling were blinding to look at. No elevator, this time. Two soldiers in a booth guarded a single set of double doors in a rock wall. Alan led him to the booth, and the van pulled away again. Alan presented a paper with a photograph of Eric on it. There was a badge, overprinted with the number five in red, and Eric clipped it to his breast pocket. Another guard opened the door for them, and Eric followed Alan inside.

Another tunnel, no side doors. Video cameras were mounted high on the walls, and turned to follow them. Fifty yards away was another set of double doors. One door opened, and a tall man in a white, laboratory coat stepped inside to greet them when they were halfway there. Tousled hair, hawkish face, he held out a hand to Eric as they approached.

"Neal Johnson, Doctor Price. I'll be you guide here."

They shook hands. "Eric, please. I haven't been called Doctor in a lot of years."

"Neither have I," said Neal. "Physics and Computer Science, right?"

"Yes."

"Aeronautical Engineering, Purdue. You were at Berkeley, I see."

"That's right. Hyperfragments and resonances, it's all ancient history. Computer Science came later."

"Maybe if you stick around you can help us figure out what our aircraft can really do. We're supposed to be getting the book on it pretty soon. Our so-called 'friends' have finally agreed to release it. I've been working blind for over a year. Have you been briefed at all?"

"A short report with drawings, and a lot of tabled laboratory test data. Not very useful."

"Well, let's get started." Neal turned, opened the door, and they followed him inside. The light there was dimmer than in the tunnel, but not by much.

It was an aircraft hanger, immense, the ceiling a hundred yards above them, the floor at least that distance across. Three black helicopters were there: two stealth craft with missile pods and Vulcan canon, the third much larger, a flying boxcar for transportation. Otherwise the floor was empty, Neal and his guests the only people there. They walked towards the opposite wall where there were two elevated levels fronted by clear glass, behind which people were moving. To their right was a massive door of corrugated metal twenty yards on a side, and closed. Left was a fenced-in area with metal-turning machinery that hummed loudly, and what appeared to be a parts storage space. The floor was first rock, then metal as they walked across it. Eric looked down at the boundary of metal. Neal saw it, and said; "Floor center rises on jacks all the way to the ceiling. We can take any aircraft in or out that way."

They walked some more, and the floor was rock again. People were watching them through the windows. Neal waved to them. "Some of our technical staff," he said. "They're curious about you. A stranger's face stands out pretty fast here."

There was another door beneath the windows. Neal paused before opening it. "Time to see the Pregnant Sparrow; that's what we call it. See what you think." Air rushed into their faces when he opened the door.

Beyond was another hanger, but smaller, and the light was dim. In the center of the floor sat a low-slung aircraft with a strange shape remindful of stealth technology: black, faceted surface, a dull, mottled finish and lots of angles, delta-shaped. No windows, ports, no sign of a cockpit, any markings or insignia on tail or fuselage. They walked around it two times, coming in close. Two standard looking exhaust pipes protruded from a thick section aft which then tapered to a sharp point like a spear.

"There are two pulse-jet engines in the back half of this thick section," said Neal, "and we've run them with JP-4 up to Mach 1. Haven't been able to push it higher than that; the thing has some kind of governor, and the guys who brought it to us have been arguing about how much to tell us. Maybe it's more money, but I hear we've already paid a fortune for this thing."

"What's in the rest of the fat section?" asked Eric.

"Can't get inside to see. Shows up hollow on X-ray. You can see joints, and two hinges on the underside. It opens up somehow, but we haven't been able to activate it."

"It shows up as cantilevered on the drawings."

"Conjecture. We haven't proven that yet."

Eric was looking close at the surface, running a hand over it. "Looks rough, but feels smooth. I don't see any markings."

"Carbon composite: nanofibers in a resin we haven't figured out yet. The Japanese are working on something similar. We haven't found a single marking. No letters, numbers, just glyphs in the cockpit. A pressure bar opens that. You can see the seam near the nose. No way to see outside; everything is heads up. We at least got the instructions on using that, but it took over a year to train our test pilots to it."

"Any idea where it comes from?" asked Eric. He touched the place where his hand had rested a while, and it was still warm.

"We're told Eastern Europe, but nobody knows for sure. The people who brought it out are kept out of sight; I've never been allowed to talk to one of them. What are you writing down there?"

Neal had turned to look at Alan, who was writing something down on his clipboard. "Recording topics of conversation, sir. Colonel Davis' orders."

Neal scowled. "Thought so. Guess I won't be volunteering anything, then. Ask me some questions, Doctor Price."

"What's the problem?" asked Eric.

"No problem. I'm just here to answer your questions." Neal's anger was barely masked. He'd obviously not expected any monitoring of his conversations with the new guy from the pentagon. Something was wrong here, and Eric acted quickly.

"Okay, show me how to get into this thing. I want to see the controls' setup."

"Watch your step. The leading edges of the wings are like dull swords," said Neal. A set of three steps on rollers, wheels blocked, was by one of the half-vee wings of the aircraft. Neal stepped up onto the wing, Eric right behind him, while Alan remained standing on the floor.

A seam was now visible, and three indentations, closely spaced, which Neal pressed with one hand. A section of the fuselage popped out towards them, and Neal pulled it back. Inside were four contour chairs in a black interior. A lit instrument panel was to their left, a tunnel on their right. Neal pointed to it, said, "There's a second compartment a few feet back, like this one. It takes a crew of eight. This is the flight deck, but we don't have a clue about what goes on in the other compartment. I personally think it's related to the fat, apparently empty section we haven't figured out either. So far, nothing works for us in there. The indicators don't even light up."

"This kind of thing keeps coming up because people have brought technology over to us without the necessary documentation. Who the hell has been handling the transfer?"

"Ask Davis," said Neal in a near whisper. He glanced outside to where Alan was waiting. "Sit here, and I'll show you the controls we understand so far," said loudly.

Eric sat down, Neal beside him. Neal took a card out of his pocket, wrote something on it, and said, "Heads up display plugs in here, and seems pretty standard. Nothing-new there. The panel indicators are fuel and power, time of flight, landing gear status, hydraulic integrity."

He passed the card carefully to Eric, and went on talking. Eric pocketed the card without looking at it.

"These switches were a mystery at first. Five commands in the right sequence activate ten nozzles under the forward edges of the wings. VTO only, and fly-by-wire. Handles beautifully, up to Mach 1, and then it just sits there, with no indication of any problem or command request. Not even a blinking light."

"How many times has it flown?"

"Four. Last time out a VTO nozzle got plugged and we had to set it down fast, so that's three tests with some success."

"I'd call it no success at all, Neal. My briefing said this project has been going on for two years."

"I know. We've been flying blind the whole time, trying to reinvent this thing. We've had no supporting information. Guys like you have come here before. They went away, and nothing happened." As he said this, Neal reached over and tapped the card in Eric's pocket, raised an eyebrow at him. "I guess they thought we could do it all by ourselves."

There was a clank behind them. Eric turned; saw Alan peering in at them.

"You finished in here yet?"

"I've seen enough here. Now show me where the fat part of the fuselage joins with the rest of this thing."

They followed Alan down the steps from the wing. A seam was visible just aft of the trailing edge of the wings, and around the bottom half of the fuselage circumference. Each end of the seam ended at what looked like the end of a large cylinder the size of a fist. "Looks like a hinge," said Eric.

"We think the entire tail section swings up, the engines with it. The rest of the section is empty space. Fuel tanks are where the wings join the fuselage, long, flat things. Small. The range with JP-4 below Mach 1 is only around a thousand miles, but we're being told the range is beyond measurement, and the speed is something we've only been able to imagine. We're either being lied to, or we just don't know what we're doing."

Frustration was obvious in Neal's voice. Eric ran his hand over the fuselage again, and said, "You've seen the wind tunnel data, and so have I. Pregnant Sparrow is a good name for this thing. Even fly-by-wire it won't survive Mach 2. I don't think it's an airplane at all. I think it's designed to fly in space."

Neal grunted. "First thing we thought of. Those engines won't even get it to a hundred thousand feet."

"Then it has to have another power source."

"It doesn't. We've been over every inch of it.

"Not the fat section." Eric rubbed his hand on the fuselage, paused, and rubbed again.

"I told you, it's empty. The engines are yoked together, and there's no other structure between them. We've used soft and hard X-rays. There's nothing there."

"The surface temperature is different on the two sides of the seam here. It's hotter aft."

"You can feel that with your fingertips? I'm impressed. The difference is only a couple of degrees ambient. We've measured it. There's a T max a yard from your hand, and then it falls off. We think it's residual heat in the engines; this thing flew a couple of weeks ago. The temperature difference was thirty degrees then. It's some kind of capacitance effect."

"Maybe, but this section has to be opened up."

"Tell that to Davis. I'm ready to cut it open if I have to, but the Colonel won't let us try that until we get the documentation we've been promised for over a year. You getting this all down, Sergeant?"

Alan just grinned, and scribbled furiously.

"I'll tell him what I think," said Eric.

"That's what we all try to do, and sometimes he even listens. Are you sticking around, or are you just here to give an opinion?"

"I've been assigned here indefinitely, but I live in town."

"I won't ask why," said Neal. "I've seen your resume, and I can use you here twenty-four-seven. All they give me are military techs, and I need scientists."

"I'll do what I can. How much do I get to see today?"

"Everything," said Neal, "including the little niche we've made for you in a red-rock wall. I thought you'd like to see the plane first."

"You were right on that," said Eric.

They spent the rest of the day touring the complex of offices, laboratories and shops stretching a hundred yards in three directions from the hangers. There were a few civilians, but mostly uniformed military. An Omega 3000 housed in a lead-shielded room woven with copper cable to shield against EMP was the brain of both analytical and machining facilities. The materials testing laboratory in particular was state-of-the-art. Eric's office was literally a hole in the wall, a niche in red-rock with desk and computer terminal, and a soft green light for ambience. A central cafeteria was housed in a cavern chiseled out of solid rock, and the usual grated floor. People complained that red dust kept getting in their food, and everyone went around sniffling and snorting from breathing the stuff. "Apparently our management hasn't heard of a thing called silicosis," said Neal.

They ate lunch in the cafeteria anyway, Eric choosing a wrapped, cold sandwich and a can of pop. People stared at the new guy on the block. Neal laughed and said scuttlebutt was already circulating about Eric being a special agent for the CIA.

Neal didn't know how close that was to the truth.

When lunch was over, they toured the library, mostly a nicely assembled computer-based journal collection on everything from materials to mathematics, and an excellent collection of science and engineering abstracts.

The living quarters for military personal were deplorable: bunks stacked like cordwood in two, long rooms, and a common bathroom with showers for everyone. Neal tried to make Eric feel guilty about living in town, and failed.

When the tour was over, Alan had filled most of the tablet on his clipboard. Neal said his goodbyes, then, "You get back here quick. I like your questions, and I think you'll make a difference here." As he said it he tapped Eric on the chest, aiming a finger so that it struck the card in Eric's pocket. Eric nodded.

Yes, message received. I'll read the card.

"See you Monday," said Neal, and left them.

Alan took him back to the van. Davis was in a meeting, couldn't see him, but said he'd call. Alan said he'd try to answer any questions, but Eric had none for him. They'd meet again at oh-six-hundred Monday, and Alan would again be his constant companion. The van took Eric back to his home the usual way. Before he'd reached ground level he'd taken the card Neal had slipped him out of his pocket and read it.

> Corruption and espionage. People being murdered here. Call me at (212) 293-6752 twenty-four-hundred. Danger for both of us.

Oh, that's just swell, thought Eric. He memorized the number, then tore the card to pieces and later flushed them down the toilet at his house.

That night, exactly at midnight, he used his cell phone and dialed the number Neal had given him. He let the phone ring twenty-four times.

Nobody answered.

CHAPTER TEN
WARNINGS

"We're honored to have a special guest today," said Chairman Brown. "He arrived early this morning, and will join us in a moment."

"This was not on the agenda," said Mister Smith, his faceless figure cloaked in a brown robe on the television monitor. "We were going to discuss the manual for the Americans."

"We *are* going to discuss it. Our guest requested time to explain certain changes he insists we make in the document."

"Insists? If we have no autonomy here, and the Green Party is truly in charge of everything, then I fail to see why the rest of us are even involved with the project unless it's only for information purposes."

The translator failed to pick up the hard edge in Smith's voice, but all could sense it in the original speech coming from the monitor.

"The technology is ours to share as we see fit, Mister Smith, but we're aware of the political impact of giving it all at once to the Americans. The advice of our friends and neighbors is desired by us, and considered necessary. That's why you're here."

"Acceptable, if true," said Smith, but then all heads of the men at the table turned when there was a soft knock, twice, on the door.

"Ah, he's here," said Chairman Brown. He arose, went to the door and opened it. The man standing there had to duck his head slightly when he came through the doorway. He was dressed in sports coat, slacks and turtleneck, all in black, and followed Brown back to the table, sitting down at his right hand.

"Good evening, gentlemen. Good to see you all together again," he said, and smiled unpleasantly with thin lips in a long, bony face.

"Our pleasure, Minister Watt," said Mister Smith. "We have missed your presence at our meetings. Your new duties have kept you far too busy, it seems."

"There are times when I yearn to be an ambassador again," said Dario Watt. It was the name they always called him, and although they knew his true name they respected his desire for a small disguise.

"The manual has been prepared, and will be delivered to the Americans in the morning. There are certain omissions in it, and I wanted to personally explain my logic in making those omissions."

There were gasps around the table. "Please do," said Chairman Brown. "I thought we were ready to move ahead with full disclosure. Has something new happened to discourage our trust?"

Watt steepled long fingers in front of his face and looked directly at the television monitor, the cloaked and hooded figures there now silent. "It's not so much a lack of trust as it is a new reason for caution. A new player has arrived on the scene; his agenda is undetermined, as is his agency. We already have corruption among the agencies involved, and now sabotage. Until these problems are resolved, there will be no full disclosure. This does not come from me, gentlemen. It comes from my president."

"Excuse me, Minister Watt," said Mister White, "but our president signed off on this project before it began. The continuing delays in full disclosure have slowed progress to a crawl, and eroded our credibility with the Americans. Does he know this?"

"I send him regular reports," said Watt.

"I think it's appropriate that we receive copies of those

reports."

"I beg your pardon?"

"I think he means that as field members of this project we should have direct input to the reporting process," said Chairman Brown.

"That, and to check the validity of the reports our president is seeing. This is a government-sanctioned technology transfer intended to establish good relations with a world power, and I do not believe our head of state would do anything to disrupt it. I suggest we file our own report as quickly as possible."

Watt's eyes narrowed. He leaned over the table, and hissed, "You've just suggested the right hand of our president is a liar, Mister White. I fear you've been away from home too long. You've also forgotten your station in this project. I am minister; you are not."

There was a sudden screech from the translator box, and then the metallic voice saying, "You can intimidate your own people, Minister Watt, but not us. We share the concerns of Mister White. There have been too many delays, and for no valid reason. That and recent events involving sabotage have encouraged suspicions among all of us in the Blue party. If we decide to withdraw from this project, our reasons will be made known to your president without going through you."

Mister Jones broke in instantly. "This is all so unfair. We all understood the Greens were in charge; it is, after all, their technology. The Reds and Blues are here only for consultation. We advise. We do not interfere, or make threats in order to get our opinions accepted. I do hear dissention among the Greens, however. Minister Watt must deal with that as befits his office. I personally support the logic of a cautious approach. It was not our intent to put this technology into commercial hands. We already have two players involved in such connections, and possibly a third. Until we get rid of them, we should proceed with caution. I speak for the Red Party when I say I support the views of Minister Watt."

"A voice of sanity. Thank you, Mister Jones," said Watt.

"You can have my resignation if you wish," said White. "I will not participate any further in this sham, and the president will be told my reasons."

For a moment there was a terrible silence in the room, then, "I think that would be most unfortunate," said Watt. "What would it take to keep you with us, and satisfied?"

"Full disclosure," said White. "At least enough material so that significant progress can be made, and rapidly."

Another pause, Minister Watt stroking his long chin with one hand while he thought. "Very well, I will tell you the omissions I wish to make, and why, and then we will hear your opinions."

Watt outlined the omissions he intended to make, and there were immediate objections from his Green colleagues and the Blues, Mister Jones remaining silent and looking uncomfortable.

"The Americans must be able to activate the field generator and obtain a minimum of vacuum state energy to achieve escape velocity. For now it's not necessary they understand the energy source. but know how to use it at low levels. Anything less is not acceptable to me," said Mister White.

"We concur," said the machine voice of the translator.

"Respectfully, sir, I also agree with that," said Chairman Brown. "All the delays have put us in a critical position. It's a poor way to gain political allies; surely you can see that. President Troik has argued the case for this project before the Peoples' Congress. Failure would be a great embarrassment to him, and we all have some knowledge of what the possible consequences could be."

"That is not our concern," said Mister Smith of The Blues. "But it's not our habit to support activities doomed to failure because of poor judgments."

"The danger is real for all of us," said White. "Our governments have made agreements on this. Our failure will be theirs, and I'd rather not spend the rest of my life hiding from them in some desert."

There was a long silence. Internally, Minister Watt seethed

with violent plans for these men who dared to oppose his judgment, but he could not risk a direct report by them to his superior, not at this time. Step back, then, and wait for an opportunity for more direct action.

"Very well, ten percent power as a maximum for now. This will give them planetary capability, but not extra-solar, enough to occupy them for decades."

"Well," said Mister White, amazed.

"Excellent," said a relieved Chairman Brown.

"Your choice," said Mister Smith. "We only advise in these matters, and I must compliment your wisdom, Minister Watt."

"Thank you," said Watt, "but I ask that you respect my position in communicating with our president. Our positions must appear to be unified at all times."

"Of course," said Chairman Brown, and heads nodded in apparent agreement.

"It's settled, then. The manual, minus the section on tensor stress modulation, will be delivered in the morning, with copies for all of you. I think we're finished here, and I thank you for hearing me out." Watt smiled, his murderous hostility now totally masked. At a great distance, not even The Blues could sense it.

"You honor us with your presence, Minister. Please convey our respects to President Troik for us, and do come again at your pleasure."

"That is a promise. Perhaps next time we can share some of the local culture together. Until then, gentlemen." Watt stood up, made a nodding bow, and left them. He closed the door behind him, and walked quickly to the van waiting to take him to port. And in his head he made plans, dark plans for all of those who had just confronted him.

Back in the room Watt had just left, there was a long silence before Mister White said, "Will he do it?"

"Yes," said Chairman Brown. "He cannot risk a complaint to the president. But I wouldn't be surprised to learn he's behind the sabotage we've been experiencing."

"That is a serious implication for a man who has always given full support to the project," complained Jones.

Brown glared at him. "Your support of our Minister has been noted, Mister Jones. Might we regard the Reds as his ally, or is it just you?"

"I represent my state, sir, not Minister Watt, and I resent the inference."

"Then allow me to share a confidence with you. It's important enough that betrayal will mean death to the betrayer. This meeting today was, in fact, called specifically for a deliberate confrontation with our State Minister.

"Mister White and I have suspected for sometime that Watt represents certain members of congress who share his initial opposition to relations with the Americans. In his heart he's a conservative; it's recorded in his entire political career. Suddenly he shares the views of a liberal president, and it has taken him to the foot of the highest seat of power. We have been warned by congressional staff about views he has voiced in private to his fellow conservatives. He seeks the powers of the presidency, and failure of this project could be a big step in that direction. Despite what he said today, we will be sending a report directly to the president, and informing him of our difficulties. Mister White is writing it."

"This is outrageous," said Jones. "I will not take part in this." He stood up, and moved to leave.

White struck like a snake, grabbing him by the shoulders and pushing him back down on his chair.

"Don't even move," White snarled.

The door opened, and a guard was there, responding to a silent alarm sent by Chairman Brown.

"Enough, Mister Jones," said Brown. "Your communications have been monitored for weeks, and the evidence shared with your government. You're going home. Ensign, please take Mister Jones down to level one for transportation off base. Staff will take charge of your prisoner at area four."

Jones sat stunned. The guard stood him up, shackled his

hands behind him and led him away.

There was a strange sound from the television monitor, and then from the translator box came, "Nicely done, and without subtlety. It is a good start in cleaning our house, but you must not expect our help in saving your lives when the good Minister seeks them."

"The letter to president Troik will be sent in the morning," said White.

"Indeed," said Chairman Brown.

* * * * * * *

Eric didn't tell Leon about the message he'd received from Neal. A vague distrust of the man nagged at him. He waited until Leon had gone out on a call, and dialed Gil's private number on his cell phone. Gil answered quickly, and Eric told him all that had happened, including the note from Neal.

"Have you told Leon?" asked Gil.

"Not about Neal, but he knows what I saw at the base, and what I think about it. The project is being deliberately delayed by whoever brought the plane to us. I need to talk to them, but it seems that Davis is the only one they talk to. Face to face, I can identify their nationality. Probably Russian. I can't think of anyone else who could even approach making what I saw."

"Don't tell Leon about Neal."

"Why? Isn't he one of ours?"

"No. He's CIA. They're more interested in finding out which commercial people are trying to get their hands on the aircraft. Remember that when you share information with him. Make another call to Neal and meet with him quick. Take a gun with you; that's an order. Some people who've helped us with information in the past have disappeared, transferred out if we believe what Davis says, and we don't. Ask Neal about the foreign nationals who came over with the plane. Maybe he can identify one for you. We hear that one of them initially briefed the engineers."

"I'm calling him again tonight. I'll get back to you."

"Anytime. If I don't answer, expect a return call. Watch your back."

Gil broke the connection. Eric spent the rest of the day assembling a phony list of international galleries as part of a brochure for interested artists. Leon did not return to the office, so Eric locked up and drove home. The house had not been disturbed, no strange odors in the air. He ran the surveillance tapes fast-forward, and nothing showed up in visible, the IR camera only turned on at night.

Dinner was two potpies and mixed vegetables. He read, and watched television. At exactly midnight he dialed the number Neal had given him.

"Yes?" The voice seemed muffled.

"Eric. I was given this number to call. Nobody answered it last night."

"Sorry. I left out the date you should call. I was at the lab. I assumed you'd call again tonight. Do you know where the high school is?"

"Yes."

"I'm parked in the lot in front of the auditorium. In thirty minutes I'll have to leave. Get here fast, and come alone. I'm not armed."

"On my way," said Eric, and hung up.

It was a ten-minute sprint to the high school, no traffic on Dry Creek Road, a few stragglers on 89A heading south towards Cottonwood. The high school was just off the highway, nestled in red rock; Eric turned in to a large parking lot and saw a single car parked in one corner overlooking the football stadium. The area was dimly lit with sodium lights.

Eric pulled in two spaces away, towards the highway from the lone car, turned off his lights, then the engine. And waited. Whoever was in the driver's seat of the other car did not move to get out, but sat perfectly still.

Eric felt the familiar stirring of hairs on the backs of his hands and neck. His hand moved automatically to the grip of the Colt

Modified at his waistband, two extra clips in a pouch hooked next to the weapon. Seconds became minutes, and still there was no movement, yet someone was there behind the wheel; even behind a dirty window, the silhouette was clear in light coming from in front of the high school's auditorium.

He opened the door and stepped outside, gun in hand. Knees bent, he quick-stepped to the car, coming up on the passenger side. Before he was halfway there, alarms were ringing in his head. The car window was worse than dirty; it was splattered with something dark. He reached the car and looked inside. Neal was sitting rigidly behind the wheel, looking straight ahead, eyes open. The window on the driver's side had a single, neat hole in it and there was a bloody wound the size of a golf ball in Neal's right temple.

Eric instinctively ducked, and tried to open the passenger door. It was locked. Back door, too. He risked another look. The locking knob on the driver's side was up, only the one door unlocked. Something strange about that, but he had to get to Neal's body. The man might have something on him, even a note, a phone number, anything. At the moment that seemed most important. At the moment he did not think that Neal's assailant would have dared to remain in the area. Still, he was a moving shadow when he went around the car in a crouch, keeping below window level and jerking the driver's door open with one hand. As he swung the door open his eyes moved towards the shadowed entrance to the high school auditorium. A bright flash there was nearly simultaneous with a popping sound, then a crunch in the window above his head. Neal's body toppled out of the car on top of him, pushing him to the ground, as there was another flash from the shadows. Neal's body jerked.

Eric sucked air, eyes focused on where the flash had come from. He extended his arm and grabbed his gun hand, lining up the fluorescent dots on front and rear sights, and locking his shoulder. He squeezed off five shots rapid-fire, the roar of the Colt shattering a peaceful night.

He pushed Neal to one side, his eyes fixed on his target, and saw a shadow move. A man ran from the auditorium entrance, heading towards the red-rock scree hill on the other side of the stadium. He carried a rifle by a handgrip. An M16. Eric had recognized the sound of it with a silencer. He'd used the same weapon with deadly purpose, and now he was the target.

Eric took careful aim and squeezed off another shot. The man jumped, but didn't slow.

Eric chased him, but at one mile altitude found breathing at full-sprint more of a challenge than he expected. The man he chased widened the gap as he headed towards the highway, and disappeared over a hillock. Eric got to the brow of the hill just in time to see a small van pulling away from the other side of the highway and heading south. He squeezed off his last shot, and was gratified by a loud clang coming from the van before it drove out of sight.

He reloaded, and waited a while in case the van doubled back, and then he walked back to the car to inspect the body of a man who had probably had important information for him. He searched both the body and the car.

And found nothing.

He had to move fast. Surely there were routine police patrols around the high school. Gil was too far away, too many delays using intermediaries. Davis could be involved in Neal's murder. That left one man.

Eric called Leon on his cell phone. The man picked up after seven rings, and sounded groggy. Eric told him what had happened, "I have to get the body and his car out of here. We don't want the police involved."

"Stay right where you are," said Leon, fully awake. "I'll make a call, and be there in ten minutes."

Eric could only wait and hope the police didn't arrive first. He used the time to find the seven spent cartridge cases from his Colt, and squirreled pistol and spare clips under the front seat of his car. He tried to rehearse a reason for being there. *I was driving home from Cottonwood, officer, and my window was down. I heard loud explosions, and saw flashes of light from the school. I thought there was a fire, but when I drove in I found this. Poor man. No I.D., no wallet. What a terrible thing to happen here.*

He heard the roar of the Humvee before it turned into the lot. Leon jumped out and pointed to Eric's car. "Get out of here. Go to my house through the tunnel, and wait for me. We'll clean up."

As he said it, two black vans pulled into the parking lot and drove right up to where Eric was standing. The four men who got out wore butch-cuts, and were dressed in slacks and woolen sweaters. Two of them picked up Neal's body and dumped it into the back of one van while the other two rummaged in the man's car.

"I've already checked it," said Eric. "It's clean."

The men ignored him. "Go on, Eric," said Leon. "We'll handle it."

Eric got into his car and drove away. Before he even got out of the lot he saw that Neal's car had been started and was backing up. He was suddenly conscious of possible police patrols, and drove carefully just under the speed limit down 89A and back up Dry Creek Road. He garaged the car and holstered the Colt again under his left arm, went down to his basement and used the tunnel to Leon's house. It was a twelve-minute walk, and when he tried the door to the house it was locked and he'd stupidly left the key behind. *What now?* His nerves were edgy. He settled them by jacking a cartridge into the forty-five and holding it loosely in one hand.

The wait seemed long, but wasn't. Eric knocked on the door every few minutes. After several tries there was a thump from the other side, and the door opened.

Leon was there, and looked angry. He glanced at the big Colt in Eric's hand. "No weapon, huh? Now get in here and explain to me what this was all about tonight."

They went upstairs, past the odor of gun oil and powder residue. Leon put coffee on, and opened a package of cookies. Eric told him Neal had said he had important information for him, had given him a number to call and when. He didn't say anything about Neal's note.

"The guy's a civilian engineer. What could he know?"

"Whatever, someone made sure we wouldn't know it," said Eric. "So you knew Neal."

"I knew *of* him," said Leon. "Project engineer since the start: Wright Patterson, NASA, MIT graduate, very capable, but still an engineer. A hardware man."

"Maybe he knew someone we need to talk to."

"Could be. Anything he said could give us a lead. Have you told me everything? We're supposed to be working together, Eric. Are we?"

"What reason would I have not to?"

"Oh, I don't know. Interagency rivalry, something I've said, my after shave, could be anything."

"You CIA?"

"My, we're blunt tonight. Did they teach you that in NSA school?"

"Wrong bait. Keep fishing."

"Don't need to. I looked you up in our mutual database. I'm sure you'll find me in there, too, if you already haven't. You know what they have listed for you? On leave for special assignment. That means you're black as hell, dear boy. Deep, deep. Well, so am I, and it doesn't make any difference what special ops units we're assigned to. We're both here to save this project. We're working for the good old US of A."

"Okay, then I'll go first. I know that commercial interests are trying to get hold of this plane. Are you involved with that in a personal way? Maybe a little something to pad a federal retirement?"

"Is this going to be twenty questions?"

"If you don't answer the first one, I'll call my operations director and get one or both of us pulled."

"I'm involved in it up to my ass, and you are, too. You just don't know it yet. I heard my party acquaintance call you for lunch, or was it a cookie?" Leon waved a cookie at him.

"Lunch. We meet tomorrow."

"Don't believe his business card. I've checked, and it's a phony. I think he's someone's lawyer. See if you agree. The offer will be tempting, since you'll actually be working with the aircraft. His name is phony, and so is the company he's supposed to own. We traced the so-called executive secretary that answers his calls to an unemployed schoolteacher in a Jersey apartment. I'm still trying to find out what company or conglomerate he's working for, and how they found out about the plane in the first place. They're probably aerospace. Davis will be up for retirement soon, and what better golden parachute than a fat consultantship."

"So Davis is in on it."

"He is the man. When I started digging he came up with an offer I couldn't refuse. Do I actually appear to be corruptible? Dear me. He doesn't seem to feel the same way about you. As a matter of fact, I think you frighten him. Which brings me to *my* first question. My turn, now. I wonder how a career military man could fear a data analyst like you, unless you're more than that. Your entire career is special ops and deep cover with a few visible assignments for tech transfer, but I've checked your academic degrees and they are real. So, Mister Price, why are you here? To analyze data on something that doesn't work yet?"

"That's two questions."

"Yuck, yuck. So answer the fucking first one first."

"I'm here to save the project, and that includes data analysis. It includes identifying our tech transfer friends, and their country or countries, and why the technology has come without documentation. It includes identifying corporate spies trying to steal said technology, and the saboteurs trying to slow or stop the project. And now we can add the murderer of Neal Johnson to the list. That enough for you?"

Leon reached out and tapped Eric's shoulder holster at his armpit. "Identify—and eliminate. You didn't mention that."

"First things first," said Eric.

"I can accept that." Leon pulled back his coat to reveal the holster there, a black grip with an extended magazine protruding from it. "At least we're on the same page. The corporate spies are mine. We find them; they die, all the way up to any CEO involved. The saboteurs are yours."

"A bit extreme. My orders don't read like that."

"Mine do, so don't interfere if we get to that point. We're supposed to be allies."

"Fair enough. Now what do we do?"

"Business as usual. Neal has disappeared, and you wonder why. We'll do an autopsy and check the slugs in his body."

"They're from an M16."

"We'll check it out, and I want to get Davis' reaction to Neal's disappearance. This could even have been a corporate hit, or it could be the saboteurs we're chasing. We have to separate out the bad guys, and then kill all of them."

"And somewhere along the way I want to see that airplane doing something that tells me this entire project isn't a waste of time," said Eric.

"Now, now, keep the faith. Someone high up thinks this is vital to national defense, or you and I wouldn't be here."

"A hired killer, and a data analyst?"

Leon smiled. "Make that three hired killers, at least. And one of them isn't working with us."

Eric had to agree with that.

CHAPTER ELEVEN
WHERE ANGELS DWELL

"You were right. It was an M16," said Leon. "Neal never knew what hit him. Military rounds. One of our people found the brass near the auditorium. The firing pin has a distinctive burr we could identify if we could find the right rifle, but there are hundreds at the base. I'll talk to Davis, and see what's possible."

"He knows about Neal?" Eric rubbed sleep from his eyes. The call had shocked him awake, and morning glow was creeping down the buttes visible from his bedroom.

"Had to. He'll make up some story for the techs about why Neal is gone. He mentioned that your background would make you a logical replacement."

"What?"

"Why not? You arrive, and shortly after that Neal is gone. There have been three people in that position in the last two years. Two resigned for health reasons, and Davis will use the same excuse for Neal. I happen to know that one of the other two guys just disappeared, and has never been found. There are lots of ways to sabotage a project, and getting rid of the technical leadership is a good one. It's mostly program analysis, Eric, and that's what Davis was told you're here for. There's a whole team of people to handle the technical stuff. It would put you at the center of base operations, and that's where you need to be. You'll be a target, of course, but at least you'll be one that shoots back. Anyway, don't be surprised if Davis calls you about it."

"Is that why you called so early? It's just past six."

"Sorry. Oh, yeah, one other thing. I think you'll like this one. Nataly Hegel called me last night and left a message. She wanted your phone number. I called her shop, left a message saying you'd call her back this morning. She's usually in there by nine."

"Okay," said Eric. *What now?* he thought. *She's probably canceling out on dinner.*

"Gotta go," said Leon. "I'll be in Phoenix all weekend. Company business."

"Sell lots of art," said Eric.

"Yeah, I will." Leon chuckled, and hung up.

The buttes now glowed orange and yellow outside his window. Eric got out of bed, showered and shaved, had toast and a banana for breakfast.

He brewed a pot of strong, Colombian coffee, and spent two hours making notes and doodles on what he'd seen on the aircraft called Pregnant Sparrow. When he was finished he set fire to the pages and burned them to ash in the sink.

It was after ten when he called Nataly's shop. A girl answered, and put him on hold. His stomach was crawling with certainty that the dinner he was to have with an exotic woman was about to be cancelled.

The phone clicked. "Hello?"

"Eric Price. Leon said I should call you this morning."

"Oh, I'm so glad you called early. Are you terribly busy today?"

Eric's heart fluttered. "Just the usual; nothing special."

"Could you take some time off? I thought we might do some hiking and climbing on the rocks near my house. I don't get a chance to do it very often. It's nothing technical. Hiking boots or good running shoes will do, and the views are wonderful."

It was not the ethereal tone of voice he'd heard before, but excited and animated.

"Sounds interesting. Is this a group outing?"

"Oh, no, it'll just be the two of us. If we leave in an hour or so, we can have lunch on the summit."

"We're climbing a mountain?"

"Cathedral Rocks. It's a thirty-minute climb."

"That's where the angels are."

Nataly laughed. "You've been reading. Maybe we'll get lucky and see one, but first you have to say yes."

"Yes."

She laughed again, and it was a beautiful sound. "Meet me at my shop within the hour. I'll get started on lunch."

"Okay."

"Bye," she said, and was gone, like an excited child. Eric caught himself smiling as he hung up the phone. *How many different people are you?* he wondered.

On a day for lounging at home, he had dressed in jeans and pumas. He closed up the house and made the twelve-minute drive to the shop. Two cars and a battered, white truck were in the parking lot, and Nataly came out the door as Eric pulled up in front of it. She carried a daypack with one hand, was dressed in jeans and a red flannel shirt. Her dark hair was tied tightly in a tail that nearly reached her waist. She waved, then pointed at the truck, walked over to it and deposited the pack behind the cab.

By the time Eric reached the truck, Nataly was inside, and pushed the passenger door open for him.

"This is yours?" He climbed in, and pulled at the seat belt.

Nataly gunned the big engine, and the tires spit gravel as she backed up. "Not a showpiece, but it can take me anywhere in the backcountry."

They drove up to the Y, and turned east. A stream of traffic was coming into town, but little was leaving. Nataly pushed the truck well over the speed limit on the narrow, winding road, pointing out shops, galleries, the turnoff to Frank Lloyd Wright's famous Red Rock Chapel. They turned on Back O' Beyond road, wound their way down into a sort of canyon and passed the turnoff to Nataly's estate. Signs warned of flash flood dangers at low spots in the winding road. Coming around a sharp corner, Nataly suddenly jerked the wheel left, and pulled into a small parking area with a Redrock Pass sign. Two cars were parked there, with Arizona plates.

Beyond the tops of trees, red rock spires loomed above them. Nataly pulled her pack out of the truck, and swung it up onto her back in a single motion.

"I could carry that," said Eric.

Nataly smiled sweetly. "Thanks, but it's light, and the exercise is good for me."

They descended to a dry wash, and then up a trail winding past cactus and gnarled pinyon to a series of broad shelves. Eric was already puffing when Nataly stopped to point at a blackened spot on the rock. "People come up here to drum and play instruments at full moon. It's a good time to meet creative people, and hear their stories."

"I'll bet," said Eric, and looked up at rocky walls towering above him. "It looks straight up."

Again that smile. "It's just a walk up, but we do start out with one interesting section."

A faint, scuff trail crossed hard rock and split into two trails heading left and right. Nataly veered right, then left up a faint, steep trail of earth and scree to a shelf along a wall, and a thirty-foot drop on one side. A crack ran up a jumble of rock at the end of the shelf. Nataly shoved a foot into it, and climbed without hesitation about twenty feet before looking back at him. Eric took the hint, and climbed after her. The rock was rough, with hand-holds everywhere. In a minute they were standing on another wide shelf, and above them was a series of shelves extending to the bases of two, monstrous spires. In another twenty minutes they had ascended the shelves, and were standing on a narrow saddle between the two spires.

Nataly took a deep breath, and audibly sighed. Eric fought for breath. "Too much time behind a desk," he wheezed, and looked out at the expanse of green mixed with rusty red below them.

"Quite a view," he finally added.

"This is my favorite place," she said softly, "since when I was a little girl."

"Steep climb for a kid."

Nataly looked at him, and for one instant seemed sad. "I used to come up here with my dad, but he's gone, now."

"Oh," said Eric. "I'm sorry."

"We were close," said Nataly. She shrugged off her pack, and looked at him with huge eyes. "Were you close to your father?"

Eric leaned her pack against the base of a rock massif. They sat down beside it, with a spectacular view to the south. Nataly rummaged in the pack, pulled out a thermos, and food wrapped in aluminum foil.

"When I got older, I guess we were. Dad was in the military. He met my mom in New Mexico. I came along before he retired, didn't see him much until I was a teenager."

"You grew up in New Mexico?" Nataly handed him a wrapped sandwich, and took one for her.

"Yeah. Albuquerque, but we moved to Taos after dad retired. Mom insisted on it. Her family had lived there before she was born."

Nataly raised an eyebrow. "Was she a Native American?"

"No, but people wondered. She had a subtle, Asian look and dark eyes, but her skin was ivory white. She was very beautiful, and soft spoken, but she had a power, that woman." *Like you*, he thought. "My dad was a tough guy, but she had him wrapped around her little finger. Me, too."

Eric smiled at a memory, but looked away when Nataly smiled with him. "They were killed in a car accident several years ago. Dad was driving, and shouldn't have been behind the wheel. His eyesight was getting real bad."

"Oh," said Nataly.

Eric forced another smile, gestured outwards with a hand. "They would have loved this view."

"But now you're here to enjoy it for them," said Nataly, and suddenly a young couple stepped up onto the saddle. They had come down along another trail that snaked around a spire beyond where Nataly and Eric had stopped to eat. They nodded a greeting, took a photograph of the view, and started off down the trail towards the parking area.

"Where did *they* come from?" asked Eric.

"I'll show you. It's a short trail."

They finished eating, and repacked the pack. Eric offered to carry it, and Nataly allowed it. She led him off the saddle to a faint trail along a shelf that curved sharply around a red rock wall and ended at a steep slope of earth and scree. Below them a gray slab of rock thrust upwards like a tongue. Eric pointed at it.

"Looks like basalt. Really stands out against all this red."

"Some people think it's an artifact of earlier life," said Nataly.

Eric shook his head. "People have an imaginative explanation for everything around here," he mumbled.

Nataly didn't seem to hear him, was scrambling up the scree slope towards a needle of rock towering high above them.

Eric hurried after her. The footing was loose and crumbling, and he was puffing again when he reached the top. Nataly had descended to a depression at the base of a rock spire between two wider massifs on either side of it.

Eric slid down scree to join her. Nataly's eyes twinkled, and she seemed amused. "You wanted to see where the angels come from, and I think it's here. I feel a kind of extra energy when I'm here."

"Right," said Eric. "I guess my receiver is offline."

"Here, take my hand." Nataly reached out, took his hand in hers and closed her eyes.

"Don't you feel anything?"

Eric's face flushed, and he was suddenly conscious of his breathing. "Your hand is either very warm, or mine is cold."

"No, no, not that. Not heat. It's violet, or purple. It comes out of the rock at my feet, and goes through me to this spire when I touch it. If there's a portal for angels or beings from another dimension, I think it must be right here."

Eric squeezed her hand, thinking she might pull away from

him. "I guess I'm just not sensitive enough to feel it," he said softly. "Sorry."

Nataly opened her eyes. A moment before they had seemed much darker. Perhaps it was a trick of light reflected from orange and red rock. She pulled on his hand, and grasped his collar to bend him forward. "Then tell me if you feel this," she said, and kissed him very softly on the mouth. It was not a long or deep kiss, but the shock of it went through Eric's body in waves.

She held his hand, her other hand on his chest, face close. He thought he saw sparkles of green in her eyes as she looked up at him.

"I felt it," he said softly. "It was very nice, but I'm wondering why you did it."

"I wanted to. I always do what I want to do. And you kissed me back."

"Yes, I did." Eric put his free hand over hers on his chest. "Nataly, you don't really know anything about me."

"I know what I need to know," she said quickly, "and I like what I see."

"So do I, but I have a history—"

"No need to talk about that, now. We're attracted to each other. For now, let's keep it simple and enjoy being together. No pressures, no expectations."

"Okay," said Eric, then leaned down to look more closely at her. "I could swear that the color of your eyes keeps changing. I thought they were brown, but now they're deep green."

Nataly smiled. "I'm just drawing energy from the portal here. Maybe someday we can go through it."

"And do what?"

"Visit with the angels, of course, or whatever creatures there are on the other side."

"I think maybe one of the angels is standing right here."

Nataly's eyes seemed to glow. She lifted up on her toes, and gave him a quick, but firm kiss. "That was sweet. Now let me show you the view on the north side."

He followed her down around the central rock spire to the

edge of a steep slope where there was a wide view of Bell Rock and Courthouse Butte in the distance. They looked at it for several minutes, Nataly's head resting lightly against him, and his arm around her waist.

"There *is* an energy here," murmured Nataly. "People come here from all over to meditate, to create, to find peace. Some come here to find their souls."

"Or to make a lot of money," said Eric.

"Is that why you're here?"

"No. Well, that's part of the reason. This is a nice place. I'm going to like it here, as long as I stay. I get moved around in my business."

"Not for a while, I hope." Nataly's head pressed harder against his shoulder.

"Not for a while," he said.

They enjoyed the view and their closeness for half an hour, then scrambled back up the scree slope and picked their way down from the saddle on rough-grained rock that gripped the soles of their shoes. They met several people coming up, faces bright with expectation of adventure, and waited for four of them before descending the steep crack down to the low terraces of rock.

In minutes they were back at Nataly's shop, and Eric was unlocking his car.

"Don't forget dinner. I'll call to remind you," Nataly said brightly.

"I'll be there. Thanks for today."

She smiled, and was gone, and Eric drove home. When he entered the house the phone was ringing. It was Leon, returning him to reality.

But that night, Eric had a wonderful dream about Nataly.

CHAPTER TWELVE
OPPORTUNITY

Eric got to The Coffee Pot at seven, but tourists already filled the little parking lot. He had to park across the street and risk his life in a sprint back across again in morning traffic. A tall man in western garb and a black Stetson identifying him as a big city dude watched Eric approach, and smiled.

"Good broken-field-running, Mister Price. Sorry we have to meet so early." The man extended a hand. "John Coulter. Let me buy breakfast for your trouble."

Coulter's grip was firm, but his hand was smooth, and he'd used a musky and probably expensive after-shave that morning.

"Thanks," said Eric. "We'll probably have to wait a while."

They went inside, and were fortunate. The first wave of diners was just finishing, and the second wave had not yet arrived. In ten minutes they were seated at a corner table, ordering coffee and three-egg omelets. The waitress brought coffee, and left them.

Coulter leaned forward and spoke softly. "Did Leon give you any hints about what to expect in this meeting?"

Eric made steady eye contact. "He said you're a good source of business contacts, and he's worked with you in the past. On the phone you said something about markets for a lot of things, including art and guns. I presume we're here to talk about art, Mister Coulter."

"That's John, please. If we can do business together, I can provide you with dozens of markets for western art: scenics, cowboys, Indians, you name it. Europeans eat this stuff up, and I have a lot of contacts over there, west *and* east." Coulter raised an eyebrow. "Eastern markets are tougher, but the right person can make a lot of money with them if he has the right product."

"You could make more money if you worked directly with the artists. Why choose a middleman like me? I get my commission before you get yours."

Coulter smiled. "The people I represent have wealth beyond our imagination, Eric. Money has no meaning to them. I am convenient, and so are you. I buy in bulk, and distribute what my clients desire. It is done privately, without fanfare. In the eastern block, a show of wealth remains impolite in elite circles. Money exchanges hands for many things without public knowledge, and not just art, as you well know."

"I beg your pardon?" said Eric.

Coulter blinked slowly, and leaned closer. "Everything is for sale: art, ancient artifacts, weapons, nuclear material, state secrets, it's all the same. Occasionally a thing is sold in error, but again, money is not an object, and that thing can be bought back for twice the price paid, or even more, if one deals with the right people."

"I don't see what this has to do with contemporary western art," said Eric, and the waitress arrived with their breakfast.

They sat in silence until the waitress left. Coulter breathed in the odors of his food. "Let's eat first. I've heard the meals here are excellent."

"Yes, they are," said Eric. He was surprised by the turn of the conversation. John Coulter did not sound like a corporate representative at all. Embassy staff, maybe, but what embassy? There was no detectable accent in his speech.

At the worst, surprise might produce an observable reaction. The two of them had eaten a few bites in silence when Eric suddenly asked, "Exactly which government are you representing, Mister Coulter?"

The man looked at something over Eric's shoulder, and chewed thoughtfully, then, "I work for people, not governments, but I must admit that many of my clients are well connected. Shakers and movers, Eric, the people who make the world go around. A man who provides for their needs can quickly become wealthy beyond his imagination. And that could be you." Coulter wiggled an eyebrow at him, and took another bite of his omelet.

"I would have to sell a great deal of art for that to happen, even if I inflated my commission for you."

Coulter smiled, took a sip of coffee, and the smile disappeared. "Let's not dance any longer, Eric. I know who you are, and why you're here. You have recently obtained access to a piece of technology that is stolen goods. It belongs to my client, and he wants it back. He's aware of the difficulty in accomplishing that, and the political consequences of retrieving his property. But he will pay any amount of money to as many people as necessary for the task. Leon is on our team, and one other person I'm afraid we consider less than reliable. He's privately made some contacts with aerospace giants who might pay him more than we have offered. He might even have to be removed. Since that could arguably be part of the assignment from your government masters, you would be an ideal choice for the job if it became necessary."

Eric felt heat come to his face, and played on it. He gave Coulter what he hoped was an expression of both anger and surprise, folded his napkin and slapped it on the table by his unfinished breakfast. "This must be another one of Leon's little pranks, Mister Coulter, and I don't appreciate it at all. It's not even amusing."

"Twenty million, Eric. That's my opening offer, and I'm authorized to go higher. Just agree to join our team. Assignments can be negotiated later."

Eric stood up. "Don't bother to call Leon. I'll tell him what I think of this myself. Maybe he should start looking for a new partner."

"Talk to him," said Coulter. "I'll be in touch."

"Goodbye, Mister Coulter. Thanks for the breakfast, but

otherwise you have wasted my time."

Coulter only smiled. Eric turned, walked away from him with the air of one offended by a foul odor or presence, and left the restaurant. He kept his posture all the way to the car, and drove back to the office in three minutes. Leon was on the telephone when he arrived, and looked up expectantly at him.

Eric pulled up a chair by Leon's desk, sat down and stared at the man until his call had ended.

"You don't look happy," said Leon.

"I'm not."

"What happened?"

Eric recited the entire conversation he'd had with John Coulter. "So, what did you tell him about me? He must think I'm pretty easy to get right to the point like that. I assume the other guy he mentioned is Davis. Since when am I supposed to eliminate Davis? You're worse that a leak, Leon. You're a flood."

Leon held up his hands. "All approved by Gil, right from the get-go. The agency orchestrated my contact with Coulter in the first place. There are a lot of things going on behind our backs. And I never said anything about you eliminating Davis. That has to be a plant, so ask Gil about it.

"At least one person outside the base knows our cover. I don't find that comfortable."

"Gil apparently thinks it's necessary. I hope your act wasn't so good that Coulter will have doubts and decide against working with either one of us."

"I know the look, Leon. The guy is not an amateur. One or both of us will be getting a call from him soon. In the meantime, I'm calling Gil, deep line."

Eric went to his desk, tapped at the keyboard. 'Saw Uncle John, and his health worries me. Please call me tonight. Eric.' He sent the message to his Aunt Emma via satellite link, then went back to work at his desk.

There were four telephone calls that afternoon, all of them for Leon, and none of them from John Coulter. At six, they closed the office. Leon looked at him darkly, and said, "If Coulter doesn't call tomorrow, I'll have to suspect your theatrics have fucked us up, my man. That will not be good for either of us."

Eric didn't offer a reply, and they went their separate ways. Leon headed uptown in his Humvee, and Eric drove home. Clouds were moving in from the southwest, and light rain was forecast. Eric checked his paper shard and thread indicators at the front door, and nothing was disturbed. There were no strange odors in the house. He changed into shorts and T-shirt, and popped two readymade chicken potpies into the oven.

His cell phone played a passage from Beethoven's Ninth, and Eric answered it.

"Price here."

"Gil. What's the problem?"

Eric told him everything about the meeting with Coulter. "Leon says you set up the contact with this guy. How much does he really know, and where does he hear I have an assignment to get rid of Davis? That's news to me. Anything else left out in my briefing?"

"The briefing was for you. The extra assignment was for whoever is running Coulter. It was in a supplemental file, and buried deep. I guess I'm a bit surprised Coulter dared to use it.

"So you're telling me my dossier has been cracked, and my cover blown. Why don't I just close up shop and head for home? Leon, too."

"Easy. It's all selective, all in the family for the little drama we're writing here. Coulter has just told us he's working for a government, not a corporation. No company has the hardware to decrypt that deep file as fast as he did. We added that file two days ago."

"He offered me twenty fucking million just to get on his 'team'. If he gives me the money, can I retire?"

"If we'd told you everything, how could you have acted so surprised and indignant? Leon says your face was nearly purple when you came back to the office. That doesn't sound like you. Something else going on?"

"I don't like being manipulated. There are too many players in this game, and God-knows how many I'm not aware of yet, and I'm not being told everything. I'd like to come out of this alive, something I was never concerned with when I worked alone. If that means I'm getting too old for this, then tough shit. I don't like other people making up the rules of the game as we go along. I make my own rules, or I'm out of here."

"Fair enough. There shouldn't be any more surprises from our end, but I don't regret not briefing you about Coulter. He's been nibbling at the hook, but today he bit it. Accessing that deep file gives us a short list of countries he could be working for. Our insiders will be looking at the most likely candidates for decrypting the file so quickly. Sit tight. Coulter will call again. And watch Davis carefully. Look for any change in his attitude towards you. He and Coulter might be tighter than we think. Or not. If Coulter's handlers want that aircraft back, Davis could be working with him or against him. It would be nice to know which it is."

"I'm not sure about Leon, either," said Eric.

"Treat him right. He's as hard-core as you are. You don't have to like him, but work with him. If you can't do that, I'll have to pull you out and give you a desk somewhere. I don't think either one of us would like that."

It was a light enough slap on the cheek, and Eric took it. "I hear you," he said.

"Good. You're the best at what you do, so do it. You could be in a central position soon. I want daily reports from now on, six p.m. eastern, this number." Gil gave him the number. "I'll pick up on the tenth ring. Otherwise, you hang up, even if I answer."

"A bit dramatic, isn't it?"

"I have my reasons. Got the number?"

"Yes."

The call terminated with a click. Seconds later there was dial tone, and Eric punched his phone off. A recording, or was someone else listening to their conversation? The number Gil had called from looked like a landline. Unsecured? The Gil Eric knew didn't do sloppy things like that without a reason.

Dinner was quick, the cleanup quicker. Eric hated mealtimes, had hated them since his long-ago divorce. It was the one time he didn't like being alone. He washed his few dishes in the sink, and put them away, and sat down in a living room chair to read a magazine.

The kitchen telephone rang, and he picked it up on the second ring. It was Leon.

"Coulter just called me. He said he was amused by your act, but I think he was checking to be sure it *was* an act. I took responsibility for everything, told him I hadn't let you know his client was the party the aircraft was stolen from, that you thought you were dealing with some corporate technology thief. I said we'd talked, I'd explained everything, and you were okay with it."

"I am?"

"Oh, yes. He wants some ideas on how that aircraft might be returned to its lawful owner. Better start thinking about it. Coulter's going out of town, wants to meet with both of us in a week."

"Okay," said Eric.

"You busy right now?" Leon's voice was suddenly back in friendly mode.

"Reading a magazine."

"Want to do something interesting?"

"Like what?"

"A little work with the handguns. I'm itching to shoot something."

"You have an extra gun for me?"

"Sure, but cut the crap and bring along whatever you have. I don't know about you, but recent events encourage me to polish my hardware skills. Besides, I want to see what you shoot."

"Right now?"

"Sure. Come through the tunnel. The door's unlocked, and cookies will be served. Coming?"

"Yes," said Eric, and hung up. *What the hell.* He retrieved the

Colt Modified and three extra magazines from a closet shelf, the Walther holstered in its usual place at his ankle. He left the room lights on, and went through the long tunnel to Leon's basement, the holstered Colt dangling from his hand. He knocked once, the door opened, and Leon was standing there in a white robe. He wore yellow-tinted shooting glasses, and held a small spotting scope with tripod in one hand. His eyes went instantly to the Colt Modified, and he smiled.

"No gun, huh? What is it?"

"Long slide Colt, Harris trigger and bushing, rubber grips."

"Nice. I prefer the Smith .41. My hands are small." Leon led him to the two metal conduits that were his shooting range. A long, black semi-auto lay on a table there. Eric put his Colt on the other table. Downrange, a bull's-eye target was brightly illuminated fifty feet away.

"What's your barrel?" asked Leon.

"Four-five-one. I shoot standard hardball. Four magazines, here."

"Won't be enough," said Leon. "I'll get what you need." He went to a cabinet behind them, came back with a box of fifty full-load cartridges, and smiled. "Five rounds load and lock. At your leisure, sir."

Both men inserted earplugs and then put on cushioned muffs. The bull's-eye of the target was a black dot that didn't even cover the front blade of his pistol's sight, and Eric was used to shooting at silhouette targets. He squeezed off five shots slow-fire. Leon fired five times in ten seconds, waited for Eric to finish, and turned on a motor that brought both targets back to them.

Not bad, thought Eric: two nines, a ten and two X's. He looked at Leon's target, saw two tens and three X's.

Leon saw his look, peered at Eric's target. "Pretty good for an analyst who doesn't carry a gun. Let's do it again, rapid fire, and I like match pressure. How about a quarter a target?"

They went through a dozen targets each, five shots in ten seconds. By the end of the session, Eric was putting nearly everything in the ten and X rings, but Leon had beaten him every time.

"I think you were actually trying there towards the end," said Leon.

"It's one thing to punch holes in paper," said Eric, "and another thing to kill a man."

Leon looked at him coldly. "I know it is."

"I bet you do," said Eric. And both men knew at that instant their relationship had suddenly changed.

They finished the evening with decaf and cookies, did not talk about private things. Eric didn't even mention his outing with Nataly. There was some small talk about new artists in town, until both men were yawning. It was only nine when Eric went back to his own house. He read for a while, spent half an hour staring mindlessly at the television, and then went to bed.

Sleep came slowly. For a while he was again focused on the black dot of the bull's-eye target, the sights aligning, the gentle squeeze of the trigger, the recoil pressure traveling along a rigid arm to the shoulder, the sights realigning without conscious effort. He drifted away finally to a place of dreams unremembered, while hundreds of yards from him Leon was visiting the golden being that was the higher manifestation of him.

Near midnight there was a click from the basement, but Eric was sleeping deeply. A stairway squeaked, and shortly afterwards a shadow filled the doorway to the bedroom. The shadow moved to Eric's bed, and took form. It was a man, his face shrouded with a hooded mask. He took a bottle from his pocket, sprayed a gentle mist over Eric's face, and waited a moment for the rhythm of Eric's breathing to slow. Satisfied, he attached three wires to Eric's forehead, and turned on a palm-sized device in his hand. The device glowed with flickering points of light on its face, and then went dark. The man detached the wires from Eric's head, and left the room.

By the time he reached the doorway, the man was once again a formless shadow.

* * * * * * *

It was two hours past her usual time for sleep, but Nataly sat mesmerized by what she saw on the computer screen as the long, violent history of Eric Price scrolled past her view. *No wonder he was divorced*, she thought. *He was never home.* This much was obvious, even from the incomplete NSA file that had been hacked for her. Several pieces were missing, each covering periods of six months to a year, missions so black they were not included in the general file.

She picked up the telephone, punched in seven numbers.

"Nataly. The file has several gaps in it. Can you fill those in for me?"

She listened a few seconds, then, "How long, then? We're moving ahead with this tomorrow, and I need to know everything I can get about him."

Nataly rolled her eyes at the reply. "That's not funny, Vasyl. You know what I mean. Get back to me tomorrow, even if you haven't found anything. Okay. Bye."

She hung up, and immediately felt a movement of cool air that washed over her face and bare arms. She tensed, but kept her eyes on the computer screen, not reading.

The cold went away, but she felt the presence somewhere behind her by the balcony of her bedroom that overlooked the pool. She forced her mind away from Eric's file, focused on what she'd read about Leon several weeks before, and what little, useful intelligence she'd been able to get on Davis.

The presence was moving behind her, right to left, coming off the balcony and inching towards the darkened corner of the room beyond her bed, all the while probing at her mind.

This was not good. She really needed to study Eric's file in private, and without interruption, and then get to bed.

Nataly suddenly turned around. At the foot of her bed, two shimmering columns of air were now changing colors to blend with the shadows. A third had just entered from the balcony, and was still a dark gray. All three flashed darkly when Nataly stood and stomped a foot hard on the floor.

"All of you, get out of this room right now! One more violation of protocol, and I'll go to the Council, and you'll be left to explain the repercussions to your masters. Now, get out of here!"

The shadows fled the room.

CHAPTER THIRTEEN
PROGRESS

Eric awoke fuzzyheaded, and his mouth was dry. Two cups of coffee cleared his head, but he pushed away a bowl of cold cereal half-eaten and settled for a piece of toast spread with peanut butter.

The van arrived at six, the driver a sergeant who said nothing beyond "good morning", and played a horrible, country western CD all the way to the base. By the end of the trip, Eric had a dull headache from it, and vowed not to allow a repeat of the experience.

Sergeant Alan Nutt was waiting for him at the elevator, clipboard in hand, took one look at him and said, "Rough night, sir?"

"Didn't sleep worth a damn," said Eric, as the elevator arrived. They got in, and descended.

"Looks like you'll be filling in for Doctor Johnson, at least until Davis names a replacement," said Alan. "Too bad about Johnson. Sure was sudden."

"I heard it was a heart attack. You never know, with these type A personalities," said Eric.

"Yeah," said Alan, and then there was a pause.

"I don't think it was a heart attack, sir. Do you?"

Eric looked steadily into the man's eyes. "What makes you think it wasn't, Alan?"

Alan met his gaze, and held it. "I just don't, sir. Johnson is the third Tech Supervisor since I've been here. The first left with ulcers, the second just left without explanation, and now this. Seems to be a hazardous job, and now it looks like you'll be doing it. I guess what I'm saying is you should watch your ass, sir."

Eric suddenly had a good feeling about the man. "I will, sergeant, and you watch yours, too. Anything else I should know?"

"If I hear it, you'll know it, sir. The word is there's trouble with the Pregnant Sparrow project: not much progress, and a lot of frustration."

"That's what I hear, too, Alan."

"You here to fix it?"

"I'll do whatever they let me do, but the documentation I have to work with is pretty poor."

"Oh, then you're in for a good surprise, sir. The manual everyone has been waiting for came in last night. Colonel Davis brought it down himself. I'm taking you right to it in Sparrow's Bay."

The elevator door opened, and they walked. Overhead a small bird flew desperately in circles, looking for a way out. Eric looked up at it.

"Overhead was open a while early this morning. They get in here sometimes, and we let'em out at night, before they crap all over the place," said Alan.

Pregnant Sparrow sat in gloom. Beside it a crooked-neck lamp illuminated a small table, and three men were standing there, looking down at something.

"Good morning," said Eric, and the men stepped aside from the table.

"Are you Price?" asked one of them.

"I am. This is Sergeant Nutt. He's here to make sure I don't say anything that'll get me in trouble."

Alan shook his head, and smiled.

"Colonel Davis says we report to you until further notice. I'm Frank Harris, Systems Analysis."

Eric shook his hand.

"Elton Steward, Materials Testing," said another man, and held out his hand.

"Rob Hendricks, Flight Operations," said another. "We've been working with Doctor Johnson on this bird for the past six months without any documentation. Today we got it, only to discover we can't read it."

Eric looked down at an open loose-leaf notebook on the table, and turned a page. "Ah," he said, a suspicion now confirmed, "that's because it's in Russian." He turned another page, scanning quickly.

"Shouldn't be hard to find a translator on the base," said Rob.

"Don't bother. I can read it." Eric riffled pages, looking at section headings. "Looks like a flight manual: pre-flight check list, start-up sequence, instrument panel. Pretty brief. I'll need a day to get through it and make a rough translation. I don't see anything about the aft section I'm most interested in."

"The empty section?" said Elton.

"I doubt it's really empty. I think it's part of the power plant." Eric paused at a page, leaned down for a closer look. "Here, it talks about a mixing plenum. The details must be in here. Can someone get me a recorder, or even a secretary? The translation of this can be quick if I have some help."

"Use mine, sir," said Alan. "I'm also pretty good at short-hand, if you slow down for me."

"We need some chairs," said Rob, and hurried away. A minute later he came back with two privates in tow, and six straight-back chairs. The men sat down around the table, Eric bent over the flight manual. Alan put his recorder on the table and sat with pen poised over his clipboard.

"Ready when you are, sir. Just nod when you want the recorder on."

The translation came in bursts of broken English, Eric's brain working directly in the Russian tongue like a native. Alan struggled to keep up, and often asked for repeats when the strange mix of Russian and English confused him. The other men were attentive at first, sitting at the edge of the circle of light, a darkened bay behind their backs and overhead. Gradually, their attention drifted in and out, the words becoming nonsensical to their minds. After an hour of this, Rob finally stood up and gestured for the other two men beside Eric and Alan to follow him.

"I think we'd best wait for a cleaned up version of what you're doing. I can't follow it, and we're not helping you any. Why don't we meet here tomorrow morning?"

Eric nodded, and said something else the men didn't understand.

A moment later, Eric and Alan were alone in a circle of light next to the shadowy silhouette of a stolen aircraft called Pregnant Sparrow. They worked hard through lunch and past dinner without a break, until a Master Chief showed up looking for Alan and took a message back to Colonel Davis about what was going on. Davis sent the man back with an invitation to use a conference room four levels up, and had sandwiches and coffee sent in for them. A computer and printer were provided. Eric finished the translation at eight in the evening.

"What a mess," he said, after hearing parts of it over and comparing with Alan's written version. Alan sat down at the computer.

"Dictate, and I'll type."

They went through the entire manuscript; start to finish, in four hours. By the end of it, two things were clear to Eric: a native Russian had not written the original document. The language was stiff and formal, without idiom, and English words had been substituted where Russian words existed. The second thing he noticed was more troubling. There was frequent mention of a mixing plenum in the context of power plant and startup, and reference to FL-7 on two occasions. But FL-7 should have been in the Flight Operations section, and that only went to FL-6, which was good up to Mach 6 and an altitude of a hundred thousand feet. The lab guys would be giddy about that, having pushed Sparrow only to Mach 1, but Eric was anything but happy. His gut was telling him that everything they were after was in FL-7, and it hadn't been given to them, yet the pages in the original manual were consecutively numbered, and nothing seemed to be missing.

As he thought it, his mind suddenly went blank. Eric sighed, and closed his eyes.

"You okay, sir?" said Alan.

"Tired," said Eric, and rubbed his eyes. It was not a physical fatigue that troubled him, but more like a hallucination. He saw an image of Sparrow's control panel, and his hand working there, moving a sequence of toggle switches and then pressing an unmarked switch on the overhead panel. The vision went away, then came back seconds later to repeat itself.

Eric stood up. "We're going back to Sparrow's Bay."

"Sir?"

"Get me in the cockpit of that thing."

"I don't know how, sir. I'll call the others back."

"No. Stay close. Write down everything I do." Eric's eyes opened wide as he watched something that was only in his mind.

They went back to Sparrow's Bay. A lone guard checked them in as they entered, and recognized both of them. Eric climbed up on Sparrow's stubby wing, shoved his hand into a slot in the fuselage, and squeezed.

There was a metallic pop, and a gull-wing panel unfolded as it swung out above their heads. Eric climbed into the cockpit without hesitation. Settled himself. Alan looked over his shoulder, clipboard at the ready.

"Draw a layout of these switches, and number the sequence I use."

Eric waited a few seconds, and then began throwing switches, seven of them, in sequence. His hand moved to the eighth on the overhead panel."

"Got it?" he asked.

"Got it, sir. Hope you know what you're doing."

"I don't, but here goes," said Eric, and punched the switch on the overhead.

There was a loud thump from the bowels of Pregnant Sparrow.

Eric waited for something to happen, held up his hands. "Still here. No balls of fire, yet."

Alan was looking aft along the fuselage. "Holy shit," he said, and then Eric felt a faint vibration, stood up in the cockpit and looked back around Alan.

The entire tail section of Pregnant Sparrow was rising, rotating, as if hinged. Eric climbed out and followed Alan off the wing as the tail section quit moving with a dull thud. They looked inside the tail section, and saw an empty shell. The fuselage it had connected to was empty back three feet to a solid panel covered with nubbins the size of baseballs, and sharp, metal vanes only an inch in height ran back to it, parallel along the fuselage.

"They've been trying to get into this thing for a year," said Alan. "We really needed that manual."

"It wasn't in the manual," said Eric, and ran a hand over the edge of a vane. It felt vaguely warm to the touch, while the fuselage surface was cool.

"So how did you figure it out?"

"I don't have a clue," said Eric. "Must have been something I read in the controls section. I'll check it again. These vanes are warm, and they're getting warmer. Ah, what's this?"

The vanes were uniformly separated by a couple of inches, but between two of them, halfway back, was a small depression in the fuselage. A black button switch there was engraved with a glyph that looked like an eye. Eric's finger hovered over the switch. A part of his mind screamed out in warning, but a stronger part was urging him on.

"This will either be enlightening, or stupid," said Eric, and pushed down on the switch. There was a click, then a faint buzzing sound resonating from the fuselage.

"Hear that?' asked Eric.

"No."

"Lean closer." Eric leaned inside the open fuselage so Alan could get closer. The fuselage was cold on his hands, but his face was suddenly warm, and it felt like the hair on his head and hands was moving in a light breeze.

"Feels warm in here," said Alan.

"And getting warmer," said Eric. His face felt flushed, while hands remained cool on the metal surface.

"Enough," he said, reached over and pressed the black button down hard. Another click, and the faint buzzing sound stopped instantly. Alan stepped back, but Eric remained where he was for another minute. The warm breeze he'd felt before was gone, and his face cooled quickly. "Did you feel a breeze in here?"

"No air movement, but my hand felt warm."

"Gone, now. Let's close it up and get some others to take a look at this." Without thinking, Eric climbed back onto the wing, reached inside the cockpit and toggled a single switch on the overhead panel.

The tail section lowered again without sound, and locked into place with a thump.

Alan looked at him with a grin on his face. "I guess that was in the manual, too."

"Must be," said Eric. "Why don't you go get the others back here while I try to figure out how I did this? I know it's late, but you might catch them up."

Alan left him there. Eric went through the manual several times, focusing on the controls section, but found absolutely nothing that even suggested how to gain access to the interior of the fuselage. The words 'mixing plenum' and 'FL-7' kept popping up, an unknown term and missing section that had to have something to do with it, at least providing a clue. So without a hint, a trigger for inspiration, how could he have seen what he'd seen, his own hand moving over the controls in the proper sequence? And how had he dared to press that black button in the interior of Sparrow's belly? What had compelled him to do it? This was not Eric the analyst, the scientist. He would not do something like that without some knowledge of the possible consequences, and yet he'd done it without hesitation.

In what seemed like a moment, Alan was back with the others. They were all excited, and demanded Eric show what he'd done.

Eric obliged them, returning to the cockpit, and without reference to Alan's notes he toggled in the switch sequence to open the bowels of Sparrow to them. The men were all peering inside before he even got off the wing. "Don't lean in too far. Might be a residual energy field there. It started to get warm inside when I pressed this switch."

The men backed up a step. Eric leaned inside the open maw of Sparrow and pressed the button switch on the fuselage. Again there was a thump, and a buzz near the edge of their audible range. Eric intended to show them the growing warmth inside, but this time something more spectacular happened. Elton Steward had left his loose-leaf notepad in the fuselage interior before he stepped back. As Eric inserted his hand into the opening to check for the first indication of warmth, the notebook suddenly snapped open, the cover standing straight up, the pages riffling until they were spread into a fan shape, each page equally spaced from its neighbors. Eric flinched, but didn't remove his hand, saw the hairs there waving as if in a breeze, felt the first warmth caress his skin.

"Here, you can feel the heat."

"I don't think so," said Steward, and took another step back. "What the hell's going on with that notebook?"

Eric ignored him. "Getting warmer," he said. Not warmer, but now hot, and the hairs on his arm and head were beginning to move. He punched the switch again, and kept his hand inside. The notebook pages collapsed, and the hairs on his hand and arm were instantly still. The heat he'd felt dissipated more slowly, but was gone in a few seconds.

He handed the notebook back to Steward, but the man hesitated before taking it. "There's some kind of energy field inside this thing when you throw that switch," said Eric. "It's not microwave. I feel the heat first at skin surface."

"And it would take a hell of a radiation pressure to move those pages like it did, and the way they ended up doesn't make any sense if it's a radiation effect," said Steward.

Eric looked at the watch on his wrist. "Not magnetic, either.

My watch is running fine. But there's an energy field inside this thing, and it's controllable. My bet is that switch I activated is just a system check. Any ideas?"

"Lots of tests we can make," said Steward. "You sure there isn't anything in that manual about this?"

"Not a word. There's a reference to a section I think has been left out."

"Still playing games with us," said Steward.

"Maybe, but we're inside, now. Let's make the best of it.

"I meant you," said Steward. "You haven't told us how you figured out how to get into this thing so quick, and we've been playing with it for months."

"Trial and error. I was just throwing switches, and it opened up," said Eric, and knew they didn't believe him.

"Right," said Steward.

Eric felt a coldness creep over him. He took a deep breath, and fixed the man with a baleful stare. "Excuse me?"

"I can help carry some equipment if you like," said Alan quickly, and stepped in front of Eric.

Steward's face went ashen. "Uh—sure—I'll show you where it is." He turned quickly, and Alan followed him away. The other men seemed oblivious to the tension of the moment. When Eric sat down at the table and began leafing through the manual, they ignored him and talked quietly near Sparrow's tail section.

A few minutes later, Steward returned with Alan. They brought with them a magnetometer, calorimeter and optical pyrometer. Eric remained confused after another quick pass through the manual, had found nothing that might have triggered his sudden, and now uncomfortable knowledge of how to open up Sparrow's belly.

Eric did it again, climbing to the cockpit and toggling the switches without a word, then going back to his study of the manual. Steward and the others set up the instruments inside Sparrow and it was Steward who punched the switch there. Eric heard the buzz, some mumbles from the men, but was focused on the operational checklist for sub-sonic flight.

Suddenly, Steward was standing beside him. Eric looked up.

"Nothing," said Steward. "No magnetic field, and nothing registered on the calorimeter. Optical T went up two degrees on the vanes and fuselage interior, and stayed there."

Eric blinked. "So put a light rubber band around your notebook and put it inside. From what we saw, the band should stretch, and you can calibrate that. The field inside Sparrow isn't electromagnetic."

Steward frowned at him, and went away. Eric went back to his reading, but Steward was back again in a few minutes. "Whatever is there can produce a milli-newton force," he said.

Something crept into Eric's mind. "Makes you wonder what it can do if Sparrow is all closed up, and we really turn it on," he said, and Steward just gave him a dark look.

"I'm sure you'll figure that out for us, Doctor Price. Do you write the report on our little tests here?"

"You're a chief scientist here. Think of me as a consultant," said Eric.

"Okay, I'll write it, and the rest of us would like to study that manual, if you don't mind."

"I'll get three copies for you," said Alan, always within listening distance, clipboard poised. "But they're only for use in this bay, on shift. End of shift, I lock 'em up."

"So do that, Sergeant. Now. Doctor Price seems to be busy with this copy."

Alan looked at both of them, then, "I'll be back in a minute, sir." And he hurried away.

Enough of this shit. Eric stood up, stepped so close to Steward their noses were nearly touching, and said very softly, "Just what exactly is your fucking problem, mister?"

Steward didn't flinch this time. "I wouldn't want to say anything to Davis' boy, would I? Johnson heads our group for months, and there's no help or information. Johnson disappears, and now here you are and we suddenly have a manual with stuff missing that seems to be in your head. Tell Davis we're sick of his stalling and his games. Either give us what we need or send us back to our civilian jobs where we can accomplish something."

"You're civilians?" said Eric. "I thought you were all government, or military."

"Just the techs. The scientists and engineers are all on loan from industry."

"Where?"

"I can't tell you that, not for any of us."

"Then private industry knows about Sparrow?"

"No. I mean, I don't think so. I didn't know until I got here. My company is making a lot of money for my services. Why should I tell you what you already know? More games?"

"No games. I didn't know, and I'm not Davis' man. I'm here to find out what's hanging up this project, and Davis is not happy about my being here, if that tells you anything."

"You CIA?"

"No. Private agency."

"Yeah, sure."

Eric smiled. "You wouldn't expect the truth anyway."

"I guess not. We've had nothing but cover-ups and lies around here. Are we ever going to know what happened to Johnson, or the guy before him?"

"Maybe, but I can't tell you where he is, or if he's alive."

"We were told it was a heart attack. I don't believe it."

"Neither do I," said Eric.

There was a long pause. Steward locked eyes with Eric and stared at him. Suddenly he blinked, let out a sigh. "Okay, suppose I assume you're actually here to help. What can I do?"

"Your job, as best you can," said Eric. "I can help with that, too. My scientific credentials are real, but I have no idea what that energy field inside Sparrow is, and throwing those switches in the right sequence today was just blind luck. Whatever information there is about it has been left out of this manual, and I intend to find out why. Have you ever seen or talked to the people who brought Sparrow to us?"

"Saw them once," said Steward. "They were right here, with

Johnson, two dark guys, Slavic accents. Russians, I think."

"The manual's in Russian."

"So you said. I'm wondering if we're dealing with Russian Mafia."

"Maybe. Everything's for sale over there. But if money has been agreed on and paid, I don't see why material would be left out of the manual."

"More money," said Steward.

"I don't think so. There's something about Sparrow they don't want us to know, and I think that energy field we just looked at has something to do with it. I heard Sparrow was supposed to have space flight capability."

"Me, too. That was the big excitement in the project."

"Well, what I've seen in the manual doesn't take us over a hundred thousand feet. It's all conventional JP-4 and boosters. But I found two references to a so-called 'mixing plenum' I bet were left in by mistake. I think we looked inside that 'mixing plenum' today, and it has something to do with powering this bird above the atmosphere. We need to quantify that energy field and identify it. And I need to get that missing material for the manual. Maybe Sergeant Nutt can help me with that."

Alan had just entered the bay through the single personnel door, and was hurrying towards them, arms loaded with loose-leaf notebooks. He stacked the books on the table, and turned to Eric.

"Colonel Davis wants to see you right away."

"You told him what happened today?"

"Yes, sir. He wants to know what you think is missing from the manual. It was supposed to be complete this time."

"This time?" said Steward, smirking.

Alan ignored him. "He's waiting for you, sir," he said to Eric.

"Shouldn't take long. Maybe while I'm gone you can estimate how much energy was in that field we observed."

"I can tell you right now it won't be enough to lift a marble to a hundred thousand feet," said Steward.

"It's a starting point. Okay, Alan, lead on."

Steward mumbled something as they walked away from him, and all Eric heard was the name 'Davis'.

They went straight to Davis' office. Alan knocked on the door jamb, and there was a sharp reply from inside, and Alan stepped aside for Eric to enter.

Davis stood up behind his desk, motioned Eric to a chair, and sat down close to it on the edge of his desk. His forehead glistened with sweat, and his eyes were red and glittering.

"How the hell did you get inside Sparrow?"

"Pure accident," said Eric, and he sat down.

"Bullshit. You did it first try, no trial and error. Sergeant Nutt watched you do it. Who told you what to do?"

"Nobody. I'm not hiding anything. It just happened. I don't know what the trigger was. I don't see any clue in the manual. It was an impulsive thing, just seemed right. And I have no reason to lie to you. The manual we got is incomplete. There's at least one section missing, something on FL-7, whatever that is. My bet is it's to do with Sparrow's space flight capability. There's some kind of energy field inside that thing when you open it up. That ship has a power source we haven't seen yet. Didn't we pay our Russian friends enough money?"

Davis blinked, paused, and looked above Eric's head. "I warned the fuckers. Now I'm going to the Pentagon."

"Warned who?"

"The group of slimes who brought us Sparrow. I've talked to three of them, but there are more. A lot of phone calls, and half the time I don't know who I'm talking to. They're having disagreements among themselves on how fast to give us what we need to get Sparrow into space. When I complained yesterday I was told getting the plane to a hundred thousand feet was the necessary next step."

"You knew the manual was still incomplete?"

"Yes, but I thought our people might get a clue from what we'd received. Getting Sparrow to open up was a surprise, Price. A big surprise, and not just for me. They already know about it. I got a short but nasty call not ten minutes ago, telling me to use whatever means possible to find out how you got inside that plane. And the call was not from the Pentagon."

"Only Nutt and I were there when it first happened. That's a couple of hours ago."

"They have eyes and ears everywhere. That's not news. They said if I don't find out what your information source is, they'll do the job for me."

"A threat?" said Eric.

"That's the way I took it. I didn't recognize the voice. It wasn't either of the people I regularly deal with."

"Do you have a way of contacting them?"

"Yes, but I can't tell you what it is."

"I'm not asking you to. I'd call them right away, and see if they know about the call you just received. They might have a rogue in their group. The mercenaries and political entrepreneurs I've had experience with don't deliver a product, collect the money, and then try to prevent the product from being used. That caller might be the source of the accidents you've been having. He might be Johnson's killer, Colonel. Get after him."

Davis gave him a hard look, but nodded. "All right, but in the meantime you don't do things without telling me, Price."

"You, too. Your friends aren't friendly. You'd better find out which people you can trust."

Davis paused, thinking, then, "Sit right there," he said, walked around his desk, picket up the telephone and punched in four numbers.

"Davis," he said. "Are you alone? Good. I want to clarify something. Did one of your people call me a few minutes ago? No? Well, I got a call from someone in your group, and I'm thinking about reporting it to the Pentagon."

Davis described the call he's received, and told about Eric's success in opening up Sparrow. He listened, then, "How long will that take? One more 'accident', I'm dumping the blame on you people, and you can explain it to the Pentagon before you go to prison."

There was a reply, and Davis' face flushed deep red. "I don't give a shit. I won't be kept in the middle. Yes, I'll tell him. Don't call me again until you have something." Davis slammed down the receiver as if to emphasize the point, leaned back in his chair and looked at Eric over steepled fingers.

"He claims they didn't call me."

"Do you believe him?"

"No. But I think I shook him up. I'm writing this up and sending it to the Pentagon right now. You'd be wise to do the same for whatever agency you're working for, before someone starts shooting."

Davis pulled a sheet of paper out of a drawer, and looked away from Eric. "Interesting that our foreign friend didn't ask how you figured out how to open up the bird."

"And what does that mean to you?" asked Eric.

"Nothing, I guess. But it might explain why he wants to meet you, Doctor Price."

CHAPTER FOURTEEN
NATALY

Eric's life had gone from mysterious to bizarre overnight, and it was apparent the so-called 'hidden base' in the backcountry was leaking information like a sieve.

He called Gil on his secure line and told him what had happened. Gil told him not to say anything to Leon about it, and refused to explain why. "I'll get back to you soon," he said, and hung up.

Gil was no sooner off the line than the phone was ringing again. This time it was Coulter. "Heard you made a big break-through yesterday," he said. "I hope Leon has convinced you by now that I can be trusted."

"I suppose," said Eric, "but I'd like to know your information source about yesterday."

Coulter laughed at that. "Company confidential. Cost is not an issue. And my offer to you still stands if you'll meet me again. No contracts, just a handshake, if you like, but you'll be held to it once you've been paid. No more worries about living on a government pension when you're too old for field work."

"You presume a lot, Mister Coulter."

"Just tell me you'll meet me again. A man has to think about his future, and we live in a dangerously insecure world. Money can buy you security *and* safety, Eric."

"You think I'm in danger?"

"We both know the answer to that."

"Maybe I'm in danger from your client."

"Exactly the opposite. His network can look out for you without you even knowing it. Come on, now. Meet me."

"Okay. Same place and time. You name the day."

"Tuesday. I get back from Phoenix the night before."

"Busy, busy."

"Yes, I am, and more than some of it is in your behalf."

"Tuesday, then, and one more thing."

"Yes?"

"No more phone calls, not on this line," and Eric hung up before the man could answer.

He was surprised when the telephone rang again a minute later. "Christ, I just told him," he said, and picked up the receiver.

It was Nataly.

"My, but you're busy this morning."

"The phone has been ringing off the wall. All business."

"Well, I'm not business. I wanted to remind you about tonight, my house."

"It's on my calendar. Should I bring wine, or something?"

"Just yourself. I hope you're adjusting to the pace of our little town. Not too boring, I hope."

"I'm too busy for boredom. A quiet, relaxing evening will be a nice change for me."

"Then that's what you'll have. See you at seven, Eric. Bye."

"Bye," he said, as the line went dead. He suddenly remembered his first date. He was in junior high school, and he'd had a terrible crush on a girl named Gracia Cole. She had a twin named Gloria, but Gracia was the quiet one of the two, and he was crazy about her. He'd finally worked up the nerve to call her up and ask for a date, and she said yes, and they chatted a while, and when he'd hung up the phone his heart had been pounding so hard he could scarcely breathe.

His heart was pounding like that right now.

A deep part of him that hadn't been used for a long time seemed to find that amusing.

He sat down at his desk and wrote a long report for Gil, with details of what he'd seen inside Sparrow, and also the new call from Coulter. Encrypted, it left for satellite link with the strike of a key.

It was very quiet in the house, only an occasional creak here and there as the temperature outside rose and then began to drop again. He was aware of each small sound, a kind of hyper-vigilance he found distracting until the report was out and he was actually doing work for his cover. He spent over an hour studying several portfolios submitted to him on disk. The week before, thanks to NSA imagination, he'd actually placed nine paintings by a young, local artist. The works had been shipped to Berlin, and would never be seen again, but an advance in the low five figures meant rent and food for the artist for over a year, and word of the sale had gotten around quickly.

Leon called at two. "We had a visitor today."

"Oh?"

"Nataly. Just stopped by to say hello, she said, but I think she was looking for you. Asked where you were, and I told her what days you were off."

"I talked to her this morning," said Eric. "We're having dinner at her place tonight."

"Just the two of you?"

"I think so."

"Well, there's no accounting for a woman's taste in men. If she only knew, oh my. Be good to her, Eric. She really is a sweetie."

"We're just having dinner, Leon."

"Of course. Any other news, maybe something dramatic that happened at the base yesterday? I hear the inside of some strange bird was revealed."

"You've been talking to Davis?"

"We're very close. Of course, you were going to tell me all about it."

"Not until I reported to Gil. It just went out."

"Must be quite a breakthrough. Davis is scared. He warned me to watch myself, said you might be in danger. Someone is upset with what you did. Want to talk about it?"

"Not until Gil gets back to me. Everyone talks to everyone around here. Security is a joke. Coulter called again, and already knew what happened yesterday. He practically offered me protection."

"Probably got it from Davis," said Leon.

"I'm meeting him again. He's signing me up, and I still think he's working for a government, not a corporation."

"Maybe. We're in a position to find that out. Davis is really scared, and the guy who shot Johnson is still running around. My bet he's military. Davis and I are searching files for people with sniper training. You coming in tomorrow?"

"Yes."

"We'll talk more then. Here comes a client. Got to go."

Leon hung up on him before Eric could answer.

Lies, lies. Eric knew his own, and wondered how many Leon was telling. The man had been around for over a year, was likely deeper than Eric suspected, and there had been more than enough time for corruption. Eric knew all about corruption, sometimes wished he'd availed himself of it early enough to retire and save a marriage. And Coulter was giving him a new opportunity. Maybe.

Eric checked e-mail; saw the message from Auntie, the text a single exclamation point. His report to Gil had been received and logged. He clearly heard a car drive by outside. His state of hypervigilence lingered on, and he felt anxious. It was more than anticipating the dinner with Nataly, not simple nervousness. Perhaps his sub consciousness was dealing with the danger Davis was warning of, or the identity of Johnson's killer, or even whom Coulter could be working for. And then there was the manual, written in Russian, but not by a Russian, and who else could make such an aircraft in the east? And why would a mercenary or turncoat leave out information when their money had already been paid? *No more coffee*, he thought. *Too much banging around in my head. I'm getting jumpy.* He heard every small sound, imagined blurred movement in his peripheral vision.

Enough of this. Eric stripped down, took a long, hot shower, and shaved. Nataly had said casual. He dressed in black slacks and a terra cotta sport shirt, and inspected himself in a mirror. The sight of his own, grim face disturbed him. *I've forgotten how to smile. Why can't I put things behind me, and just let go?* The smile he tried looked forced, and didn't show in his eyes. *Oh, I'm going to be great company tonight.*

For an hour he cleaned up the kitchen, the magazine and newspaper mess in the front room, and made up his bed for the first time in five days. The stalling was sufficient; in traffic, it was twenty minutes to Nataly's place. The sun was low, and the buttes east of town glowed yellow to orange-red. There was the usual snarl at the Y, the crawl across Oak Creek, then acceleration out of town. A few minutes, and he turned on Back 'O Beyond and wound his way up into the high rent district, then the turn on the unmarked road that was a driveway and wound his way up to the entrance gate. The guard there smiled and waved him through the opened gate. Four hairpin turns, and he parked in the gravel lot near the pool. Suddenly he was anxious again. *I should have brought flowers, or some little thing for her. I should have asked Leon about it.* By the time he reached the massive front door of her palace, his heart was hammering hard.

Nataly opened the door before he could knock on it. Her long, black hair fell over one shoulder, held in a tail by a band of gold filigree, and her dark eyes were lined in purple. A golden, sleeveless dress clung to her figure. "Eric," she said, in a tone that made him feel welcome and missed, and she extended both hands as she said it, and her grip was warm and firm and lingering. His hammering heart slowed in an instant as she led him inside and shut the door behind them.

"It's such a beautiful evening. I want to watch it on the balcony." Nataly hooked her arm in his and led him across her vast living room to the balcony overlooking the pool, and looking out at the nearby peaks of Cathedral Rocks. Spires glowed red there. *Where the angels come through their portal from another dimension,* he remembered.

They sat down at a table covered with a tile mosaic of a red rock scene. A servant arrived, a young Native American with a finely arched nose. Nataly ordered tonic water, and Eric asked for a beer. Nearing sunset the view was breathtaking: deep red spires close by, and a sky painted in yellow and orange.

"I've never seen views like this anywhere but here," said Eric. "It seems to me these so-called vortex sites are really just beautiful places that inspire people with romantic notions."

"Have you read any of the books from my shop?" asked Nataly.

"All of them are interesting, but I don't believe in a magnetic grid, or real vortices. The rocks have enough iron grains to make a nice rust, but that's it."

Nataly smiled. "Well, you did warn me you're a skeptic. Any good scientist is."

"I'm an art dealer, not scientist," said Eric, then thought to add, "but I read about lots of things, including science. Art, mathematics, music, science, it's all right-brain activity."

Nataly gazed at him. Near dusk, her dark eyes seemed black. "I suppose you're right, but I've never met an art skeptic before. Art either moves you or it doesn't, but it still exists."

The servant came with their drinks. Nataly raised her glass. "To sunsets," she said, and their glasses clinked.

His apprehension was gone. Eric was mystified by how relaxed he suddenly felt. "Thanks for the invitations. In my normal routine, I just don't get out much."

"Neither do I," said Nataly. "It's self-inflicted, of course. I have nobody to blame but myself. Having a party in my own house is somehow different. I'm in control, and it's my own territory. I get many invitations, but it's usually for some charitable cause. My money is always welcome."

There was a sorrow in her voice that touched him. "Well, I don't have that problem, and I don't get many invitations. I've always been busy, and away a lot. It's hard to make friends that way, or—or to keep a family." Eric looked down at his hands.

There was a pause, then, "I've never been married, or had any family other than my father," said Nataly. "My mother died when I was very small; I don't remember her, but I look like her. Father used to say that. He missed her terribly."

"And you miss him?"

"Yes, I never felt alone when he was here."

"Some people like to be alone. I thought I was one of them until my wife left me. I miss my daughter, too. I wasn't there while she grew up, and so she didn't want me at her wedding. I wouldn't want me there, either. I know I can't do anything about it, now, but I wish things had been different. And it's my fault, all of it."

Eric jumped when Nataly leaned over and put a hand on his. "I'm sorry," she said.

He didn't move his hand, felt her warmth flowing into it. He smiled, and said, "This is no time to hear my sad story."

"I disagree. Anytime is good. Stories get less sad with the telling, and we all have them. Do you believe in auras, Eric?"

"No. It's another new age thing."

"Well, I can see yours. It's quite clear against the dark background out here, a touch of red, but mostly blue. I saw it the first time I met you, and it hasn't changed."

Eric bit his tongue, avoiding an answer that might offend her. Nataly leaned closer, her hand still on his. "I want you to do something for me tonight."

"What is it?" he asked, and looked into the dark depths of her eyes.

"Tonight I want you to put aside what has happened in the past. Tonight there are only the two of us, good food and drink and pleasant conversation. I want to know the real you, Eric, without the sadness, without the dangers you see in life."

"Dangers?"

"It's in the aura, all of it, the fear, the vigilance. I want you to let go of it, just for a while. I know you don't believe this, but humor me." She lowered her chin, and smiled a smile that made his heartbeat quicken. He felt a warmth creep up his arm to his shoulder, and over to his chest.

"Okay," he said, "but only to humor you."

She patted his hand, and withdrew her own. "Good," she said. "Now, tell me how you became involved in the art world. Are you an artist yourself?"

"Hardly. I'm too left-brained for that. I'm better with numbers, statistics, that sort of thing. I have an M.B.A. I've done some actuary work. After the divorce I wanted something new that would keep me in one place. I met Leon through a friend, and he got me into sales. I've had to learn a lot about art in a hurry."

"And here you are," said Nataly. Her eyes seemed to change shape when she smiled.

"This town—this place, it still seems unreal to me." Eric gestured at the dark spires of Cathedral Rock as he said it.

"There are many mysteries here," said Nataly.

"Oh, I've been reading about those. I've even thought about looking up Bob Terrell, the guy who wrote some of the books. I hear he lives uptown."

"I know Bob well," said Nataly. "He often signs books in my shop. I can introduce you to him."

"As long as he understands I'm not a believer."

"What, in UFOs?"

"In all of it: UFOs, hidden portals to other dimensions, angels, the whole bit. People see something strange, and then their imaginations run away with them."

"If you've read the books, you've seen the photographs."

"Could be fakes, or real phenomena, I don't know, but it's all become mixed up with new-age commercialism."

"Including auras, and crystal resonances?" Nataly said softly.

Eric suddenly realized he was treading on dangerous ground. "More phenomena that could be real or faked. I've heard of respectable scientists who claim to have seen auras, but I've never held a crystal in my hand and felt anything other than rock. I know crystals can have vibrational resonances; we used to use them in radios. It's the idea of resonances tuned to a person that I find hard to believe. I'd have to have physical proof to be convinced."

"I'll take that as a challenge," said Nataly, and her eyes sparkled with delight. "You've just told me some things I can use to entertain you after dinner. Would you like another beer?"

"I'm fine," he said, then, "I'm curious about your house. It must be custom built."

That was good for ten minutes of conversation without Eric having to think of anything clever to say. It was also informative. Nataly's father had not been some rich industrialist. He'd arrived in Sedona in the forties, a kid with a few dollars in his pocket. He'd worked for a grower for several years, living a Spartan existence, bought land and become a grower himself. By the time he met Nataly's mother Maria he had a hundred acres of fruit trees and grapes, and had purchased the property overlooking Cathedral Rocks. Maria was part German, part Havasupai. She was barely out of high school and working in a grocery store when her itinerant family moved on without her. For Nataly's father Donald it had been love at first sight. For Maria it had been survival first, then love. They were married after a courtship of three months, but Nataly had come along much later. She grew up in a doublewide mobile home where her mansion now stood, went to school in Sedona, some college in Prescott, then home again to start her business.

"You've lived your entire life in Sedona?"

"Yes," she said, and then, as if reading his mind, "All that I know about the world has come from schooling and reading. I've felt no need to travel, but it might be interesting someday."

"I've traveled in business, spent most of my time in meetings and hotel rooms, alone, and little time for sight seeing. Traveling on vacation, without appointments or even a cell phone is the way to go."

The servant arrived to announce dinner. Eric moved quickly to slide her chair back as she stood. Again, she hooked her arm in his and walked him to the dining room. Two places facing each other had been set at the end of the massive oaken table that seated fourteen. Small salads awaited them. They sat. In candlelight, Nataly's eyes seemed amber, her arms copper and glowing.

"I wish you could have met my father," she said suddenly.

The tone of her voice when she said it made Eric's face flush, and he hoped she didn't see it in the dim light.

"Being missed so much is a tribute to the person. I've never experienced that."

"He's only been gone four years. To this day we don't know the cause. Some kind of rapidly developing pneumonia that killed him overnight. He was a healthy man."

"Did you have an autopsy done?" Eric felt a crawling in his stomach, but took a bite of salad and chewed thoughtfully.

"Yes. There was no sign of viral or bacterial infection. The doctors were mystified. They say he died of natural causes, but can't tell me what they were."

Her eyes hadn't left his since they'd been seated, and she hadn't taken a bite of food or even lifted a fork. "What else could it be?" he asked.

Nataly smiled meekly. "Delusions of a daughter who can't accept the death of a father she thought would live forever. I even thought of murder, but who would want to kill a retired man who spent a lifetime growing fruit? I was silly with grief at the time."

Now Nataly began eating, and didn't look at him. She took two bites, then said softly, "It was only weeks later when we began hearing reports of strange sounds and lights in the canyons. People were reminded of the military base rumors from twenty-five years before, and I found myself trying to connect it somehow with my father's death. I'd driven myself to the edge of something very dark, and dangerous. I sought help with several spiritual practitioners in town, and began meditations. It brought me back from a bad place, and I'm grateful for it. Do you practice any kind of meditation, Eric?"

How easily she changed the subject, he thought. She had presented him with a mystery she thought he should hear, but why would she think that of a man who sold art, a man she'd only recently met? He seemed to intrigue her, and though flattered, Eric wondered about it.

"No. I run each morning, and have a small set of weights I use at home. I sleep well at night. That's it."

"Well, if you're going to live here, someone is going to have to introduce you to our culture, and I'm volunteering if you're willing to learn something new." Nataly rested her chin on steepled fingers, her face glowing in the candlelight.

"Sounds interesting," he said.

"Oh, that was a *nice* smile. You're finally relaxing."

They both laughed at that, but Eric's mind was still dwelling on what she'd told him moments before. She was beautiful, sophisticated in an ethereal way, and intelligent. He did not think she would reveal a negative about her character without reason, knowing full well that her suspicions about her father's death might be interpreted as a negative.

Soup arrived, was consumed, and taken away. The main course was a prime rib that filled his plate. They ate leisurely. Mostly he listened. Nataly talked about the local tourist industry, and the reasons Sedona was considered by many to be the new age capital of the country. "Many come here to relax and be pampered. For others, it's a place to find something higher than themselves, and to discover who they really are."

"Or who they want to be," said Eric. "I guess I'm still working on that."

That look again, a steady gaze, her dark eyes looking for a way into his soul. For one instant it seemed like she was inside his head, studying him.

"We all have things to hide, Eric. Some of them are dangerous things, but it doesn't mean we can't change. It doesn't mean we don't deserve what we want."

Whoa, he thought. *Here we go again.*

Nataly blinked, looked down at her plate. "I'm sorry. That was too personal. I shouldn't have said it."

"No problem. You say what you think. Most people don't. Most people are hiding out. At least that's the kind of people

I usually deal with: the collectors, gallery owners, even the artists. They're all playing a part, like life is a stage play. I do it too, when I'm with them. I don't think I have to do it with you, Nataly. Why is that?"

She smiled. "Oh, now you're looking serious."

"I am serious."

"And I can't answer your question. I like talking to you. You're a good listener. I sense intensity in you, a hint of danger, but you have an emotional, vulnerable side. You show it in your eyes, you know, when you talk, when you listen. You're not as deep as you might think. I like that."

"Now I'm flattered," he said.

"Well, you should be." Nataly turned and beckoned to her servant, who was waiting at the doorway with a silver tray holding two plates of baked Alaska lit by candles. He served them, and went away.

The ice cream made his sinuses ache for only a moment. Eric was full, but not uncomfortable. He leaned back and sighed. "I haven't eaten like that in a long time."

Nataly stood up, held out her hand. "There's brandy in the living room."

It seemed so natural to take her hand in his, to feel her fingers squeeze. She led him to the front room, now illuminated dimly by four bulky candles, one in each corner, and there was the odor of sweet grass. Curls of smoke drifted from a closed, brass pot with holes in its cover. A window was decorated with a stained glass panel lit from below, showing stars and a crescent moon. A soft, rhythmic sound came from overhead, a beat of drums, and a high-pitched harmony of voices far away.

Nataly let go of his hand as they sat down close together on a plush sofa. She poured brandy for each of them from a crystal bottle. "Do you hear the drums?" she asked softly.

"Yes. And singing."

"Yavapai singers. Close to my mother's tribe. She didn't practice the old ways, but taught them to me. It's part of who I am."

"Then Boynton Canyon is sacred to you?" said Eric, trying

to show some local knowledge. He was rewarded with a smile.

"Yes, it is. The first people came from there, if you follow tradition."

"Lots of UFO sightings in that general area, too."

"Yes." Nataly leaned closer, put a hand on his arm. "Would you like to see an aura?"

"What?"

"You're skeptical about auras. I want you to see one."

"Oh—that. Well, sure. My mind was going in another direction just then."

"Brandy first," she said, handed his glass to him. They drank. "First, another candle." She lit a tall candle on the table in front of the sofa, blew softly on it, and the flame wavered. She leaned up against him, her head touching his shoulder, and he smelled a pine scent from her hair. She blew ever so gently, and the candle flame danced in the breeze. "Watch the flame," she whispered.

He looked at the flame to please her, saw the black wick, the wavering glow around it, felt Nataly's warmth creeping into his arm and shoulder. The sound of the drums seemed to fade until he could actually hear the occasional sound of air escaping Nataly's pursed lips. His heartbeat slowed, and his right hand, which had been clenched, now opened up and lay as if paralyzed on the sofa beside him.

"That's it, Move with the flame. There is nothing else. Keep your eyes on it, now, while I move."

Eric lost concentration for one instant as Nataly stood up and stepped around the table. She was watching him, and he immediately moved his eyes back to the flickering glow now blurred in front of him.

"Keep looking," she said in a near whisper, and Eric went with it, feeling himself sink deeper and deeper into the sofa. Time seemed to stand still. There was a faint rushing sound in his ears, and he thought of molecules colliding. His fingertips began to tingle, and then his legs, then higher, nearing erotic pleasure until Nataly spoke again.

"Now look at me," she said.

Eric raised his eyes from the glow of the flame. Nataly was kneeling on the floor three feet from the table, and facing him. Her eyes were closed, and her arms were crossed over her chest. Behind her, bookshelves and a sand painting were barely visible in gloom. The candle flame dully lighted the front of her, and at first there was nothing else to see but her serene beauty.

But as Eric watched her, Nataly began to glow in a new way.

Her skin first glowed faintly golden, but then the glow moved outwards and took shape like a gold fog, dynamic, with tendrils reaching out from it. Now the tendrils grew, and there were new colors: yellow, red, and a touch of blue. In seconds a beautiful pattern with cloverleaf symmetry surrounded her kneeling form, swirling in gold and shades of orange and red, with faint wisps of deep blue.

"My God," said Eric, so softly it was less than a whisper.

And Nataly opened her eyes. The glow of emerald green there gave her eyes an almond shape, and Eric's breath escaped him.

"See me," she said, and it was the sound of a singing, crystal bowl, "and remember."

She closed her eyes, and the colors faded, the glow dimming. The candle flame itself seemed to dim, and Eric was floating away as his own eyes closed and there was darkness, then a spot of light, and he was moving towards it. The light grew, and became a man, a golden man, sitting in lotus position, eyes closed.

Eric saw himself sitting there, naked, with golden skin and hair, and then there was a voice, saying, "This is who you really have been, and will be again," and the seated man opened his eyes and smiled. He gestured with a hand. "Please sit for a while, and I will teach you what I can, for the moment."

Eric vaguely remembered that he sat down in the vision. He could never recall what happened next. But he remembered a warm feeling when something soft and moist brushed his lips.

He opened his eyes. There was a faint beat of drums, the high-pitched sounds of an ancient song. Nataly was sitting close to him on the sofa. Her eyes glistened in candlelight as she leaned forward and kissed him softly on the mouth.

"I think you drifted off there for a while. Did you see my aura?"

"Yes. I never could have imagined the colors, and then they faded, and I guess I dozed. That was incredible, Nataly. You were beautiful."

She kissed him again, longer this time. "We're all beautiful, Eric, but sometimes we have to look for it. Would you like another brandy?"

"Better not, if one drink could put me to sleep."

"I'd like to talk a lot more, but I suppose you have to get up early in the morning."

"Oh, it's not so late," he said, and then glanced at his watch.

It was twelve-thirty.

"My watch is off," he said.

Nataly looked at her watch. "It's just after twelve-thirty. You were sleeping so soundly I didn't want to wake you."

"Two or three hours? I'm so sorry. This is worse than embarrassing."

Nataly squeezed his arm. "I allowed it because you needed it. I watched you the whole time. Now we have an excuse to get together again."

Her face was close, and Eric looked straight into her eyes. "I'd like that. I want that."

"When?"

"I'll call you tomorrow at your shop. I'll know my schedule, then."

Nataly nodded, and Eric leaned close. "I had a wonderful time tonight. Sorry I nodded away."

"Don't be. It was wonderful to be with you, Eric. I felt very comfortable." Without hesitation, Natalie put a hand on the back of his neck, drew him closer, and kissed him firmly and long.

Eric heard his own intake of breath as Nataly made a little sound in her throat.

Their lips parted, breathing quickened. Nataly touched her

forehead to his. "You'd better go."

She waved goodbye at the doorway, and Eric drove home in a kind of daze. He went straight to bed, and slept soundly.

But that night, he had another conversation with the golden man.

CHAPTER FIFTEEN
ALIENS AMONG US

Eric awoke and felt a wonderful calmness. He remembered only last remnants of the dream that had awakened him. A golden man was floating in air above a body of water showing white caps, and above him was a single eye in emerald green. He knew there was a significance to the eye, was certain he'd seen it before, and the effort to remember where awoke him.

The house was quiet, and he lay there a moment, coming back to consciousness. The sheets were not their usual tangled mess around his legs, so he knew he'd slept soundly, and that was a rare thing.

He remembered Nataly's kiss, and the smell of her hair, and the way she'd glowed in the darkness, eyes closed, so serene. His chest ached when he thought of her, and his eyes suddenly stung. *My God, what is happening to me? I've never felt such power in a woman. I thought I'd had enough of women who try to get inside me. Why is this so different?*

Whatever it was, he had to see her again. His watch said seven. To call her now would be far too early. She's be in her shop soon enough. *I'll call her at eleven. We'll have lunch. I'll open the office this morning, get things done early. And I've got to tell Gil about Nataly, her suspicions about her father. No, why did I think that? It has nothing to do with why I'm here.*

Eric shaved in the shower. Breakfast was coffee and a protein shake, consumed as he e-mailed Gil on closed link. He gathered up the art portfolios he'd been working on the day before, finished dressing and headed for the door.

His computer blinked at him with a red envelope icon. Gil. The message came up with a keystroke.

'Got your message. Nothing to be concerned about, but we're doing a background check on Nataly. Be careful about what you say to her. Gil.'

Eric's face flushed. *Oh, oh.* He typed 'Got it', and sent the reply on its way.

The BMW spit gravel as he accelerated away from the house. A minute down the road he realized he hadn't set his usual intruder alarm in the house, but he didn't turn back. It was seven-forty-five when he reached the office. It was quiet in the room, and the scent of Leon's cologne lingered. Eric called up the list of phantom markets NSA Phoenix had provided him with, matched them with the portfolios in his briefcase, and scanned in samples of each with prices.

Leon arrived promptly at nine. "My, what got into you this morning?" he asked, and raised an eyebrow at Eric. "Was last night an inspiration to do good works?"

"I think I'll just keep you in suspense," said Eric.

"Ha! I bet all you did was listen to her talk about UFOs and aliens."

"Nope. I'll have to ask her about that some other time."

"Ah, so what are you doing for the firm this morning?"

Eric told him.

"What would we do without our Phoenix friends?" said Leon, and sat down at his desk.

They worked without talking for over an hour. Leon's computer pinged twice. Suddenly he turned, and said, "Davis wants to see you first thing in the morning. You're meeting one of our foreign benefactors. How did you wangle that?"

Eric shrugged. He still didn't trust Leon enough to tell him details about breaking into Sparrow, and wondered if he was being fair. He hadn't mentioned that to Gil when he'd filed his report on the bird, but had said the report was for Gil's eyes only.

When Eric remained silent, Leon said, "I expect to hear all about that meeting, Eric. If I don't hear about it from you, I'll be very disappointed. Davis will talk, and I intend to verify what you tell me. We're working together, remember?"

"How could I forget?" said Eric, and didn't look up.

"Oh my, we really *are* in a mood today."

Leon was quiet after that. Eric finished his scanning, assembled the formal looking proposals for five non-existent galleries, and sent them away. Purchase requisitions would return within a day, all suggested prices realized, and Eric would be a local hero again.

It was nearing eleven, and Eric's skin was crawling with anticipation. He reached for the telephone, but it rang before he touched it.

It was Nataly.

"Hi. I was about to call you," he said. "Do you have time for lunch?"

"Pick me up at the shop," she said. "I called your house, but the line was busy."

Alarms went off in Eric's head. "Must have been another call coming in. I came in early this morning. How about going to that veggie place down by the high school? I can leave right now."

"Fine. I'll be waiting. Did you sleep well last night?"

"Sure did."

"No strange dreams?"

"Well, there was one I thought strange, just before it woke me up."

"You'll have to tell me all about it. See you soon."

"Bye." Eric hung up the phone, feeling lightness in his chest, not excitement, but a kind of apprehension.

Leon grinned at him. "Bet I know who that was. Another date so soon? Oh, my."

"Did you call my house this morning?"

"No."

"Well somebody did, and only you and Nataly have that

number. The line was busy when Nataly tried to call."

Leon's grin disappeared. "Interesting."

Eric pushed away from his desk. "I should be back by one. My contribution to the art world is done for the day. I have to wonder what happens to the paintings we're supposed to have sold."

"There's a cover story for each, if the artists ask questions," said Leon. "Otherwise, I don't have a clue. Say hi to Nataly for me, you bad boy."

Leon was reaching for the telephone as Eric left the office.

It was seven blocks to Nataly's shop. She was waiting outside. Her hair hung well down her back and she was dressed in black sweater and a peasant skirt with swirls of orange and red. When she got in the car he immediately smelled pine. "Hi," he said, and heard the softness in his own voice.

She didn't answer right away, but smiled beautifully and fastened her seat belt after putting a book in her lap.

"Some reading material for lunch?"

"It's for you," she said. "You'll probably find it amusing."

It was only four blocks to the deli, and they parked on gravel, and went inside. A young woman was behind a counter, chopping up something on a board. Eight tables in the room, three now occupied by people eating sandwiches and reading magazines or books. Nobody looked up.

They ordered sandwiches, organic chips and bottles of juice. Nataly handed Eric the book she'd brought along. "Yours. Part of your education in our mythology."

"Aliens Among Us?" Eric riffled some pages.

"Now, now. You promised you'd keep an open mind. I think it's fascinating to think that aliens are actually living here among us, and we're all blissfully unaware of it."

"They're probably just here for our women," said Eric, and blinked rapidly at her. "Can't say that I blame them."

Nataly smiled, and punched him gently in the arm.

They sat down on high chairs at a round table, their knees touching. Eric bit into a sandwich of cucumber, hummus, and sprouts on dark, wheat bread. Nataly uncapped her bottle of juice.

"So, tell me about your dream," she said.

Eric told her everything, in detail, as much as he could remember.

Nataly nodded. "Good. You've had a connection with your inner self, your higher self. As you go from one lifetime to another, he is the constant. What did he tell you?"

Eric chewed thoughtfully. "He said something, but I don't remember it. He just floated there, with that green eye above him. What's with the eye?"

"I don't know," said Nataly, and then her eyes seemed to sparkle. "It could have been the Earth Mother, watching over you."

Eric shook his head.

"Well, you have to admit it's imaginative. It's that kind of atmosphere that attracts so many creative people here. There are no stigmas about beliefs in our town."

"Including UFOs and little green men," said Eric.

"I've read that some are more like a bluish gray. Graylings, and there's more than one kind. If you read that book, you'll see there are as many as sixty different alien species living with us at the moment. Some are real friends, especially the Paladians. It's said we're descended from them, but their home world is in another universe in another dimension. It's all in the book, Chapter six."

"God," said Eric, and turned some pages.

"Other species are hostile to us, like the shadow people and the reptilians, but fortunately for us they don't have the power the Paladians have. Chapter nine. The Trills and the Kraal live in a kind of uneasy truce with us that was made by the Paladians and is enforced by them."

"Lord, how do they think up these names?" Eric had turned to chapter nine, was skimming a page.

"The names differ from book to book. When you get into it, you find many divergent opinions among those who believe in an alien presence here. Even the differences are fascinating."

Eric was actually reading a page in chapter nine. Nataly ate silently for a moment, then said, "I'll give you the book if you promise to read all of it. I'll try to answer any questions you have."

"You make it sound important," said Eric.

"We take our mythologies seriously. If you're going to live here, you should at least know what they are."

"I really don't know how long I'll be here," said Eric.

"I want it to be a long time," said Nataly, and she reached over and put a hand on top of his.

Eric looked down at her hand on his. "All you know about me is that I can't stay awake after a beer and a brandy."

"I know more than you think. I really like you, Eric."

He looked at her. Up close, the lighting seemed to make her dark eyes a mixture of purple and phalo-green. "I like you, too," he said softly. "I still remember you from last night, glowing in the darkness. You're magical, Nataly."

She squeezed his hand. "That's sweet. Sometimes I feel much less than magical. I'm a sensitive, Eric. I feel things, sense things I often don't understand. Right now I'm feeling apprehension, a feeling I've had before when someone was watching me and I didn't see it. This time the feeling involves you, and Leon. It started last night, right after you left. I really called you this morning to see if you were all right. For some reason, it frightened me when I couldn't reach you at home."

Her hand was tight around his. He put his other hand over it, looked closely at her. "Be patient with me, Nataly. There are things about me I'd like to tell you, but I just can't do it right now."

"I know," she said. "Just be careful, and promise to call me when you can. Please."

"I promise."

"Good. So, let's get back to the book."

"Oooo, Trills, and Kraals, and Paladians, oh my!"

"What?"

"Lions, tigers and bears?"

"Oh—yes. I saw it on television. If you accept the mythology, all these species have disguises of one kind or another. The Kraals are reptilian, but can telepathically control what we see by suggestion. The Trills use cloaking devices that make them seem like shadows or blurred movement in open air. The Paladians, of course, are our distant cousins, and look much like us. They're said to be beautiful people."

Eric ran a thumb over the palm of her hand, and smiled. "Do you ever have a chance to get back to the mother ship?"

Nataly smiled back, and sighed. "I'm trying to be serious. Haven't you ever thought something was moving at the edge of your vision, but when you turned, nothing was there? Read chapter eleven. How was your sandwich?"

"Excellent, but meatless, and I'm a carnivore."

Nataly narrowed her eyes, and Eric's heart skipped a beat. "I believe that," she said, "but it was your choice, this time."

"Next choice is yours."

"No hamburgers. They sit in my stomach for a week. When?"

"I'll have to call you, maybe late in the week. I'll give you a couple of days warning."

"Okay, We'd better go. Marie is running the whole shop for me. Thanks for lunch."

She squeezed his hand. They got up, left the deli, and made the short drive back to Nataly's shop. She unbuckled herself, turned and kissed him firmly on the mouth. Her eyes were open and, so close, he could see flecks of emerald green in their depths.

"Bye," she said, got out of the car and went into her shop without looking back.

Eric sat there stunned for a moment, looking at the door to the shop, then darted into the steady stream of traffic on 89A for the drive back to his office.

Leon was waiting for him. He scowled when Eric came through the doorway. "Hope you enjoyed your lunch. I have some news to share with you."

Eric put Nataly's book down on his desk. "Lunch was great," he said, and then a small lie, "Nataly says hi."

Leon's smile was more of a smirk. "It's about your home phone line being busy this morning. I've done some research on it, and have a confession to make."

"You called me," said Eric.

"No, I didn't, and neither did anyone else. It wasn't an incoming call. Someone was in your house, and placed a call from there. I even have the number called. I was about to check it out, but maybe you'd like to do it."

"And just how do you know all of this?" asked Eric, and his heartbeat quickened.

"Oh, that's the confession part, dear boy. Nothing personal, but your home phone is tapped, and so is mine. The recorder is in the tunnel between our houses. Orders, need to know, you're new on the project, and all that. I called the Phoenix office while you were at lunch. They downloaded the recorder, located the call, and gave me the number. Here it is."

Leon handed Eric a piece of paper. "We really are a mistrusting lot, aren't we? In fairness, I think you should check this out."

Eric looked at the paper. "This is a local number."

"Yes it is. Maybe someone ordered a pizza for you."

"Funny," said Eric.

Leon went back to his desk. Eric sat down, took a deep breath and let it out slowly, then punched in the number on his desk phone. Leon watched him closely. Eric listened a few seconds, then looked up at the ceiling, and said in a high, falsetto voice, "Oh, I'm terribly sorry, sir. I have the wrong number." He hung up, sat back, and smiled.

Leon looked astonished. "What?"

"A man answered," said Eric, "asked who was calling, please. A familiar voice, Leon, especially since he was supposed to be out of town today."

"Damn it, Eric, who was it?"

"It was John Coulter, our friend and benefactor."

Leon steepled his fingers in front of his face. "Well, well," he said.

* * * * * * *

Eric returned home at six with a bucket of deli chicken from the market. Nothing seemed disturbed, and there were no strange odors in the rooms. His computer was in hibernation, as he'd left it. The telephone answering service was cleared. He checked closets and drawers. Nothing seemed displaced, no marks on doors or windows. The tunnel door in the basement was still locked from his side. If someone had searched his house it had been done by a professional, or not at all. Eric spent two hours searching under tables, in lamps, air vents, any place conceivable in which to hide a surveillance device. He found nothing, including the tap on his own phone, which was disturbing.

He called Leon, found him at home. "Everything's clean as near as I can see, but I need an electronic scan for bugs. Do you have the equipment?"

Leon didn't have it, said he'd have it in a day. "Sleep tight," he said, and hung up.

It was midnight before Eric got to bed. He'd eaten too much chicken, and his stomach was protesting the overload. He chewed up a handful of antacid tablets and read from Nataly's book for over an hour. He wanted to read more, but the van would arrive at six in the morning to take him to the base.

That night his sleep was mangled with dreams about switches and control panels, little gray men with bulbous eyes, and snakes crawling over his legs as he lay paralyzed on soft ground that sucked at him. When he awoke at five, the room smelled musty, and it took him minutes to sleepily untangle himself from the bed sheets.

"Oh, this is going to be a terrific day," he said, and staggered to the bathroom.

CHAPTER SIXTEEN
MISTER BROWN

The ever-present Sergeant Nutt opened the door for Eric, and Davis scowled at him from behind his desk. "Don't bother sitting down. I've just been informed we're meeting down the hall. There's too much light in this room."

"What?" said Eric, as Davis stood up.

"Our Mister Brown, as he calls himself, wants the room to be darkened for your meeting. I guess he doesn't want you to see him clearly, which seems silly to me because *I've* seen him in full light and so have several others. Or maybe he's just jerking my chain again. Let's go."

Davis pushed past Eric at the doorway, and Sergeant Nutt quickly closed the door behind them. Davis led them down the long hallway to a door marked 'Conference' and rapped on it softly.

There was a muffled reply from inside, and Davis opened the door. They stepped inside and Nutt shut the door, plunging them into near darkness. Overhead light panels had been turned down to dim, and there were no other lights on the long conference table that filled half the room. A man was seated at the far end of the table, a silhouette in the gloom.

"Where would you like us to sit?" asked Davis.

The man's voice was soft, with a heavy, Slavic accent. "No reason for you or sergeant to remain, Colonel. My business is with Doctor Price. Thank you for bringing him to me."

Eric was surprised when Davis didn't argue for at least

leaving Nutt to take notes. "Very well, if you feel there's nothing I can contribute, but I'd like to see Doctor Price right after your meeting is concluded. Sergeant Nutt will remain outside in the hall to accompany him back to my office."

"It will only be few minutes," said the man known as Mister Brown.

Davis and Nutt left, and the door closed. Eric was suddenly aware of the soft sound of air flowing from a vent in the ceiling, and a high-pitched tone at the edge of his audible perception.

"Please sit," said the man, and a black-gloved hand pointed to a chair near the end of the table. Eric sat down two places away from his host, his eyes adjusting rapidly to the low light.

"You may call me Mister Brown," said the man, "but is not my true name."

"I understand," said Eric. "I'm grateful for this meeting, Mister Brown. I have several questions I hope you can answer for me."

"I'm sure you do. One moment, please," said Brown. He leaned forward, and Eric could see a small nose, sharp, a well-sculptured, handsome face wearing what looked like sunglasses in the low light. Brown placed an object shaped like half an ellipsoid on the table in front of him, and pressed something on it with a long finger. Eric felt a kind of pressure in his head, and immediately the sounds of air flowing from the vent, the high tone from something else, both were gone.

"We are private, now," said Brown. "Our conversation is not to be shared with anyone, including our dear Colonel. Do you accept this?"

"If you feel it's necessary."

"I do. There are so many players in this little game of ours. It has become complicated. You must wonder why I want meet with you."

"Yes."

"You're new to base personnel, but have demonstrated interesting insights."

"If you mean what I think, insights are usually generated

by trial-and-error experimentation. It doesn't take genius to do that."

Brown smiled in the gloom. His lips were thin. "Ah, you uncover my reference quickly. I've done my research, Doctor Price. I know who and what you are, and why you're here. Our good Colonel only knows a partial truth."

"Maybe you can explain what you mean by that. I'm a scientist, an analyst, and I've been sent here to troubleshoot a project that appears to be deliberately stalled by the people who originated it. I believe that includes you, Mister Brown."

"To say the project is stalled, Doctor Price, is inaccurate, as is your description of yourself. The project has been sabotaged, and you're here to stop it. We want to work with you."

"We?"

"The organization I represent. We brought you the star craft at great risk to our lives and our government. It was supposed to be a cooperative effort to solidify a union of states. If the project fails, the effect will be the exact opposite, and we believe that is the motive behind the sabotage. We have suspicions, but no proof. It is the kind of thing you're expert at, Doctor Price, both you and your partner, though we're not certain about his loyalties."

"You mean Leon?"

"I mean one of the deepest agents ever put into the field by your government. You, of course, are also on that list. The trust you've been granted is extreme. We want to make use of that. I will not show you the credentials of your partner; it would not be proper protocol. But this is what we know about you, and your assignment here."

Brown fumbled at something at his feet, came up with a thick file and pushed it across the table to Eric with a gloved hand. The sleeve of his jacket pulled up on his arm, revealing ivory white skin that seemed to glow in the dull light.

Eric read the file quickly, was astounded by the detail. His entire career was summarized there, from Russia to Viet Nam to Turkey, then Germany and a killing mission to Israel that had only been known by Gil and whoever had given the orders.

"I hope you are impressed," said Brown. "There is another file about your personal life, if you'd like to see it."

"Don't bother," said Eric, then very softly, "If you believe what's in this file, then you know I could kill you in one second just because you've read it."

"I believe that, Doctor Price, but I assure you it would be a bad experience for both of us. As I said before in a circuitous way, we feel we can trust you, and wish to join forces in removing the opposition to the star craft project. We can be a valuable information resource."

"Ty sajchas govorisk bez aktcenta. Ato interesno!" said Eric. "Your accent has gone away. I find that interesting."

"I'm fluent in several languages, including Russian and English, but I represent several countries, not one. My ethnicity isn't important here. You'll have to accept that, or we won't be able to help you."

"I can do that, but you're trying to convince me your origins are in Eastern Europe. You've read my file, you know how much work I've done there, and I have a pretty good idea about what kind of technology those countries are capable of. The aircraft you brought to us doesn't fit. I don't think it comes from the east. You called it a star craft. What am I supposed to do, think you come from Alpha Centauri or something? Or maybe you're just trying to oversell your product. I'm beginning to wonder about that."

"No matter. The point is we have brought it here, where we think it has the best chance to be adapted for peaceful purposes. It is a star craft, Doctor Price, not an aircraft."

"I've been told it can fly in space, but the material we've been given shows capabilities of Mach 4 and perhaps a hundred thousand feet. That doesn't come close to technology we have right now, Mister Brown. We've either paid a lot of money for nothing, or you're withholding information on us. Which is it?"

Brown reached up and removed his dark glasses. In the dim light his eyes glistened, seemed only a shade darker than his skin. "I hear your frustration, and admit there have been some communication problems. There have also been problems of trust. Some of your people have mixed agendas in this project, and look for ways to become wealthy from it. That is not acceptable. We feel it's not a problem with you. There have also been deliberate lapses in communication we must take responsibility for. These are being corrected, but security requires sensitive information regarding star faring operations that cannot be conveyed in written form."

"Star faring operations? Please. Just tell me when we can expect to get the information we need to use the technology we've paid for."

"We have methods outside of the ordinary. One was tested on you, and worked nicely. You might think it was luck that gave you access to the interior of the star craft, Doctor Price, but it was not. You were told what to do, and you did it."

Eric remembered the kind of vision he'd had of his hand playing over the switches in Sparrow's cockpit. There had been no fumbling or hesitation in performing the proper sequence. "Are you saying I've had some kind of hypnotic experience without knowing it? I like to think I'm a little more aware than that."

Brown smiled. "Your awareness cannot be questioned. Just be aware that revelations you have in the near future are not by your own doing. There will be many of them, Doctor Price. And believe me when I tell you we're going to take you to the stars."

"Sounds nice, but for now I'll settle for a complete instruction manual that can get us above our atmosphere. The stars can come later."

Brown leaned back in his chair, and laughed. "What else can I say, Doctor Price? You haven't believed anything I just said, but more will be revealed. In return, you will do something for us. There is a man you're in contact with. He calls himself John Coulter. We suspect this man is not a friend. We believe he's working for the person we think is trying to sabotage the star craft project. We want you to encourage Coulter, and do whatever you can to meet his employer in person, to bring him out of the darkness, so to speak."

"And then what?" asked Eric.

"We might ask you to do what you have done before. It's an option your employer has given you to stop the sabotage. Your orders come from the highest levels of your agency; it's all in the file."

"And *then* you'll take us to the stars," said Eric.

"That's the agreement. Your belief in what I say must come later. Revelations will appear, but you must write nothing down, and your life will be in extreme danger from this moment on. Our adversary has eyes everywhere. All progress you make with the star craft will be known instantly to him unless you work absolutely alone, and that doesn't seem likely or even possible."

"Seems to me it would be quicker to just tell me who you want killed, and let me kill him."

Eric said it as a simple statement of fact, was unaware of the sound of menace in his own voice.

The slight smile on Brown's face disappeared. He paused, looked away for a moment, then, "It's a possibility, but I'll have to consult with my colleagues. We're fairly certain about our suspicions, but the man in question comes and goes, and the information you need to locate him is currently beyond what I'm authorized to tell you. I'll contact you again later, Doctor Price, but it will not be here. This must be the last private meeting we have that others are aware of."

"Okay, but Colonel Davis will want me to brief him about this meeting. What can I tell him?"

"Say nothing about Coulter. Davis thinks he's an agent for industrial firms who promise a large retirement contribution for access to the star craft. For the moment you must allow people to think your breakthroughs are due to your own brilliance and luck. Tell Davis nothing about our input. You're free to tell him everything we've talked about regarding sabotage and the elimination of those responsible for it. Embellish if you wish; you seem to have an adequate imagination."

"Including murder?"

"Of course. It will be no surprise to him." Brown retrieved Eric's file, pulled a briefcase from beneath the table and snapped it open as he pushed back on his chair. He pressed down on the ellipsoid he'd placed on the table; picked it up, put it in the briefcase with the file.

"I assume you know where we are in understanding how to operate your aircraft," said Eric.

"Star craft, yes. The field you've detected is only a standby signal, but you're correct in thinking it's related to the main power plant. Like I said, Doctor Price, more will be revealed." Brown stood up.

Eric was surprised by the height of the man, well over six feet. "When?"

"Soon." Brown extended a hand. "Very soon. Good hunting, Doctor Price, and be alert about protecting yourself. I'll get back to you."

Eric shook Brown's gloved hand, and the grip was firm.

Brown turned and exited the room through a back door Eric hadn't noticed before. Alan Nutt was waiting right by the hallway door.

"Hear anything?" asked Eric, and smiled.

"No sir, but I can't say I didn't try," said Alan, and smiled back.

"Now take me to your leader, Sergeant Nutt."

"Yes sir." And Nutt led him down the hallway to Davis' office.

Davis looked startled. He came around his desk, sat on the edge of it, and motioned for Eric to sit down. "That didn't take long."

Eric sat. "I think he was mainly looking me over. He had my entire file, and wanted me to know he had it. Any ideas about who gave it to him?"

"Not from me. What did he want from you?"

"He wants me to kill someone," said Eric, and nearly laughed at Davis' reaction: the darting of his eyes, the Adam's apple bobbing as he swallowed hard.

"Who?"

"The guy responsible for the sabotage on the base, probably the same guy behind Johnson's murder. He thinks it's one of his own people."

"Figured that," said Davis. "I've only seen three of them, including Brown. Shifty-eyed, never speak English when I'm around, heavy accents when they talk to me. Don't trust any of them. Did he identify a target for you?"

"No. We have to draw the guy out into the open to get at him. Brown says he comes and goes, but didn't explain how. Are there ways to get in and out of the base I don't know about?"

Davis' reaction was uncontrolled. His face flushed, and he looked over his shoulder as if to see if someone were watching him from behind. "There are two hundred miles of tunnels on this base, and lots of places to hide. If whoever you're looking for is right here, it'll be like trying to find him in Phoenix."

"Brown said he'd help me. Seemed to think he knew how to find the guy. Any ideas?" Eric was watching Davis closely, now, looking for any reaction.

But Davis was calm again. "Might have. Let me think about it. Is that all you and Brown talked about?"

Nice recovery, thought Eric. "No. He was impressed by my luck getting inside Sparrow. There's supposed to be more info in the manual that we got. He's going to check on that, and correct it."

"I've heard that before."

"He said he'd get back to me soon."

"You let me know when that happens, Price. I mean it."

"Sure, and I mean it, too. If you withhold any information I need to nail your saboteur, my complaint will go directly to the Pentagon, and you can expect an early retirement."

Davis snarled. "I'd expect that from you. I knew you were a killer from day one. Thought I might be your target. Still think it."

"I never lied to you about my credentials, Colonel. I just left out a few things. And killing you has never been part of my assignment. I really do want this project to succeed."

"So do I, Price, or I wouldn't still be here. This is my last assignment; I know that. There's no glory, the public will never know about it, I'm just trying to end a career successfully."

And maybe put a lot of private money aside, thought Eric. "I understand, Colonel," he said.

"So where do we go from here?" asked Davis.

"Nothing changes, except cooperation between you and me. I'll work on Sparrow as before, but I want more time on the base to get around for any leads on our bad guy. If I find him, he's dead, witness or not. From this day on I'll be carrying, on and off the base. You need to authorize that with security. Without it, I'm out of here."

"Done," said Davis. "I'll get back to you on expanding your base access. I have to talk to Brown first."

"Checking up on what I just told you?"

"That, too. There are things you should know that Brown and his people will have to approve first. It has to do with how Sparrow was brought in, and how we get parts for it."

Eric stood up. "Okay, talk to him. I want to know something today, and I'll be in the test bay with Sparrow until evening."

"I'll call Sergeant Nutt when I have something."

"Only in the test bay. I don't want him shadowing me everywhere I go on the base. It draws attention to me."

"I'll talk to Brown, like I said. Right now, you stick to the test bay."

Eric sighed. "You have one day to get me what I want. Otherwise I call my boss, and leave you to handle the mess by yourself."

Davis nodded. "Fair enough."

Nutt was waiting right by the door again when Eric exited the room. He grinned. "Listened for gunshots, but didn't hear any."

"My faithful companion," said Eric. "You can now spend the day with me in the test bay, but be ready for a call from Davis.

I'm sure you can find other things to do besides following me around and recording my profound thoughts."

"Oh, I don't know, sir. Interesting enough duty."

Eric slapped him on the shoulder.

They took the elevator down to bay level. The light was low, and Sparrow was a dark shape in the center of the vast floor. A helicopter was near one wall, probably brought in through the massive, rolling door in the ceiling. A bright light beneath its belly looked like someone working with an arc welder there.

The little lamp was lit on the table next to Sparrow. The instruction manual was there, closed, a piece of paper protruding from it like a bookmark. Steward had left a one-page report for him on the field measurements. No electric or magnetic fields had been observed, all measurements made mechanically and crudely by looking at forces between closely spaced panes of cardboard. Steward's estimated uniform energy density of three joules per cubic meter in the opened belly of Sparrow was large compared to quantum levels, but ridiculously low for powering a spacecraft.

Eric opened the manual where the piece of paper protruded. It had marked the section referring back to an apparently missing piece of the document. When he'd placed the paper there it had been blank. He was surprised to see writing on it, printed in a small, neat hand. He unfolded the paper, and read it.

'If you have questions, ask the golden man, and the answers will be revealed to you.'

Oh, my, thought Eric.

CHAPTER SEVENTEEN
THE GOLDEN MAN

They ate Mexican uptown and went back to Nataly's shop. Marie was working the counter when they entered, and smiled at what she thought was secret knowledge.

They went in the back and Nataly made green tea. Eric put her loaned book down on a table.

"Have you finished it already?"

"I've put myself to sleep with it the past three nights."

"Oh, it bored you."

"Not at all. Well written, and easy to read. Very interesting."

"But you don't believe any of it."

"Sorry. I guess I have a bookkeeper's mind. The distances between stars are just too huge. I doubt we'll ever get together with other intelligent societies, even though I think it's likely they exist. And if they *were* here, I don't see why they'd pick on places like Sedona, or some guy's front yard in Switzerland. It doesn't make sense."

"I don't see why distance is important," said Nataly, and poured tea. They sat down at a round, glass-topped table with a plate of cookies on it. "I mean, alien societies could be far advanced and have ships that travel much faster than ours."

"Up to a fraction of light-speed, sure, but mass goes to infinity as you reach light speed. You can't go beyond that."

"I've heard of Einstein, Eric. I just think there are a lot of things scientists don't know yet. It limits our thinking. What if we had a way to travel across a galaxy in the blink of an eye?

Then we could all get together."

"That's why science fiction is so popular," said Eric, and bit into a cookie. "No limits there, and good entertainment."

"I think it's fun to think about things like that," said Nataly.

She leaned close, and munched a cookie between sips of tea. Her eyes fixed on his, flecks of emerald green swimming in dark brown. "You didn't believe in auras either, until you saw mine. Didn't that change you?"

Eric reached over and touched her cheek. "I don't know what I saw, but I sure haven't forgotten it."

Her eyes widened. "You don't need an explanation?"

"No." He touched her chin with a finger, and she grabbed it. Her eyes seemed to darken, and flecks of green were enhanced by it. Eric felt a small ache in his chest.

"I don't either," she said, and kissed his finger. "When can you come over again?"

"I don't know. The next few days look bad."

"Oh."

"I mean I'll let you know in the morning. I might have to be out of town."

"Okay." She looked down at Eric's fingers clenched in her hand. Eric wondered if she could feel his strong pulse in it.

"I'll try, I promise. I want to come over. I like being with you, Nataly." *Oh, man, why did I say that?*

Nataly brightened, squeezed his hand. "That's what I really wanted to hear." She reached out and caressed his cheek. Eric felt blood rush to his face, and for an instant time seemed to disappear as he experienced a brief lapse of consciousness like a waking dream.

Eric blinked. "Sleep was tough last night. I couldn't turn off."

"Dreams?"

"Yeah, that too. Bizarre stuff. I was flying in one of them, arms stretched out like I was a sailplane. Then I was talking to a guy with gold skin. We were having what I thought was a deep, philosophical conversation about something, but when I woke up I couldn't remember any of it. Had trouble getting back to sleep after that, kept hearing every pop and creak in the house."

Nataly frowned, and fumbled in her purse. "I can give you something to help you sleep. I use it myself."

"I don't use sleeping pills," said Eric.

"Oh it's not that. More of a relaxant. Here, try it tonight, two tablets at bedtime. It's herbal." Nataly took two pink tablets from a vial in her purse, wrapped them in a piece of paper napkin and handed it to him.

"Okay," said Eric, and put the little package in his shirt pocket to appease her. Inwardly, he had no intentions of taking any pills for sleep. Deep sleep made you vulnerable. Deep sleep could make you dead.

They finished their tea, and rinsed out the cups. "I'll call," said Eric, tilted her chin up and kissed her softly. Nataly leaned into the kiss, and then grinned at him. Marie gave him another grin at the front of the shop when he left.

There were four cars in the parking lot. A man sat behind the wheel of a silver Mercedes. He'd been looking at Eric, but looked down when Eric saw him.

John Coulter.

Eric walked straight to the Mercedes, and tapped on the driver's side window. Coulter looked up, smiled, rolled down the window.

"Well, Eric, how are you?"

"Are you following me?"

"No. I went next door to get my glasses adjusted, but the parking lot there was full. I see you're discovering our new-age shops. Have you met the owner of this one?"

"Yes. Leon took me to a party at her home. You and I met there. Remember?"

"Isn't she a beauty? I haven't had the privilege of meeting her."

"Well, I'll have to introduce you sometime. Are we still on for Monday?"

"Ah, well, it's actually fortunate us meeting like this. I was going to call. Can we put it off until Friday? Two other cancellations messed up my schedule. That's why I'm in town today."

Right. "Sure. Same time and place?"

"Yes." Coulter smiled. "Bring a pen. I'll have a contract for you to sign."

"I'll do that," said Eric, and stepped back as Coulter started his car. The Mercedes backed up, turned, and headed south on 81A, tires spitting red scree in the parking lot.

Leon was in the office when Eric returned. Eric told him about meeting Coulter.

"I don't like it," said Leon. "He was supposed to be out of town. He might be watching us."

Eric bit his tongue to keep from telling Leon what Mister Brown had said about Coulter. "He's a dirty guy, Leon, hiring us to do dirty things. We have no reason to trust him."

"I know. Eyes open, mouth closed. You armed?"

"Yes."

"I did notice the hard lump when I brushed by you yesterday. Hear something?"

"No. It seemed like the right thing to do. You?"

Leon smiled, lifted a pants leg to show the Smith .41 holstered at his ankle. "Want me to follow you on Friday?"

"I don't want to chance it, but you might want to pick him up after the meeting and see where he goes. We need to find out who he's working for. If possible, we should put a twenty-four-hour tail on him."

"There's a gallery next to the restaurant. I'll be in the parking lot, and follow him when he comes out. I won't use the Humvee."

Eric sat down on the edge of Leon's desk. "Any progress on what happened to Johnson?"

"Not a clue," said Leon. "Military round, standard weight bullet. Someone just out of boot camp could have fired it so accurately at that distance."

"Someone young. He ran like a rabbit," said Eric.

Leon blew out a breath of air. "Things are heating up, but I don't see why. The only thing new is you coming here. What else could it be?"

Eric's decision was made before he realized it. "Yeah, there is something. We got a new instruction manual for Sparrow."

"I know that from Davis. It still isn't complete," said Leon.

"No, but there are some leads. I got inside Sparrow, Leon, opened it up. There's some kind of strange energy field inside. We're trying to identify it. People think I'm a wunderkind for opening it up, but it was just luck or intuition or both."

Leon frowned. "I won't ask when you did this; the answer would probably irritate me."

"Yeah, it would."

"Still don't trust me?"

"I'm trying to. Davis is on the take, and you're pretending, and now I've had an offer. We don't get paid top dollar, Leon. I have no illusions about the temptations of bribery."

Leon nodded. "Okay, that's honest. Can't say I haven't had the same thoughts about you. I guess actions will have to speak for us. Let's start with Friday."

Leon held out a hand, and Eric grasped it. No limp greeting for the garden club ladies, the handshake was bone hard.

They went back to work at their desks, doing a mix of local cover and agency work. Eric had asked Gil for information on John Coulter, and sent a reminder. Two new portfolios were assembled and sent, and there was a call of thanks from an excited artist who'd just received a check for eighteen thousand dollars.

Eric followed Leon down Dry Creek Road, turned in first, and garaged the car. An overhead camera the size of a laundry marker watched him unlock the door to the house, and enter it. Four other cameras watched him move from room to room, checking the placement of hair-sized threads at strategic places. In the basement, he played the day's recording of all cameras, and then erased them. Nothing was amiss. No phone calls had been received, and there was no electronic news from Gil.

The house was terribly quiet, and the walls seemed to be moving closer together. Eric put on a classical CD at low volume, put two potpies in the oven and boiled some frozen vegetables.

Eating alone was again a thing to be dispensed with quickly, as it had been since the divorce. Thinking about Nataly, imagining her sitting across the table from him, helped.

He rinsed his dishes, put them in the dishwasher with their cousins from breakfast and meals of the previous day. Some brainless sitcom was on screen when he turned the television set on, and he flipped channels for twenty minutes before turning it off. One of Nataly's loaned books remained on the coffee table. He'd read it, but looked through it again: strange lights over Sedona, magnetic vortices, portals to other dimensions, aliens living in his own backyard, blah, blah, blah. He snapped the volume shut, put it on the coffee table and leaned back in the embrace of an overstuffed chair. For a moment he dozed, but came back startled by a sound from the basement that could have been a door opening or closing. He pulled the Colt Modified from its underarm holster, snicked off the safety and pulled the hammer back from half cock. The floor creaked once as he padded to the basement stairs on stockinged feet. The downstairs lights were still on. Eric put his back to the wall, went sideways down the stairs, gun leveled.

The door to the tunnel was closed. When he first glanced at it, Eric detected blurred movement to the right, but when he looked directly nothing was there except two boxes and a broom in a corner. He unlocked and opened the tunnel door. Nothing. Closed and locked it again. He was not feeling foolish; instincts honed by twenty years of life-threatening work were telling him to remain observant. He sniffed the air, but there was nothing obvious. The quiet was absolute. He stood motionless for minutes, eyes scanning back and forth. Even as he ascended the stairs again, the Colt held lightly in his hand, he felt an apprehension about having missed something.

Eric sat down in his chair again, put the Colt on the table in front of him. He sat that way for an hour, feeling as if he'd had six cups of strong coffee. And when the telephone rang, a shudder ran through him from head to toe.

"Hello."

"Hi. Just called to say good night. I'm going to bed early."

It was wonderful to hear her voice. "Not me. For some reason, I'm jumpy tonight."

"Take the pills I gave you. What's wrong?"

"I don't know. Every sound makes me hyper-alert."

"The pills will help. Do you have to go out of town?"

"No. I would have heard something today, but it could be anytime."

"How about tomorrow night?"

"Sure. Why don't we eat at my place? I'll fix you a pot pie, and show you my etchings."

"You live on those horrible things. Okay, pick me up at five. Marie can close up."

"I'll be there. Sleep tight."

"You too. Bye."

A click, and Nataly was gone, but suddenly the world was good again. The jumpiness was still there, but didn't seem important anymore. His watch said ten, early for bed, but if he stayed up his hyper-vigilance would only get worse, and for no good reason he could see.

The little piece of folded napkin was still in his pocket. He unfolded it, took the two pink tablets Nataly had given him to the kitchen and washed them down with a glass of water.

He undressed, and brushed his teeth, checked the doors, windows, the video recorder downstairs. The pills seemed to be working, the jumpiness fading, and no more imagined movement in his peripheral vision. The house was thankfully quiet when he finally crawled into bed at ten-thirty and turned off the bed stand lamp. He felt relaxed; a tingling that began in his toes and worked its way upward. He heard a car go by outside his house, recede in the distance. From far off came a mournful call of a dog or coyote on the prowl.

There was a lapse of consciousness for some length of time, and then he was aware again. His eyes were closed, his skin warm against the sheets. When he willed his eyes to open they didn't respond. He wondered if he was on the edge of dreaming, but could smell traces of cooking odors in the air. He felt a tingling again in his legs, a pleasant feeling, and he sighed.

The vision began with a sound like gently bubbling water, and then it was as if a curtain was raised on a brightly lit stage. Eric felt the muscles of his closed eyes tighten at the brightness. There was a pale blue sky, a giant eye of emerald green hovering there above a golden man. The man was seated in lotus position on a green rug that floated on a layer of mist over an endless pool of bubbling water. He was dressed from head to toe in a net of shimmering white cloth that filtered the brightness of his golden skin.

Eric realized with a start that he was looking at himself, though the eyes seemed extraordinarily blue.

"Hello," said the man, and smiled. "We've not formally met before, though I've wished for it."

It was his own voice, but affected, and Eric suppressed a laugh. He could feel the cool air in his bedroom; hear the occasional creak as the house settled in the night. "This must be a waking dream," he said, and felt his lips move. "I know I'm not asleep."

"Not exactly," said the golden man, "but in this state you can receive the information I have for you, and remember it when necessary. We don't have much time. There will be a disturbance, but you will not come to harm. You must focus on what I have to say, and we'll protect you."

"We? You're me; I can see that, an interesting illusion I'm conjuring up for myself. Nataly's new-age stuff is getting to me. Interesting." Eric could not remember being so relaxed, and willing to go along with the flow of what was happening.

The golden man's voice was sharp. "This is not some amusing dream. Now listen to me carefully. The star craft you call Sparrow must be flown again, and you must fly with it. The information you need is here; it's only necessary that you look at it, and it will be stored in the proper place in your mind." The man made a swirling gesture with one hand, and a framed page of text and symbols appeared to one side of him. The text was already scrolling when Eric looked at it, accelerating as he focused, a near blur of text and diagrams rushing past his view. He was drawn to it, mesmerized, though other things suddenly tempted his senses. He felt motion in the air around him, and there were sounds: a rattling, a crack like a hammer hitting stone, a pounding on a wall or floor in his house.

"Concentrate!" said the golden man.

It was more than pounding. It was the sound of a struggle coming from the basement. Eric's eyelids fluttered, and flashes of darkness obscured for one instant the data scrolling in front of him.

"Ignore it! You're safe! We're nearly finished!"

There was a crash, and the pounding stopped. Eric smelled a strange, coppery scent, and the blur of words and diagrams suddenly ceased. The golden man stared at him with concern, but had not changed his position. The large, emerald eye above him was gone. Eric felt uneasy by its absence, and wondered why.

"The danger is past. I'll make a small correction when we're finished," said the golden man. "Your confusion is understandable. Don't be alarmed by it."

"Don't be alarmed? I'm in a waking dream, talking to myself while something or someone is crashing around in my house, and my legs and arms won't move and I'm supposed to be reading something that's a blur to me. Who or what are you?"

"I'm you," said the golden man, "the essence of you, if you wish. I hope we can meet again, just the two of us, but for now I must channel for our friends. What you do for them you do for yourself, and for all humanity. We are honored."

"You're a figment from my reading and Nataly's new-age mysticism, all of it. Enough of this, now. I'm going to sleep."

The golden man closed his eyes, and nodded. "That is best for now. I'll complete my task, reinforce what has been given to you, and give you a restful sleep with simple dreams. But in the future I hope you'll think of me, and search me out again. We have issues to discuss."

"Sure," said Eric, and again felt his lips move. A strange scent remained in the air, and there were faint scuffling sounds close by. He tried opening his eyes, moving legs and arms, but nothing would respond. His mind was suddenly fuzzy, and as consciousness faded he felt his right leg jerk once.

When he awoke in the morning he was instantly alert, jerking back the covers and leaping from the bed. Everything he'd experienced the night before was instantly remembered. He checked the doors, the windows, even the floor around his bed. Nothing was disturbed. He browsed the kitchen, the bathroom, found a faucet dripping slowly, and tightened a cold-water handle to stop it. The lights on the alarm clock on his nightstand blinked at him. There had been a power outage or surge in the night. He looked up at one corner of the ceiling, saw the faint red spot of light from the camera there, still on, but the recorder could have been affected. If there had been loss of power, the alarm clock indicated it had been shortly after eleven, soon after he'd retired.

His suspicions were confirmed when he went down to the basement. The video recorder was off, sitting on standby, and the tapes ended just after eleven. He remembered the sounds he's heard, and he'd been without surveillance, totally vulnerable, yet nothing had happened to him other than a bizarre waking dream.

He turned to go up the stairs again, and saw a dark spot at the inside edge of the lowest step. He touched it, felt a soft crust, then liquid. The color was right; he sniffed at the liquid on his finger.

It was blood.

CHAPTER EIGHTEEN
CONCERNS

The lights were low, the video monitor on the table darkened. Mister Brown and Mister White sipped tea and spoke in near whispers. They had checked the room for listening devices, Brown had activated his random wave generator, and they were reasonably certain they were alone in the room.

"You seem certain we can trust him," said Mister White.

"I do. He's been evaluated at all levels. There are no commercial interests pulling at him. His loyalty is to his government, and his experience is just what we need."

"He's a killer."

"Yes, he can be that. He has also survived by his wits for many years. It won't be simple to predict his reactions or movements. Natasha will give us what she can, but her time with him is limited."

"Her father would be proud," said White.

"Indeed, but I'm concerned about her. She has developed feelings for the man, and I don't want to see her hurt."

"She's an adult. And there are certainly no racial issues."

"That's not what I mean. You know me better than that. I just hope her attachment to Mister Price doesn't go too far. At worst he could soon be dead. At best he will be gone when his job here is finished."

"So what's the next step?" White leaned closer.

"We have to tell him about the portal. I'm convinced our saboteurs are using it to come and go. Davis has not cooperated with us in the placement of guards. He insists his people cannot stand in total darkness for hours at a time. And even when the bay is active I can't get him to regularly photograph all personnel coming in and out of the portal. It's too simple to hide a face from a video camera placed only at one position."

"So how can Price help with that?"

"If he knows how parts and key personnel get in and out of the base he can talk to Davis as a security expert and pressure him for better surveillance. He also needs access to the portal bay if he has to pursue someone. He at least has to know where it is."

White grasped Brown's arm. "He cannot be told the exact nature of the portal. If he reported that to his government there would be a panic. It could destroy everything we've worked for."

Brown patted White's hand. "I agree it could shock people in the agency he works for, but I know for a fact that people much higher than any agency know all about the portal and its origins. And they are the people who initiated this project with us. For now, it's enough if Price knows where the portal is and can get to it. But if he ever has to use it we'll have to tell him everything. Do you agree with me?"

"Yes, for now. Even Davis doesn't know the mechanics of the portal. He just thinks he does."

"But he'll have to allow Price access to the bay so he can see its operation. I'll talk to him right away. Things will be happening fast, now. Price has what he needs to fly the star craft. If that leaks out, our adversaries could make a move quite soon. Make sure our people are never far from Price. We just came close to losing him."

"Will you tell the others?"

"No. We still can't be sure there aren't other conspirators acting with Watt."

"Why not have Price kill him right away?"

"Not until I know their overall plan, and everyone behind it. Watt surely knows our suspicions. For now, I think sabotage will cease, but I worry about assassinations. And it could happen to any of us. I'm going to see Davis, and demand that he introduce Price to the portal bay. Hopefully he'll do it quickly before Price demonstrates his new knowledge of the star craft. Things will likely be chaotic after that. I'll want regular reports from your people on any reactions from Reds or Blues. It has been far too quiet lately."

"I really don't think they're involved. Watt is working alone, or with secret service personnel loyal to him," said White.

"I tend to agree, but let's keep a close eye on our so-called allies anyway."

The two men shared a laugh about that, and adjourned their meeting.

* * * * * * *

Outside it was close to sunrise. Inside, the control room was nearly dark, and only one man sat at the console. It was the time of low priority transmissions, and only a few people were in line. Dario Watt had presented his authorization, and enjoyed an herbal tea while waiting his turn. His aide sat with him, a small man with a prominent nose. Dario smiled pleasantly at him.

"I'm sure you have a good explanation for me, Degan. It was a simple mission. How could it have been such a failure?"

Degan swallowed hard. The sight of such a smile on Dario Watt's face could mean death to the receiver. Only honesty and humility could save his life.

"I have no explanation, Sire. They were ready for us, and cloaked when we came through the tunnel. Three of my people did not return, and another was slashed badly. We didn't even get to the first floor of the house. They either knew we were coming, or were there on permanent guard. Only a handful of us knew about the operation at the last moment, Sire. There couldn't have been time for a warning."

Watt nodded. "They're using him. Something else must have been going on, and we were unfortunate to arrive at the same time. Back off for now, but be ready to move at an hour's notice.

Has your team returned?"

"For medical treatment. I'll have them early tomorrow. We have a little house in Cottonwood."

"That's close enough, but I want one of your people, cloaked if necessary, to be with me at all times."

"I understand, Sire."

"No, you don't. I've raised the suspicions of the Council, and they are also capable of murder."

"Yes, Sire."

"Things are not going well, Degan. I'm considering action that could require as many as twenty men. I'll leave the recruitment to you, but it must be done within a week. The loyalty of these people must be beyond question. The future of our government, perhaps even our civilization is at stake."

"It will be done, Sire. See you on the other side." Degan left, and went down the stairs to the transmission area.

A few minutes later, Dario Watt also descended the stairs to the narrow room below the control console. One wall glowed orange, then yellow as Watt walked up to it. He stood for a moment until the surface of the wall turned brilliant white with ripples of blue, and then he stepped into it and was gone.

CHAPTER NINETEEN
THE PORTAL

When Eric got to Sparrow's bay a cluster of men awaited him. Nutt was there with his clipboard. Flight Operations Chief Rob Hendricks was accompanied by two techs Eric hadn't met, and there was a new man with a buzz cut. He wore fatigues, sleeves rolled up, captain's bars on his collar. Hendricks introduced him to Eric.

"Eric, this is Captain Ted Dillon, our chief test pilot. He's the one person who's been able to get this bird off the ground. I've told him all about you."

"Not everything, I hope. Captain, I have a few hundred questions for you." Eric managed a friendly smile, and shook hands with the man.

"Sir. Colonel Davis said you might want to risk your neck in this thing." Dillon patted Sparrow's fuselage as he said it.

"Yes, I'd like a ride. I'm not a pilot, Captain. I just want to see what you can do with her."

"Not much so far. Sparrow is VTOL and handles like a helicopter with too much load aft. The tricky part is getting her out of this bay." Dillon pointed up at the ceiling. "After that it's like flying a Harrier, nice and smooth, but I haven't been able to push her past Mach 1. I have an opinion about this aircraft, sir, if you'd like to hear it."

"I would," said Eric.

"I think it's a piece of junk, sir. Looks like stealth, but has a normal radar signature. It doesn't seem to be equipped for fly-by-wire, but should be, especially for takeoff and landing. Flies like a bumblebee at low velocity. Weird design. Even the controls look like they've been cobbled together by a five-year-old, and most of them don't do anything."

"Eric found a use for some of those switches," said Hendricks.

"Yeah, I heard," said Dillon. "You were lucky, sir. In my business, randomly throwing a bunch of switches like that in a strange aircraft can get you killed before you leave the ground."

"I agree with that, Captain. That's why I want you there in the seat next to me when I try out a few ideas in flight. Do you know what we found inside Sparrow?"

"I told him what we have so far," said Hendricks.

"He says you think this bird has two power plants," said Dillon.

"One conventional, and one for space."

"Space? No way, sir, not with that engine. Sluggish as hell, especially near Mach 1. I had to keep pushing the nose down."

"Like there was too much mass aft?"

"Yeah, something like that."

"I'd like to see it first-hand, and run some tests. When can we do it?"

"Colonel Davis says it's your call, but he wants a detailed briefing on any tests you want to make in flight. I'd like that too, sir."

"I'll have it tomorrow. Will you take me up?"

"It's part of my job, sir. Another part is being cautious enough to bring us back alive. I'm in charge up there."

"Understood, Captain, as long as you're willing to take some risks."

Dillon chuckled. "Just *being* in that thing is a risk, sir."

Eric slapped the man's shoulder, then, "let's take a look at that cockpit, and I'll show you what I found."

The two of them climbed up onto the stubby wing of Sparrow and squeezed together into the cockpit. Dillon was a small man compared to Eric, but their shoulders were pressed tightly against each other. Dillon smiled at him. "They put guys like you in bombers."

"Not if I can help it. I prefer my feet on the ground. Brief me on the controls you use. I want to make a diagram."

Dillon showed him what he'd used in powered flight: startup sequence, VTOL, landing gear, transition, pitch, yaw and trim, all of it without computer. All controls occupied the left half of the cockpit. Eric went through the overhead switch sequence, opened up Sparrow behind them, and closed it again. He wrote everything down, showed it to Dillon.

"Not much," said Eric. "Two-thirds of these controls are for other things, and the manual tells us nothing about them. This one, for example."

Eric flipped a switch by his left knee. There was a thud, and five rows of red lights flared right in front of him.

"Jesus," said Dillon.

"Oops," said Eric. "Well, we're still here."

"Don't do that again, sir. Better turn the switch off again."

"Wait a minute. Only this one panel lit up." Eric drew a quick picture in his notes. "Everything here must work together. There are glyphs by each switch." Eric wrote each of them down, unfamiliar markings like ancient runes. As he did it, his mind seemed to wander for an instant, his hand moving as if by habit, without the slightest hesitation or sense of caution. He threw the first switch in each of four rows, and all lights on the panel went from red to green. Sparrow shuddered for one instant, and there was a high-pitched whine, either low in intensity or at the edge of the range of human hearing.

"Hey, what are you guys doing in there? The whole aircraft just shook!" called Hendricks from outside.

"Found something new," said Eric. "Keep your eyes open."

"Are you nuts?" growled Dillon."

"Not with a green board in front of me."

One switch on the panel remained unlit, and Eric threw it. There was a metallic creak from behind them, and a single light glowed green on another panel by Eric's right knee. He wrote something else down while Dillon watched him, ashen-faced.

"Something's happening out here," cried Hendricks. "You'd better take a look at it."

"Just *tell* us," said Dillon. "We're busy in here."

"The plane is heating up! There's heat radiating from the aft section of the fuselage, and the metal is getting hotter by the second!"

Dillon looked angrily at Eric. "Well, what now?"

Again no hesitation, some kind of strange instinct guiding him when Eric said, "This is as far as we can go on the ground. We'll have to do the rest in flight." He reached out and began throwing the same switches again, in reverse order. The lights went from green to red, then off.

"And you really expect me to fly with you when you do crazy shit like this? Sir!"

"You're the test pilot, Captain. Are you telling me you don't want to see what'll happen when we go through the rest of this?"

"Okay, it's cooling down out here!" yelled Hendricks.

Dillon let out a breath of air through pursed lips. "Not if it kills me. But this isn't luck, is it. I watched you close, and you've been told what to do, I'm sure of it. You didn't even flinch."

"Maybe," said Eric, and remembered what Brown had said to him. It had all seemed natural, rehearsed, a task repeated a thousand times, and he knew why. It was a startup sequence to power Sparrow into space, the initiation of a power plant only hinted at in the bowels of the craft. He'd been right to shut down when he did; to go further would have unleashed a terrible power in the closed bay. The sequence to follow was in his head, a panel of switches by his right knee, a handle at the top, a quarter turn, and then—what? It ended there, for the moment, but he knew it would have to be done in flight, and high in the atmosphere.

"I have to trust you. You're the only person who has flown this thing. The question is whether or not you can trust me. If you follow my directions we can take Sparrow into space, and there won't be any Mission Control to help us. You'll be the pilot of this thing, not me. I'll be relying completely on your flying experience to get us down alive."

Dillon's eyes narrowed. "I've flown in space, and back again. It wouldn't be a first for me."

The man was a military pilot, not an astronaut. "Aurora?" asked Eric.

Dillon blinked slowly. "So when do we take this bird up all the way?"

"Just as soon as I can get Colonel Davis to clear the test. There's nothing about this in the flight manual. I'll have to convince him I know what to do. I can't write it down for a permanent record. Look at these notes, and memorize the sequence. I'm destroying the notes after we climb out of here, and I don't worry about forgetting what's in them. Don't ask why."

Dillon took the notes from him, studied them a minute, handed them back. "Okay, Got it. Now what?"

"We get out of the plane, act like we had a nice chat, and make up a story about how we got that panel to go green. I'll do the talking. I'm probably a much better liar than you. It's part of my training."

"I'll bet it is," said Dillon.

"Let's start with a diversion," said Eric. He flipped some switches; Sparrow shuddered, the aft fuselage opening again. "Get a probe in there, and look for residual radiation!" he called out.

Eric followed Dillon out of the cockpit and off the wing to the ground. Two techs were already leaning inside the open maw of Sparrow's belly to place instruments there.

"So, what was all that heat about?" asked Hendricks.

"Just throwing switches again, and suddenly an entire panel went green. That's when you started yelling about heat."

Hendricks looked at Dillon, but the man just shrugged as if it was all a mystery to him. In the meantime, Eric wadded up two small pieces of paper in his hand and shoved them in his pocket. Sergeant Nutt was watching, saw him do it, and raised an eyebrow.

"I need to see Colonel Davis right away," Eric said to Nutt.

"Sir," said Nutt, and pulled out his field phone.

Hendricks tapped Eric on the shoulder to get his attention again. "I'm not buying the good luck act, Doctor. Where are you getting your information?"

Eric thought fast, and decided a partial confession would be better than a lie. "I'm not at liberty to say. Sorry, that's the best I can do. I *will* tell you that tests from now on will have to be done in flight. Captain Dillon and I were just talking about it. We're taking Sparrow up as soon as we get approval from Davis."

"So why you? Why have the rest of us been kept in the dark?"

Eric shook his head. "Wish I knew. Politics, personalities, who knows? The decision came down from the people who brought Sparrow to us. I don't know what they're thinking."

It worked. Eric could see it in Hendricks' eyes. For the moment, the explanation had logic to it, though questions were sure to come later.

"Then maybe they should make an effort to know us better," said Hendricks. "There aren't any politicians here."

"Doctor Price!" called Nutt. "Colonel Davis wants to see you right away."

Eric nodded, as a tech came back from inspecting Sparrow. "No radiation, outside of IR, but the metal's still warm in there, around one-ten."

Eric answered the tech before Hendricks could open his mouth to reply. "In space, there won't be any T increase. Decay time is nanoseconds once the field is powered down in vacuum. At full power and one atmosphere we could melt the airframe in a hurry. That's why we can't go further with testing unless we get Sparrow above the atmosphere."

The tech stared at him, and Hendricks scowled. Nutt came up, put a hand on his arm. "Got to go, sir."

"And when you come back, maybe you can let us in on more of your secrets," said Hendricks.

"I will. I know this isn't fair to you guys, but I didn't ask for it. It's just the way it is."

Hendricks glared at him, and turned away. The two techs looked nervously in other directions. Nutt took Eric by one elbow and hurried him away.

"Shit!" said Eric. "I can't blame them for being pissed."

"Nothing new," said Nutt. "It was the same with Johnson. He was getting information the rest weren't. It's the only reason we got Sparrow off the ground."

"Davis never said anything about that."

"You didn't hear it from me, sir. Oh, I didn't have a chance to tell the Colonel what you just did with Sparrow. He wanted to know if I was with you, and said he had to see you right away."

"So I'll surprise him," said Eric. "This base seems to be full of surprises."

They left Sparrow's bay, took the elevator up and Nutt knocked on Davis' door. There was no answer for a moment, so Nutt knocked again. "Come!" came a reply, and Nutt opened the door. "Doctor Price is here, sir."

"Send him in."

Eric entered the office, immediately smelled a vaguely familiar, musky odor, as if incense were burning nearby, but saw nothing like that. Davis was sitting behind his desk, chin resting on cupped hands. "Have a seat, Doctor. I think you're going to like this."

Eric sat. "What is it?" The sweet odor was even stronger where he was sitting. He noticed the door to the adjoining office was ajar. Was the smell coming from there?

"You wanted more access to the base, and you just got it. Our foreign friends seem to think you're the man to nail our saboteurs, and need to know counts for everything around here. I suppose you've wondered how we got Sparrow into that bay in the first place."

"Yes, but I know the ceiling opens up. A cargo helicopter could drop a load through there."

"True," said Davis, "but that's not the way it happens. We have a special port in a neighboring bay. Everything comes through there, and I've been instructed to show it to you. Mister

Brown was very insistent. You must have made quite an impression on him."

"If I did, it wasn't obvious to me, but I just had another breakthrough with Sparrow, and I need your approval for some flight tests."

It was as if Davis hadn't heard him. "Do you want to see the delivery port, or don't you? It's Brown's idea, not mine. If it were up to me, I'd keep you out of there. Too many people already know about it."

"Of course I want to see it. Right away. But if you let me make some flight tests, I think we can have Sparrow in space this week. Captain Dillon was with me today, and we found out how to activate most of the controls. The rest we'll have to do in flight."

"I thought the manual was still missing what you needed."

"It was—is, I mean. But we figured it out."

"Figured *what* out?"

Eric told him, making it sound like he and Dillon had done it together in a systematic way until they had a green board and heat was boiling from the fuselage.

"Jesus," said Davis.

"We had to shut down. Whatever field is in that thing, we'll have to be in near vacuum to bring it up to full power. I need your authorization to make the necessary flight test. Dillon is with me on this."

"You want to fly it with Dillon."

"Yes."

"You're not a pilot."

"Dillon can fly. I'll conduct the power up procedure."

"More magic insights, is that it, Price?"

"Brown didn't seem to think so. Maybe I actually know what I'm doing."

It was like a slap in his face. Davis flinched, and glared back at Eric. "Well, you did impress the right person. He made that clear to me, and my orders are to keep him happy."

Orders from where? thought Eric, "I can have a briefing

ready for you by the end of the day. All I want to do is a run up to full power, and then pull back. No maneuvers, no performance evaluation, nothing like that."

"Keep it short. I'll consider it. Are you done, now? Can we do what I just brought you here for? I thought it was what you wanted so badly."

"The port, you mean. Yes! Right now, if you have the time."

"I'm making the time. Only a handful of us are allowed in that bay. The rest are foreign personnel."

"Foreigners in a top-secret U.S. military base? That has to be a first."

"It isn't," said Davis. "There are a lot of perks for bringing over valuable technology, and a lot of trust. We get the technology. We don't ask how they bring it over, and they don't tell us. You'll have to see this thing to understand what I mean."

"When?"

Davis stood up. "Follow me."

They left the office. Davis ordered Sergeant Nutt to return to Sparrow's bay. At the elevator, he turned to Eric and softly said, "Where we're going is near Sparrow's location, but we're taking another route. I'll show you the connecting passage on the way back."

They took the elevator down to the reception platform at tunnel level. Two guards stood by a jeep. Davis led Eric to the jeep, saluted, and got in the driver's seat. The vehicle jerked as Eric sat down, backed up, turned into the tunnel and sped for a hundred yards to a turnout on the left. They parked there, opened a metal door in red rock. Hot air rushed out at them.

They were in a machine shop, a hallway separated from the shop area by a wall of transparent polymer. Several men were in the shop, watching work turning on mills and lathes. Beyond them was a wall flickering with the reflected light of an arc welder.

At the end of the hallway were three doors, all with cardkey locks, otherwise unmarked. Davis chose the center door, ran his card through the slot of the lock, and opened it. A short hallway led them to a guard in a plas-steel-enclosed booth. Another guard, armed with an M-16, stepped into the booth behind him. Both men regarded Davis and Eric somberly until Davis had swiped his cardkey and punched in a sequence of seven numbers. There was a loud click, and a door adjacent to the booth opened up.

They stepped into a room the size of a large closet. Another door was across from them, a red light blinking on a panel there. Davis closed the door behind them, turned to Eric. "Just for the record, if I'd changed one of the numbers I punched in back there, you would now be dead or dying."

Eric smiled back at him. "Nice of you not to do that," he said.

They waited a few seconds, and the light on the panel opposite them turned green. Davis opened the door, stepped aside for Eric to enter ahead of him.

Heads turned when he entered. Four men sat at a console looking out through glass at banks of lights hanging from a high, rock ceiling. The men were all young, with hard, chiseled features. Two turned away after only a glance, but one studied Eric for a moment with startling, blue eyes.

Eric and Davis stood behind the men and looked out on a bay half the size of the one housing Sparrow, but full of activity as they watched. Overhead cranes moved freight boxes the size of Humvees to flatcars on tracks. Men walked back and forth with smaller cargo pushed on hydraulic lifters, a large stack of boxes and crates awaiting their attention along the rock wall of the bay.

"Another shipment just came in. It'll be a while. Want some coffee?"

"Sure," said Eric.

"How about you guys?" asked Davis, and tapped the shoulder of one of the men sitting at the console.

"No thank you, sir," said the man. "We must prepare here."

Not Russian, but Slavic, thought Eric.

Davis brought Eric a foam cup of black coffee, and pointed out towards the bay. "We're the only two Americans in here, now. We're not allowed down on the bay floor, but you can see everything from here. Most of the people you see will be leaving soon. The portal itself is that entire wall on the other side of the floor."

Eric looked, but saw only a rough rock wall, floor to ceiling. "Pretty well disguised," he said. Out of the corner of his eye he saw one man at the console studying him, but the man looked away when Eric turned around.

"There's a large tunnel beyond the wall, but I have no idea where it leads to," said Davis. "I don't like admitting that, but it was all part of the deal to bring Sparrow in."

"This whole project must go far up the command chain," said Eric.

"At least Chief of Staff," said Davis. "And all my orders come down through the Pentagon."

"Think it might go as far as the White House?"

Davis shrugged. "Could be."

A line of men was now forming on the floor below them. A second line formed quickly, with men steering hydraulic lifters. The lights in the ceiling suddenly dimmed, and several red lights went on along the walls close to the floor. The cab of an overhead crane moved back to a wall, a door opened, and a man descended a ladder there to join the others.

"Should be any minute, now. They all leave together."

The lights in the ceiling dimmed further. The men at the console were murmuring into their headsets, their hands moving over panels in front of them. If there were sounds in the bay, Eric couldn't hear them through the thick window of the room. The floor was now in gloom, and though Eric's eyes adjusted quickly it was now difficult to pick out individuals in the lines of men.

The far wall suddenly glowed deep red, then orange, faint but distinct. Davis pointed, said, "The glow is a kind of protective barrier. I've been told it would be dangerous to touch the wall right now."

The effect only lasted seconds, the orange glow overwhelmed

by a blue glare rising from floor to ceiling in rippling waves and lighting up the entire floor for one instant before disappearing in a blink, and where the wall had been was now inky blackness. The two lines of men marched straight into the blackness, the lifters rolling along with them. When they were gone, the blue glare descended again, a blinding thing. Eric blinked once, twice, and saw only rock on the far side of the floor. The ceiling lights remained dim, but he could see the floor was now empty.

"Quite a show," said Eric.

"Sometimes I wonder if that's *all* it is. Brown says it's an electromagnetic door they'd like to develop here for their own profit if we can complete the Sparrow project with them," said Davis.

"Capitalism is contagious," said Eric, but looked down at a folded piece of paper that had suddenly appeared on the floor by his feet. The men at the console had finished their jobs, pushed back their chairs to stand up. The man nearest Eric, the one who'd been glancing at him from time to time, leaned over, picked up the paper and handed it to him. "You have dropped this," he said. In the low light, his blue eyes seemed violet in color.

Eric acted by instinct. "Uh—thank you," he said, and pocketed the paper.

They all left the console room, Brown's people and Eric behind Davis, turning in opposite directions in a hallway. "Where do they go?" asked Eric.

"They have quarters near here. We don't go there, either. They even have their own cooks," said Davis.

They went through two cardkey-controlled doors and descended in an elevator to a small bay filled with crates. An unlocked door led them into a corner of Sparrow's bay, a few techs still crawling over the craft in the center of the floor. Dillon was still there with Hendricks, studying something in the flight manual.

"Get that briefing to me. Keep it short," said Davis, and walked back towards where they'd entered the bay.

Eric told the others he'd been on a tour, and had to write a brief on the flight tests he wanted to make. Dillon and Hendricks gave up the table to him, and went away with the manual. The techs continued work inside Sparrow, disconnecting instruments used to measure heat flux earlier in the hour. Eric used a legal pad on the table, scribbled a few words, and pulled the folded paper from his pocket. He unfolded it, and a small photograph of a man was there. On the paper were words written in neat, block lettering.

'The man in the picture is considered dangerous to our project. If he's ever seen in the portal area he should be immediately detained and arrested.'

It was signed 'Mister Brown'.

Eric looked again.

The man in the photograph was John Coulter.

Why am I not surprised? thought Eric.

CHAPTER TWENTY
NEGOTIATIONS

Light rain made the streets slick, but did not deter speeders. By a stroke of exceptional luck, Eric found a space in the little parking lot and darted into it. It was just after sunrise, but the Coffee Pot was full. A line of people waited by the door, others crowded in the adjacent souvenir shop.

John Coulter was seated at a table in the back of the restaurant, and waved vigorously at Eric when he arrived. Eric sat down, shook rainwater from his furled umbrella, and put it on the floor beside him.

"I bet people don't even slow down when it snows here," said Eric.

"Not that I've noticed," said John, reached over and shook Eric's hand. "Lots of empty country out here. People like to get through it as fast as they can. Takes big city folks some time to get used to it." He took a long envelope out of his briefcase, and handed it to Eric. "Here's your contract, as promised. Don't open it here. Read it at your leisure, edit as you please. If you don't like the consultant fee I put in there, write in your own number. I'm easy, and it isn't my money. My client expects the information and services he needs, and your loyalty in providing both. The contract is a formality, of course. It's only for the eyes of the signers."

"And who are the signers?"

"Yourself, my client, and I'll sign as witness to your signature. My client's cipher will be a scribbled symbol, since he must remain anonymous."

Eric paused to open his menu, and then said, "I understand why your client wants anonymity, but I have a problem with it."

Another pause of a few heartbeats, and Eric studied his menu.

"And why is that a problem, Doctor Price?" said John softly.

Eric looked over the top of his menu at John's steady gaze. "I'm used to knowing who I work for, and what their motivation is for asking me to do what I do."

"This is private enterprise, not government. The motive is money, and recovery of stolen property. What more do you need?" John Coulter had a way of narrowing his eyes when he smiled, and it was not pleasant to look at.

"I don't like working with intermediaries. Orders have a way of being corrupted when they're relayed by someone."

"I transmit my client's wishes without corruption, Doctor Price. If I had ever made a single error he would no longer employ me. I could even be dead. You'd be less likely to get accurate information directly. My client's use of the English language is quite poor, and I must translate for him."

"I speak Russian and Polish fluently, also German and French and others. Take your pick."

"Ah," said Coulter, trying to look surprised. "I'll have to mention that to my client, but it'll make no difference. His identity must remain unknown to you."

So I tried, thought Eric. "My point is that it might become a problem if I'm ordered to do something nasty enough to require a surcharge. I don't like people negotiating for me with the big boss."

Coulter hadn't opened his menu, was studying Eric's face as a waitress approached them with a silex of black coffee. "Why don't we order, now? Perhaps an advance payment and a trial assignment would show our good faith before you sign anything."

They placed their orders, and the waitress went away. Coulter pulled out a business envelope bulging with content and heavily taped over the flap. He pushed it across the table to Eric. "Call it a retainer," he said.

Eric hefted the envelope. "Retainers are for services to be rendered in the future, so what is this for?"

"Information, Eric. You are associated with the transfer and development of a technology that will have considerable potential on the open market. My client's stolen product can control that market if development here is successful, but it seems there have been considerable problems with that. It has recently come to our attention that since your arrival several technical breakthroughs have been achieved. They have been achieved through your own insights and inspirations, far beyond what others have been able to do. Your talents are of interest to my client, and your knowledge of the project would be vital in his development of a commercial prototype. The project leader's salary would make a federal pension look like pocket change, believe me. But to develop the prototype he needs information in complete detail about every breakthrough you achieve, as it happens. He also marvels at your recent successes. Any references you can give, or names of people who have made useful suggestions, would also be useful to him. We have gone as far as we can with the written materials you've had to work with. With your sudden insights, we know you are close to flight-testing. We want to know how you'll be proceeding with that."

Coulter pulled a disk from his briefcase. "Use your home machine to make your reports. Put them on this disk, and erase the originals, and call me when you have something. My number is on the disk. Send nothing electronically. I want your first report within two days. If that seems too soon, then inspect the contents of that envelope."

Now Coulter handed him a key. "This goes to a postal box at the post office by the Y. When you've called me, put the disk in the box, and I'll pick it up when I can. When you call me, all you have to say is that the package is ready, and hang up."

"I love drama," said Eric. "Maybe we should adopt code names for ourselves."

Even as he said it, Eric knew he'd gone too far in antagonizing someone he already knew was not a friend.

Coulter's reply was soft, yet crisp. "I'm not trying to amuse you, Doctor Price. This is serious business, and people have been killed for working with us. The same could happen to you."

Eric's face flushed. "*Who* has been killed?"

"A man who was doing very much like what you're doing now. You have essentially replaced him."

"Johnson?"

"That was the name he used. He was murdered, you know. You were there."

"My, how you get around. I suppose Leon told you that."

"We have many sources, Eric."

"Whoever killed Johnson tried to kill me. You must know that, too. For all I know, your client arranged the killing and now I'm being set up for the same treatment."

"Utter nonsense. Johnson was our most valuable asset in the early stages of the project. We think military people killed him. They're the ones you need to watch out for."

"Including Colonel Davis?"

"We're not sure about him. He's an opportunist."

"And I'm not?"

Coulter smiled. "You might be. You have to prove your worth to us, Eric. The envelope there is a token of our faith in you."

Eric smiled back, and pulled the envelope to his edge of the table. "Okay, I'll have my report in your mailbox by tomorrow morning. Just remember that if something critical comes up, I intend to deal directly with your boss."

"My client," said Coulter. "I'll see what he has to say about that. He might even be willing to accommodate you."

"Fair enough," said Eric.

Eric pocketed the two envelopes, and a waitress arrived with their breakfast.

* * * * * * *

"You think it could be true about Johnson?" asked Eric.

"No, but at this point I don't trust anyone, past or present," said Leon.

They'd closed the office for the day, and sat at Leon's desk. The envelope Coulter had given to Eric contained ten thousand dollars in crisp, one-hundred-dollar bills now arranged in five neat stacks. They'd read the contract together. "Nothing sinister, no specifics, more like a consultant's contract," said Leon. "I signed one just like it, but my offer was better. I guess he thinks my tastes are more expensive than yours."

"When's the last time you saw him?"

"A week ago. We met for lunch. He's been around town. Yesterday I saw his car in the parking lot at Nataly's place. He was just sitting there. Didn't you see him there once?"

"Yes."

"I wonder if Coulter knows you're seeing her?"

"I wouldn't be surprised. He seems to know everything else."

"Either that, or Nataly knows him. I don't think I'd like that. I know you two are getting close, but I expect you not to share our little secrets with her."

"Of course not."

"It wouldn't be safe for her."

"No threats are necessary, Leon. If she knew what I was really up to here, she'd probably run like hell."

"I hope so," said Leon. "The other possibility, of course, is that Coulter is watching her. It might be part of checking up on you."

"I could ask Nataly if she knows him, claim he wants to do some export business with me."

"Yeah, let's do that. I want to trust her. I want to trust you, too, but you're still not telling me things. Maybe some new orders from Gil would help."

"What things?"

"Your new breakthrough with Sparrow. Davis had to tell me. He says you're going to fly that thing. That's major news, Eric, and I didn't hear it from you. I've complained to Gil just this morning. Maybe he can clarify for you what our relationship is supposed to be like."

It would serve no purpose to tell Leon that Eric was following Gil's orders in not telling him everything. "Okay, let's see what he says. Are you telling me everything *you* know? For example, do you really think John Coulter is a lawyer for a big corporation, and if we help him he'll make us rich?"

Leon smiled. "He's more of a business partner, maybe. He seems to be serious about the money."

"Tempting, isn't it?"

"Yes, it is. How about you?"

"I guess I've risked my ass for my country for so long it doesn't make any sense to sell out now. Coulter is no friend of ours, and he lies through his teeth. He tried to tell me Johnson was working for him, and was murdered because of it."

"Bullshit," said Leon. "My office knew more about that guy than he knew about himself. His whole life was science."

"Yeah, but he was killed with a military weapon."

"Which you or I could buy on any street corner in any large city."

"So why would Coulter tell me something like that?"

"To make you think you aren't the first. Others have trusted him. You're part of a team. I don't know. I sure don't believe him about Johnson."

"So we stop stalling about putting a tail on Coulter, find out where he goes and who he's seeing. My feelings are getting nasty about this guy."

Leon raised an eyebrow. "Mine, too. Say, we've found something we agree about. Can we be friends, now?"

"People like us don't have friends, Leon."

"Oh, I don't know. You have Nataly."

Eric swallowed hard. The remark had hurt, and he wasn't sure why. "I have no illusions about that. When the job is finished, I'll be out of here. Nataly needs a responsible person in her life. She deserves it."

"She deserves love, Eric. We all do."

"Well, I haven't had much luck with that," said Eric, and

heard the bitterness in his own voice.

"Sorry," said Leon. "Look, why don't I keep an eye on Coulter for a while. I can get help with it. You just deliver your reports, and keep them honest, at least with anything Davis might know. And when Gil orders you to trust me, you do that, too. No more charades."

"We'll see," said Eric, and nodded as if he agreed. It seemed like a positive way to end the conversation. But when he got home that evening, he found an encrypted e-mail from Gil saying that due to a recent understanding between NSA and some office in the Pentagon he should keep Leon informed of all recent breakthroughs made on Sparrow, and the identities of any new players he came in contact with, including the mysterious foreign operative known as Mister Brown.

This surprised Eric, because he had not yet told Gil about his meeting with Brown, or the sudden breakthroughs with Sparrow.

So how had Gil found out about these events?

He was still thinking about it when he went to sleep that night. And shortly after that, Eric Price had still another conversation with the Golden Man.

* * * * * * *

Nataly knew that continued apprehension could make her sick, but all meditative techniques had failed her so she resorted to a non-prescribed sleeping-aid that made her groggy in the morning. She'd slept deeply over the night, but then the call came at six and upset her again, and she couldn't get back to sleep. She arose, drank strong coffee and reread the local newspaper for the third time, checked her e-mail and found a sweet, two-word message from Eric there. 'Miss you', he said.

I miss you, too, the real you. I'm not in love with the killer. Oh, Eric, how I wish things were different for us.

Nataly sipped coffee and walked the floors of her house, checked doors and windows for any sign of incursion. There had been no cloaked entries since the IR sensors had gone in, but outside the residence the devices were so sensitive even a rabbit could set them off and The Council had sent out a tactical team several times to investigate strong disturbances. She could not resent them. It was the same team that had saved Eric's life.

She checked the recorders in a downstairs closet. There had been two signals last night, quite small, both down by the pool. Rabbits were attracted to that area, and she'd put shields over the plants there to protect them from nibbling. The signals were not the reason for Vasyl's call. "Things are heating up. We need to talk," he'd said, and hung up on her.

Things were always heating up for Vasyl, but like it or not, Nataly felt connected to the man and his cause, if only to honor the memory of her father and his origins.

The sun was peeking over the summits of distant buttes when she had a breakfast of dry toast and a banana. She showered quickly, toweled herself dry, and examined herself in a mirror. The curves of a twenty-year-old were there, but the woman was forty-five. *What would Eric think if he knew that?* she wondered.

The forecast was for a sunny day, but the morning at six-thousand feet would be cool. Nataly dressed in jeans and a wool shirt, added a Gore-Tex shell when she went outside. She wore cowboy boots instead of her clumsy hiking shoes, good enough for a short walk and certainly more stylish to any tourist who might happen to come by.

She left the Mercedes in the garage and took the truck, her white and battered four-runner with nearly a hundred thousand faithful miles on red-rock scree. Traffic was light going into town, and nonexistent up the Schnably Hill Road to the outlook parking area. She parked there, waited in the truck a few minutes, then got out and strolled up the winding trail to the ridge overlooking town and buttes beyond. Someone had recently placed red rocks there in the pattern of a medicine wheel, and she sat down next to it. The air was crisp, and Nataly breathed deeply, feeling the energy of the place, the energy that had brought her father to it so many years ago.

A few minutes later there was a crunch of a step falls behind her. She turned and saw Vasyl's smile. He was dressed in jeans and flannel shirt and wore a wide-brimmed straw hat to shield him from even the morning sun.

"Good morning, Natasha," he said, and sat down beside her, put an arm around her, gave her shoulder a squeeze. There was an expression of deep caring in his light brown eyes. "I hope you're sleeping better these days."

"The pills help, but they're not natural. I feel drugged half the day, and then worry the other half. When will this be over, Vasyl?"

"I wish I knew. Doctor Price has made the progress we hoped for, thanks to you. The Americans could have what they want within a month, if Dario Watt can't find a way to stop it. The man has hidden himself away. We suspect he's still here, along with agents under his control. We're certain he'll make a move before a flight test is made. We have teams watching Price and Davis, and we're putting one on you."

"Me? Why me?"

"You're associated with Price. I'm sure Watt knows it. You could be used to intimidate Price if you were taken hostage. Even now you could be watched by someone who works under cloaking."

"There have been no incidents at the house since the IR sensors were installed."

"You can be followed anywhere, Natasha. We only want to protect you."

"And Eric too."

Vasyl put an arm around her again. "Yes. I hear softness in your voice when you say his name. We certainly didn't plan for that."

"I know. I suppose you think I'm foolish."

"He's a dangerous man, Natasha."

"A part of him is worse than that, and frightens me. But when I look inside and see who he really is, the way he was before the wars, the training, the personal losses in his life, I cry for him.

I cry for his heritage. Not out of pity, but sorrow over such a gentle, loving soul who has been dragged through circumstance into a terrible existence. The person inside, the real person, cries out for serenity and love."

"I've never envied empaths, or any exceptionals like your father was. You have his soul, Natasha. I can't feel what you feel, but I see you giving your heart to a man who is paid to kill, a man who has neglected important people in his life. I don't want to see you hurt."

"The man I love will never hurt me, but he must be allowed to show himself. He is not who you see."

"Oh, Natasha," said Vasyl, and pulled his arm away from her. "You can be so frustrating."

"It will be easier for you if you don't try to run my life," she said, and smiled.

"Very well, but we're still going to watch you. It'll be best if you see less of Price until the flight test is made. He needs to focus on that task. I want you to report anything that looks out of the ordinary, anything that makes you feel you're being watched, even if it turns out to be our own people."

"There *is* something," said Nataly. "I've seen a man in my shop's parking area several times, now. He never comes into the shop, just sits in his car a while and then drives away. Could be he's been shopping next door, but then Eric was in my shop one day and stopped to talk to him on the way out. I'd nearly forgotten that."

"What does he look like?"

"Broad shoulders, and his head goes nearly to the ceiling of his car. Dark hair and eyes, square face, basically a nice looking man."

Vasyl's eyes narrowed. "We'll check on it. Don't go anywhere with him if he ever approaches you."

"Vasyl, I—"

"Please, Natasha, do as I say."

Nataly sighed. "All right, but I *will* see Eric, and you can't force me not to. I'll make excuses about being busy until his flight test is over. I'll do that for Eric's sake. I've done a lot for you and the Council, Vasyl. You owe me."

Vasyl smiled, and took her hand in his. "Yes, I do, and I owe your father even more. He was the first."

Nataly squeezed his hand. "The first in this town, you mean. I think he would have liked to see people reach the stars. At first, it was only political with him. I'd better go. Maria can't make change before she's had two cups of coffee."

They walked back down the trail to the parking area. Vasyl hugged her, pulled away in his black van, turned uphill and drove away from town in a cloud of red dust.

Nataly got into her truck, turned on the ignition, and thought, *I just told my best friend that I love Eric Price.*

And I do.

CHAPTER TWENTY-ONE
WARNINGS

Dario Watt held a strategy meeting with his deputies. Four men arrived with him at the conference room overlooking a portal bay bright with lights reflecting off titanium-strutted plas-steel walls. It was early, the bay just beginning to gear up for the day's travel schedule, and only a few people walked the floor. As a minister, it had been ordinary for him to arrange a meeting before departure, and his deputies were familiar faces among portal staff. They were the last four men he could trust. All others had abandoned him, including his president, men who claimed to be visionaries but were willing to sacrifice the security of their world just to make a show of it.

The door was closed, and a deputy made an electronic sweep while the rest waited patiently. "It's clean," the man finally said, and sat down with the others.

Watt sat at the head of the table, and folded his hands together in front of him. "Thank you all for arriving promptly. I'll keep this short, and we'll continue our usual meeting schedule on the other side. Things are speeding up there. I wish I could bring you good news, but the facts are otherwise. The opposition has somehow become aware of all our plans, or is able to anticipate them. I've not been able to locate White since his arrest. He might have told them something, but plans we've made since then have also been uncovered."

"Do you think we have a security breach on this side?" asked a deputy.

"No. I trust all of you completely. Our adversaries are skilled, and numerous. Our moves must be pre-planned and quick. It's clear to me we must abandon any plan to return the star craft safely. It will have to be sacrificed. The fault is my own. I overestimated American greed for money, and forgot about pride. Every government operative I've tried to buy, even Davis, is now working against us. The fools can barely conceal lies from each other. The council is controlling Price, trying to use him to gain access to us, and feeding him information about the star craft. Price will have it flying in space within weeks unless we eliminate him. That will be difficult. We tried it once, and you all know what happened."

"They were cloaked, and we didn't expect them," said another deputy. "Now they'll be watching him all the time."

"True, but we'll have to try. My plan involves multiple diversions. The Council has a limited number of armed personnel, but in the event of failure we should be prepared to move to the next stage. If the star craft flies, it can be destroyed in space, but that is complex. It is better to destroy it on the ground. One of your people must go through and see to that. A simple explosive keyed to the startup sequence can do the job."

"And if *that* fails?" asked another deputy. His voice dripped sarcasm, and Watt frowned at him.

"If you have better ideas, we'd like to hear them now."

"It's not that, Minister. We're too few in number. We need a force behind us."

"Ah, but I have such a force. That's the one thing White managed to do before his arrest. He found a sympathetic ear among the Blues, and put me in touch with a mercenary force more than happy to take our money."

"Kashmires?"

"A few. They're a mix of several nations, well armed, around a hundred of them and battle hardened. I can call them up on a day's notice, but only for a major operation that will be our final option if everything else fails."

"We'll destroy everything," said a deputy.

"Star craft, base and portal, all of it will be obliterated by the explosion. The required ordinance will be massive. We'll bring it through the portal in a shipping crate, preset to detonate. The mercenaries will provide cover for the operation."

"What about the Council? Do we just leave them there to die? It could be politically offensive to our neighbors."

"I personally don't care. Let them rot, or get home the best way they can. And there will be no future contact with the Americans. The explosion will kill all of them in the base, and even the nearby town is likely to sink out of sight into the ground. I have faith that our constituency will understand the need for this, as well as the need for new leadership."

"If you're wrong, we'll all be dead men," said a deputy.

"Better that than to allow these people to spread their corruption to the stars," said Dario Watt.

* * * * * * *

Leon intended to follow John Coulter when he could, but two weeks passed by and he was unable to locate the man. Each day, before and after his office duties, he searched the town for Coulter's black Mercedes, and never found it. Coulter didn't call him, and hadn't called Eric.

"I don't like it," Leon said to Eric. "The guy has dropped out of sight right after giving you a pile of money. Something has spooked him. Has that guy Brown contacted you again?"

"Nope. Not a word. I thought he might. We're flight-testing this week. Ground rehearsal is tomorrow. Dillon still thinks I'm nuts. Hell, *I* think I'm nuts. These images come to me, and it's always the right thing to do. I'm beginning to think I can actually fly that bird."

"You probably can. Brown hinted at it. I think you're being programmed for it, all the information you need is being fed to you through hypnosis or some other weird process we don't understand. Your dreams have something to do with that. I bet they were doing it with Johnson, too. Otherwise, I don't see why they'd pick on you."

"Maybe that's why he was killed. Brown didn't say anything about him. Maybe they were getting Johnson ready to fly Sparrow and our resident saboteur had to kill him. He nearly killed me on the same day. That would have *really* set us back."

"Are you still carrying?"

"Waist and boot, when I'm in town. Davis won't let me bring anything into the base, but I've somehow acquired a Beretta 92F there."

"Hang on to it," said Leon. "What do you say we close the office early. I want to widen my search area for Coulter, and you have a big day tomorrow."

"Fine with me," said Eric, and locked his desk.

They left together, turning in opposite directions on 89A. Leon headed uptown and cruised the tourist area, went back to the Y and east to Oak Creek Village and the parking areas near Bell Rock and Courthouse Butte. Traffic was growing heavier as he returned to Sedona, and went back south on 89A to the high school. He spent the better part of an hour doing the Red Rock Loop, slowing at every side street and dirt road. If Coulter had changed cars, Leon was wasting time.

Frustrated again, he sped back to Dry Creek Road and turned towards home. In his haste, and in heavy traffic, he failed to notice the black Mercedes sitting in the parking area in front of Nataly's shop.

* * * * * * *

When the UPS truck arrived, Nataly asked the driver to pull around to the back of the store so he wouldn't risk hitting one of her closely-spaced displays with his loaded hand-truck. He complied, and unloaded several heavy cartons at the back of the store. Nataly left Marie in charge of the register and went back to open and inspect each carton for damage as it was brought in. Everything had arrived safely. She signed for everything, and the driver went away.

There was a carton of colorful crystal specimens from Mexico, and two boxes of Brazilian quartz. She opened them up and lovingly unwrapped each piece. A scepter of yellow quartz with rutile inclusions sang to her, and several others near her resonance were warm in her hand. Time stood still as she sensed the vibrations of each piece, but as she opened another carton the curtain between the back room and her shop was suddenly pulled aside and Marie was standing there, rolling her eyes and being dramatic again.

"Oh, God, you *are* here. I told him you'd gone out. He's been waiting up front for half an hour."

"Who?"

"Some man. He said Eric sent him over to pick you up."

Nataly blinked. "That's not right. Eric would call first. We didn't have anything scheduled for now."

Marie sighed grandly. "I'm only telling you what he said."

"Okay, tell him I'll be there in a minute."

Marie returned to the front of the store, and Nataly resumed her unpacking of the box she'd been working on.

"The last thing Eric would do would be to send someone to pick me up for any reason. He'd come himself. What do I do now?" she said out loud. But before she could answer herself, the curtain was pulled aside again and a man was standing there. He was tall, and wore an expensive looking gray suit with a power tie. His face was square, quite handsome, and his eyes were deep brown. He smiled.

"I'm sorry, Miss Hegel. Didn't Eric call you? We're supposed to meet him at Toucan's in fifteen minutes, and if we leave now we might make it on time." The man looked around the room as he spoke, but remained standing by the curtain.

"Eric didn't call me about anything. Who are you?" Nataly felt hairs moving on the back of her neck, and her entire body was suddenly tense.

The man took a card case from his vest pocket and handed her a business card. "John Coulter, Miss Hegel. My business is mostly import and export of art, artifacts, and antiquities.

Eric and I go back a couple of years. I've had some luck selling art for him, and he suggested your store as another source of artistic treasures. We were supposed to meet today to discuss it, and now I find out he didn't tell you about it. This is very embarrassing. I'll call Eric from Toucan's and have him pick you up, as he should have. The meeting will only take an hour. I see you're quite busy here. That yellow crystal is exceptional, by the way. Such beautiful things in your store, just what I'm looking for. Can you spare the time?"

"I suppose," said Nataly, still tense. The man's eyes seemed fathomless, without expression. But it wasn't the thing that bothered her the most about him.

"I'll see you later, then. Dinner is my treat for both of you."

Coulter walked away before Nataly could answer him. She watched him through the curtain. The man said something to Marie that made her smile, and then left the store. He got into a black sedan and left the parking lot, headed south, in the opposite direction from Toucan's.

"Now I'm scared," said Nataly. "That man is one of us, and Eric has never mentioned him to me. I'm calling Vasyl."

She punched in a number on her phone, and waited, then hung up. "Not there. I'll have to bother Eric."

Eric had left the office, and she got only the message service. "I suppose he could be on the way here," she said, and at that instant, the back door of the room was jerked open and John Coulter's bulk was filling the doorway.

"Like I said, Natasha, you are coming with me," he growled, and lunged towards her.

"Leni!" she screamed, and leaped backwards.

John Coulter encountered an invisible force in mid-lunge that first snapped his body upright and then slammed him on his back on the floor. Coulter rolled, scrambled to his hands and feet with unusual speed for a large man, and was ready to charge again as Nataly cowered in the corner. And then his eyes widened with sudden surprise and fear.

The air in front of Nataly seemed to shimmer, and then boil, and the figure of a man appeared starting with his head and then down to his feet. He was dressed in black from head to foot, his face covered with a deep purple shield, and he held a short, stubby weapon that he now raised towards Coulter.

"Shit!" snarled Coulter, and with one leap he reached the door and was through it.

"Let him go!" said Nataly. An engine roared behind her shop, and gravel crackled against the wall. The man who'd suddenly appeared now stood at the doorway, looking outside.

"Black Mercedes, 500 Series, and I have the license number."

"Vasyl didn't answer when I called." Nataly choked back a sob, and her eyes were brimming with tears. "Oh thank you, Leni."

"I have another number for him. I'm not leaving you now. Dry your eyes. I'll report this to Vasyl. He'll know what to do."

"If you hadn't been here—what did he *want* with me?"

"You would make a good hostage. Eric would do what he was told. It was anticipated." Leni smiled. "What just happened only justifies all the lonely hours I've spent in this empty room without even something to read."

Nataly laughed, put her arms around Leni and hugged him. "My protector with the face I never see," she said.

"And never will," said Leni. "I think it's safe to work up front now. I have to make a call, and recharge for cloaking. Expect me to be wandering the store. I'll try not to bump into anything."

Nataly heard the soothing tone of Leni's voice, but knew that inside the man was a coiled spring.

She returned to the front of the store. Marie looked at her strangely, but said nothing. Nataly wanted to call Eric and tell him what had happened, but knew she shouldn't. He had work coming up that would not be helped by worry.

She didn't even think about calling Leon.

CHAPTER TWENTY-TWO
GROUND TEST

Eric felt excited, but also had a nagging apprehension that had begun the day before. At first he'd thought it a lack of confidence about the ground test, but the procedure was so clear in his mind it was like the test had already been successfully performed. Perhaps it was Nataly he worried about. They'd had lunch once in the past two weeks, and she'd been her usual ethereal and affectionate self, but when he'd called the next day she was suddenly very busy. There were times when he felt the woman was peering into the very core of him. Her gaze would become intense, she would squeeze his hand warmly in hers and, for Eric, everything except Nataly would cease to exist. Maybe she'd finally seen what was really inside him: a merciless killer for political masters, a man who could only live for himself in order to survive.

In two decades he'd never had such intense feelings for a woman, a longing that went far beyond the physical. And there were moments when he felt Nataly returning those feelings with a look, a touch, and a light brush of her lips on his. The thought of it made his eyes moist.

He didn't want to lose her, even after the mess at the base was finished.

The van bumped hard in the usual place on the usual road and there was the usual decent to the tunnels below high desert buttes. Twenty minutes later Sergeant Alan Nutt, his faithful base companion, accompanied him to Sparrow's bay. Several people were waiting for them.

Steward was there, and Frank Harris for Systems Analysis, but today it would be Rob Hendricks' show. As head of Flight Operations it was Rob's responsibility to write procedure for all ground and flight-testing, but unlike Steward, his ego never got involved in the work. Eric liked him, though Rob didn't accept the 'Good Luck' theory of Eric's breakthroughs with Sparrow any more than Steward did. He reacted in a different way. He simply assumed that for reasons unknown to him people who knew how to get Sparrow into space were feeding Eric information, and it made common sense to go along with what they said. He'd even said openly he thought trying to find out why Eric was The Chosen One was a waste of time.

Rob had asked Eric to write up the ground test procedure, and Eric complied, with the proviso there could be only one copy, to be kept in Sparrow's cockpit at all times. Davis had strongly objected to that, but gave in when Rob promised to somehow obtain another copy. He told Eric this, and Eric had seen the logic. If there was an accident, Eric might be killed and the procedure record burned up with him, leaving the rest of them with nothing. The people who'd brought Sparrow to them had demonstrated all too much that they couldn't be counted on for vital information, at least for the rest of the team. In the end, Eric had allowed one disk copy to be stored in Davis' safe. If Brown objected to that, he'd have to deal with Davis.

Captain Dillon was inside Sparrow when Eric arrived, and two techs were standing on the wings to look in at him.

"Morning," said Eric, and Hendricks gave him a look of surprise when he climbed right up onto Sparrow's wing and nudged a tech aside.

"Aren't you going to give us a briefing?" called Hendricks.

"You have the procedure, and so do I. Let's get to it. Morning, Captain; have room for me in there?"

Dillon was already throwing switches, and the ready light on his side of the cockpit was green. "All set, sir. Climb in."

Eric climbed into the seat next to Dillon, and strapped in. A tech handed his headphone to him, and he put it on. The entire procedure to the limit of their knowledge was on a single sheet of paper on a clipboard, all of it drawn only from Eric's memory. He put the clipboard in his lap.

The roar of heavy engines was a momentary distraction. Four fire trucks pulled up alongside Sparrow on both sides and targeted the craft with four-foot nozzles prepared to spray foam. When the trucks were in place, both techs saluted and got down from the wings. Dillon touched a lever on his side of the cockpit; the canopy above them levered downwards and locked in place with a snap. The red interior light went on and seemed too dim until Eric's eyes adapted to it.

"Here we go," said Eric, and threw five switches in rapid succession. They could hear the whine from Sparrow's aft section even with the canopy closed. When the sound was steady, Eric threw the final switch on the board, and a single light glowed on a panel by his right knee.

"Should be getting some heat now," said Eric.

Hendricks responded instantly. "Warming. T at twenty-two and climbing. We're going to the trucks."

Eric nodded at Dillon. "Powering up."

Dillon's left hand moved a lever forward, and soon they could hear the whine of conventional turbines rising in pitch until there was a thump, then a steady vibration in the cockpit. At that instant, a second light went on by Eric's right knee.

"Ah, hah!" he said. "That is reassuring. Now bring it up to half thrust."

Dillon pushed the lever again, and cockpit vibrations seemed to smooth. A switch light at the top of the panel by Eric's right knee turned green when Eric threw it.

"That's it, we're done. The rest has to be done in flight. Power down, and shutting down. How's the heat out there?"

"T went to fifty, but leveled off when you went to half-thrust. I wish we knew what the hell we're doing here, Price." Hendricks did not sound pleased.

"So do I, Rob. I'm just following directions." Eric followed the switching sequence in reverse as Dillon powered down, and a minute later there was no sound to be heard except for their nervous breathing.

"That took about five minutes, and I was up half the night worrying about it," said Dillon.

"The real stress test comes when we're in the air, Captain. That's when we find out what that last panel is there for. All we know now is that it's ready to do it when we reach half-thrust. God knows what would have happened if I'd thrown those switches before then.

Dillon smiled, and shook his head. "I've been doing first-flight on high performance aircraft for fifteen years, sir, but I've never been in one where we had no idea what was going to happen when we threw a switch. It's not what I'd call good engineering procedure."

"Anything that works is good engineering," said Eric.

The two techs had returned to Sparrow's wings and helped Dillon and Eric climb out of the cockpit. On the ground, Hendricks looked glum, and folded his arms as he made his judgment. "That has to be the shortest ground test on record. Tell me, please, what we just accomplished."

"We didn't blow up," said Eric.

"You have the startup procedure verified up to liftoff," said Dillon. "When can we fly?"

Hendricks paused, and tapped his foot. "It'll have to be at night. I'm thinking Sunday, or early Monday morning."

"We could do it any night. We'll be at altitude in less than a minute. There's no security issue." Dillon was clearly anxious to see what Sparrow could really do.

"Sunday is soon enough," said Hendricks, and that looked like the end of the discussion. Eric raised an eyebrow at him.

"There are some things we want to look at first," said Hendricks. "When you were powering up, the fuselage T was increasing fast, but suddenly leveled off. At that point we saw something strange, like a thermal plume, all around the aircraft. The air shimmered. Maybe it glowed. We have it all on film, optical and IR. I want to compare the two views. I don't think it was a thermal plume. Didn't you feel anything unusual when you powered up?"

Eric shook his head, but Dillon said, "It got quiet and smoother, just before we hit half thrust."

"That's when the green bulb lit up on our mystery board," added Eric.

"I'll run stress and temperature data correlations with what we have on film. I want to know everything I can before you fly. It'll be Friday before we have it all written up, and Saturday will be flight check and fueling. We might be able to lift off early Sunday morning. That is the earliest."

Dillon smiled wanly. "Yes sir."

"This means both of you will be staying here Friday through the weekend, and maybe Monday. I hope you haven't made any other plans, but if you have you'd better change them."

At least Nataly wouldn't have to find an excuse for not seeing him this weekend. "I wouldn't miss this flight for anything, Rob," said Eric.

"And it's long overdue," said Dillon.

Steward and the two techs had opened up Sparrow and were crawling around inside with their instruments. The fire trucks pulled back and parked in a corner of the bay. Sergeant Nutt came up to Eric with an expectant look on his face. "Colonel Davis, sir, right after the test, he said."

"Okay," said Eric. He turned to Dillon, held out a hand. "See you on Friday, Captain."

The men shook hands, and Eric went away with the sergeant to make his report to Davis, and indirectly to the mysterious people who had brought Sparrow to them.

He wondered if he'd ever have the chance to talk to Mister Brown again.

* * * * * * *

By noon the techs had finished their measurements on

Sparrow, and closed her up again. Elton Steward sat at the little table by the aircraft and analyzed data on his PC for another two hours. Rob Hendricks showed up, talked with Steward a while, Steward folded up his PC and the two men left the bay together.

There was little activity in the bay the rest of the afternoon. A welder was busy on the arm of a crane, high above the floor, and a crew cleaned up an oil spill near the large baffled door. Four guards continually patrolled the perimeter of the bay every day until lockdown. Late afternoon, on separate occasions, three uniformed men came out of the door that led to the neighboring portal bay. They crossed the bay and went out another door, taking a shortcut to the parking area by the main tunnel in the base.

As lockdown approached, the baffled door rolled upwards ten feet, and three men came in with a forklift. The welder who'd been working high above them stopped what he'd been doing and climbed down the crane's ladder to the floor. The arc-welding-unit power supply was picked up on a pallet and carried away.

The four guards checked to be sure all personnel doors were locked, and went out through the baffle door. The door rolled downwards, hit the floor. Magnetic locks engaged with a loud snap, red lights went on near the ceiling and strobed slowly. The lights that had been on all day now dimmed until there was only a strobing, red gloom in the bay. Lockdown would last until oh-five-hundred the following morning.

Sparrow sat silently in gloom for over five hours until, suddenly, the door leading to the portal bay opened again. Four men came out of it. They wore military fatigues, and carried heavy black satchels no larger than briefcases.

The men walked up to Sparrow. Two climbed up onto the wings, and opened the cockpit. A minute later the aft section of Sparrow rotated upwards, and the other two men climbed inside with their satchels. They worked for over an hour, then climbed out again with satchels now held lightly in their hands. They waited patiently. It was another hour before the men inside the cockpit were finished with their work.

Sparrow's fuselage was closed again. The other two men emerged from the cockpit and closed it up, stepped down from the wings.

The four men talked softly for several minutes, reviewing what they'd done, and then they walked back to the door leading to the portal bay and made their exit.

It was quiet in the bay for exactly one hour, and then, quite suddenly, the figures of two men materialized out of clear air right by Sparrow. They wore helmets with opaque facemasks and were clothed in black from neck to foot. Both carried short, stubby weapons, and one was talking on a cell phone.

The men waited by Sparrow for twenty minutes, and then the personnel door leading eventually to the office of Colonel John Davis opened up, and a man entered the bay.

The man was Sergeant Alan Nutt.

Alan walked over to the men and shook hands with them. There was a murmured discussion that went on for several minutes, and then Alan stepped up onto Sparrow's wing and opened the cockpit. He reached inside without hesitation, there was a thud, and Sparrow's aft section opened up again.

Alan went back to inspect the inside of Sparrow with the other two men. There was another discussion, and Alan crawled inside Sparrow until only his feet were visible. He worked at something for several minutes, and called out. The other two men grabbed his ankles, slowly pulled him out and helped him stand. Alan was holding something the size of a shoebox away from his body at arms' length, and gingerly put it down on the table by Sparrow.

The three of them went back up on Sparrow's wing, and Alan got into the cockpit. He remained there for half an hour. Sparrow's aft section levered shut, and soon after that there was a brief whine from the craft. Alan got out of the cockpit, and closed the canopy. He stood on the wing, and made a call on his cell phone. He talked to someone for several minutes before hanging up, and then turned to his companions. They listened intently as he talked, and then they all climbed off the wing.

Alan walked to the table to retrieve the box he'd taken out of Sparrow. Behind him the other two men disappeared from view, their images rippling, fading, then gone from the feet up.

Alan picked up the box, again held it well out from his body, and marched to the door leading eventually to the nearby portal bay. He punched in a code to open the door, went through it, and closed the door behind him.

And Sparrow's bay was quiet again.

CHAPTER TWENTY-THREE
BRIEFINGS

Arthur Evans splashed cold water on his face and wiped it dry with a towel. He combed his hair and put the comb in a glass on the shelf in front of the mirror, studied himself, and decided the long, daily walks were doing some good.

The door opened, and Len was standing there. "Gilbert Norton is here, Mister President. He's waiting for you in the office."

"Thanks, Len. I want you there, too. Take some notes for me."

"Yes, Mister President." Len opened the door wider, and stepped to one side. Arthur clapped him on the shoulder as he walked past. He liked Len: quiet, unassuming manner, a good-looking kid, and sharp as a tack.

It was only a few steps, and he opened a door leading to the oval office. Gil had been sitting in a chair near the big, mahogany desk, and stood.

"Morning, Gil. Good to see you again." Arthur shook his hand. "You know my aid. He'll be taking some notes so I'll remember what I'm supposed to do."

"Hi Len," said Gil; Len smiled faintly, and sat down on a leather couch.

"I appreciate your time, Mister President."

Arthur sat down behind his desk, and then Gil sat down. "Sounds like things have really been heating up," said The President.

"We're getting close. The flight test is the end of the week. They'll be going for a hundred thousand feet and what Eric Price is calling hyper-flight. I don't know what that means, and Eric claims he doesn't either. He just expects Sparrow to achieve extreme speed."

"That man has been quite a surprise," said Arthur. "We sent him there to find and eliminate a saboteur, and instead he's become a chief scientist for the project. How did that happen?"

"I don't know, and neither does Eric. The insights come to him in bursts. He thinks he's been somehow programmed with hypnosis or even telepathy. A woman he's been seeing could be involved, but we've checked her out and she seems totally clean. There has been an attempt on Eric's life, but we feel he was in the wrong place at the wrong time. Johnson was his prime contact at the base, and was trying to tell him something; Johnson's assassin was still there when Eric arrived; we figured he tried to kill two for the price of one."

"And the killer is still on the loose."

"He is, but we're not aware of any new sabotage. The project has been moving ahead quickly. We've been checking out one suspicious individual who is bribing personnel for information on the project, but we can't find anything on him, even a birth record. The man claims to represent corporate interests. Quite frankly, Mister President, I think Eric Price knows more about him, but is holding back. And I think his explanation for his scientific accomplishments is a bit convenient. His knowledge could only have come from our foreign associates, but if Eric has made contact with them he's not telling me about it."

"Are you telling me he's unreliable? Do you want to recall him?"

"Not at all, Mister President. He's doing his job. I've always had a policy of giving field agents free hand in day-to-day oper-ations. If Eric isn't telling me something, he has his reasons. And his achievements in moving Shooting Star ahead have been outstanding."

"Success of the project is what this is all about, Gil. If the man has your trust, he has mine. Is there anything else I should know about?"

"No, Mister President. That's all I have for now. I'll call after the test flight. That'll be early Saturday or Sunday morning."

Arthur stood up, and Gil stood with him. Arthur walked around the desk and shook hands with his old friend again.

"I'm encouraged, Gil. Things were stumbling along until we got your man in there. I'm amazed at how much he stirred up in such a short time. But it's hard for me to find the words to express how important this project is to me, and to humanity, for that matter. If what we've been promised is true, we can go to the stars. The perspective of the entire human race could be changed overnight. This belongs to all of earth's people, Gil, not just one nation."

"I agree," said Gil, "and I think your attitude is the reason they brought Shooting Star to us in the first place, and not one of the other western countries."

Arthur squeezed Gil's hand again. "And I don't intend to betray that trust, old friend," he said. *You think you understand, but you don't*, he thought.

"Anything I can do, call me." Arthur took Gil by the elbow, led him to the door. "Say hi to Jean for me."

"She misses the quiet dinners we used to have," said Gil.

"We'll have them again, after I survive this second term."

The door closed, and Gil was gone. Len sat on the couch, an empty note pad on his lap. He looked expectant. Arthur's expression was suddenly serious. "Okay, let's get our Mister Brown in here and find out what's really going on."

Len left the office. Arthur returned to his desk, sat down, and riffled some pages of a folder without seeing them. He checked his appointment calendar and made a few doodles on a notepad.

There was a soft knocking on the door, and it opened. Len leaned inside and said," Mister Brown is here, Mister President."

"Send him in, Len, and please wait outside."

A tall man came into the room. The dark blue business suit he wore had been carefully tailored for him. *Eye-candy for my receptionist*, thought Arthur. At the doorway, the man bowed, and clicked his heels together as the door closed behind him.

Arthur stood. "Vasyl, it's good to see you again. I've just been hearing good things about our project. Please, sit down."

Vasyl sat. "There have been problems, but we're gradually working through them."

"I've been particularly interested in the progress made by an operative of ours named Eric Price," said Arthur.

Vasyl smiled. "Yes, he has created quite a stir."

"How so? I've read the man's file. No doubt he's a fine scientist, in addition to his more violent skills, but I find it hard to explain the breakthroughs he's achieved in such a short time. Surely you've been feeding him information you couldn't trust other people with."

"We have, sir."

"But why? There were others you could trust, like Johnson. The lack of information transfer has slowed progress to a crawl until now."

"Johnson was murdered, sir, because we gave him key information directly and by ordinary means, and he was unable to keep it to himself. We didn't want the same thing to happen again. Price has been advised subliminally and with key words or visual patterns to bring information to a conscious level when needed."

"But why Price?"

Vasyl smiled. "Because he's one of us."

"WHAT?"

"An incredible coincidence, I know. And Price has no knowledge of his heritage. One of our people was the first to see it at a party Price attended. I'm afraid her attraction to him is a bit of a problem right now, but she has been our information conduit and we have to trust her. Price seems quite taken with her."

Arthur was amazed. "What webs we've woven here, even without knowing it. But when you get down to it, we're all the same people."

"Watt is also one of us, sir, but I do not claim him. Now

he's dropped out of sight, and we anticipate more sabotage or worse. I'll spare you the details, but there has been more than one attempt on Price's life, and with the flight test only days away we're expecting another. There was an attempt to place a bomb on the star craft just yesterday. I have only a few cloaked personnel, barely enough to cover the star craft and portal bays, and then there was a kidnap attempt on one of our people in town, the woman Price is attracted to.

"I have three people with cloaking capability to cover all our town operatives, including Price. I need four times that, and I need a visible permanent force at the base. Davis is not cooperating. He insists our people must leave at the end of each working day, and the guarding of the bays is hopelessly inadequate. Davis says he will not tolerate the continuous presence of foreign troops in his command."

"You want me to order it? Officially I haven't even been informed about this project. The Pentagon sees it as a minor issue of technology transfer from turncoats. Only a few even know how advanced that technology might be."

"Including the man who just walked out of your office," said Vasyl.

"Yes."

"And he's in charge of your deepest security operations. He could make a request. You wouldn't have to know details. It would be a diplomatic gesture to a friendly, foreign power."

"I've known Gil a long time. Hell, I trained him, and I know what he'll say. The presence of foreign troops on a highly classified base is a bad precedent. Why not order Davis to use his own people, and stiffen up the guard for the project?"

Vasyl sighed, and shook his head. "We don't trust his people. Watt has been spreading money around like butter, and he's infiltrated their ranks just like we have. When something happens, Watt knows it within hours, and we've only identified a couple of his sources. I need to have our own people there, in force, and before the flight test."

Arthur leaned back in his chair, and drummed the fingers of

one hand on his desk for a moment. He fixed his gaze on Vasyl, and then said, "I realize I'm a bit out of practice in the clandestine world, but I hear you telling me that Watt and his followers might attack the base with considerable force of arms."

"It's a real possibility, sir. We have to be ready for it, at least for the next two weeks. Flight-testing has to be done in two stages, or we could lose the star craft, and it would take us years to bring in another. Governments come and go, and our next one might cancel the entire project."

"Only a fool would do that." Arthur rocked in his chair, and studied Vasyl's face. The man was calm, but his eyes betrayed the anxiety within him. Arthur had known him for nearly two years, but they had met formally on only three occasions. Vasyl had the good looks and manners to charm anyone, but he had the daring of a combat officer and the attention to detail of an accountant. Arthur liked him.

"All right, I'll talk to Gil right away. Everyone will know the order has come down from me. We don't have time for arguments."

Vasyl visibly relaxed. "Thank you, sir. I realize this is a political risk for you."

"Blowing my nose in public is a political risk, Vasyl. Everything is headline news in this country."

"Our people will never be seen outside the portal and support bays, and they'll be dressed as American marines. When should I activate them?"

"Give me until midnight. If I haven't called, then do it."

"Yes sir."

"I really appreciate what you've done, Vasyl, and the personal sacrifices you've made for us. It's hard to spend an entire tour of duty away from family. Any children?"

"One girl. She just turned four. I've been collecting dolls for her—and some jewelry for my wife."

"Well, this will all be wrapped up soon, the way things are going, and we'll see you back at home. Maybe I'll get a chance to visit you there someday. I should get back to the Old Country at least once. My people came here so long ago there's probably no family of mine left across the big sea anymore, but it couldn't hurt to look."

Arthur stood up, signaling that the audience with The President had ended. Vasyl stood, and the men shook hands. Arthur walked him to the door.

"We're making history, Vasyl," said Arthur. "Unfortunately, the public might never know the who or the how, only that suddenly we can travel to the stars. I think that's a good thing."

"I agree," said Vasyl.

Arthur opened the door for him, and clapped him on the back. "Then let's do it," he said, and Vasyl went away.

Arthur returned to his desk and took a cell phone from a drawer, punched in numbers and listened.

"Gil?" he said softly. "Something has come up, and I need you back in my office right away. I hope it's not too inconvenient."

He laughed. "Ah, good. See, there's an advantage to slow cab service on occasion. Give me ten minutes, and come right in."

Arthur hung up, punched a button on his intercom. "Dorothy? Gilbert Norton will be returning soon. Send him right in when he arrives."

The President of the United States took pen and legal pad, and began scribbling an order with language terse enough to make even the toughest Pentagon obstructionist obey without argument.

He was still scribbling when Gil arrived.

CHAPTER TWENTY-FOUR
VISITORS

The more Leon searched, the more he worried. John Coulter had dropped off the face of the planet only days after giving Eric a substantial amount of money and talking about assignments. Coulter knew that Eric and Leon were close. Leon expected a call from him, an assignment, maybe even another unmarked envelope stuffed with fifty-dollar bills. He waited a week, and then called the cell number Coulter had given him. There was no answer, so he left a message. He sent e-mail to the address on Coulter's business card, but it was returned immediately with the admonition 'user doesn't exist'. In retrospect, that was the first warning that something had gone wrong.

For over two weeks, he'd roamed the streets mornings and late afternoons in search of Coulter's black Mercedes. Those wasted hours were only added to by repeated phone calls that went unanswered. The man had disappeared. Something had spooked him. It had to have something to do with the meeting Eric had had with him, but Eric remembered nothing unusual. Coulter had told him what he wanted, and paid him handsomely for it.

Leon made inquiries with any person he knew had seen Coulter in the past. He went to the Coffee Pot, Shari's, The Planet, described the man who'd been there before with Leon. Nobody had seen him. He even asked Nataly, thinking Coulter might have come to her shop when Eric was there. Nataly hadn't seen the man, didn't know who he was. She looked away from

Leon when she said it, distracted by something.

"When you see Eric, tell him I came in to flirt with you."

"I haven't seen him for a while, Leon. We've both been busy."

Something in her tone of voice bothered him. "You two okay?" he asked, and meant it as a friend.

Nataly smiled faintly, put a hand on his arm. "I think we're trying to figure that out."

"Well, don't take too long."

Nataly patted his arm. "I'll keep an eye open for your friend, and let him know you're looking for him."

Leon left her in a dark mood, and went back to his office after another fruitless drive around town. He was surprised to find Eric there, clacking away at a keyboard.

"I thought you'd be at the base today."

"Nope. I go in tomorrow morning. I'll be spending the night there before the flight."

Leon sat down. "Still no Coulter. I've asked all around. Maybe he changed cars."

"Maybe he's sick, or dead," said Eric.

"Right. Maybe you'd better take it seriously. My stomach is crawling. Something is up."

"Either that or Coulter has skipped town. I have enough to think about right now."

"That's sort of what Nataly told me today."

"What?" Eric stopped typing, and looked at him, eyes narrowed. When he looked like that, Leon always felt hairs moving on the back of his neck.

"She said you've both been very busy lately. She sounded kinda sad."

Eric's smile could be nasty when he wanted it to be. "You in love with her, Leon?"

"No, but if I was I'd sure be with her a lot more than you are. And if you hurt her you'll see what a royal shit I can really be."

"Threat noted," said Eric, and went back to typing. After a few seconds, he looked at Leon again. "Sorry. I'm sensitive about Nataly right now. We're taking a little break to cool down."

"That's stupid," said Leon, and went to his desk.

"Maybe," said Eric, and began typing again.

They worked the rest of the afternoon without talking. Eric finished his work first, and turned off his computer. "I'm going home early and going to bed early. I'll call you if I live through the flight."

"Good luck," said Leon, and didn't look up. The door closed, and Eric was gone.

A few minutes later the telephone rang, and Leon answered it.

It was John Coulter.

"Well, hello. I've called you a couple of times. What's up?"

"I just got back from Phoenix. Something *has* come up, and I need your advice about it before I do anything foolish."

"That sounds ominous. What's the problem?"

"It has to do with someone we both do business with. We have to meet. I don't want to talk about it on the phone."

"I'm about finished here. Where, and when?"

"How about your house? I don't want to meet in public."

"You have my address?"

"Sure. I know where it is. I've been by there on my way to the canyons."

"Okay." Leon looked at his watch. "I have four-twenty now. Meet me at my house at five. Just pull up to the gate, and I'll buzz you in."

"I'll be there," said Coulter, and hung up.

So Coulter had been out of town, and Leon had been wasting a lot of time searching in the wrong place for him. The problem he wanted to talk about had to be Eric. Shit. Whoever employed Coulter had probably become suspicious when Eric wanted to deal with him directly. *I can think of a way to explain that: Eric is an asshole who hates authority and makes end runs when he doesn't get his way. The money will make him back off. He loves it. What else can I say?*

Leon thought about it for several minutes, then shut down his computer and locked up the office. The Humvee's tank was nearly empty from the entire fruitless running around. He gassed up a block away from the office, drove four more blocks south and turned west towards the Canyons on Dry Creek Road. Out of habit, he watched his rear-view mirror every time he made a turn.

A black van turned with him, and was following five car lengths behind. Leon sped up, and the van kept its distance. He slowed to the speed limit and kept it there. It was only a few minutes before he reached his house. Coulter's black Mercedes wasn't there. Leon put on his turn signal to make a left turn and pressed on the gate activator above his head. He slowed, and the black van slowed behind him, coming close. Now Leon could see the man who drove the van.

It was John Coulter.

Leon turned into his driveway, and Coulter followed. They parked up close to the garage. Coulter got out of the van before Leon had shut off his engine.

Leon got out of the Humvee. "What happened to the Mercedes?"

"In a shop in Phoenix. The van is a loaner. This will only take a few minutes, Leon."

"So let's go inside."

Leon unlocked his front door and turned off the security alarm next to it. They entered, and Coulter closed the door behind them. Leon put his briefcase on the couch, and turned to face his guest.

Coulter was standing there with a black automatic in his hand, and it was pointed at Leon.

"What the hell is *that* for?" asked Leon.

"Just in case you're also part of my problem, Leon. I haven't been able to read you as well as the man I'm after."

Coulter backed up to the door, and opened it. Six men came into the room. They were dressed in black from head to toe. Deep red plastic-looking masks covered their faces, and they carried ugly, black and stubby weapons that looked like machine pistols. It was as if they'd been in his house before. They walked straight to his basement door, opened it, and went down the stairs.

"Guess they wouldn't fit in the Mercedes," said Leon, and smirked at Coulter.

"I don't think you realize how close you are to dying," said Coulter, and carefully aimed his pistol at Leon's head. "You and Price are probably in it together, but I'm going to give you one chance to show some loyalty and give me a reason to keep you alive."

"The last I heard, you gave Eric Price more money that you've given me in a year. And now you don't trust him? That doesn't sound smart to me."

"Money does lots of things, including diverting people's attentions. Makes them easier to read, Leon."

"Whatever the hell *that* means."

Coulter took a step closer, and lowered his gun to aim at Leon's chest. "What it means is Price isn't selling. He's digging for the identity of my employer, and has no intention of providing what I've paid for. He's a spy, just like you, Leon; only he's more open about it. That makes him dangerous, so I'm eliminating him, and if you don't help me I'll eliminate you too."

"Bribery is one thing, but murdering a federal officer makes you a dead man," said Leon.

"Words can't describe how much that frightens me. Now get down the stairs."

"Why?"

"You're going to lead us through that tunnel of yours to your neighbor's house, and then you'll get him down to the basement so we can kill him there. And when that's done, maybe, just maybe I'll believe you're working for me."

"Bullshit. All you have is suspicions. Eric has never given me a reason to think he'd cross you. He wants a good retirement as much as I do."

"Leon, if you don't move quick I'm going to kill you right here. I don't want it that way, but I'll do it." Coulter straightened his arm, and Leon saw a tendon bulge in his hand as he began squeezing the trigger.

"Okay. Okay! I'm moving, but I think you're wrong about Eric, and getting rid of him is just going to mess things up."

"That's another reason to kill him. Get going."

Coulter waved his gun, and Leon went to the basement door and down the stairs. His own weapon was loaded and locked, but the safety was on, and the holster it was in was velcroed to his ankle. He would need a big distraction to get to it, and now, as he came down the stairs, seven men were watching him.

"Very nice," said Coulter, and he looked around the room. "You must get a lot of practice."

"I keep my hand in it," said Leon, and was careful to keep his hands in sight. Coulter and his thugs had stupidly not bothered to search him for a weapon. If Coulter had the slightest bit of trust in him right now, it was the only card Leon had to play.

Coulter opened a cabinet door and saw six pistols hanging on hooks there. He selected one, a Sig forty-five, checked the chamber and magazine to be sure it was unloaded, and handed the weapon to Leon.

"What's this for?"

"You're going to lead us through the tunnel and knock politely on the door at the other end. If nobody answers you'll open the door with that gun in your hand. If somebody *does* answer you'll be standing right there, ready to shoot, but of course you won't be able to do that. You might get lucky. Price might be able to control his instincts, and not shoot you, *or*, anyone guarding him might be smart enough to see what's going on before they blow you to pieces. Either way, we're coming out that door right behind you, and Price is going to be a dead man."

"And if I get through this alive, can I anticipate any kind of a reward for my participation?"

Coulter's smile was more of a sneer. "You'll get to live, for starters, and just maybe there'll be another donation to your retirement fund."

Leon paused a moment to let Coulter believe he was thinking about it, then, "Okay, let's get it over with. But I still think you're wrong about Price."

"Yet you'll still help us kill him," said Coulter. "Your loyalty is outstanding."

"I'm loyal to one person," said Leon, "and that person is me."

Coulter waved his pistol towards the tunnel door. "Then by all means, let's proceed."

Leon stepped up to the door and opened it. The tunnel lights flickered, and then came to full brilliance. The air smelled of paint and oil and something sharp, like a solvent. The vent pumps came on almost immediately, and the walls vibrated with a dull throbbing.

Coulter's men bunched up behind Leon, and Coulter trailed behind them. After a few steps he ordered his men to form a widely spaced line behind Leon. "Watch for tripwires. Stay on the catwalk, and don't touch anything else."

"That sounds like you've been in here before," said Leon.

"Shut up," snarled Coulter. "No talking the rest of the way."

The tunnel ran straight for fifty yards, and then curved slightly to the left. There were no buttresses or cutouts where Leon could jump to and pull out the weapon strapped to his ankle, but he was looking for them, anything he'd forgotten. He was searching the walls as he came around the curve in the tunnel. For one instant he thought he detected movement at the edge of his vision, but when he looked ahead nothing was there, just another hundreds of yards of tunnel and the door at the end of it.

The nearest man was only a few feet behind him. Leon glanced over his shoulder, was surprised to see that Coulter was now several yards behind them, his forehead glistening with sweat. The man looked scared. He looked ready to run.

Eric was armed. If Leon could warn him, the attackers could be shot down one by one as they went up the basement stairs. That meant getting the door open. But what if Eric was right there, waiting for them? A single, lucky shot and Leon could be dead.

The tunnel was nearly soundproof, but not perfectly so.

Gunshots would certainly be heard in the basement, and maybe upstairs. If Leon could start and maintain a firefight in the tunnel for even a few seconds, it might be warning enough. He thought about it, watched the tunnel exit coming closer and closer. He looked back again; saw Coulter twenty yards behind, and slowing. *What the hell?* Leon looked forward again, lost some balance and stepped off the catwalk. As he did it he felt something heavy and sticky brush up against his left side. It shocked him, and his heart pounded hard. He stepped back on the catwalk. The man behind him had closed up, was within arm's reach. And Leon suddenly knew what he had to do.

It was five yards to the door, and Eric's basement. Leon slowed, felt a man's body and the hard muzzle of a weapon press against the back of his head. He reached out to the door, turned the lock, the doorknob, and pulled back hard.

"Eric! Watch out!"

Leon slammed back against the man behind him, and twisted. There was a muffled explosion, and he felt searing pain in his right side. He got his arm around the man's neck, as there were two more explosions, then a staccato of gunfire down the tunnel. Leon pulled up under the man's chin, then jerked to the right and heard a satisfying snap. The man slumped. Leon went down with him, scrabbling for the gun strapped to his ankle.

Leon's gun came loose from his holster and he thumbed the safety without thinking. Coulter's men charged as Leon twisted around his human shield and emptied the magazine of his pistol as fast as he could pull the trigger. One man staggered and went down, but the other three kept coming, and Leon felt the terrible impact of three bullets in his chest. He watched his pistol fall from his hand, and slumped against the doorway as the three men trampled on his legs getting past him. Down the tunnel, Coulter had disappeared, and two other men were still struggling.

There was a long burst of gunfire from behind him, and then Leon's hearing failed as he plunged into cold oblivion.

CHAPTER TWENTY-FIVE
FIREFIGHT

On the drive home, Eric realized why he'd been short with Leon. The guy really *did* care about Nataly, and was being protective of her for good cause. *Who am I kidding?* he thought. *A paid killer with my track record can never give her a happy life. Divorced over neglect, estranged from a daughter for the same reason, I'm a poster child for government slavery. Be honest with yourself, for once. You've hated your job for years, but are afraid of doing anything else. The idea of doing something in the private sector terrifies you.*

Terrific. Having thought all that, he was still crazy to see Nataly, touch her, even hear the sound her voice. And he really *did* have other things to worry about.

His plan was to throw a pizza in the oven, boil some peas, and have some ice cream after. Nothing cerebral in the evening, some junk TV, a beer, and bed early. There was no preparation to worry about. The entire startup sequence was clear in his mind—up to a point. That point was when the green light lit up on that third panel by his right knee. Up to that point his instinct was telling him that Sparrow was going to go very fast and very high.

And then what?

Eric thought about Nataly getting ready to close her shop. She was so meticulous about everything, always ended up staying open longer than planned. It was about that time when he pulled into his driveway. He garaged the car and went in the house through the side door. He turned on the oven and left it to heat while he went downstairs to scan the surveillance videos for the day, and checked the little string still lodged safely at the top of his front door.

In fifteen minutes the oven was properly heated. Suddenly weary of pizza, Eric took two potpies out of the freezer, put them on a tray in the oven. A handful of peas and some water in a pot, and dinner was on its way. He got a beer from the fridge, opened it, and walked to the front room to turn on the TV. Just as he got there he saw Leon's Humvee rush by the house, followed seconds later by a black van. Unusual. There were few houses beyond his, and it was getting late for hiking in the canyons. Or maybe Leon had a guest.

He turned on the television, and sipped his beer. The pies would be ready in twenty minutes. Eric checked his watch, went to the stove and turned on the burner under the peas when the pies were nearly finished.

The sudden explosions he heard were muffled, but distinct. It took him a heartbeat to recognize them as gunshots, and they were coming from the tunnel in the basement. He thought he heard someone call his name. That thought was not complete as he gripped the long-slide Colt in his hand, jerked from the shoulder holster without conscious reaction.

He leaped to the basement door and opened it. The tunnel door banged open at that instant, and someone lay crumpled in the doorway. Gunshots echoed in the tunnel, and three men dressed head to toe in black crowded their way through the doorway into the basement. They looked left and right, waved machine pistols, but neglected to look upwards.

Eric went down on one knee, arm rigid, shoulder locked, and fired seven rounds into the heads of the three men below him. The far wall of the basement splattered red with their blood. Eric scrabbled at his shoulder holster as he released the Colt's empty magazine, then slammed another magazine home and worked the slide. There were two more shots from the tunnel, then a gurgling scream, and silence.

Eric crab-walked down the stairs and kept his aim on the tunnel door. He jumped to one side, stepped up to the door, dared a quick glance down the tunnel, then a longer look. There was no movement. Two men were crumpled by the doorway, two others in black were sprawled steps away, and there was an isolated puddle of blood beyond that.

From upstairs came the roar of a vehicle rushing past his house, and Eric remembered the black van following Leon.

Leon. Oh, shit.

And then, right where he stood, someone groaned.

Eric looked down. At first he saw only a man on his back, face masked by a solid, opaque plate, arms to his sides. But there was a third arm jutting from beneath the man's waist, a coat-sleeve shimmering gray.

Eric rolled the masked man over, and stared with dismay into Leon's face. There was a blue pallor to his cheeks, and his chest was soaked with blood. Leon's eyes flickered open. He smiled weakly.

"Heard—shots. Didn't think—got you," he gurgled.

Eric pulled Leon's coat aside, saw three entrance wounds there, two high in the chest, one lower, close to the heart.

"I've got to get you medical help quick. You're losing a lot of blood."

"S'okay. No pain. Just cold. Coulter did this. Wanted to kill you. Did—what I could—Eric."

Eric watched Leon's life pumping out of him with each heartbeat. The base had no hospital he knew of, only an infirmary. He could call Davis, and wait half an hour for someone to come. There was no surgery in town. The nearest was in Cottonwood, another half-hour down the road. And it would take over an hour to get him to Phoenix, even if a helicopter was called.

Leon didn't have half an hour. Eric considered his options for two heartbeats, and decided.

"I'm taking you to Cottonwood, buddy. This'll have to hurt."

Eric picked the man up like a baby, and Leon groaned.

The groaning stopped halfway up the stairs, and Eric felt

Leon's head fall against his back. There was an ache in his chest, a sense of futility as he carried Leon into the garage and lowered him into the back seat of the car. Leon's skin was horribly tinged blue, and his breathing made sinister bubbling sounds. Eric had seen the signs before, in a far away war the newspapers had never heard of. He could try as hard as he could, and had to do that, but the result would be the same. Leon would be dead in a matter of minutes, and they were too far from a hospital to save him.

Eric gunned the engine, thumbed open the garage door and the gate at the same time. The tires squealed as he backed up, but one look in the rear view mirror and he slammed on the brakes hard.

Military vehicles were pouring in through the gate, and blocking his way out.

Eric opened the door so hard the hinge shrieked. "I've got a gunshot victim here! He's bleeding out!" he shouted. There was a Humvee, two vans and a jeep, all in desert beige, and the sight of the man in the jeep astonished him.

It was Sergeant Alan Nutt.

Eric gaped at him. Men poured out of the vans and Humvee. Alan gave orders, pointed, and some of the men ran right by Eric and headed for the garage.

"Is the door unlocked?" asked Alan.

"Yes," said Eric. He hadn't even thought about locking it. "My partner has been shot up bad. He needs immediate surgery." He opened the back door of the car.

"He'll get it," said Alan. Two men came up from behind him, carrying a stretcher. A second stretcher was being carried into the house.

Leon didn't make a sound when they put him on the stretcher and carried him to a van. Eric felt a lump in his throat when Alan put a hand on his shoulder. "We'll do what we can," said Alan.

Eric swallowed hard, and tried to distract himself. "How did you know we needed help here? You must be hooked in live to the surveillance cameras, but even so you got here awful fast."

"We'll talk later. Are you okay?"

"Yes. I got three of them. Leon got three others, and I know who was behind the attack. His name is John Coulter, and the next thing I'm going to do is kill him."

"The next thing you're going to do is fly Sparrow," said Alan. "Get in the jeep. I'm taking you straight to the base and under guard until the flight. Give me your keys. We'll clean up here, and lock the house for you."

Eric gave Alan his keys. Alan gave them to a corporal returning from the house. Two stretcher-bearers were with him, and they carried a man covered with a blanket. His eyes flickered, and he looked at Eric as he passed by him.

"We turned off the stove, sir. Your dinner was burned," said the Corporal. He took the keys, and went back to the house.

Eric nodded at the man on the stretcher. "Where did *he* come from? I looked in that tunnel, and Leon was the only person alive in there."

"Guess you didn't look close enough, sir," said Alan, and took Eric's elbow to steer him towards the jeep.

Eric went with him, got in the back seat of the jeep. Men were now carrying body bags out of the house. The injured man was put into the van with Leon, and the van sped away. The body bags were put into the other van, and the doors closed.

The jeep carrying Eric went out the gate, turned left, and sped towards the canyons, Eric sat in the back, counting numbers in his head.

Two injured men, and six body bags made eight people.

But including Leon, Eric had only seen seven.

* * * * * * *

At a distance, they followed the van that carried Leon. As Eric expected, the van was returning to the base. It raised a cloud of dust ahead of them once they were off pavement and bouncing on red earth and scree. When they arrived at the fenced-in hut that was an elevator, the van had gone underground, and they had to wait ten minutes for the gate to open again for them. They descended, raced along the main tunnel and passed the van parked at a cutout near the entrance to the portal bay. The back doors of the van were open, but nobody was inside.

Alan said nothing to him the entire trip, looked back at him a few times, and once reached back to pat him on the knee as if to say "It'll be all right."

But it wasn't going to be all right. Eric knew a mortal wound when he saw one, and had heard the last words of dying men. Leon had been shot defending a man who'd treated him like shit on more than one occasion, and now that man was feeling badly about it.

They were approaching the main parking area, and the jeep slowed. Eric leaned forward, and said loudly, "I saw the van back there. Is there another clinic nearby?"

Alan turned, but didn't look at him. "It's upstairs. There's another set of elevators."

The jeep stopped. Alan got out; pulled the seat forward for Eric to follow him, and the jeep sped away.

Alan smiled wanly. "Guess we had to throw your dinner in the trash. Aren't you hungry?"

Eric thought. "Yeah, I guess I am."

"Me too," said Alan. "Second shift is just finishing up in the mess. Let's see what they have."

They went to an elevator, Alan punched the button for level two, and the doors closed.

"You're taking good care of me, Alan," said Eric.

"Thanks. Just doing my job."

"You forgot your clipboard."

Alan smiled. "Yeah. Didn't need it this time."

"Oh, I thought taking notes was your job."

The elevator stopped, and the doors opened.

"I do whatever needs to be done, sir. Let's eat."

They turned left out of the elevator and walked a few yards to the mess hall. A few men in fatigues were sitting at long tables, talking after their meal, and mess was still open. Alan had his tray filled with meat, potatoes and veggies. Eric followed suit, and added a sliver of apple pie. They both got coffee at the end of the line, and sat down at a table away from the other men.

They ate quickly, and it was Eric who finally broke the silence.

"There are several questions I'm not asking, Alan, because I'm pretty sure I'm not supposed to know the answers. After tomorrow's test I might be a bit more demanding."

"I understand, sir. This has been a rough day for you. If you feel overwhelmed by it and can't sleep tonight I hope you'll tell us. You have to be on top of things early in the morning. The flight can be postponed if you're not ready."

"I'm paid to be ready, Alan," said Eric, "and eventually I *will* get the answers to my questions."

"Yes sir, I'm sure you will." Alan met Eric's steady gaze, held it, and Eric knew he was not talking to a soldier who made his living writing notes on a clipboard.

"You ever been in a firefight, sergeant?"

Now Alan smiled. "I think you know the answer to that one, sir."

"Well keep me alive until the flight test, and maybe your job will get easier."

They finished eating, and bussed their dishes. Alan took him back to the elevators, and they went up three levels. There was a long hallway with closed, numbered doors. Alan went to number ten, unlocked the door, and handed the key to Eric. "Someone will come for you at oh-three-hundred, sir. There's a beer and some snacks in the fridge."

"Thanks. See you in the morning?"

"I expect to be there, sir. Wouldn't want to miss it."

Alan turned, and walked away.

The room was simple, but not Spartan. There was a TV and a CD player, a selection of music from rock to classical, a few magazines, including *Sedona Monthly*. He opened the lone beer in the fridge, but left the cold meats and cheese he found there. Music, or sound of any kind, didn't appeal to him at the moment. He sat down on a sofa, sipped his beer and read the Sedona magazine. There was an ad in there for Nataly's shop. He suddenly wanted to call her, but there was no telephone. He wanted to tell her about Leon. He wanted to tell her how lousy he felt, how much he missed her, how much he loved her, and—

Whoa!

The thought remained. *My God, I'm in love with her. I have to tell her before she pushes me away.*

He resolved to call her right after the flight test.

Eric finished his beer and went to bed near twenty-one-hundred. There was absolute quiet in the room. Eric could hear the rush of blood with each pulse of his heart. He tried not to think about Leon, and failed. He imagined himself sitting with Nataly, her head on his shoulder. He kissed the top of her head, smelled pine, and she looked up at him with eyes a man could drown in.

He slept. Twice he came awake enough to know he was in a dark room. He'd been talking to Nataly, and John Coulter was there too, laughing about something that made Nataly angry with him. The Golden Man had appeared. Eric had asked him a question, but the man just smiled and didn't answer. Eric felt uneasy about that, an uncomfortable pit-of-the-stomach reaction that could have been fear. Nataly appeared again, and kissed him, and then he said how much he loved her. She frowned and didn't answer him, and then he felt something worse than fear.

He felt despair.

CHAPTER TWENTY-SIX
FLIGHT

The alarm made a terrible screech that shocked Eric awake. He'd only slept around five hours, but he didn't feel groggy. He splashed cold water on his face, and used soap to shave with a razor he found in a cupboard. He dressed, and nibbled on some cheese, and at exactly oh-three-hundred there was knocking on his door.

Two military policemen escorted him to the elevators and down to Sparrow's bay in the bowels of the base. When he first entered the bay, a cold blast of air shocked him. The bay was dark except at the center of the floor, where Sparrow and a crowd of men were illuminated with deep red light. Eric smelled JP-4, looked up and saw stars twinkling where the ceiling had been rolled to one side.

Two techs came up to him and he was hustled away from Sparrow to a side room where he spent over an hour being fitted with pressure suit and helmet. The last time he'd had one on was in the back seat of a Blackbird on route to a special killing for Uncle Sam.

The techs took him back to Sparrow, and fussed with his suit on the way. Techs were swarming over Sparrow, and Dillon was waiting for Eric by one wing, all suited up.

"Good morning," said Dillon.

"A bit early for that," said Eric.

"If this was Area 51 I'd be in the air by now."

Eric smiled. "Ah, hah. Suspicions confirmed."

There were no preliminaries. Eric stepped up onto Sparrow's wing behind Dillon, but climbed into the cockpit first. The pressure suit seemed to mold his body comfortably to the shape of the seat, and a tech leaned in to buckle his chest harness. Eric put on his helmet, but left the faceplate up. It was already uncomfortably warm in the suit.

There was a voice inside the helmet. "Radio check, Eric," it said. It was Rob Hendricks, soon to be their link to home.

"Roger, Wilco and out," said Eric.

"Cute. Well at least you're awake."

Eric wondered if Dillon and the others here for the test had heard about Leon and the firefight at Eric's house. Nobody had said anything about it yet, and Alan hadn't been in the bay when Eric arrived.

Dillon climbed in, and got settled while a tech fussed with him. For a moment, Dillon ignored Eric and studied a few lines of notes on a scrap of paper.

Eric pointed at it. "Nothing about our startup boards, I hope."

Dillon shook his head. "Nope, this is manual stuff, some notes on VTOL sequence. It's like flying a helicopter until we've cleared the bay."

The techs finished their fussing, saluted sharply and left. Dillon hit two controls with the flat of his hand and there was the rising pitch of a turbine whine as the canopy closed around them, and they were bathed in deep red light.

Eric's heart thumped harder than normal for several beats, and he breathed deeply to calm it. This was no static ground test, but flight in a strange aircraft that might or might not have awesome capabilities and be a deathtrap for its occupants in either case. The fact that Dillon had flown the thing to Mach 1 was little comfort at the moment.

Dillon looked at him. "Your eyes are getting big. I promise not to kill us until you start throwing all those switches, so if we blow up I can tell everyone it was your fault."

"Gee, thanks."

"You're welcome. Face plates down. Let's do it."

Eric pulled his faceplate down, felt it snap into place as Sparrow rocked beneath him and there was a sudden sinking feeling in his stomach. The darkened cockpit above his eye level suddenly lit up in a holographic display of their outside surroundings in wide angle. Dillon's hand moved slightly on one of several touch plates on the control panel, and they were lifting straight up. The cockpit vibrated softly, and beyond it was the faint whine of conventional turbines.

"Quiet in here," said Eric.

"Virtually soundproof," said Dillon, and his hand moved again on the touch plate.

The edges of the opened ceiling passed them, and fell behind, and Sparrow continued to rise for another minute before Dillon's left hand made a quick motion and Eric was pushed back into his seat.

"Leveling, going to quarter thrust," said Dillon, and Eric realized he was talking to flight com without Eric hearing the response.

Now would not be a good time to lodge a complaint, he decided.

Dillon pulled Sparrow's nose up, and went to quarter thrust. It was like the takeoff of a commercial aircraft, and Eric relaxed, even when their climbing attitude began to approach vertical.

"Half thrust," said Dillon.

Not too unpleasant, but unpleasant. Eric breathed deeply, a tightened diaphragm pushing against the invisible weight on his chest. The first, bright stars appeared ahead of them, and Sparrow shuddered.

"Mach 1, going to eighty-percent," said Dillon.

"Ooof," said Eric, and struggled to breathe, reached out a hand towards the panel in front of him.

The stars outside got brighter, and a new, green star lit up on the panel. Dillon turned his head towards Eric, his face invisible inside the helmet. "Going to startup sequence—now."

Eric threw the first switch on the panel. "One," he said.

A new light appeared, but nothing else happened.

"Two," said Eric, and threw another switch. The green light went on at the top of the panel by his right knee, as it had on the ground test. It was suddenly quiet in the cockpit. The weight on Eric's chest fluttered, and then lessened, though Eric knew their acceleration hadn't changed. The strangeness of it didn't escape him, but now his hand was poised above the next switch, and somehow he knew what would happen next."

Eric threw the switch. "Startup complete, and go to full thrust."

Dillon's left hand pushed a lever forward until it locked in place.

There was no shudder, no feeling of acceleration. It was as if they were floating, the stars ahead frozen in place, but on the lower left of the holodisplay movement blurred two rows of numbers. Dillon gestured at the screen, changing scales until the indicators could be followed and read.

"Whoa," Dillon whispered, then said loudly, "Passing Mach 6 at twenty kilometers, and accelerating. We're feeling no g forces here, and no vibration. Smoothest ride I've ever had. Mach 7, going to 8. Our fuel gauge isn't showing any change from when we began the startup sequence."

"Three more lights just went green on the second panel startup took us to. I didn't touch a thing," said Eric.

For the first time in the flight, Eric heard a reply from the ground.

"Say again," said Rob Hendricks.

"Three lights on the second startup panel went green together without me touching the switches. It happened at Mach 8, I think. There's one switch left, and a pressure plate with a radiating sun glyph on it. Don't ask me how I know, but I'm supposed to throw that switch now, and that's as far as we're going today."

"Mach 10, and climbing," said Dillon. "We're at thirty-five kilometers, sir. Have to admit I never thought Sparrow could do it."

"So throw that switch, Price," said Hendricks, "and then

we'll talk about the pressure plate."

"There's nothing to talk about on this flight. We have to figure out how to get home first." Eric threw the switch without hesitation, and saw Dillon's body tense in anticipation of something dramatic.

It was hardly that. There was no change in acceleration as Sparrow continued a vertical climb, now passing Mach 12 at an altitude of forty-four kilometers. A new icon appeared on the holodisplay, just above Eric's left knee. It showed the globe of planet earth. A light blinked from the western part of North America. Icons below the globe were labeled 'zoom' and 'set' and 'enable'. Eric gestured with a finger, and zoomed in on the blinking light, now appearing in a topo map of canyons and buttes.

"The base," said Dillon softly.

"And home," said Eric. Another gesture, a cursor moved to the blinking light, and Eric gestured to 'set' with his finger. The holodisplay flashed bright green, and was quiet again.

"That's it. We're done," said Eric.

"Now what? We're still climbing."

"Throttle back completely. Sparrow will do the rest."

"More advice from the angels?"

"More advice from the guys who gave us this thing. If you ask how I'm getting it, I'll just give you a blank look. Throttle back, and turn us around."

"That I can do, but deceleration might require more fuel than what we have left. This speed is way beyond what we expected."

"Don't worry about it. We're okay."

"Right. Flight com, Doctor Prices advises we terminate test and come down. We have a new icon on our holoviewer that is giving us the base location, and Price is saying we'll be brought in automatically. I can use the verniers to turn us around, but we're now at Mach 13 and fifty-four kilometers. I'm a bit concerned about adequate fuel for a deceleration burn, but Price says it's not a problem. Please advise."

Hendricks' response was immediate. "Price is correct.

Proceed with reorientation at zero throttle."

"No arguments? My God," said Eric, and forgot his mike was on.

"No need for argument, Doctor Price. I'm getting some advice at my end, too. There's a Mister Brown standing right next to me. He says you're doing fine."

"Well I could use some extra input right now. My instinct is telling me to enable the base-homing icon when we're reoriented, then sit back and relax, and that isn't making any sense to me."

There was a pause, then, "Mister Brown didn't say anything. He just smiled."

"Shit," murmured Eric.

Dillon throttled back, but there was no sensation of it. It had been like floating in a comfortable womb since completion of the startup sequence. Dillon's hands played over four pressure plates on the control panel. Stars moved. A crescent moon swept past their view, and then the bright blue panorama of planet Earth with puffy, white clouds off in the far distance at a rapidly approaching terminator. Directly below them it was still dark, but with clusters of lights showing from Phoenix and a fainter band that was probably Los Angeles.

"Okay, now what?" said Dillon.

Eric swallowed hard. "We let Sparrow do her job." He reached out to the base-locator icon with a finger, and touched 'enable'.

There was a thump, and Sparrow shuddered.

"We're doing a burn," said Dillon, amazed. A minute later he pointed at the gauges on the holoviewer. "What the hell? We're down to Mach 3, and no fuel has been used."

"And no g forces," said Eric. Sparrow must have us in some kind of protective field, and we're not burning conventional fuel, we're tapping that energy field in her gut. I bet we've been using that since startup."

Sparrow shuddered again. "Mach One," said Dillon, "and falling fast. We'll top out around sixty kilometers."

And seconds later they were falling.

"Phoenix is right where it was a few minutes ago," said Eric. "We're not just falling, we're flying."

"I'm not touching anything," said Dillon.

"Neither am I. Maybe we could play cards."

"You must have enabled a descent program. Look at the drift corrections on the icon. We're being guided in, and the engines aren't even on."

"The engines we understand, you mean. Better tell Hendricks."

Dillon called in, told Hendricks what was happening.

"Brown says to just ride her in. Your job is done. He says the next flight will be a simple extension of this one, but you'll be going to full power."

"Whatever that means. Let me talk to him," said Eric.

"I can't. He left here a minute ago."

"I want some explanations from someone," said Dillon. "I've been flying this thing on faith alone, and I won't do it again."

"Understood," said Hendricks, and broke off contact.

"Can't blame you," said Eric. "It was an exceptional risk just taking my word on what to do."

"So why did I do it?" said Dillon, and raised his hands. "Look at that. I'm just sitting here, and Sparrow is right on a glide path to the base. Did you know *that* would happen?"

"No, I didn't. I just knew which switches to throw, and when."

"That guy Brown, he's one of the people who brought Sparrow over to us. I met him the day I was oriented. Didn't say much, just pointed at things, and it seemed enough. Did he brief you?"

"I think so, I just don't know how. The one time I met him we talked about other things. Stuff comes to me in my sleep. Could be hypnotic suggestion, but I don't remember being hypnotized, and I have no idea why I was picked to receive the information. You're not the only one operating on faith around here. I've never flown anything in my life."

Dillon looked at the holodisplay. "Not even a vibration. We're down to four hundred miles an hour at forty thousand feet without a care in the world. God."

"Would you really give up the next flight if nobody answers your questions?"

Dillon chuckled. "Not a chance, but don't tell anybody that. Twenty thousand feet, and right on approach path, and nobody has told me if I'll have to bring her in on hover. I should be concerned, but I'm not. Brown said to ride her in, and that's what I'm doing, and why the hell haven't those green lights gone off?"

"I think they're all tied to the propulsion system in Sparrow's belly. I think it has something to do with dark energy."

"What?"

"Dark energy. It's seventy percent of the total mass-energy in the universe. I personally think it's vacuum-state-energy, particles popping in and out of existence. Our benefactors have found a way to tap into it."

"That sounds pretty advanced for the Russians," said Dillon.

"Yeah, that's been bothering me, too. I'm trying not to think we're dealing with little green men in disguise."

"Ten thousand feet. There's the Grand Canyon. The terminator is chasing us. Sparrow to Flight Com, we're coming in on auto. Advise, please."

"Right on glide path, and just ride her in," said Hendricks. "Maybe we won't need pilots anymore."

"That'll be the day," said Dillon. He hadn't relaxed during the entire descent, body rigid, hands hovering near the controls.

And then, quite suddenly, one-by-one, the green lights went out on the panels by Eric's knees. There was a whine, and a smooth vibration in the cockpit. Eric's buttocks pressed into his seat, and his stomach fluttered. The holodisplay flickered and disappeared, and they were flying blind.

"Oh shit," said Dillon, and grabbed his knees with his hands.

Eric felt Sparrow slide sideways, hover, then descend. There was a thump, a settling in his stomach, and the whine went away.

"Touchdown," said Hendricks, "and looking good. Congratulations."

Two techs were on Sparrow's stubby wings before Dillon popped the canopy open. Red light flooded them. Far above, the roof of the bay was sliding closed. A red-tinged cloud floated beyond it. The techs saluted smartly, and began fumbling with chest harnesses. Dillon pressed his helmet off, and grinned at Eric. "We've got to do this again real soon."

"I don't think that'll be a problem," said Eric, and flinched at a pinched ear as his helmet came off.

Hendricks was waiting for them on the floor, and he looked pleased. A small crowd applauded as Dillon and Eric stepped down off a wing and shook hands with their flight com. Eric immediately spotted Sergeant Alan Nutt in the crowd. Nutt smiled at him and gave a mock salute with two fingers. He held his usual clipboard and two thickly filled manila envelopes under one arm.

"Everything was seamless," said Hendricks.

"Pretty much, once we knew how to use that icon for the return trip. You can thank Doctor Price for that," said Dillon.

"Another revelation, Doctor?" said Hendricks.

"I don't know what else to call it."

"Relax. I asked Brown about it, and he said subliminal methods had been used by his people to feed you information in a secure way at critical points in our testing. But he would not tell me why you were favored over others to receive it. At this point I don't even care. We're scheduling a full-power test one week from today."

"Yes!" said Dillon.

"And for once, I don't have a clue as to what will happen," said Eric.

Hendricks paused, perhaps for dramatic effect, then, "If I believe what Mister Brown told me today, we will be taking our first step towards the stars."

Dillon wiggled an eyebrow at Eric. "We'd better pack a lunch."

Everyone laughed at that.

Eric was still checking when Sergeant Nutt stepped up to him and handed him the thick envelopes he'd been carrying. "You might need more than lunch, sir. Here's your operations manual for the final test. There are copies for both you and Captain Dillon. You should be ready to recommend a flight profile in three days."

"Thank you, Sergeant," said Eric. He opened the envelope, took out two slender volumes bound in hard covers and handed one to Dillon. Neither man bothered to open their manual. "Right now I'd really like a hot shower and some breakfast. I'm starving," said Eric.

And euphoric, he thought.

A sudden thought, and Eric drew close to Alan Nutt, whispered, "Anything new on Leon?"

"He's critical, sir. They're working on him right now. I'll let you know when there's something new."

Later, after he'd been bathed and fed, Eric retired to a conference room to do a quick overview of the new manual he'd received.

What he read there both shocked and thrilled him. Apparently the effect was the same for his pilot, because halfway through Eric's read there was a pounding on the door and then Dillon was there, gibbering with excitement.

"Do you believe what it says here? I've been testing high-performance aircraft for a decade, and I never even dreamed of this!"

"Me neither. I think we better be conservative about our flight profile."

"Over my dead body we will."

"I was afraid you'd say that," said Eric. "No matter. I think a higher intelligence has already decided our profile for us."

"I think maybe you're right," said Dillon, "but we'll file one anyway."

And they did.

CHAPTER TWENTY-SEVEN
DECEPTIONS

There were times when being military liaison was worse than a boil on Alan's ass, and listening to Davis rant and rave had been one of them. But in his years of diplomatic service, Alan Nutt had learned to know when it was safe to simply tune out a diatribe and go to a higher, peaceful state while his antagonist vented a spleen, so to speak.

It had taken Davis several minutes to vent his anger; all the while believing Alan was actually listening. Whatever, it had worked. A few minutes later, Davis was teachable again. The threat to the base was real, and required a substantial force to counter it. A foreign power that had gifted a priceless technology would provide that force at no cost, if only to protect their investment. What was there to be debated and discussed? The orders had come from the oval office. Davis could obey them, or relinquish command. End of discussion.

The argument had soured his stomach, and Alan was not in the mood for conversation or even comforting words for a man he really liked. Eric was working with Dillon in Sparrow's bay, finalizing a flight profile. If Alan came through there he would have Eric all over him about Leon, would have to say nothing was new, again, but the man was in good hands, et cetera, et cetera. To say nothing was new was truth, of course, but Leon had been rushed through the portal, and Alan had no idea what had happened to him on the other side. Eric's pain over his friend was horribly real, and came in powerful waves that Alan could not contend with at the moment. He avoided Sparrow's bay, went back to the main tunnel and took the back entrance past the machine shop to get to portal bay.

Three men were at the console when he arrived. They stood, and Alan motioned for them to be seated again. The bay below them had been cleared of all personnel, and was empty. Quarters had been readied on level four, and two service elevators would be used. The duty roster was divided into three shifts of thirty men, ten of them cloaked at all times.

It was ten minutes until activation. Alan poured himself a small cup of coffee from a thermos, and made small talk with the console operators to put them at ease in his presence. It was their first rotation away from home, and they were far too conscious of his rank when he was with them. It had nearly led to problems of explanation for him when Davis had been present on two occasions.

"You all must be getting anxious to go home. It's nearly a year, right?"

"Yes sir," said one man, a boy, really.

"Stuck down in this hole, no suns, no salt in the air. I'm working for surface leave, and the council is listening, but it won't happen until we're flying. I think it'll be soon."

The three young men smiled, but nobody spoke.

"A young person can go nuts down here. No women."

That earned a reply. "What are they like up there, sir?"

"The women? Oh, same as home, maybe a little more outspoken and aggressive, some gorgeous, some plain. Same people, Ensign. Remember that."

"I do, sir. I'd just like a chance to find out for myself."

"I'll work on it," said Alan, and patted the kid on the shoulder. Towards the end of the console, a board suddenly lit up. Heads turned.

"Incoming signature. B-42, sir."

"That's the one. Let 'em in, Ensign."

Fingers played over the console boards. The bay below darkened, and a wall shimmered red, then flashed brilliant blue in rippling waves. Alan exited the control room and went down a spiral staircase to the bay. As he walked towards the brightly glowing wall he saw the dimples come and go on its surface as the first, cloaked personnel came through. He counted ten, and stepped up close to the quiet ripples of the portal.

"Welcome to Hole-in-the-Ground, gentlemen. Good to have you with us. Looks like a 1694 day."

"A sunny day," came a voice out of clear air.

"Very good," said Alan, and looked at his watch. "I have ten-forty-two. Officer briefings and a lunch with the Council are at twelve hundred. Noncoms will be served in the Mess. I'm taking you straight to quarters to get settled in first."

The air shimmered, and the figures of ten men appeared in front of Alan. They were dressed in fatigues, were burdened with heavy field packs and helmets with darkened faceplates. All carried stubby, black automatic weapons. The man nearest to Alan put a hand to his throat and said, "Proceed," then held out his hand and smiled.

"Good to see you again, sir. It's been a couple of years."

"Jack," said Alan, and shook his hand. "Haven't you had enough yet?"

"It was either this or a desk, sir. How about you?"

"One more tour after this one, someplace where I can get a sunburn, then home. We could have a bad situation here, Jack."

"I understand, sir, but for once our Intel is good. Watt's outfit has been porous for the past year; people are positioning themselves to be in the President's favor when arrests begin. His mercenaries are good, but they won't have time for rehearsal. We'll be ready for them. I don't know about you, but I never did like Watt, even when he was the President's right hand. Shifty-eyed, always said exactly what people wanted to hear."

"He wanted to be President," said Alan. "He still does. The obsession has run away with him."

"Too bad," said Jack. "Our orders come direct from Blue Tower, sir. There was some argument about mining the portal and the bay here to lower the risk to our own personnel, but in the end they accepted the value of keeping the portal intact for the star craft project. No prisoners are to be taken. That includes Watt."

"I agree," said Alan, "but we'll have to find him first. Let's get you settled."

Three lines of men had marched out of the portal and arranged themselves in three platoons behind the single squad of men who had been cloaked. Jack turned to face them.

Alan whispered, "Elevators are to your left. One platoon at a time. Cloaked personnel remain here until the rest are settled."

Jack barked a command, and one platoon moved off. Ten men spaced themselves at regular intervals around the bay, and disappeared from view. Jack went with the first platoon, came back later for the second, then the third, and Alan joined him for the ride up in the elevators.

The flickering, shimmering wall in the bay went to orange, then red, and was rust-colored rock again. The lights went out, plunging the bay into darkness. Above the floor, a dim red light went on in the control room.

A door snicked shut, and the portal bay was peaceful again.

* * * * * * *

Dario Watt had done all he could to create a positive atmosphere for the meeting. The boardroom was large, with variable lighting from brilliant to near darkness. The air conditioning was more than adequate and the chill would serve to shorten debate on any trivial matters that arose. Most importantly, the air would remain fresh, the odor of his guest neutralized and swept away. The slightest hint of it would be offensive even to the least sensitive of the few men who had remained loyal to Watt, those men who were destined to serve on his cabinet once he had taken power. Privately he agreed with their beliefs in ethnic purity, but now was not the time to indulge in it, a conclusion he knew was not lost to any of them.

The meeting began promptly at seven, and Watt used the

half-hour he'd allotted himself to explain why it was necessary to move so quickly, that once the star craft was in space it
would be virtually impossible to destroy it with the resources
available to them. Everyone seemed to agree, and there were
no questions or arguments. The longer they waited the more
chance their operation would be discovered by a president who
had previously shown no mercy to dissidents. Discovery meant
death for all of them.

At seven-thirty there was a knock on the door and Watt
himself answered it. Ustiss Kroic had dressed himself in military blues, and saluted sharply. Watt ushered him in and seated
him by his side at the end of the big conference table. The five
other men had seated themselves near the other end, in anticipation of Kroic's arrival.

"I hope you had a pleasant trip," said Watt.

Kroic's voice was the sound of a small engine needing
tuning. "Only because we arrived with embassy personnel in
the dead of night. There were few people to gawk at us. My
troops arrived before us on a private jump ship."

Kroic paused, and absently scratched an unusually thick
scaly patch on his face with a long fingernail. "It is very dry
here," he said.

"Misters have been arranged for your quarters," Watt said
pleasantly, then, "What I would like for this meeting is a brief
summary of your strategy for the operation, and the probability
of its success."

"Of course," said Kroic. "I must first say that based on the
information I've been provided there will be little opposition to
a lightning strike. The bulk of my force will be used to trans-
port ordinance for destruction of the target. There is only a
police force to contend with, but the ordinance comes in four
large crates that must be moved quickly to optimize positioning
for maximum effect. The bays are separated by twenty feet of
rock. The individual weapons are moderate in yield, but shock
reinforcement will take out both bays and a one-mile section of
tunnel simultaneously. I guarantee this."

"Won't the weapons be detected when they come through?" asked a man at the far end of the table.

"Our intelligence efforts have indicated the portal has never been equipped with radiation detectors at any wavelength. The one installed for the Americans is an older, commercial model, not military. The crates will be brought through as supplies for the base, and preset to detonate within a few minutes. Half my force will be cloaked, the rest disguised as laborers."

"Really?" said another man. "And how will you do *that*?"

"By the judicious use of thin polymer masks, and darkened face plates. We wouldn't want to frighten anyone." Kroic's voice dripped hostility, and matched the tone of his inquisitor.

The odor that burst from Kroic's body was like fecal matter in moist earth, and Watt fought hard to suppress a gagging sensation. "The plan is excellent, but ordinance placement is critical. Your people must remain until that is accomplished, and the portal must be closed before detonation. Do they understand the risks?"

"Yes," said Kroic, his voice a low rumble. "They are professionals, all of them. Their courage is beyond question."

"Portal shutdown and detonation must be synchronized," said a man in gloom at the end of the table. "Our own facility can be destroyed if there's an error in timing."

"Our plan includes a twenty minute window. I will carry a remote that can reset the timers, but you must control the portal. We must be in constant communication."

"Absolutely," said Watt.

"If all goes well the crates will be delivered and properly placed, and we will leave without incident. At worst there will be a limited exchange with a small contingent of guards and police and we will withdraw under fire. The end result will be the same, but you must keep the portal open during this time."

Kroic half smiled, half scowled at the men at the other end of the table, and it was an unpleasant thing to see.

"I will be there to oversee everything," said Watt, and gestured to the others. "We will all be there, gentlemen. That's two days from now, the usual morning transmission at nine. Our usual friends have been paid, and the preparation bay will be open only for our group at eight. The transmission will not be logged in; officially there will be a two-hour portal hold for maintenance. Unofficially this is a private, black market operation, and the people we've dealt with have supported such in the past. There can be no hint of a military operation until it has begun. Weapons must be out of sight, and disguises intact."

"As I've been instructed," said Kroic.

"Yes, and now I'm sharing it with the rest of you."

There were questions. Watt could see it in the eyes of the others, but they all held their tongues.

"Are there any questions for Commander Kroic?" asked Watt, and saw the mercenary's posture go rigid beside him.

"No?" He turned to Kroic. "Funds have been deposited as you instructed."

"They are received, and will be distributed. It is a generous sum."

"The future of our civilization is worth it," said Watt.

Kroic made a strange sound in his throat, but said nothing, and stood up to leave.

"Thank you for coming, Commander. We'll see you in two days."

Kroic nodded, walked in his heavy-footed way to the door, and left the room.

A long silence followed. Watt poured a glass of water and drank it slowly.

"He disgusts me," said a voice in the darkness.

"I know, and you made little effort to hide it. That is stupid, my friend. We have no supporters for what we're doing. They will surface, of course, when we are done. Until then we work with whomever we have to, and you'll be wise not to jeopardize it. Besides, our association with Kroic and his mercenaries will soon be terminated."

"So? You've paid him, and the money can be traced."

"There is no money. The accounts have been terminated."

"But he checked them!"

"Electronically. Better that he did it in person. I collected on a small political favor that was long overdue."

"If he finds out he'll come after all of us."

"He won't live to find out. There is going to be a premature shutdown of the portal during operations, a minimum of five seconds before detonation. It will be much sooner than that if the operation goes too smoothly. In any case, our mercenary colleagues will not be returning to serve as witnesses against us. The blame for the entire operation, in fact, will be theirs."

"Their government will deny any involvement."

"Let them. Any hearings will show they have indirectly supported mercenary operations in the past. They are not friends of ours. It will be another challenge for the new president to show the people who our true friends are."

The others were now silent. Watt detected discomfort. "You all knew there were risks from the beginning. Have you lost faith in me?"

"I would feel better if we were far away on other business when the operation commences. I don't see why any one of us has to be there. Even you, Dario."

It was the same man, Elias Trent, who continued to question the plan. The others remained silent. Watt wondered if the man acted alone, or as a spokesman for the other four.

"I must be there to order portal closure, and you will be there to concur with my decision. There will be no operation without the presence of all of us. Two days from now—at eight—prep bay. If you are not there I will send someone after you, and you will never miss a meeting again. Am I being clear?"

A pause, then, "Yes, but you need not threaten us, Dario. We became involved to rid ourselves of a president who works to give away our sovereignty, and we will see it through."

"Thank you, Elias. That is reassuring. I'll see you in two days, gentlemen. Try to relax until the moment is upon us. We are making history."

The other men nodded silently, stood, and followed him out

of the room. They went their separate ways, Watt taking an escalator up one floor to his Ministry office, the others descending in elevators to the street level below.

Or so he thought at the time.

* * * * * * *

Across the street from the Ministry building, five men huddled around a corner table and sipped tea.

"What do we do now? He's crazy. There will be war over this. The president will dig out the truth and be a hero," said one man.

"The president has more than a few enemies. We can expose the star craft project without destroying it, and then the threat will be real. We can win in the polls, but if we kill people we'll lose," said another.

Elias Trent leaned closer and said, "I can warn them about the attack, give them the time and strategy so they can be ready for it. I have an old friend stationed at the base, and he will believe what I say. If you agree, I'll send the message today."

"The mercenaries might succeed anyway."

"It will be up to the Americans. The best we can do is warn them. It's really the only thing we can do," said Elias.

"Then do it," said one of the conspirators. "It could mean our lives when we're at the mercy of the court."

"Our president might be more forgiving than we think," said Elias. "Our lives will be in more danger when the operation begins, but we must be there for it. At the first sign of trouble I'm running. Follow me if you wish, or not."

The other men left Elias at the table, and hurried away. Elias made a call on his headphone, then typed a message on his pocket computer and loaded it on disk. A few minutes later a man came across the street from the Ministry Building. He wore the cap and coveralls of a stevedore who worked portal shipments. He came straight to Elias' table and sat down. Elias handed the disk to him.

"Wear your IR when you go through. Locate any cloaked guard and tell him this is for Commander's eyes only, and urgent. If you can't deliver it, get right back to me so I can try another way."

Elias handed the man several folded credit notes. "For your trouble," he said.

The man said nothing, pocketed money and disk, and went away.

Elias sat for a few seconds, and then made another call.

"The time for the attack has been set, and I just sent them a warning. I'll have to be there, otherwise Watt will call it off and my usefulness will be over. Yes, the others have agreed, but they're scared to death of the consequences. I think a show of mercy might be politically wise if we live through this."

Elias listened a moment, then, "I appreciate that, sir. It's my job, and I knew the risks when I started it. Maybe I'll get lucky. Goodbye, sir, and thank you for the opportunity to serve you."

He broke the connection, and felt the sting of tears in his eyes.

His president had been sobbing while he praised what Elias had done for him.

CHAPTER TWENTY-EIGHT
CONFESSIONS

The guard smiled and waved Eric through the gate. Clouds had moved in and were threatening rain, and that meant lightning. Tires squealed as Eric negotiated the hairpin curves up to the summit of Nataly's butte. He'd offered to pick up something for the meal, and stopped by Safeway for a quart of peppermint ice cream, which was her favorite. She had given cook and houseboy the night off, so they would be alone. They hadn't seen each other in two weeks. Eric felt a terrible apprehension. As much as he loved her, as much as he wanted her, there were things that had to be said.

He parked by the pool. By the time he reached the front door the first raindrops were falling and there was a distant rumble from the south. The nearby spires of Cathedral Rocks were already shrouded in mist. Nataly opened the door, and her smile was enough to brighten the sky. She slid into his arms as he stepped inside, looked up at him and said, "Hi, stranger," very softly.

Eric kissed her cheek, her lips. "Sorry I've been so busy."

"Me too." There was a sudden gust of wind, Nataly reached out and closed the door behind them.

Eric handed her the little bag containing the ice cream. "Your favorite."

That smile again. A table had been set by the balcony window, and candles were lit. "I had to bring everything inside," she said.

Lightning flashed outside, and the beamed ceiling trembled.

"Good thing," said Eric.

Nataly put the ice cream in the freezer, came back and took his hand and led him to the big sofa in the front room. A CD was playing, some kind of chants, very deep. "What's that?" Eric asked.

"Tibetan throat singing," she said, "very relaxing."

They sat. Nataly leaned her head against his shoulder. "I've missed you."

"Me too," he said. The vibrations of the singing seemed to resonate with something deep inside him.

"I have a roast cooking. It'll be half an hour until dinner. What should we do until then?"

Eric looked down at her. Her lips were parted, and her eyes sparkled playfully. A wonderful feeling started in his heart and worked its way across his chest. He sighed, and stroked her lower lip softly with a finger.

"I have a suggestion, but it might take longer than half an hour."

"Oooo," she said, and snuggled closer.

"Better not. Dinner will get burned."

"Let it."

Eric leaned over and kissed her softly. "Can't resist a good roast, and I can't resist you. I'm in love with you, Nataly."

"I love you too," she murmured. "What are we going to do about it?"

"I don't know."

"You don't know? You *still* don't know?"

How easily the lies came to him. "The job is uncertain. Leon is visiting the corporate center in Phoenix to plead our case. We might have to close the office here."

Nataly frowned. "So what happens? You move to Phoenix?"

"Maybe."

"A two hour drive. There are people here who work in the valley, but live here. They come home weekends, or work from home."

"The company is expanding, going more international. I'd be

gone all the time." Eric had a hard time looking at her when he said it; her gaze was so intense. Sudden anger was there.

"So quit, retire, whatever you want to call it. A job should never interfere with the rest of your life, Eric, unless the job *is* your life. I want to think that isn't true for you anymore."

"You have a business. You work long hours."

"But I leave it behind when I come home to this big, empty house."

Nataly reached up and folded her arms around his neck. "I want to come home to *you*, Eric. Live with me."

For one second, the room seemed to spin around him. "Nataly, I—"

"I'm not asking you to marry me, unless you really want to. I just want to be with you, all the time. Be my business partner, my life partner. Life can be grand for us here, Eric. It's where we belong."

"I don't know where I belong."

"You belong with me. I don't know where else I could find someone like you, and I'm not letting you go. You said you love me."

"I do." Tears blurred Eric's eyes. Nataly's arms were tight around his neck, her breath hot on his face. "But if you really knew me you wouldn't talk like this, you'd run for your life." *I can't tell her. I'll lose her. I'm living a lie.*

Nataly's eyes darkened. "You can't live a lie with me, Eric Price. I know exactly who and what you are, and have been, and it makes no difference to me. I want to spend the rest of my life with you."

Eric grasped her shoulders and held her at arms' length. "What? Just what do you think you know about me?" *An intuitive, that's what she is. She's guessing.*

"I know everything: the agency you work for, your history with it, the people you've killed, everything you're doing at the base. I helped you do it. I helped to give you the information you needed. I'm part of it, Eric, and I've been living a lie too. I know about your John Coulter. He is an enemy of the entire human race. He tried to kidnap me to intimidate you, but he failed. My friends protected me, and they've protected you. I've known the man you call Mister Brown since I was a little girl. It's nearly over, Eric, and then you'll be gone. I won't let it happen. I *won't!*"

Nataly grimaced. "Ouch! You're hurting me."

Eric's fingers were digging into her shoulders. Everything was coming apart. She was a plant, a way to get to him from the very beginning. The quiet dinner, the vision of her body glowing, the golden man, that's when it had begun. She had burrowed into his mind like a mole, and programmed him for her masters.

"It's all been a setup from the start. You didn't have to say you loved me. You had me hooked good, lady. I'd kill you right now, except it looks like you're working for the good guys. So who are they? Where are they from? You must be a sleeper, planted here at birth." Eric shook her for emphasis. Tears were streaming down her face.

Nataly closed her eyes as tears gushed. "Oh Eric, I *do* love you, I really do. Now I've ruined everything. When you started making excuses again I just lost it. I shouldn't have said what I said. Oh God, the Council will be furious. Vasyl will be furious."

"The people you're working for?"

When she opened her eyes they were blazing green. "I'm not working *for* anyone. I'm working with my own people, *your* own people, trying to help the human race reach the stars."

"What?"

"Let go of me!" she shrieked with a fury that shocked him, and he released her.

Nataly put her head in her hands, and sobbed. "It wasn't supposed to be like this. I was never supposed to fall in love with you, but even that first night I saw the part of you that is like me, and—and, well, I have a human heart, too. It was so easy to give it up."

She was talking in riddles, he thought. "If this is supposed to make me feel sorry it isn't working. So you're an agent for the good guys on my side, whoever they are. You've been a conduit for information I needed. You didn't have to make me get crazy about you. You mind-fucked me, Nataly. That isn't the first time a woman has done it to me, but I sure never expected it from you!"

Eric's voice cracked, and tears burned his eyes. Nataly looked at him and broke into hysterical sobs. Eric watched her helplessly, was embarrassed by his own tears.

"Don't worry, I'll get over it. Over the years I've built up some good armor plate in my head. And when the pressure gets too bad I can always go out and kill someone. That's who I *really* am."

Nataly shrieked, and fled from the room. A door slammed.

"Well, I think it's safe to say that dinner is off." Eric stood up, took a deep breath and let it out slowly. He wiped his eyes with a hand. "That's what I get for thinking things could be different."

Coldness spread across his chest, but it felt like his heart was being cut in half. "Don't bother!" he shouted. "I'll let myself out!"

Eric left the room with the table set with delicate china and illuminated by candlelight. The odor of nicely cooked meat wafted from the kitchen, and there was the distant sound of sobbing from behind a closed door. The tears that gushed again made him furious, and he slammed the door so hard behind him it sounded like something fell off the wall and hit the floor inside the house.

The guard at the gate saw him coming and opened the gate quickly, leaned out of the kiosk to wave at him but jerked back inside as Eric roared past in his car. He ran two stop signs and a light getting home. He pulled the telephone cable from the wall, had two beers for dinner, and cleaned his guns. The smell of Breakfree and powder solvent was somehow calming to him, as if he were preparing for a firefight.

He went to bed early and fell exhausted into sleep. There were no dreams about starships, Nataly or a golden man this time.

He was alone again.

* * * * * * *

Nataly heard the front door slam so hard it shook the house. Her instinct was to run after him, but her body refused to move. She hurt all over, and the pillow's surface at her cheek was soaked. She lay there for a long time, wanting to think it was all a bad dream and soon she would wake up. The real Natasha was not capable of such foolishness, but could imagine it.

Reality returned, and with it the consequences. In a moment of blind frustration she had not only lost a love she would never find again, she had jeopardized a project her people and her father had worked long and hard for. Yes, it was Eric's fault, in a way. She sensed his love, but also his reluctance to commit, always leaving a door open so he could flee from a relationship. It was like a switch had been thrown, and suddenly she'd lost all patience, had an emotional meltdown she hadn't even imagined before. This was not Natasha. But who was it?

Natasha returned to her at that instant. She couldn't change what was done, but she could warn others about it. She rolled off the bed, snatched the telephone from the nightstand and dialed.

Thank God he was there. "Vasyl, something horrible has happened."

She told him everything, with every detail.

"Oh Natasha," said Vasyl. "This couldn't have happened at a worse time. I should never have gotten you involved. Don't try to contact Eric again until after the flight. I'll do what I can."

Vasyl hung up on her before she could reply.

She went out to the kitchen and found the roast still cooking and beginning to burn. A small voice urged her to throw it in the trash. She ignored it, wrapped up the meat in aluminum foil and put it in the refrigerator.

She went to the living room, blew out the candles on the table, but left the table settings where they were. The storm outside was breaking, and the clouds to the southwest were beautifully tinged red.

A kind of numbness overtook her. Nataly undressed and went

to bed. The entire pillow surface was soaked with her tears. She turned the pillow over, and soaked it again.

CHAPTER TWENTY-NINE
THUNDER IN THE BAY

There had been many emotional experiences in his life, but sitting home alone for a day and a night after the fight with Nataly now ranked among the worst of them. Eric had reconnected the phone the morning after, but no calls had come in. He was crazy to think she might call. It was all a sham, a ruse to accomplish the tasks of the people running her. Naming Vasyl had possibly been a slip. A Russian name. She was undoubtedly a sleeper, probably trained in Siberia before she was an adult. They would have done well to keep up her psychological profile. She was still young, and lonely. Maybe she really had fallen for him, and in doing so made a mess of things. Her masters might think Eric would now be so distraught he couldn't do his job. *I will not give them that satisfaction*, he thought, but a secret part of him also knew he would be protecting Nataly.

He survived the day by taking two five mile morning and evening runs in the back country, penetrating so far into the wilderness area that he spooked a javelina that ran squealing from him. Once, he had to leap high over a rattlesnake basking in the morning sun. The exercise left him catatonic for part of the day, and that night he slept like a dead man.

Next morning the usual van arrived for him at five, and by six he was taking the elevator down to Sparrow's bay.

The doors opened, and four guards were standing there. "Emergency, sir," said one of them. "We'll walk you to the bay."

The guards walked on either side of him the few yards left

to the personnel door of Sparrow's bay. Four more guards were standing there at port arms, looking grim.

"What's the problem?" asked Eric. "I have a flight coming up in the morning."

"Sorry, sir, it's been scrubbed. Sergeant Nutt will explain when he gets here."

"What?" Eric's face flushed with anger. *Hell, she told someone what happened, and now they're going to pull me out of the assignment. How stupid can things get?*

"Red alert, sir. The base is being locked down. That's all I can say."

Mother of God, if I can't have a relationship then at least let me have the work. Oh great, now I'm pitying myself. What the fuck is going on? Eric was tempted to force his way past the guards, but then there was a call from behind him.

"Eric! Hold on. I'll get you inside."

Sergeant Alan Nutt walked towards him, a cheerful smile on his face, and clipboard in hand. "Sorry, but we've had to delay the flight a couple of days."

"Why?"

"I'll show you," said Alan.

The guards moved aside. Alan opened the personnel door, and Eric followed him inside.

The bay was in chaos, people swarming everywhere. The big door was open and a flatcar had been brought in on the rails. The shop and welding space was empty, equipment packed in crates along the wall, and the big crane hovered far above Sparrow, lowering a giant hook towards it. Men were crawling all over the craft, attaching a web of cables and chains.

"We've received word that the base will be under attack in a matter of hours. We're moving Sparrow to a safer place in case the fight spreads to this area," said Alan.

"Attack by who? This base is nuke proof from the surface."

"It's not coming from there. We've been warned that a mercenary force will be coming through the portal to place nuclear weaponry here and detonate it. The fight will be in the portal bay. I just came from Davis. He wants you out of it."

"That's bullshit. I came here to get rid of saboteurs, and now they're out in the open and you want me to disappear. That's not going to happen, Alan."

"Colonel's orders, sir."

"I don't work for him. All you have is military police. You'll need all the help you can get. How many are coming at us?"

"Maybe a hundred."

"You might have half that in military police."

"We have what we need. One more man won't make a difference. You're needed to fly Sparrow. It's been decided, sir."

"Like hell it has. I'm seeing Davis." Eric walked away, but Alan hurried to catch up to him.

"He won't see you."

"I'm not asking."

"Sir, the fight could take out several bays. We can't risk your life or Dillon's. You have to stay with the star craft."

"You didn't tell me who's behind the attack, sergeant. These are the people I was sent here to stop." Eric punched a button, and an elevator door opened.

"One of Brown's own people. Looks like one man has been behind everything from the start." Alan looked nervous, his eyes darting around as the elevator ascended. "Sir, this stink you're making is going to get me in trouble."

"Sorry, Alan. Hazards of the trade."

The elevator doors opened. Alan grabbed his arm, but Eric pulled him along the few steps to Davis' office door and pushed it open without knocking.

"I tried to stop him, Colonel," said Alan.

Davis stood up from behind his desk, and slammed both hands on it. "Even NSA can't give you the authority to enter a commandant's office without knocking, Price. Now get the hell out of here and try it the *right* way!"

Eric walked up to him in a fury, and whatever was showing in his eyes made Davis sit down hard. "I don't give a shit about your protocol. I want to know why a firefight is coming with the guys I'm after and I'm being sent away someplace else."

Davis' eyes seemed to cloud over. "What?"

"He can't be involved, Colonel," said Alan. "If he's killed we'll be set back weeks or even months. We're running out of time."

"I was sent here to kill bad guys, and you're not letting me do it. I think you can kiss your retirement goodbye."

Davis glared at Alan. "Now wait a minute. We didn't talk about Price. What did you tell him?"

"We cannot risk his life, Colonel. I forbid it."

Davis' face went purple. "You *forbid* it? I am the commander of this base, whether you like it or not, and *I* do the forbidding around here. If Price wants to fight, let him fight. I don't give a shit whether he lives or dies. Dillon can handle everything from here on."

"We had a agreement, Colonel. You agreed to—"

"I am in charge of this base. Get the hell out of here, sergeant. I'll talk to Price without your interference."

"I'm going to the Council right now," said Alan.

Eric was astonished. Alan's eyes blazed, and his fists were clenched. It was certainly not a good way to retain rank. "Price had better be here when I get back," said Alan. He turned, left the room, and didn't bother to close the door behind him.

"Close the door," said Davis, and Eric closed it.

"We need to talk."

"Yeah?"

"That little scene should show you the kind of crap I've had to deal with around here. He goes to the Council, they go to the Pentagon, and I get new orders. I'm not running anything here."

"No insubordination in today's military, I guess."

"He's not one of mine," said Davis, and sat down again. "He works for Brown and the other guys who brought us Sparrow. Brown's spy, I'd call him, and he's smooth, moves freely among our personnel, and knows everything. Might be American, but I don't think so."

"Is he telling the truth about the base being attacked?"

"I believe it. I've never seen him so emotional, near panic. He's scared, and that means we should be scared. They never let our people into the portal bay, just the control area. My police will set up a perimeter beyond there, in Sparrow's bay and the main tunnel. He says they don't need us to repel the attack. Maybe he'll use that electromagnetic shield thing on the portal."

"I've seen it," said Eric. "That red glow, but when it lifts off all you see is inky blackness. How far back does the tunnel go? Maybe they have people stationed inside it."

"Never got near the thing," said Davis. "They could have an army in there, for all I know. End of a career, Price. That's why the Pentagon put me here. Fuck 'em, I'm still in charge. You want a fight?"

"You bet. Alan says they know who's behind the attack, and when they're coming. I want to be there."

"I can get you into the control area. That's the best I can do."

"Close enough. When?"

"Right now. The attack is expected in two or three hours. It'll take nearly that long to get Sparrow out of there."

"Let's go."

"Wait," said Davis, opened a drawer and took out a photograph, handed it to Eric. "If you see that guy during the attack, do me a favor and shoot him in the head. He's the man behind everything bad that's been going on. I want him dead, and so does Brown."

Eric looked at the photograph, and shook his head. "I'm not surprised. This guy has been giving money to my 'business' partner and me. He wants intel on Sparrow and our test results. Says it belongs to a client of his who wants it back."

Davis' face flushed. "He told me a big aerospace company wanted to develop Sparrow as a commercial carrier. Big money for me, he said, and I even bought it until the sabotage started. At least you collected your bribe. All I got was shit. So kill him."

"If I see him, and that's unlikely. We'll be fighting his hired help. Guess his client wants Sparrow destroyed if he can't get it back."

"Where'd you get the picture?" asked Eric. It showed the head and shoulders of John Coulter in suit and tie, a slight smile on his face. Eric handed the photograph back to Davis.

"Got it from Brown. He said if we ever saw this man we should shoot him on sight."

"Well I'll certainly oblige him if I get the chance, but it looks like Brown doesn't want me to have that chance."

"Screw Brown. Let's get out of here," said Davis. "I'll get you some weapons on the way."

They left the office, stepped into an elevator and descended one floor. "Confession time," said Eric. "I have a small auto on my ankle and something bigger squirreled away in that little niche you gave me that I hardly ever use."

"That's tunnel level. We'll go there last. Right now I want you looking like you belong here. Fewer questions that way," said Davis.

The doors opened. Davis led him down a curving hallway to an area caged in by heavy wire mesh. He punched in a code on a panel lock and the door clicked open. Inside were rows of shelves floor to ceiling and racks of M16 rifles. Davis pointed to three shelves loaded with boxes, boots and heavily padded helmets. "Sizes on the boxes. Grab an issue, boots and helmet. I'll give you five minutes to look like a soldier."

Eric found what he needed and stripped down while Davis selected two rifles from the racks and extra magazines in pouches on a shelf near them.

It took him seven minutes to dress, and squeeze into a vest. Davis slung a rifle over his own shoulder, handed the other to Eric and gave him an appraising look. "Okay, you're a private again. Hopefully they won't notice you're missing a name patch. I'm assigning you to guard duty in the portal control room."

He handed Eric a belt loaded with magazine pouches. "Load and lock, private."

Eric put the belt on, pushed a magazine into the M16 and worked the slide. "I still want my other handgun," he said.

Davis nodded, loaded his own weapon, and locked the supply cage behind them. They went down one level to a short hallway where Eric had been given a small desk and chair in an open niche in red rock closed by a barred door, making it look like a cell. Eric retrieved the long slide Colt he'd kept there since the attack on Leon, but left the military Beretta. At times like this, the stopping power of the forty-five seemed appropriate for the job.

In the tunnel area men and vehicles were hurrying every-where. Heads didn't even turn at the sight of two more helmeted soldiers carrying rifles. Davis led Eric to the door they'd used before to gain access to portal bay, a door from a dock formed by a cutout in the main tunnel. Eric suddenly remembered seeing the ambulance parked there when Leon had been taken away. Opposite the transparent wall of the machine shop was a set of elevator doors that had likely taken Leon up or down for treatment. But was he still alive?

They went through the card-key door, and two soldiers watched Davis slide his card at the second door and punch in his code. A few yards ahead Davis pushed open the door to the control room, and they stepped inside.

"Security. I'm placing a guard in this control area. Stay out of the way, private," growled Davis.

Four young men were hunched over the control panel, and barely looked up when they entered. It was the same four Eric had seen before, including the one who had passed him a message. But there were no signs of recognition from a brief glance. The men seemed totally absorbed by their work, and with his helmet pulled low Eric had a faint hope he would not be recognized. Davis gave him a thumbs-up and exited the room, leaving Eric standing in a corner next to two thermoses of something and four empty cups. He unslung his rifle and moved it to port arms to assume his role. The other four men played hands over the control panel, jabbered something incoherent into throat mikes, and didn't look at him.

The floor of the portal bay was relatively quiet, a few people walking here and there, and one wall shimmered red. The floor was empty of crates or other containers. Eric pressed himself back into his corner when he saw Alan Nutt come out a side door and walk over to the shimmering portal to talk to two military policemen stationed there. The conversation was short. Alan walked around the periphery of the bay, still talking. Suddenly he put a hand to his ear, and looked straight up at the control room. He scowled, shook his head and walked back to the door he'd entered by. He was still talking when he exited the bay.

Eric tensed. The young man who'd passed a message to him earlier now turned to look at him.

"You're not supposed to be in here, sir. We have a bad situation coming up."

"I know all about it, son, and I'm here to defend this base like you are. When the shooting starts I need to be down on the bay floor. How do I get there?"

"Right behind you, sir, but when the door closes you can't get back inside."

The seam ran near his left shoulder, so narrow he'd missed it, and there was a small finger latch for opening the door.

"Anything else I should know?"

"It's a spiral staircase down to the floor. The commander knows you're here, and says to stay close to a wall until the targets are identified. He's not happy with you, sir."

"Neither am I, son, but it's my fight too."

The kid gave him a faint smile and turned back to the console. Nothing unusual happened for the next few minutes except that four men set up a row of posts near the end of the bay and hung a light canvas between them. When they were finished, Alan Nutt came out again to inspect it, then exited. One part of the bay was now screened off from the other, and the reason was obvious a few minutes later. Dozens of armed marines came out of the door Alan had exited by. They pressed themselves back against the walls, two men deep, each holding stubby weapons with long magazines and wearing goggles making them look like two-legged insects.

The bay was still, and quiet. Nothing moved. The kid who had spoken to Eric now glanced at him, and Eric saw fear there. He'd seen the look before on a kid making his first combat jump, a kid who was dead before he hit the ground.

Eric counted just less than twenty minutes until a red light blinked on the control console, and there were soft murmurings by the operators there. Other lights flickered, and the bright overhead lights of the bay dimmed to near darkness. The shimmering red wall flashed to a rippling blue and was quickly an inky void on the other side of the bay. Streamers of deep blue remained, flickering in and out. The men who came out of the darkness appeared suddenly, men in khaki overalls and lowered faceplates, and they guided powered forklifts laden with crates. *Supply delivery*, thought Eric. *What's so dangerous about this?*

The answer was not long in coming.

A steady stream of forklifts came out of the darkness without incident, deposited their cargo by a wall and turned to go back to the portal. At that moment three more forklifts appeared, and the bay was plunged into chaos. An alarm sounded with ear-splitting intensity and red lights strobed from the walls. The three forklifts moved left and right, mixing in with the earlier machines now trying to return to the portal. Behind them came three more, this time accompanied by dozens of armed men in marine uniforms. The men opened fire with automatic weapons and sprayed the entire area with bullets.

Eric gasped at the sight of gunfire being returned out of clear air from the walls around the bay, and then the marines behind the screen charged in, firing as they came.

Eric saw Alan Nutt come in behind them. He grabbed the latch of the door, slammed it open to the rattle of continuous gunfire, and hurried down a steep, metal staircase to the bay floor.

* * * * * * *

Deep in the bowels of the ministry building, the portal

rippled in shades of blue. The assembly floor was packed solid with hydraulic lifters bearing crates, and Kroic's heavily armed troops pressed in tightly behind them. Their faceplates were down, hiding the ridiculous masks they'd used to disguise their true faces from both friend and foe. The odors of their bodies remained mercifully close to the assembly floor.

On a balcony two meters above the portal floor Dario Watt stood with his four lieutenants and the two portal operators he had heavily bribed for the operation. According to Watt's plan, the lifetimes of the bribed ones were now less than a day. There would be no witnesses to show ministry involvement in an operation to be seen as instigated by an unfriendly government and carried out by Kroic and his mercenary soldiers.

Three of Watt's co-conspirators looked frightened to death, but Elias Trent seemed calm, even stoic, now that the hour had come. Perhaps Watt had underestimated the metal in the man. He had given all of them communicators, but only for listening. The power to command was his alone.

"One minute to initiation," Watt said softly. A portal operator nodded, one hand reaching towards the console.

"We're ready," said the gravelly voice of Ustiss Kroic.

Watt looked, but didn't find him in the crowd below. Dressed like the others, Kroic had the only detonation transmitter on his person, could set the timing in an instant, but only one time. This he would do when the American portal bay had been penetrated, and only then would he withdraw his forces.

The portal strobed red, and was blue again. Contact had been made, could not be interrupted at the receiving end. They were now committed.

"Go," said Watt.

The lifters and their operators went in first, then the three devices and a platoon of support troops, Kroic himself somewhere among them. At the rear of the assembly, twenty soldiers activated cloaking and disappeared from view, their exit only shown by transient ripples in the portal's surface. Communication was instantaneous. In high order n-space, the speed of light was astronomically high, and there were no time delays.

"Receiving fire! Cloaked defenders!" shouted Kroic.

"Press on, Commander," said Watt encouragingly.

There was a delay of a minute. Watt glanced at his colleagues. All four looked stricken.

"Heavy fire! A marine unit is here! One device is in place. I'm setting the timer for ten minutes. Pulling out in five. Acknowledge!"

"Acknowledge," said Watt, and looked at his watch.

One minute went by, then two, three, four and five.

Watt reached out to the console, and slapped his hand hard on it, palm down.

The portal operator jumped back in horror.

The portal rippled, went to red, then blue again, and was gone.

There was a horrible silence. Watt's colleagues, the portal techs, nobody dared to speak.

Watt smiled. "Now we wait—around five minutes. And then we check to see if the American's portal address is still operable." He turned and saw his colleagues, including Trent, edging away as if they were ready to run. "Only then do we leave, gentlemen. Stay where you are," he growled.

The men stopped moving, and stared at him.

They waited a full seven minutes, and then Watt turned to the frightened young tech standing next to him. "Reactivate the portal."

The tech took a step forward, was not yet in reach of the console when the portal opened up with a flash of red and blue.

A lifter came out of the portal, bearing a single crate.

At first sight of the crate, Watt glanced back at his colleagues in shock and surprise.

His colleagues were not there.

He looked back; saw two men pushing the lifter.

Heat seared Watt's forehead when he recognized one of them.

CHAPTER THIRTY
THROUGH THE PORTAL

Eric hit the floor in a crouch. Gone was the scientist, analyst, the gentle soul saddened by a lost love. All of it was swallowed up by something dark and purposeful and deadly within him. His heart was hammering hard and the fire of adrenalin burned in every vein in his body. He pushed himself back against a wall to survey the action, looking for a focus, and at first he wasn't seen.

The men who came out of the portal with crates that had set off the alarms had been caught in a terrible crossfire by Alan's hidden marines and also invisible sources all around the room. Most of them had gone down, some on one knee, firing wildly. Men pushing powered lifters had been shielded from the initial fire, but were now dropping one by one. Lifters roamed randomly around the bay without guidance, though one had been steered to a wall to Eric's right and parked there deliberately.

All firing was wild, and target identification treacherous. The invaders were dressed like marines, but the material of their uniforms seemed lighter or more highly reflective, even in the dim light, and they wore darkened faceplates. Eric focused on the faceplates, went to a kneeling position and squeezed off two rounds with his M-16. Two men dropped where they stood, face plates shattered. Another man closer to him turned and charged, firing a burst from his stubby, black weapon. Eric calmly fired twice as bullets smashed into concrete and metal above his head. The man pitched forward and slid on the floor, coming to rest a yard from Eric's position. His faceplate was ripped away and with it something white and shredded to pieces by sharp polymer. His cheek was against the floor, eyes yellow and open, staring accusingly at his killer. The face was brown, with scales like a large fish, and the open mouth showed a row of fierce-looking needle teeth.

What the hell?, thought Eric, but at that instant a horrible wave of fire came from the portal, and nobody was there to be seen. Bullets splattered all around him and he saw marines go down. Flashes of fire were coming from the area just in front of the portal, flashes out of clear air. There was a roar of fire from the marines to his right. Eric flipped the lever on his M-16 to auto and emptied a magazine, swinging the barrel back and forth to cover the space in front of the portal.

Bullets seemed to explode in midair, and men shimmered into view, staggering, and falling to the floor. Flashes of fire continued to spew forth from the air around them. Illusion or technology, but there were invading soldiers there, invisible to the naked eye, and it seemed that Alan's marines were seeing them while Eric could only shoot at fire flashes. Eric emptied another magazine before more men appeared out of nowhere to fall dead on the floor. The fire flashes stopped near the portal, but there were several shots from Alan's marines before an order was screamed and there were other sounds in the bay.

People were yelling and milling around. Several men had attacked three of the crates with pry bars and were vigorously dismantling them. Alan Nutt was screaming at the top of his voice, "Find the timer! Check all the bodies! *Move!*"

Eric stepped up to a marine who was rolling a corpse over with his foot. "What are we looking for?"

The marine showed him the palm of his hand. "About this size. Should have big numbers—like a clock."

Wood splintered under the prying of crowbars. Men were racing from body to body.

Suddenly the portal flashed brightly, went to red, and was gone.

"What happened?" shouted Alan, and he looked up at the control booth. The men there just shook their heads.

"I want that *timer*!" screamed Alan.

Two of the three crates of interest fell apart simultaneously, revealing a metallic cylinder hanging from a frame in each. "Four minutes!" yelled someone. "Four here!" yelled another. Two men were now hunched over each cylinder, working furiously.

Eric was going through the pockets of a dead man when the third crate fell apart, but the sound that startled him was a shout from a marine only steps away who got up from a dead invader and held something up in his hand. "Got it!" he yelled. "Two minutes-ten!"

Alan grabbed the thing away from him, saw Eric and glared angrily at him. "Two minutes, people, that's what you have!"

"Two minutes to oblivion was Eric's guess. The cylinders were the right size for missile warheads with medium to high yields. The portal had sensed their radiation. There would be no pain for Eric, no time for it during the nanoseconds of ionization, but the people in town wouldn't be so lucky. Even all the dense rock above the portal bay would not contain three high yield explosions. And Eric was helpless to do anything about it.

Others were not.

A pair of marines worked on each cylinder with focus and determination. Their lack of hesitation made Eric think they were familiar with the devices they worked on. He counted seconds, was down to a minute-twenty when he stepped over the body of the man the timer had been taken from. The marine who'd taken it was still there. Eric looked down; saw yellow eyes, crinkled, scaly skin and sharp teeth. He pointed to the body, and asked, "Who are these guys?"

"Dead snakes," growled the marine, and then added, "The best kind."

One minute.

Eric took another step towards the growing crowd around one cylinder. Alan was there. Eric heard him say, "No time for caution, just jerk it out of there," and then there was a shout from the men around him.

"Got it! Clear!"

"Clear!" came another shout from across the room.

Men were still working on the third cylinder. "Almost there," yelled someone.

"Twenty seconds," called Alan.

A platoon of marines stood grim-faced where they were. Not one man flinched, but there were audible gasps when the call came.

"Clear!" A man held up something that looked like a pencil with a ring on the end of it.

There was nervous laughter from all over the bay. "Twelve seconds, gentlemen. Good job," said Alan. "Now, I want this one rearmed and the timer programmed for ten seconds on activation. Nail a few boards around that thing. We're gonna give 'em a taste of their own slime if we can ever get that damn address. Don't we have it yet?" Alan was looking up at the control booth again and waving a hand. A kid in the booth gave him a thumb's up.

"We're going to push this thing back through the portal and light up their day. An extra push will help. I need a volunteer."

Hands went up, but Eric hesitated. A ten second delay on a nuclear explosion, and they were going to push it into a tunnel? Maybe twenty miles in, and the bay would be safe, but how did they expect to get out in ten seconds?

While Eric was thinking, Alan chose a marine, and talked to the man while several marines were crudely hammering together a crate around the rearmed device. Alan had the timer in his hand, was explaining something to his volunteer. Eric was wondering how much extra thrust one man could give to a powered lifter when it was suddenly apparent to him that two men were doing the job and Alan himself was the second man.

Commanders didn't go on suicide missions. That was too stupid for any military unit in the field, so what fact was Eric missing?

The crate was picked up on a lifter, turned sedately and headed towards the portal, which suddenly flickered and flashed on. Alan operated the controls, had the timer in one hand, and leaned a shoulder against the machine like his volunteer was doing.

"Good luck, sir!" shouted someone, and several marines saluted as Alan passed by them. The lifter accelerated, now within twenty yards of the portal.

Suddenly there was gunfire; two repeating flashes of fire came out of clear air from the left side of the portal. Alan cried out in pain, and his marine volunteer went down flat on his face.

The return fire was terrible, a hundred guns focused on one small area. Two figures shimmered into view by the portal, orange fluid gushing from their heads and bodies as they collapsed to the floor.

Alan clutched his free shoulder and pushed hard on the slowing lifter.

Well, screw this, thought Eric. He dropped his rifle and sprinted the few steps to the lifter, slamming a shoulder so hard against it that Alan nearly fell away.

"*You* again. Just can't stay out of it," grunted Alan.

"You hurt bad?" asked Eric.

"Shut up for once, and push."

"How far?"

"A few yards now."

The rippling blue surface was close. Eric dug in his heels and pushed harder. There was a buzzing sound like static, and then a pull and a brief sensation of cold and blackness as the shimmering surface swallowed them—

And spit them out into a room with bright lights at the ceiling and a balcony on which three men stood, two of them young, the other older and quite familiar.

John Coulter saw him, and his mouth opened in an 'O'. He looked behind him, and then lunged towards an instrument panel on the balcony.

Alan pressed something on the timer, and slid it on the floor into a corner of the room as Eric jerked the long-slide Colt from its holster and snapped off a shot at Coulter.

The bullet struck Coulter in the throat. He made a gurgling sound and clutched at his throat with both hands.

Eric aimed carefully and shot the man in the chest. Coulter toppled against a railing and went down on his knees, coughing blood.

"Come on!" Alan pulled Eric back by the shoulders, and there was a sensation of cold and blackness.

They fell onto the concrete floor of a dimly lit bay filled with marines, and behind them the face of the portal went from blue to red, and was gone.

Alan lay on his side, gripped a shoulder sleeve now soaked in blood, and smiled weakly. "Got the bastard," he said, and passed out.

"Medic!" screamed Eric, and several men arrived to help their wounded commander.

* * * * * * *

Outside of the portal bay only a handful of people knew what had happened until after it was over. The only indication of anything unusual had been the automatic lockdown of the bay. Davis had been in touch with the control room when the smoke cleared, and by the time Eric got to Sparrow's bay efforts were already underway to return Sparrow for flight. Dillon was there, and so was Davis, and a flatcar loaded with crated equipment was rolling into the bay on tracks.

"Well it's good to see you didn't get your ass shot off," said Davis. Eric guessed he was trying to be funny, but it wasn't.

"We lost a bunch of marines in there, Colonel."

"*We* didn't lose anyone. Foreign troops on the base weren't *my* idea, Price, but I guess it's good we had them here. I hear Nutt was wounded."

"Shoulder. The bullet went through. They said I could see him later this afternoon. He's the commander of that marine unit, Colonel."

"I know. Right in the middle of it. I guess I envy him. At least he has a command. Well, damn it, so do I. Sparrow will be back in this bay by dinnertime, and you have a flight test in two days. No more delays. Will you be ready for it?"

"Absolutely," said Eric.

"Good. Dillon has two copies of a briefing delivered personally by Brown. Get it from him. I'm going back to the office."

Davis suddenly smiled, and held out his hand. "I really am glad to see you alive, Price. Glad you could help shoot up some bad guys for us."

Eric shook the man's hand, and Davis walked away. Eric was left with the distinct impression that Davis hadn't heard the whole story yet, including Eric and Alan's dive through the portal.

He found Dillon by the flatcar, and the man knew even less. "Haul it out, haul it back in. False alarm, I guess. Davis says we have a definite go in two days, and this time I believe it. That guy Brown delivered these to me personally just a few minutes ago. One copy is for you."

He handed Eric a thin, loose-leaf notebook. "Got time for coffee?"

"Sure," said Eric.

They made the walk to Mess. Halfway there, Dillon asked, "That's a marine field uniform you're wearing. How come? You're not military."

"Davis wanted me to look like everyone else when he thought an attack was coming."

"And it didn't?"

"Well—"

"Don't worry about it. I just wonder why you smell like a gunnery range. Need to know is the rule, and my job is to fly Sparrow, so don't tell me anything."

Dillon had coffee. Eric was ravenous and had a chopped steak topped with two eggs. For a few minutes they ate silently while Eric leafed through the notebook.

"Looks like we'll be robots again," said Dillon. "The whole flight is programmed once we reach space. All you do is throw a switch or two."

"What's N-space?" asked Eric.

"Never heard of it until now."

"Says here our turnaround is N-space/Ariel sector 3."

Dillon just shrugged his shoulders. "Like they told us last time, I guess. Just sit there and enjoy the ride."

Maybe Alan can give me a clue, thought Eric. After the meal, Dillon went back to watch over the transfer of Sparrow. Eric got his kit, took a shower, and changed back into civvies. He asked for directions, and took an elevator up three levels to where he'd been told sickbay was located. He asked the corporal at the reception desk if he might be able to see Sergeant Alan Nutt, a patient there.

The corporal checked a card tacked up at a corner of the desk. "Sergeant Nutt is in room twelve, sir, but if you're Doctor Price you're supposed to go to room five first. Can I see some I.D.?"

Eric showed it to him. The corporal came around the desk and led him down the hall to room five. "In here, sir."

The room was dark. There were two beds, and one was empty. A man lay in the other bed, back turned to Eric.

"Excuse me? I'm Eric Price. I was told to come to this room. There might be a mistake."

The man rolled over. "No mistake, dear. You're invited."

Eric's heart thumped hard twice at the sound of the man's voice.

"Leon?"

"Back again. Don't turn on the light. Something in my meds is making me sensitive to it. Get over here. I heard what happened. Let's see if you still have all your parts."

Eric grabbed a chair, pulled it to the bed and sat down. Leon stuck out a hand and grinned at him. Eric grasped the hand softly in his, and held on. "They wouldn't tell me anything. I really thought you were dead."

"Nearly was, I guess. They had to pump me full of blood, and the surgeons did the rest. I'm amazing."

"I didn't realize they had that kind of capability here."

"They don't. I just got here. Weird trip, I was all doped up. One second I'm looking up at bright lights in a hospital and the next second it's dim lights from the ceiling of a rock cavern. I'm in the base, right?"

"Yes."

"I wasn't treated here. It was a huge hospital, everything in soft green, and the most gorgeous nurses I've ever seen. Not all of them women, by the way. Brought out the naughty in me once I was feeling better. I know I was shot several times, but they had me walking by the third day. They say I won't even have scars."

"Medicine has come a long ways," said Eric.

"In a hurry. Say, a sergeant Nutt is being treated here, and told me about your little firefight. You okay?"

"Not a scratch. They tried to destroy the base with a nuclear weapon, but we were ready for them. There were no survivors on their side."

"Yikes. That's not good for intel."

"We know who was behind it, Leon. It was John Coulter. I shot him twice, and he was spitting blood when we blew him up."

"Good riddance. So now it's over?"

"All over. The final flight test is in two days, and then you and I can go home."

Let's keep the money Coulter gave us, and celebrate."

"We'll have to ask the bosses about that, Leon."

"You're just being difficult again." Leon smiled, then, "How's Nataly?"

"We had a fight. She was a plant for the guys who gave us Sparrow. She fed the information to me that I thought came from dreams. The rest was a sham."

"I don't believe it. Did she admit to that?"

"No. She insists she loves me, but it's only part of the lie."

"Oh how I wish I had your psychic and mind reading abilities," said Leon. "You've never lied to anyone, of course. It's good to see you alive, Eric, but I still think you can be such a prick."

Eric laughed. "I love you too, Leon."

Leon put a hand to his chest. "Oh, I believe my heart just fluttered. Do yourself a favor. Make up with Nataly and marry her. The clandestine world of government secrets will be safer without you."

"Maybe," said Eric, and stood up. "I want to see Sergeant Nutt before I get out of here. I'll come back again to irritate you."

"I'm out of here in three days," said Leon, and squeezed Eric's hand. "Give Nataly a kiss for me."

Leon frowned at him when Eric smiled in silence.

Alan Nutt's room was a few doors down the hall, and Eric knocked on the doorjamb before entering. Alan was propped up on two pillows, writing something on his clipboard. His left arm was held rigidly against his body in a sling.

"Hi Sarge, or should I just call you 'sir'?" Eric walked to the bed, and shook Alan's good hand.

Alan smiled. "Alan will do. Did you go to room five?"

"Yep. Good news. I assume your people took care of him."

"My people?"

"You, Brown, the people who gave us Sparrow. I've seen a lot of weird things today, Alan. I shot a guy who looked more reptile than human. One of your marines even called him a snake. I saw men appear and disappear. I went through what I thought was a tunnel entrance, and in a blink I was in a building somewhere. I watched you command a military unit which I'm willing to bet money isn't one of ours, and then Davis tells me you're one of Brown's people. How am I doing so far, Alan?"

"Pretty good. I really was a Sergeant once, though we don't call it that."

"Who's we, Alan? I don't think you guys are from anywhere around here, and by that I mean anywhere on this planet."

"Took you long enough to figure that out."

"I've had my suspicions for more than a while"

"Actually, what you say isn't quite accurate. We've been around here a long time, and off-and-on for a *very* long time. Sorry to disappoint you, but we're not little green men with big eyes. Or was that little *gray* men?"

"I think it was gray. The mythology also includes shadow people and reptilians, and then there are the beautiful ones with long earlobes. Is that you guys?"

Alan grinned, and pulled at an earlobe. "Don't think so, Eric." He chuckled and closed his eyes. "God, this is the most wonderful dope they gave me. I feel like I'm floating. I should be screaming at you about today. The entire skirmish was to protect Sparrow and the test flight crew, and there you were, inserting yourself into the middle of a firefight. Brave, but stupid. Oh yeah, thanks for the help in returning the bomb to its rightful owner. I'll never forget the expression on Watt's face the second before you shot him."

"Who?"

"Dario Watt. Our president's right hand at one time."

"I knew him as John Coulter. He was—"

"I've heard the whole story. Don't bother. Hey, I really want to sleep, now. You have the big flight coming up, and Brown will answer all your questions when it's over. You'll have a new perspective by then."

"How's that?"

Alan was drifting off. He pointed at the ceiling and wiggled a finger. "You'll see how really big—it is—out there."

Eric left the sleeping man and also found Leon asleep. With the new flight schedule he had an overnight leave to catch up on mail and phony office business, would be back for a full night and a day at the base before flight. On the way to the tunnel he peeked into the bay and saw Sparrow just coming back into it on a flatcar. A van waited for him at the dock by the elevators, and drove him back home. It was hot on the surface, and not a cloud in the sky. He turned the air conditioner on and worked on the computer for two hours, catching up on lies. He thawed out some fish and fried it for dinner because the potpies had been used up. With evening came television and boredom, and sudden loneliness that was like a punch in the stomach. At that instant he finally noticed there was a message on his answering machine. He punched the play button.

"Eric, it's Nataly. I just heard what happened today. They tell me you're okay, but I need to hear it from you. Give me a call. I promise I won't pick up. You won't have to talk to me. Just tell me you're alive. I love you."

Something seemed to break inside him. His eyes teared up, and he stared at the answering machine for a long time. Twice his hand moved towards the telephone and twice he pulled it back. Finally, he erased the message and went to bed early.

The oblivion of sleep should have drowned his misery, but instead his dreams that night were full of a woman he still loved.

.

CHAPTER THIRTY-ONE
ARIEL

Everything was routine and uneventful until Eric threw that final switch.

The flight had begun on time; it was oh-two-hundred at liftoff. Eric and Dillon had easily memorized the routine and gone through it several times on the ground. There was really very little for them to do. They would take Sparrow to maximum thrust at the top of Earth's atmosphere, as they had done before. At that point the real flight would begin, all of it pre-programmed but initiated in steps they would participate in through interaction with their holoscreen. Only one travel program had been loaded into Sparrow, and it was called 'Ariel'.

The flight profile was a mystery, two columns of six numbers labeled N and t, running from 2 to 15 in N and 1 to 7 in t. No units were given. Brown had been in touch with them by telephone during their reading, but had only deepened the mystery. He did say that t was time in seconds, but N referred to light velocity in the space they were in, and there was a well-defined sequence of spaces and travel times for any particular destination. Dillon had made a crack about 'Warp Factor Six' at one point, but Brown either didn't understand it or find it amusing.

Their job was to initiate the program, and enjoy the ride.

Dillon lifted Sparrow smoothly out of the bay, took her to quarter, half, three-quarter thrust while Eric activated each program panel in turn. Brown was in contact with them moments after liftoff and had assumed flight officer duties this one time, though Hendricks was right beside him.

There was the roar of conventional engines, followed by silence and a feeling of lightness as before, and then they were at full thrust at seventy kilometers altitude and a speed of Mach 13 and Eric threw the switch to activate the one panel they had not used in the cockpit.

For two days and nights Eric had waited for the appearance of the golden man with some new revelation for him, but the only dreams he'd had were about Nataly, and nothing else had come. For the first time since he had begun work on Sparrow, he had no idea what would happen when he toggled a switch.

He tensed, reached out with a finger, and pushed.

A second holoscreen flashed into view in front of them, overlapping the other. There were strange glyphs for icons, but all were labeled in English.

"We have a new display," said Eric.

"Good," said Brown. "Now go to 'Menu'."

Dillon glanced over at Eric from time to time, but kept Sparrow on a near vertical trajectory at constant velocity.

Eric gestured, and a new column of icons appeared.

"Got it."

"Go to 'Define Home'."

Another gesture, and another icon was just below his finger. "And then 'enable'?" said Eric.

"No!" shouted Brown, and Eric jumped.

"If you enable at this point, Sparrow will come straight back home from your present position. Go up two icons."

Yikes. "Ah, 'Define Program'."

"Yes, Do it."

Eric gestured. At each gesture a green light had gone on at the panel by his right knee. Two lights remained unlit. An icon came up that looked like the planet Saturn.

"A new icon, a planet with rings," said Eric.

"Ordinarily a whole list of programs would come up, but there's only the one right now. We'll gradually add to the list over the next few years once we teach you the use of N-space mapping."

Eric had the impression Brown was now speaking to someone else. "Do I activate the new icon?"

"Yes."

Gesture. One light unlit.

"And now 'enable home'?"

"Very good, Doctor Price. Captain Dillon, you may now relax. Sparrow will take you where you're destined to go."

A single icon replaced the others, a single circle in red-orange labeled 'Begin trajectory'.

"You are going on a long journey, gentlemen," said Brown, "the length of which cannot be defined. We have now come full circle as a people. Congratulations to all of us. You will experience very brief delays in communications, but they should not worry you. Sparrow is in full control. Enjoy the journey, and your star craft will bring you safely home as programmed, in exactly one hour. Begin trajectory, Doctor Price."

And Eric gestured again.

"Just give me a second to grab onto my ass," said Dillon, as Eric moved his hand.

The icon disappeared and the overlapping holoscreens dimmed. In those first seconds of their journey there were only the pinpoints of stars and a faint, distant glow showing the boundary of earth's atmosphere. There was the sensation of floating they had felt before, not weightlessness, for it had been there when they were under thrust. Now the feeling intensified, as if Earth's gravity were being sucked away beneath them. A high-pitched humming that quickly went beyond their audible range broke the silence, and the fuselage of Sparrow creaked around them, as if under sudden stress. Outside, the stars disappeared, and for the time of two anxious heartbeats there was total darkness. A bright light flashed past their view, then another, and from behind the cockpit a sound like scratching on metal.

"Oh, shit," said Dillon, and Eric swallowed hard. His hands gripped his knees and he felt like a live mouse was running around inside his stomach. He took a deep breath, and forced it out hard.

"I think now we're *really* under power," he said

Outside Sparrow lights flashed past in a blur of blue, yellow and red, and then there was a continuous smear of something deep violet as there was an audible thud behind them and a strong shock passed beneath their seats. The space outside Sparrow went from a curtain of purple to one of red in exactly seven seconds by Eric's habitual counting, and stars reappeared, a flood of them stretching in a band across their view. Most of the stars were blue-distant, hot and giant. There was a metallic groan deep within Sparrow's hull, and suddenly the stars were a deep red and barely visible.

Brown's voice was a shock to them. "Final stage, gentlemen. You're nearly there."

"Yeah, and where's *there*?" asked Dillon, but Brown was gone again.

Eric had counted fifteen seconds when the stars outside turned blue and white again, but they were dimmer than before. A yellow glow began at the right-hand border of the holoscreen, and intensified. A bright disk slid into view, lemon yellow, three black spots arranged near its center, edges tinged red. It was about the size of a quarter held at arm's length.

"Star," said Eric softly, "and close to us. Hope the Ariel program knows it's there, and doesn't dump us into it."

"Not likely, Doctor Price," said Brown, and his voice was again a startling thing. "I must admit that you passed straight through several stars along the way, but there was no time for interactions. The star you see is a special one for my people and myself. In a moment you'll see why. We call it Elder. It's hotter than your sun, but not by much, and a bit older."

"Your home star," said Eric. "We should be getting pictures of this."

"And I'd like to know where we are," said Dillon, and turned to Eric. "If this isn't some elaborate, phony setup, he's saying we've traveled a lot of light years in a minute or two."

They waited a few seconds, but there was no reply from Brown.

"Hello?" said Eric.

Again a pause, then, "Ah, yes, the star craft is recording everything. As of now you are also being recorded in local space, and your remarks will certainly be released to the public. Ariel should be coming into view in a moment as your star craft reorients itself for the return home."

Elder had slid off the left border of the holoscreen, but a new glow was now forming where the star had first appeared. And as they watched in amazement a most beautiful planet came into view. The disk was powder blue, but mottled in green, orange and light brown, landmasses arranged close to the equator and surrounded by seas. Two distinct rings surrounded the planet, white and sparkling, and Sparrow was close enough for them to see wispy, white clouds dotting the surface.

"My family is down there," said Brown softly. "We call it Ariel."

Eric suddenly realized he'd been holding his breath, and let it out. "It's beautiful," he said. "I could be looking at Earth, except for the rings."

"Maybe you could say a few words of greeting, Doctor Price," said Brown. "Unfortunately they cannot hear me. It's just the beginning, you see. Two peoples are meeting with knowledge of who they are for the first time. Anything simple will do. My people have waited years for this. Our president's plan to bring us together has been major news, and hotly debated. It could have resulted in total societal disruption if Dario Watt had been successful. The star craft is a gift from my people to yours, so we can come together at last. Tell them what you think about this. The channel is now open."

Eric's stomach trembled, and he felt a burning in his fingertips. He glanced at Dillon, but the man looked terrified and shook his head. "Not me," Dillon mouthed.

What to say at a time like this? Something friendly, and short, a greeting to Brown's people, Alan's—Nataly's. *Oh Nataly.*

The few seconds he thought seemed like minutes, and then he swallowed hard, took a deep breath and spoke with a soft, steady voice directed from somewhere inside him.

"My name is Eric Price. I come from a planet called Earth, or Terra, very far from you. My people have always wanted to travel to the stars, but our technology has only allowed us to travel to planets and moons in our own system. Now we have received a gift from you, the gift of a star craft that has brought us to your planet. I'm told it's called Ariel. It reminds me of my home. We don't have rings like Ariel, but we have a single, large moon to admire at night. On behalf of my people I want to thank you very much for your gift. I hope it will bring us together soon, and that we will be good friends. I bring best wishes to you, from Earth, until we meet again."

Eric paused, wondering what more could be said.

"Very nice," said Brown. "Wait a moment before speaking again, please."

They waited. Dillon grinned at him. "One step for man," he mouthed.

"We can talk freely now. The channel has been closed. Thank you, Doctor Price."

"Glad to do it. I meant what I said, but I'm sure it will also be politically useful to your president."

"There is that," said Brown. "He went through much difficulty to bring you here. Unfortunately, it is now time to leave."

"I still don't know how far we've come," said Dillon. "How many light years is it?"

Pause. "As I said, that cannot be defined, Captain. The Ariel program lists six universes, including your own at $N=0$. You are now at $N=2$ and went through orders up to fifteen on your way here. Each universe has different physical constants, of course. The N value is used in a multiplier times your light speed value."

"So where we are, the light speed is twice what it is on Earth?" asked Eric.

"No, it is a hundred times the value on Earth. The N is the power of ten times your value."

"Up to fifteen?" Dillon was astounded.

"The upper limit seems to be twenty-one for stable universes. The portal uses eighteen. The concept of distances in light years has little meaning to us. It's travel time that counts, and your trip consumed just over seventy-four seconds, including deceleration to your present location. Return to your own space will take a few seconds longer."

"We're not even in our own universe," said Dillon.

"That is correct, Captain."

"Good Lord."

"It's quite complex, I know, but we'll teach you the use of N-space maps, and we have current listings of populated worlds we'll share when you're ready. There is also the power plant to learn. The theory involves a coupling between gravity and electromagnetic fields, but the technology is rather straightforward. This will take years, Captain, and I hope you and Doctor Price will be able to participate."

"As long as I can fly," said Dillon, but Eric was silent.

"Good. We'll talk about it in a few minutes. Enjoy the trip home."

There was a click as Brown's voice faded away, and Eric felt that peculiar lightening in his stomach again. The image of Ariel shuddered, then sped away until it was only a pinpoint of light. *Wish we could have stayed longer*, thought Eric, but then the holoscreen displays came back again with icons dimly lit. Outside there was blackness, then veils of colors, then lights flashing past in blue, red, and blue again.

"Down the rabbit hole," said Dillon, and chuckled.

He's having a good time now, thought Eric, but inside he was feeling a strange sadness. *I couldn't have imagined such an adventure. I should be euphoric right now. Why do I feel so badly about going home?*

But only a minute later, the sight of planet Earth on his holoscreen nearly sent him into tears.

"Pretty little world; let's go there," said Dillon, and then Brown's voice was back again.

"Right on time. Keep your eyes on the screen, Doctor Price; to be sure each panel is closed as a phase is completed. Everything should be automatic."

"Right. I've been wondering what we could have done if something had gone wrong while we were in one of those higher-order spaces."

"There are procedures, and also a fail-safe that will put you back into the space of origin. This will all be a part of the training in later stages. Today you have made the easiest of all possible flights, and the one we're most familiar with. Relax. Sparrow is bringing you home nicely."

"I've come in on auto before, but at least I had to make a dead stick landing," said Dillon. "I want to really *fly* this thing."

"Of course, Captain. There will be opportunities for that. See you in a few minutes."

Dillon was quiet during the spiraling descent through the atmosphere, but kept his hands on the controls, feeling each change in pitch and yaw. Eric's attention was held by the holo-screens as he went through the switch sequence in reverse. Sparrow dropped to a hundred thousand feet before chasing the terminator and catching up to it in seconds before dropping again. The lightness within them had gone away at first descent, and now they were buffeted by the turbulence of passage through thickening air. In the last minute of descent they were coming down vertically, and a huge cluster of lights lay near the horizon. Below them was darkness with a few peaks and buttes dimly illuminated by a setting moon.

"We see you. The bay is opening." An unfamiliar voice.

Slightly south of their position, a dim red hole suddenly appeared on a flat just west of jagged peaks. There was a thud, and a whine as Sparrow's lifters cut in, and they seemed to float towards the hole until it was beneath them and no longer visible. Eric grunted when they dropped rapidly, and then slowed. He saw the edges of the bay ceiling pass by, the red glow on rock walls, and felt the soft concussion of landing pass beneath him.

Dillon popped the canopy and techs were already swarming

the wings. One saluted Dillon. "Lots of excitement here, sir."

The ceiling was closed by the time they were unstrapped and out of the cockpit. Eric followed Dillon out. There was applause from a small crowd gathered around Sparrow. Smiling faces. Davis was there, Hendricks and his crew, Brown, and a man who looked much like him.

Alan should have been here, thought Eric. He stepped onto the wing and ran his hand along Sparrow's fuselage. There was no sign of scarring or burning, even after reentry from space.

Davis was the first one to shake his hand. "Now I can retire", he said, and Eric knew instantly the man was serious. "I'll need a debriefing, but Brown wants to talk to you first. He says it's important."

"While the flight is still fresh in your mind," said Brown, who had come up behind Davis. "It'll only take a few minutes, Colonel."

"I'll be in my office," said Davis, and he joined a small group of people crowded together around a computer to look at pictures that had been transmitted during the flight. An image of Ariel floated in blackness there. As Eric walked past them, Rob Hendricks stuck out a hand. "How does it feel to be spokesman for an entire planet?" he asked, and grinned.

Eric shook his hand. "Hasn't sunk in, yet. I'm a little numb."

Brown took him by the elbow and steered him away. Seeing Brown in normal light for the first time, Eric thought the man had the good looks of a celebrity, a sort of dark, brooding look.

Another man who could have been Brown's brother approached them, held out his hand, and Eric shook it.

"This is my closest colleague, Mister White," said Brown. "He has been my right hand on this project."

"So glad to meet you at last," said White. "I must admit I had some doubts about you at first, but I should not be surprised at your performance. Your heritage demanded it."

Eric nodded politely, thinking the man was simply complimenting an American ally, but Brown squeezed his elbow and pulled him away. "We can have dinner together this evening, but now I have private matters to discuss with Doctor Price. Please excuse us."

"Of course," said White. "I'm sure he has a thousand questions."

"Nice to meet you," said Eric, as Brown pulled him away.

"He does love to talk, especially about Ariel. Davis will be there, and two other members of the Council. I think you'll find the evening most entertaining, but now some private things need to be said. I'll even buy you a cup of coffee."

The man actually smiled. "Okay," said Eric.

They went to Mess Hall and found a corner table. Eric spooned sugar into a tall cup of coffee, and Brown drank tea.

"First there's the matter of project continuation. We want you to be a part of it."

"Any trained pilot can work with Dillon, and he'll certainly agree to it. You don't need me for anything. I did what I came here to do. I'll likely be reassigned soon," said Eric.

"Not if we request your services here. Reliable support for this project goes to the highest levels in your government. It's the reason we brought Sparrow to you in the first place. You're a scientist, an analyst, and the first to fly Sparrow in N-space. Your voice is the first from earth to be heard by the Arielian people. And there is one other thing, probably most important."

Brown paused and frowned, but Eric remained silent.

"There's no subtle way to say this, Doctor Price. In every practical definition, you are an Arielian. It would take a DNA sequencing to show the difference between you and a pure human strain. The only differences appear in viral fragments. We're cousins, so to speak. We share a common ancestor, gone long before either of our written histories begin."

Eric smiled. "I think I read that somewhere."

"Our contact with humans goes back at least ten thousand years. Our people have stayed here for many different lengths of time, but the times have become longer in recent centuries. Breeding with humans has been natural; many Arielians have had families and lived out their lives here. There are records we could have checked to find you, but it was only after Natasha discovered you that we did that. You are second generation, Doctor Price. Your grandmother on your mother's side was from Ariel. She was a cultural anthropologist who spent half her life doing field work on Earth."

"My mother was a native American," said Eric.

"She was half Arielian," said Brown. "She gave you that spiritual quality we've never understood in ourselves, that quality that connects our souls. Poor Natasha connected with you so quickly, well before you discovered your feelings for her, and now she's miserable because of something I asked her to do to help her own people on both sides of her heritage."

"Nataly?"

"Yes. Her father came from Ariel as a young man, looking for land of his own. He was an important contact in the early stages of our project. We suspect he was murdered because of it, but I think it's now safe to say that justice has been served. I've known Natasha since she was a little girl, Doctor Price. I feel her misery, and yours as well, and I bear the guilt for it."

Brown was looking at him closely, his forehead creased with the signs of worry. "Knowing what you know now, would you have done the same for your people?"

"I think I would have told the whole truth to someone I loved, and who said they loved me."

Brown shook his head. "You all had to believe you were dealing with an Earth-based power for as long as possible. Dealing with an alien power is either unbelievable or too frightening. We have experienced that problem on Ariel. It came close to destroying us. We didn't intend to inflict that on Earth's people. The whole truth can gradually be released as our relationship grows. Natasha loves you with all her heart, Doctor Price, but she did what she had to do. Her soul has been bruised, and so has yours, and I will suggest a cure, if you're willing to listen."

"I'm willing," said Eric.

CHAPTER THIRTY-TWO
PARTNERS

Nataly dressed in a Santa Fe skirt and a sleeveless white blouse for the occasion. She brewed a pot of coffee, and then arranged her business plan and a few sketches of the proposed gallery on her desk.

The call from Vasyl had come the previous evening. Whenever she heard his voice, now, she anticipated bad news about Eric, but this time it wasn't so."

"Is this about Eric? Is he leaving?"

"He's still thinking about it, Natasha. I promise I'll let you know when he decides something. No, this is about a project you've had in mind for quite a while. You remember Leon, of course."

"Yes! Is he getting better?"

"He's recovering nicely. I went to see him, to thank him for saving Eric's life, actually. The man talks and talks. He mentioned your ideas about a gallery addition to your shop, and said you'd need a partner to help run it."

"Leon and I actually talked about that," said Nataly. "I already knew he was a CIA agent at the time, but I think he has a genuine interest in art. Is he retiring from government service?"

"Oh no, this isn't about him. But, you know how it is; he has a friend of a friend from Phoenix who would be interested. Leon has talked to him. The man will arrive in the morning. I thought I might bring him up to meet you around noon? I think it would be good for you to have a new, creative project, Natasha. You need a distraction. I want you to stop being so sad."

"I know you're trying to help, Vasyl, but I'm not a little girl anymore. I'll get over it." *It's just my soul that's dying*, she wanted to say. "Sure, bring him over. If nothing else, I can get a second opinion of my ideas."

"We'll be there at noon."

"Vasyl?"

"Yes?"

"I thought I might at least hear a goodbye from Eric. You've talked to him. Has he said anything about me?"

"No. We talked, though. I told him everything about you, about your father."

"You didn't!"

"Yes. He also knows his own heritage, now. I told him about his grandmother. I'm trying to get him to remain with the project, Natasha."

"What was his reaction?"

"A bit stunned, I'd say. He has a lot to think about. Be patient with him."

"I'm trying," she said. *It's easy to be patient when your heart isn't crumbling into pieces over something you have no control of.* "See you tomorrow."

Now it was noon, and Vasyl was habitually prompt. There was a pleasant coffee odor throughout the house, and it was a sunny day. Nataly opened the doors to the balcony, put three coffee cups and saucers on the table there.

The doorbell chimed four times, and she went to the door and opened it.

Vasyl was standing there with a slight smile on his face, and Eric Price was standing next to him. Nataly felt heat come to her face, and a little gasp escaped her.

"Okay, so I lied just a bit," said Vasyl.

Eric's eyes glistened. He held out his hand. "Hi. I'm Eric Price. Mister Brown here says you might consider the application of a total idiot to help you run an art gallery you're planning. I'm here to apply for the job."

Eric blinked. A tear edged up in one corner of an eye, and hung there.

His hand was cold when she touched it. She squeezed lightly. "Why don't you come inside, Mister Price?" Her chest was so tight it was hard to speak, but the instant she touched him delicious warmth surged within her, and she willed the flow of it to her hand and into his.

Eric brushed past her to go into the house, and Nataly turned again to usher Vasyl in behind him.

Vasyl was gone.

Nataly closed the door. Eric had walked to the balcony and was standing there with his back to her. She walked up to him, reached up to place her hand on a shoulder blade.

"Eric," she said softly.

"I've been a damn fool, Nataly. I'm still carrying baggage I should have dumped a long time ago. I had no reason to feel betrayed, but I felt it anyway. I don't know how you can love a person like me."

She rubbed his back. "But I do love you."

Eric sniffled. "I love you, too. I tried to deny it, and it just made me miserable. I'm supposed to be Mister Tough Guy, with lots of walls. I didn't want to get hurt again, so I hurt you instead."

Nataly grasped his arm and turned him around to face her. His eyes were red and puffy, and he looked at her with an intensity she'd seen before and had dreamed about seeing again. And then he touched her, his hands, now warm, sliding softly up and down her arms.

"I'm still here," she said. "I've been waiting for you to come back to me." She reached up and put her arms around his neck, pulled his head down towards her, and kissed him.

It was a forever kiss, soft and deep, and time became irrelevant, a folded-up dimension. Two souls kissed, and expressed the bond between them that would not be denied.

Their lips finally parted, and his cheek was pressed warmly

against hers. "I'm back if you really want me," he said.

"Oh yes." Nataly squeezed him tightly, and held on for long seconds.

"Your friend told you one thing that's true. I'm looking for something to do here."

"Are you leaving the service?" Nataly looked up at him and ran a finger across his cheek.

"Not just yet. I called my section chief, and he'll approve a phase-out to retirement over five years while I work as a consultant on what they're now calling the Ariel project. I'll be on call, but I doubt I'll spend more than half time at the base. Leon really did tell us about your gallery project. He's already been reassigned. He'll be gone in a week, and there will be no more tax-payer-funded-art sales for local artists. But the Phoenix office really did set us up with some good contacts. I think those will be useful if I get involved with a new gallery here."

Nataly kissed him quickly, and smiled. "So, do you want to be my partner?"

Again, there was that intense look that made her heart sing.

"In every way," he said, and pressed her to him.

"We probably should have some sort of contract," she said, and curled a leg around his.

"Whatever you want," said Eric.

"I'll show you what I want," said Nataly, and she led him through the house to the bedroom and the big brass bed where they would conduct their first business together.

EPILOG

"It was quite a hassle, Gil, but we got it done," said Arthur Evans. "I'm sorry I had to deceive you for such a long time, but if I'd told you everything you'd have switched to the Democrats and kicked me out of office."

The President of the United States listened, then laughed. "I only let my antennae show after the fourth martini. There just isn't any real difference between us, Gil. We come from the same stock, and nearly all of us born off Ariel are a mix. My blood is so diluted the people in the old country will call me Earthling. Your Eric Price will get a better reception, I bet. His was the first voice from Earth that they heard, and he's a lot closer to pure blood. That will be something to watch when he arrives in the star craft. As for me, I'll be sent through the portal, quick and dirty, after the initial excitement cools on Ariel. Not spectacular, but dignified. It's a nice way to end my presidency."

Evans listened, and shuffled papers on his desk. Len sat in a chair near him, waiting patiently.

"I'm not aware of anyone who had previous knowledge of Price's heritage, Gil. It was just blind luck." Evans lifted an eyebrow at Len, and the young man smiled, acknowledging the lie. "I think phasing him out with such interesting work was both wise and kind. It sounds like he's found a new life, and he deserves it. You too, Gil. Lets both of us retire and go fishing."

The President laughed again, and hung up the telephone. "Gave him a shock, I did, and he's one of my oldest friends. Fortunately, he has a good imagination. What generation are you, Len?"

"Fourth, Mister President."

"Gad, even my aid is closer than I am to the old world. I'd better look it up; I think it's eight or nine generations for me. They'll ask me about it on Ariel. Want to go with me?"

"I'd be honored, Mister President."

"Then let's do it. What's next for today?"

"Senator Banesfield is here to argue for more wheat subsidies, and then there's lunch with the Syrian delegation."

"Ah," said Arthur Evans, "that will certainly bring me back to Earth in a hurry."

* * * * * * *

"You're glowing again," said Eric, and ran a fingertip over her lips. They had just made love, and lay on their sides, facing each other.

"So are you," said Nataly. She gestured above his head. "There are some nice gold streamers here, and some red, but I still see a little patch of blue. We have to fix that."

"As long as it takes. We have the rest of our lives."

Nataly smiled. "We never talked about age. I'm not so young as you think. I'm actually a year older than you."

Eric pulled her to him again, and kissed her softly. "Ohh, a mature, knowledgeable woman. Teach me what I need to know."

Nataly giggled, but then there was a sound, a distant, high-pitched whine they heard together. "Oooo, I've got to see this," said Nataly. She struggled out of Eric's embrace, threw back the covers and ran naked towards the front room of the house. Eric was right behind her when she reached the balcony doors and opened them. They stepped out onto the balcony and Eric enveloped her in his arms as they looked towards the high buttes to the west.

A star colored red and orange was rising slowly above a butte, then stopped and floated slowly north before rising again. Colors brightened as it accelerated its vertical climb.

"Someone going home. Maybe it's Vasyl," said Eric.

"No, he'll use the portal to the presidential building, and so will the rest of the council."

"I'll be going in on Sparrow. Vasyl wants to make a show of it."

"He would."

The star flared, and then rose faster and faster, dimming with altitude. There was a bright flash, the star winked out and was gone.

"Someone is sure to see it and call the police," said Eric.

"And the report will be ignored as usual," said Nataly, and leaned back against him.

"Maybe someday both of us can go to Ariel. In a way, it's like going home."

"Home is right here—with you," said Nataly, and she looked up at him.

Eric growled, and Nataly squealed as he swept her up in his arms and carried her back to their bedroom, and they made love again in a cloud of swirling colors.

AFTERWORD

Sedona Conspiracy is a work of fiction. I made it all up. A couple of restaurant names are real, or close to real, and the food is good. Area descriptions are accurate. I own two timeshares in Sedona, Arizona. I paint, drum and play didj there with friends. It's one of my favorite places on this planet. It's also considered by many to be the New-Age capital of the country.

New age culture, including UFOs, angels and aliens, is rich in Sedona. The literature is huge, and ranges from quackery to serious reporting. A lot of levelheaded, no-nonsense people have seen strange things in the Sedona area, and will tell you about it. They'll tell you how the Sedona Fire Department once went into the backcountry to fight a raging fire and was turned back by armed soldiers in black Humvees. And in my own experience, hiking near the end of Long Canyon one day, I heard what sounded like a 747 taking off nearby. Okay, I'm a professional skeptic, a trained physicist who spent thirty years teaching and doing research in physics, but I'm the first to admit that theories are never proven, only disproved. And the mind must always be kept open to new possibilities.

Sedona Conspiracy started out with a 'What If'. What if all of it is true? What if there really is a secret military base in the Sedona backcountry, and aliens really are living among us?

The rest was pure fun. Hope you enjoyed it.

SOME FURTHER READING

1. Dongo, Tom, *The Mysteries of Sedona. The New Age Frontier.* Tom Dongo, Sedona, AZ. 1988

2. Dongo, Tom, *The Mysteries of Sedona. The Alien Tide*, Hummingbird Pub. Co., 1990

3. Nichols, Preston B. and Moon, Peter, *Encounters in the Pleides: An Inside Look at UFOs*, Sky Books, 1996

4. Andrews, George C., *Extraterrestrials Among Us*, Llewellyn Publications, St. Paul, Mn. 1986

5. Chatelain, Maurice, *Our Cosmic Ancestors*, Golden Temple Productions, Sedona, Az. 1988

ABOUT THE AUTHOR

JAMES C. GLASS is a retired physics and astronomy professor and dean who now spends his time writing, painting, and traveling. He made his first story sale in 1988 and was the Grand Prize Winner of Writers of the Future in 1990. Since then he has sold six novels and a short story collection, and over forty short stories to magazines such as *Aboriginal S.F.*, *Analog*, and *Talebones*. Jim writes science fiction, fantasy, and dark fantasy. He now divides his time between Spokane, Washington and Desert Hot Springs, California with wife Gail, who is a costumer and healing dancer. There are five grown children and eleven grandchildren scattered around the country. Jim also paints mountain, desert, and red rock scenics in oils and pastels, and is often heard playing didgeridoo and Native American flute. For more details, please see his web site at:

www.sff.net/people/jglass/

Made in the USA
Charleston, SC
08 March 2012